Ans	_____	M.L.	_____
ASH	_____	MLW	_____
Bev	_____	Mt.Pl	_____
C.C.	_____	NLM	_____
C.P.	_____	Ott	05/07 to lms
Dick	_____	PC	_____
DRZ	_____	PH	_____
ECH	_____	P.P.	_____
ECS	_____	Pion.P.	_____
Gar	_____	Q.A.	_____
GRM	_____	Riv	_____
GSP	_____	RPP	_____
G.V.	_____	Ross	_____
Har	_____	S.C.	_____
JPCP	_____	St.A.	2/10
KEN	11/06 (Cable)	St.J	_____
K.L.	2/07,	St.Joa	_____
K.M.	_____	St.M.	_____
L.H.	_____	Sgt	05/08 (Mary)
LO	12/07	T.H.	_____
Lyn	9/06 Sturtz	TLLO	_____
L.V.	_____	T.M.	_____
McC	_____	T.T.	_____
McG	_____	Ven	_____
McQ	8/07	Vets	_____
MIL	_____	VP	12/06 Thom
	Kine 08/08	Wat	_____
	_____	Wed	_____
	_____	WIL	_____
	_____	W.L.	_____

The
Cotton
Queen

Also by Pamela Morsi
in Large Print:

By Summer's End

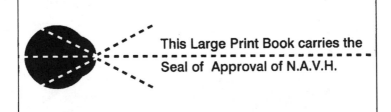

This Large Print Book carries the
Seal of Approval of N.A.V.H.

The Cotton Queen

Pamela Morsi

Published in 2006 by arrangement with Harlequin Books S.A.

Wheeler Large Print Hardcover.

The text of this Large Print edition is unabridged.
Other aspects of the book may vary from the original edition.

Set in 16 pt. Plantin by Elena Picard.

Printed in the United States on permanent paper.

Library of Congress Cataloging-in-Publication Data

Morsi, Pamela.
    The Cotton Queen / by Pamela Morsi.
        p. cm.
    ISBN 1-59722-236-4 (lg. print : hc : alk. paper)
    1. Mothers and daughters — Fiction. 2. Life change events — Fiction. 3. Texas — Fiction. 4. Domestic fiction. 5. Large type books. I. Title.
    PS3563.O88135C68 2006
        813'.54—dc22   2006004963

For the people of McKinney, Texas:

Although
the characters and premise of
The Cotton Queen
are wholly a work of fiction,
the strong bonds of community
and warm, welcoming nature of
the city's citizens
is,
pleasantly, factual.

Thank you all so much.

National Association for Visually Handicapped
---------------------- *serving the partially seeing*

As the Founder/CEO of NAVH, the only national health agency solely devoted to those who, although not totally blind, have an eye disease which could lead to serious visual impairment, I am pleased to recognize Thorndike Press★ as one of the leading publishers in the large print field.

Founded in 1954 in San Francisco to prepare large print textbooks for partially seeing children, NAVH became the pioneer and standard setting agency in the preparation of large type.

Today, those publishers who meet our standards carry the prestigious "Seal of Approval" indicating high quality large print. We are delighted that Thorndike Press is one of the publishers whose titles meet these standards. We are also pleased to recognize the significant contribution Thorndike Press is making in this important and growing field.

Lorraine H. Marchi, L.H.D.
Founder/CEO
NAVH

★ Thorndike Press encompasses the following imprints: Thorndike, Wheeler, Walker and Large Print Press.

Cotton Days
McKinney, Texas
2004

It was still early on the morning of what had been forecasted as a very hot summer day. Rachel Jerrod saw her mother the minute she pulled the car into the driveway. It would have been hard to miss her. Alana, or Laney as most people in town called her, was dressed in the most brightly flowered capri pants ever to leave a retail store. They were matched up with a baggy, red-orange T-shirt that hung down almost to the knees. Her feet were encased in drab olive garden clogs and on her head was a wide-brimmed straw hat decorated with a huge sequined flower.

Rachel simply shook her head and rolled her eyes. Her mother was so weird.

As soon as she spotted Rachel, Laney rose to her feet and waved excitedly. She was speaking before Rachel was even out of the car.

"Let me see, let me see," her mother said, indicating her daughter's hair.

Rachel turned slowly, giving the full three-sixty.

"Nice, very nice," Laney said. "You look wonderful, as always."

"I can't say the same for you, Mom," Rachel replied. "What are you wearing?"

Her mother looked down at her clothes as if noticing them for the first time.

"I'm just trying to be cool and comfortable," Alana said. "Besides, I'm gardening."

"Well, you shouldn't be," her daughter said. "You'll get all hot and sweaty and you'll have hat hair for the parade."

Laney laughed, refusing to take offense. "I was thinking of wearing the hat for the parade," she said. "It will come in handy on that hot sidewalk taking photos."

"Mom."

There was a whiny quality to Rachel's utterance, familiar to anyone who's spent time with a seventeen-year-old girl.

"Come back to the deck," Laney said. "We've got a smidgeon of time all to ourselves, we should enjoy it. There's still a breeze out there and plenty of shade. You'll get more sun than you want this afternoon."

The two walked the length of the driveway to the backyard and up the steps to the wooden deck off the family room.

"I'll fix you a nice breakfast," Laney said. "You ran out of here this morning without so much as a bite."

Rachel shook her head. "Nothing to eat," she told her mother. "I'm already so jumpy I could barf."

"Well, how about a nice cup of coffee," her mother suggested. "Hot drinks are cooling on a summer day."

"Caffeine to cure the jitters, Mom? I don't think so. Besides the stuff is supposed to be terrible for the skin."

"Then I'll brew a pot of healthy, herbal tea," Laney said. "It'll calm your nerves and quench your thirst."

"Okay," Rachel agreed.

Rachel seated herself at the round patio table beneath the umbrella. She was staring out over the backyard — her own backyard since second grade. It was a very ordinary place. If one of those fancy brass history placards were placed at this location it would have to read: *No truly important event has ever occurred here.* But this backyard was where Rachel had her swing set as a child. Replaced by a volleyball net when she was a teenager. She'd hunted Easter eggs among the shrubs. And last year, she'd had her photo taken with Clint Howell among the leaves of autumn before their date to the homecoming dance.

Nothing truly important.

But Rachel had begun to wonder about the unimportant things. The things no one really examined. The events that no one wrote down. She had become curious about the day-to-day happenings that added up to a life. On the cusp of her own entry into womanhood she'd begun, perhaps for the first time, to look outside herself and her little circle of girlfriends for answers about what the world was like and what her place in it might be.

A knock at the French doors had Rachel jumping to her feet. She hurried over to open them up for her mother.

"Here we are, sweetie," Laney said as she carried the tray to the table. "I cut up some melon and I found these tea cookies in the pantry. I know it's white sugar, but you've got a big day ahead of you and we can't have you keeling over in a faint. That's very unqueenlike."

"Yeah, I'm sure these small-town gossips would have a field day with that," Rachel said.

"Oh, it gives them something to do," Laney said. "Otherwise they'd have to create drama in their own lives."

Rachel laughed.

"The yard looks great, Mom," she said, indicating the abundance of flowering shrubs grown as large now as trees. "The colors are fabulous this year."

Laney looked out and nodded.

"Wet spring, hot summer," she said. "It's the best combination for Crepe Myrtles, and McKinney *is* the 'Crepe Myrtle Capital of the World.' "

Rachel laughed. "I thought it was the 'Diamond Stickpin in the Lapel of Texas,' " she said.

Laney shrugged. "That, too."

"So I stopped by to see Grandma this morning," Rachel said.

Laney chuckled. "I suppose she was in fine spirits," she said. "This being her big day and all."

"She tried on her dress for me," Rachel said. "She looks fabulous. And she's really looking forward to the parade."

"I'm sure she is."

"I told her that you were dragging your heels," Rachel commented carefully.

"Then you misspoke," her mother said. "Dragging heels indicates reluctance. I'm

11

not reluctant. I'm refusing."

Rachel made a little puff of annoyance.

"Mom, everything's ready and we've put so much time into it," Rachel complained.

Laney shook her head firmly. "I never agreed to this, you and your grandmother agreed and thought you could just force me into it. She was able to do that twenty-five years ago, but I'm not so much a doormat these days."

"Doormat? You, Mom? Not likely."

"Perhaps malleable is a better description of how I was," Laney said. "Rigid is more my stance with your grandmother today."

"Okay, so what's the deal between you and Grandma?" she asked.

"There's no *deal* between us," Laney said. "We're fine."

"You never talk to each other."

"Don't be silly, I talk to her," Laney answered. "I talk to her several times a week."

"Oh, yeah, I know," Rachel responded dismissively. "I can probably quote the whole conversation verbatim." She put her hand up to her ear like an imaginary telephone. " 'Hello, Babs. How are you?' " she began, mimicking Laney's more formal tone. " 'Fine, Laney,' " she replied in the croaky voice of an aging matron. " 'And yourself?' 'Fine. Do you need anything?' 'No.' 'Well, call me if you do.' "

Laney smiled, but not with a great deal of humor.

"Very amusing," she commented dryly.

"She's an old lady, Mom," Rachel said. "She's not going to be around here forever."

"Oh for heaven's sake, Babs is sixty-five," Laney said. "She'll probably live to be a hundred."

"I hope she will," Rachel said. "I hope she has thirty years left. But I guess it wouldn't matter if she had thirty minutes if her own daughter won't give her even one summer afternoon for something very special, something that she's dreamed of and hoped for for a very long time. Something that would mean so much to her and to me."

Laney laughed aloud at her daughter's sincere intensity.

"Is she giving you guilt lessons?" she asked Rachel. "You're sounding more like her every day."

"No, Mom," Rachel said. "I'm not the one that's like her. It's you. You're the one who's just like her."

"Me? I'm not like my mother."

Rachel nodded. "You are both stubborn, single-minded and determined to have your way."

"Oh, please, it's not that bad," Alana insisted.

"It is that bad," she said. "It hurts you. It hurts Grandma. And it hurts me to watch the two of you."

"She and I just have very different views on this queen thing," Laney said.

"You didn't want me to be this year's Cotton Queen," Rachel said.

"That's not true," Laney told her. "It wasn't that I didn't want it for you. I didn't want you to be pushed into it."

"I wasn't pushed into it," Rachel said. "It's an honor and a privilege to represent the people of McKinney."

Laney rolled her eyes. "Rachel, honey, save it for the acceptance speech," she said. "It's a small-town beauty pageant that has about as much meaning in terms of your long-term happiness as a bug splat on your car windshield. A woman's life is not a reign of glory. I want to protect you from that kind of thinking. It's not smiling in the spotlight and having every eye gaze upon you in awe. The things that make up a life, a real life, involve lots of hard work, plenty of disappointments, tremendous failures, horrible twists of fate and fortunate accidents. I know that it's tempting to think that if you're a nice person, a good person, a deserving person and attractive as well, that the world just falls at your feet. You get chosen as Cotton Queen, you wear a fancy dress, people applaud and you live happily ever after. That's not how it is."

Rachel's brow furrowed.

"Mom, I'm not an idiot. I know it's not that simple."

"No," her mother agreed. "It's not."

Babs

I remember how I laid my finger upon her tiny open palm and she clutched her little fingers around it. My daughter, just fifteen minutes old, wrapped in a little pink blanket in my arms.

"She's beautiful," Tom said beside me. He was still dressed in fatigues, having hitchhiked from the air base in Biloxi as soon as I'd gone into labor. Twenty-two hours of contractions had allowed him to make it to the waiting room in time to meet up with his parents and field requests for pink-ribboned cigars.

"I know you wanted a boy," I told him.

Tom laughed and shook his head. "I can't imagine ever wanting anyone else but her," he said.

That's what I loved about Tom. One of the many things I loved about him. He always seemed to be so pleased with me and with everything I did. I swear, if I'd presented the guy with a five-limbed, harelipped gorilla, he'd have said she was the prettiest child he'd ever seen.

But it was no stretch for him that day. She was perfect.

"I don't think Thomas Henry Hoffman, Jr., will work for her name, though."

Tom laughed ruefully.

"Do you still want to name her after your mother?" he asked me.

I looked up at him, serious but open to discussion. "If it's all right with you."

"I didn't know your mother," he said. "But I know you and how much you loved her. It will be a fine name for the baby to live up to."

"You don't think it'll make your mama jealous?"

He shrugged. "This is her ninth grandchild," he said. "I don't think it's all that big a deal for her."

"Maybe we could use her name for the middle."

"Alana Helen Hoffman." Tom voiced the name thoughtfully. "I like it," he said. "But it's too big for this little bit."

I smiled down at my baby once again.

"Oh, we'll shorten it till she's big enough to manage such a mouthful," I told him.

"We'll call her Ally or Laney."

"Laney," Tom said. "I like that."

And so it was that seven-pound, two-ounce Laney Hoffman entered into life in McKinney, Texas, in the summer of 1958. It wasn't a perfect summer. Tom was in the Air Force. He'd joined up hoping to get into mechanics training. He thought that would offer him big opportunities with a big private company like Pan Am or TWA. That was our plan.

Unfortunately much of it involved me living in the small apartment above my uncle Warren's Pennsylvania Street Coin-Op Laundromat. He let me live there free just for opening the door at 6:00 a.m. and closing at midnight. Between time, I had to keep the floor clean, the change machine full and run interference on washer backups, overloads and plumbing calamities, all of which were common.

But I didn't mind, especially that summer when the courts mulled over public school integration, and Elvis spent his days in the Army. I took my Laney in her little carry basket to work with me and I spent every spare moment singing to my little girl, playing with my little girl. It worked out well. Much of the time we were alone. And even when the laundry was full of people, the whirr of the washers and *fft-fft-fft* of the dryers enveloped us like a cloud of privacy. It was Laney and me against the world. We were a powerful pair that summer. Nobody could ever come between us.

I hadn't known all that much about caring for babies. I had, of course, put in a million hours babysitting my cousins.

I was an orphan, though I guess I didn't think of myself that way at the time. Orphans lived in big brick institutions waiting for someone to adopt them. I'd not spent one night in such a place. I'd lived with Uncle Warren and Aunt Maxine.

I don't remember much about my father. He was a soldier in the Second World War and died in Holland in a place called Arnhem. That's all I know about him. I'm sure he must have had parents, siblings, someone. But I never met any of them. My family had been my mother and me. When she died I was fourteen, and I went to live with her brother, Warren Barstow.

He and Aunt Maxine were nice to me, but they had plenty of children already. Warren Jr., whom we called Renny, was five. Pete was four. And the twins, Janey and Joley were toddlers. I was immediately put to work.

I was pretty certain that if there had been anyone else available, my aunt and uncle would never have taken me in. But there was no one. So I was determined to never make them sorry for the decision to keep me. I was Aunt Maxine's right hand in the house. I was in charge of the children whenever she needed me. And I earned my own clothing and spending money working for Uncle Warren wherever he required help. He owned a half-dozen little struggling businesses in McKinney and, sooner or later, I ended up working at all of them. I did my time polishing at his Shoe Repair Shop. I packed clothes in plastic at the Spotless Dry Cleaners. And I served up ice cream at Dairy Hut.

Of course, I also kept up my grades, joined 4-H, attended pep rallies and ball games. I wore saddle oxfords and bobby sox during the week and white gloves and a pillbox hat on Sunday. I tried to do and be everything that I thought was expected of a perfect teenager.

I think they were pleased with me. I think they were proud of me. And they tried to encourage me. If I got straight A's, the whole family would go downtown on Friday night for dinner at Dutton's Café and a movie at the Ritz. When I won the blue ribbon at the County Fair for my begonias, they fenced off a huge plot in the backyard for my personal flower garden.

My senior year, I was first runner-up for Cotton Queen. I was disappointed that I didn't win, of course. LaVeida Raymond was chosen over me. It wasn't because she was prettier, but because her family was more important. I was philosophical about it. At least I was a member of the Queen's Court for the annual Cotton Days Parade. And if, by chance LaVeida had come down with some terrible disease, I'd have been able to step into her place. But she stayed completely healthy and I maintained my place as runner-up.

Aunt Maxine sewed me a beautiful formal in pink chiffon. Uncle Warren went all the way to Denton to borrow a convertible from a dealership for my ride in the downtown parade. It was, up to that moment, the most exciting experience of my life. It was a rare occasion when I was the center of attention. My mother's funeral was the only other time I could recall and that scrutiny had been very unwelcome. But riding down the streets of McKinney, waving at the crowds gathered on the sidewalk, was a moment of triumph, a moment

21

of self-confidence that crystalized for me the direction of my life.

I was not the only one thinking about my future. A few weeks after the parade, Uncle Warren gave me his advice.

"A woman's only chance in life is to marry well," he told me one day as we worked together in the shoe shop. "Smart or dumb, pretty or plain, it's the man she marries that makes the difference."

He fitted the heavy work boot he was mending onto the shoe form of the straight stitcher.

"If a girl was really looking out for her future," he pointed out, "she'd look no further than Acee Clifton."

He bent over the sewing machine for a moment or two, allowing me to take in that thought and consider it. Uncle Warren had lost his left leg in the war, the artificial one that the Army had given him as a replacement didn't bend and, as he worked, it stuck out from the side of his bench at a curious angle.

"Acee Clifton?" I repeated the name as a question.

Acee was in my class, but he was not the kind of fellow that really caught a girl's eye. For one thing he was short. Not shorter than myself, I suppose, but he looked short and he was pudgy. He always seemed to have his nose in a book. In a high school where football and basketball were studied far more intensely than science or math, Acee was the least athletic guy in my class. Somehow I couldn't see him as future husband material.

The sewing machine stopped. Uncle Warren looked over at me, his expression sober and serious.

"I wouldn't have you aiming too high," Uncle Warren said. "I don't think there's any sense in a girl trying to get above her raising. But Acee's got money, family connections and a good mind. He's going to be someone someday. If those silly girls down at the high school had any sense at all, they'd be tearing down his mother's door to get a date with him."

As far as I knew, Acee hadn't had many dates.

I thought about what Uncle Warren said. And I spent more time just observing Acee, talking to him, trying to get to know him. But I also wanted a second opinion. So I went to Aunt Maxine.

She was ironing on the back porch. She claimed to enjoy the task, saying that she found it relaxing. Of course, she was still hot and sweating from the effort, even though it was already a breezy, crisp fall afternoon.

I told her what Uncle Warren had said.

Aunt Maxine shrugged. "He's trying to be practical," she said. "Women will have their romantic dreams, we all do. But the truth is, the man you marry pretty much determines your station in life."

She set the iron up on its end and took a deep breath of hesitation before continuing.

"Your uncle Warren is thinking you are like your mother," she said, biting her lip as if uncertain about revealing what she intended to say. "She was a truly sweet person, but she should have married again. There's no doubt that she loved your daddy, but that doesn't always come along in life. It certainly doesn't come along often. She'd have been far better off finding herself a good man who knew how to make a living, than pining away as a young widow and working herself to an early death. I'm sure Uncle Warren just doesn't want you to make the same mistake."

I nodded, thoughtfully.

"So I shouldn't marry for love?"

"No, no, I didn't mean that at all," Aunt Maxine said. "I think the only way to marry *is* to marry for love. Just try to fall in love with somebody . . . somebody like Acee Clifton."

Truly I tried to follow her advice. I was kind and polite when I saw Acee at school. I even made a point of choosing him as my partner in science lab. But I was a girl. Girls couldn't take the lead in that sort of thing. And I was never much of a flirt.

In the end, it didn't matter. I went on a Christmas hayride with Tom Hoffman. He was a farm boy who sat two rows behind me in World History. He played on the baseball team. But he wasn't one of the top athletes in the high school. He was just a sort of regular guy. He was tall, almost six feet and had blond hair that was too curly to be attractive. He kept it cut short and slicked down with Brylcreem. He had a great smile, though I can't say for sure what was so great about it. His teeth weren't any whiter than anyone else's and he had a gap between the front two wide enough to whistle through. I hadn't really thought about dating him, but when he asked me, well, I was pleased to go.

It was a cold, frosty night. I was dressed in a sweater and rolled up dungarees. Aunt Maxine didn't really approve of young ladies wearing slacks, but on a hayride, you couldn't really wear anything else.

On the way out into the country it was all carol singing and group laughter. I could have been alone or with anyone. But it was Tom who sat quietly beside me, enjoying the banter and occasionally offering a word or two of his own shy, clever wit.

We stopped for hot chocolate at the Manigault's farm. Tom put his hands around my waist to help me down. When we went inside, the other boys held the hands of their dates. Tom escorted me with four fingers at the small of my back. It made me feel so feminine and at the same time so fragile.

All of us teenagers thought ourselves quite grown-up and sophisticated. But we played silly parlor games and giggled and ate gingerbread like kids.

A brightly decorated sprig of mistletoe hung down from the door frame into the dining room. Several couples made a game of "accidentally" getting caught under it. Those trysts involved a lot of laughter.

Tom made no attempt to steer me in that direction. I was both pleased and, I admit, a little disappointed. Aunt Maxine, as well as my girlfriends, had always made it clear that it was "fast" to kiss a boy on the first date. That should really be avoided. Still, I sort of wished that he would, at least, try. When Mr. Garmon, the Sunday School Superintendent and our driver, came in to announce that it was time to load up for the trip back to town, kids began hurriedly lining up in the hallway for a last chance at the risqué game. Tom led me outside. We were the first people back to the wagon.

I sat there, trying to smile but feeling a little let down.

Tom must have read my thoughts.

"I'm not much for mistletoe," he said.

I nodded. "It's silly and childish," I told him, primly. "And we hardly know each other."

"I just . . ." He hesitated. "I just want the first time I kiss you to be because you want to kiss me, not us showing off for our friends."

"I do want to kiss you," I blurted before I thought.

Tom smiled. He leaned toward me, his hand on my jaw and our lips met. It was somehow perfect. His mouth was not too hard or too soft. He tasted like ginger and chocolate. I wasn't afraid. I was excited.

Other people began arriving and we pulled apart. But not far. We bundled up together under one blanket. His arm around me, holding me close. It felt wonderful.

On the ride home several couples were openly necking. We didn't do that, though we did steal a few more kisses.

"I've liked you for a long time," Tom admitted to me. "When you were in Queen's Court in that pink dress, I thought, 'she's the prettiest one of those girls.' "

"So you think I'm pretty?"

"I know you are," he answered. "But you're smart and sweet, too. That's the kind of girl I'd want for a girlfriend, if I was thinking to going steady or something."

"Are you thinking to going steady?"

"I might."

He grinned at me then. Even in the moonlight I could see that gash of dimple in his right cheek. He had dimples on both sides, but his smile was slightly crooked and the right side showed up more distinctly.

"I don't think my uncle Warren likes the idea of going steady," I told him.

"Then maybe he shouldn't do it," Tom said.

I giggled and he planted a playful little peck on my nose.

From then on out, I was Tom Hoffman's

28

girl. I wouldn't have anyone else.

The night of the senior prom he asked me to marry him. I agreed and we tied the knot that summer in a little ceremony at church, just his family and mine.

"Both my older brothers are farmers," he told me. "By the time they get my father's land and split it up, there won't be enough to support one family."

I listened and nodded as if I understood.

"I'm good with my hands and with machines," Tom said. "I thought about working on cars, but if I go into the Army, I can get training for free."

Ultimately he decided on Air Force and airplane engines. It was a very good plan.

We didn't plan on having Laney. But, as soon as I held her in my arms, I couldn't imagine anything in the world that could have made me happier.

Laney

The one thing that I know most about myself is that I am nothing like my mother. Nothing. Not anything. We're completely different.

What I suppose, since I'm pretty sure I wasn't adopted or accidentally switched in the hospital, is that I'm like my dad.

The first memory I have of him is olive drab fatigues and big, heavy boots. I remember running toward those boots, arms outstretched. I was scooped up into the air and twirled around as I giggled.

Daddy was so tall and he had a deep voice. He smiled all the time and when he laughed, it came from somewhere deep inside him, somewhere that was full and content and extremely at peace with the world.

I was certain then, as I am certain now, that Tom Hoffman, my daddy, loved me.

His years in the Air Force, our years in the Air Force, were brief in retrospect. But at the time it seemed that it was everything. Mama, or Babs as I call her now, stayed home in McKinney for the first couple of years. My father was an infrequent visitor, dependent upon the head of his unit for leave. After he finished mechanics school he was promoted to Airman Second Class. We lived on base in California. I'm not sure where exactly. I have no memory of that, either. But there are lots of photographs, wonderful photographs. Babs in her pedal pushers with me in the stroller. Daddy on his hands and knees as I, apparently shrieking with delight, rode on his shoulders. Me playing in the sand on the beach as Daddy watched, a beer in one hand and a cigarette in the other. There is even a whole photo album devoted to what is described as "Our First Trip to Disneyland." It turned out to be our only trip.

It had been an idyllic childhood, I suppose. It ended too abruptly.

I was playing in the yard. I had a brand-new red tricycle. I hadn't figured out how to pedal it yet, so I just pushed it to the spot I wanted and then sat down on it. I suppose I'd been pushing when the car with the men drove up. I hadn't noticed them until they were knocking on our front door. I was accustomed to seeing men in uniform. All my parents' friends were in service. I didn't think anything about it until Babs began screaming.

To this day, I can hear that sound in my memory as clearly as I did then. It was a horrible, lost, almost inhuman sound. It frightened me. I jumped off my trike to run to my mother. When I realized that was where the terrible cry emanated I stopped short. I was just there a few feet away from her, frozen to the spot. Babs had nearly sunk to the ground, as if her legs would not hold her. It was the grasp of one of the men that kept her from actually falling. The other airman was closer to me. Somehow I must have mistaken his neatly pressed navy dress slacks for my own father's leg. I ran up to him and clasped my arms around it, like I always did. And just like always, he bent down and pulled me up into his arms. I felt a moment of pure bliss and complete safety.

Then I looked into his face. This man wasn't Tom Hoffman at all.

"Daddy?" I questioned him, hoping he was wrong.

"I'm so sorry, little girl," he said.

That was all he said. That was all anybody said. Without further explanation, my mother began a hurried packing. Everyone we knew, close friends and mere acquaintances, showed up at our house to get everything into boxes and loaded up on a truck. It was a quiet, subdued atmosphere with lots of effort and almost no laughter.

Then we were on an unexplained flight back to Texas. It was a military hop from our air base in California to one near my grandparents.

A sad-looking old man met us as we got off the plane. He seemed a little disappointed that I shied away from him.

"Of course you remember Grandpa Hoffman," Babs insisted.

So I nodded as if I did.

I didn't know him at all. And Babs didn't seem to know him that well, either. Neither he nor my mother had much to say to each other.

We waited as they unloaded a big box covered in a flag. Two lines of airmen saluted it before they put it in a long black station wagon.

We got in my grandfather's pickup truck and drove the long way to their farm in near silence.

There was nothing quiet about that evening. We had dinner in the Hoffmans' kitchen. We were interrupted a hundred times by the telephone and people at the door. The house was full of flowers. So many it was kind of sickening. Who could eat fried chicken when all you could smell was mums and gladiolas.

Babs put me to bed early in the front bedroom. The house was old and creaky and unfamiliar.

"I'm scared," I admitted to her.

She rubbed a hand across my forehead.

"I'm going to sleep with you in here," she told me.

"Really?"

"Uh-huh." She was nodding.

"I have to talk to your grandma and grandpa for a while and then I'm going to come in here and snuggle up beside you. Would you like that?"

"Yeah."

"So don't you go hogging all the bed, 'cause there's got to be some room for me."

"You can sleep right here," I told her, indicating the mattress right next to me.

"Okay, that's where I'll be," she said. "But right now, you have to go on to sleep and I have to talk for a while. Okay?"

"Okay."

She leaned down and kissed me on the end of my nose.

"It's just Mama and Laney against the world," she said.

She left me then and went into the kitchen. I tried to sleep, but I couldn't really. It felt so early and I heard every noise in the place. I soon became distracted by the raised voices in the back of the house. I was curious. I listened intently, trying to keep up with what they were saying, but I couldn't. Some people's voices carried better than others. I could hear my grandmother pretty well and Mom only when she sounded angry. But there were other people talking and I couldn't make it all out.

I slipped out of bed and sat down on the floor next to the door. That wasn't much better. I opened the door. I could hear more. Down at the end of the hallway the light from the kitchen shone in on the floor. As I crawled closer, it became clear that it wasn't just Babs and my grandparents. Several of my aunts and uncles were in the kitchen, as well. But it's my mother's voice that I heard distinctly.

"I know what I'm talking about," she said. "None of you have ever been a child who's lost a parent. I have. I know exactly what it means and how it feels."

"She'll need to say goodbye," Grandma said. "No matter how painful it is, she'll need that for the rest of her life."

"No." My mother's voice was calm, but adamant. "The memory of that body in the coffin will supersede every other memory she has of him. Laney is not going to that funeral, even if I have to stay here with her myself."

That sounded good to me. My mother and I would stay together, while these other people went to the funeral. It sounded okay, so I made my way back to bed. I snuggled up under the covers and fell asleep waiting for her to join me.

The next day began before I was ready. Babs was sitting at the dresser in her underwear, hooking her hose to her garter belt.

"Is it time to get dressed?" I asked.

She turned to smile at me. Even smiling she looked sad.

"Yeah, you should probably wash up and get dressed," she said. "I'm going to have to go somewhere this morning."

"You're leaving me here?"

She nodded. "I'll only be gone a few hours," she said. "You'll stay with Aunt Grace and Aunt Lurlene. And you'll have lots of cousins to play with."

She was right about that.

My Hoffman cousins were, as Grandma would have said, numerous as ticks on a dog. I didn't actually know any of them. But as things often are with kids, after only a few minutes I was having a very good time.

The Hoffman farm had a very strange yard. It was bigger than any I'd been in in California with lots of small buildings and sheds and fences. There were contraptions made with pipe that you could walk on or hang from like a monkey. There were chickens and guineas running loose everywhere. A big old dog lay bored and unconcerned by the back-door step. There were a half-dozen cats in the barn. And an outside water trough with huge goldfish in it.

Two girls about my age, Cheryl and Nicie, were my immediate playmates. Nicie, Cheryl explained to me, was an "only child," which meant she had lots more toys than Cheryl. But Cheryl was bossy, so she decided what we would play and which of Nicie's toys we needed. That seemed okay to me.

The older kids had all gone with the parents in the cars. So the games that were usually mostly theirs, like "kick the can" and "tag," could be played by us younger kids without the usual fate of always being IT. We were running and shrieking, laughing, having a great time. We took our turns, each of us chased or were being chased.

I was standing against a tree catching my breath when Ned, Cheryl's brother, came up.

"Do you want to climb that tree?" he asked me.

Ned was two years older than me and being noticed by him felt like a very big deal. I'd never climbed a tree. The ones in our yard in California had been just sticks with leaves.

"It's too high," I admitted.

"I can lift you up," he told me.

I said okay and a minute later I was on the first big bough of the giant catalpa. I found a safe perch where I could see everything and didn't feel like I was falling. I could see the roof of the house and the cotton fields beyond the barn and the dirt road that went out to the highway.

"This is great!" I told Ned.

He nodded. "It used to be a good place to hide," he told me. "But now Grandma always looks here first."

I didn't know why anyone would want to

hide from Grandma, but I made no comment.

"Look what I brought," he said.

He held out a shiny silver tool.

"Take it."

I did. It was very heavy, a long piece of shiny metal with what looked like open mouths on each end. My daddy had a big box of tools that he carried with him to work. I was never allowed to play with them. But Ned was older than me, I thought maybe it was okay for him to have tools.

"What is it?" I asked.

"It's a wrench."

"Wrench," I repeated.

"They use it to tighten up screws," he said. "You just fit the head of the screw in here." He showed me with his finger. "And then you turn it."

I nodded.

"My daddy has some like this," I told him.

Ned nodded sagely. "I know," he said. "It's what killed him."

I glanced up at him sharply. I don't remember one person saying to me, "Your father has died." Nobody had told me, I'm sure of that. I'm not sure when my mother had been planning to. But Ned had beaten her to it.

"My daddy's not killed," I told him.

"Of course he is," Ned said. "Why else would we all be here? Why else would your mama come to the farm without him? All the grown-ups are at his funeral right now. That's what they do for dead people. They have a funeral. He's dead all right. And this is what killed him. Uncle Carl told my dad. Just a common wrench."

I tried to hand it back to him.

"It's not true!"

"Is so," Ned insisted. "Somebody left it in the plane's engine. When they revved it up, the thing went flying out and killed your dad just like that." He snapped his fingers.

"You're lying!" I screamed.

He grabbed the wrench out of my hand and stuck it in his back pocket.

"Am not."

I grabbed hold of the branch beside me and began wildly trying to kick Ned out of the tree.

"Liar! Liar! Liar!" I screamed.

My aunts heard the commotion and came running over.

"What are you doing?" Aunt Grace scolded me. "Stop that right now, you'll make him fall out of the tree."

I was crying by then. Crying because I

was angry. Crying because I was scared.

"What's going on here?"

Aunt Lurlene's question was directed at Ned.

"She's . . . she's just afraid to fall out of the tree," he said. "I didn't do nothing, she's just a scaredy-cat."

"I'm not! I'm not!"

I kicked him again and this time I caught him off guard and he did fall out of the tree. Fortunately we weren't that high and Aunt Lurlene was right beneath us and caught him easily.

When she did the wrench fell out of his back pocket and landed on the ground beside them. Both women gasped, as did the older children standing around.

Aunt Lurlene grabbed the boy by the scruff of the neck.

"Ned Hoffman, when your father gets home, he's going to wear you out!"

It was that instant that I knew it was true. It all made sense. Ned may have meant meanness, but he'd spoken in honesty. My father was dead.

Suddenly I heard that terrible howl again. That awful sound that my mother had made. It had frightened me so much the day the men had come to the door. I could hear it again, only closer, louder, more intense than before.

It was years later, looking back, before I realized that it must have been coming from my very own throat.

Babs

Those months after I moved back home to McKinney are vague and unclear in my mind. Tom. I still cannot think of him without the sense of anger and injustice I felt at his happy, optimistic life being cut so cruelly short. He had all the hopes and dreams and aspirations that buoy the rest of us. But he saw almost none of them come to pass. It was so unfair. When so many, to my mind, utterly useless people continue to live and thrive in the world, it was unconscionable for a higher power to strike Tom down. It made me furious.

But I couldn't think about that.

Having lost my mother at an early age, I knew that I didn't have the luxury of dwelling on what had happened or what might happen. I had to concentrate on the moment that was presenting itself and live through it in the best way that I could.

Then there would be another moment and another. It was the only way to keep going.

It wasn't easy.

Tom's family was in conflict with me, I felt, about everything. The Hoffmans held strong opinions about proper behavior. They thought they knew what and how things should be done and felt no hesitation in doing them their way. The Air Force had taken Tom away from home. They had seen him only rarely in the last four years. But they still considered him to be *their* son, to be just like them. And somehow Laney and I were relegated to the position of latecomers. We were related to the family only by marriage. The concept that Tom belonged to me and my daughter, perhaps more than he belonged to them, never crossed anyone's mind.

When I arrived in McKinney, all the arrangements had been taken care of, the funeral had already been planned. The only thing my mother-in-law asked me was whether I had an appropriate dress for the service.

"Tom wouldn't want a funeral," I explained to them. "He never liked them himself and he knew how hurtful they had been to me."

My protestation was whisked away as if I'd never made it.

"There has to be a funeral," Papa Hoffman said. "Everybody has a funeral."

"No, everybody doesn't," I told him. "I'm sure a graveside service would be plenty. A military guard and a few nice words from the pastor would be quite sufficient."

"Every Hoffman who has ever died in McKinney has had their funeral at the Lutheran church," Mama Hoffman informed me. "We can't do less for our Tom."

"I'm not asking you to do less," I insisted. "I'm asking you to do different."

"It would look like we were ashamed of Tom," his brother Carl said.

"Anyone who would think something like that is beneath the notice of this family," I told him.

My words were useless. They wouldn't hear of it.

"Well, at least we don't have to bury him in some anonymous nondescript cemetery in town," I said.

"What?"

"You have your own cemetery, here on the farm," I pointed out. "Tom took me out there, where your grandparents are buried."

"That place is full," Papa Hoffman said. "We're not burying anyone else out there."

"Why not?"

"That little top of the hill with the tree was perfect for a graveyard," Alfred, another brother, said. "But it's full of graves. There's no room for more."

"You could expand it," I said. "There's miles of cotton fields all around it."

"That's good cotton ground," Papa Hoffman said. "We don't waste good ground for burials. He can be buried in town."

"No one ever goes to that old plot," Mama Hoffman said.

"I would," I assured her.

They held their ground, literally.

But there was one point where I got my way. One detail that I wouldn't give way on.

"Laney will not be at this funeral." I stated it unequivocally. There was no room for argument, but argue they did.

"The child has to be at her father's funeral," Mama Hoffman said.

"Why?" I asked.

The entire Hoffman clan was staring at me as if I'd lost my mind.

"Because Tom's her father," Skipper, the youngest of the Hoffmans answered. "I'd want to be there for my father."

"And you are an adult," I pointed out. "Funerals can be traumatic for children. I don't want Laney to have to go through that."

"Well, of course you don't," Mama Hoffman said. "None of us want that for her. None of us want it for ourselves. Do you think I get any pleasure out of burying my own son? I'd love to just pretend that this funeral is not happening, that my boy is not gone, that his future has not been wiped out. I could just go on about my life, like I didn't know. That would be a whole lot easier. But I'll go there and I'll publicly mourn my son. It's my duty out of respect for his life. Laney must do her duty, as well."

"Laney is four years old!" I told her.

"But she's a Hoffman," Papa said. "Hoffmans aren't sniveling whiners. We face what we've got to face."

"You don't know what she's facing," I insisted. "None of you buried your parents when you were children."

The argument went on and on. But, I was not giving in. I began wearing them down.

"Lurlene and I were going to keep the youngers home with us anyway," Carl's wife, Grace, said finally. "She's about the same age and one more won't be any trouble."

Neither of the elder Hoffmans liked the solution very much, but they were exhausted and could fight me no longer. I didn't feel particularly victorious.

"I don't know how you could put Mama and Papa through that," Tom's sister Jean Anne whispered to me angrily as she was leaving. "They are burying their son tomorrow. Did you forget that? You're always just thinking about yourself."

I believe that up until that moment I'd thought myself welcomed into the Hoffman family. But right there, I felt the welcome mat being rudely snatched from under me. If a family doesn't allow the widow to think about herself and her child, then I'm not sure I know why anyone would even want a family.

Clearly it was, "me and Laney against the world."

The funeral was everything that I hate. The family seated in the front row to be observed by all. Extended passages about fleeting life and eternal glory. Long mournful hymns by trembling sopranos. And, at the end, the procession of mourners to view the open casket. Thankfully the family went last.

The corpse lay stiff and silent, his dress blues, stark against the white satin. There was not so much as a scratch on his cheek to mar his tan complexion. His face was in uncharacteristic repose, the laugh lines wiped away. He looked like my Tom, but not so much. I felt a strong sense of relief that he only resembled the man that I loved.

It's just a shell, I thought to myself. It's the place where Tom lived, but it's not Tom.

That seemed good. It seemed like something positive that I could take away from the moment. Something that I could live with over the long run.

Then my gaze drifted down to his hands. Hands do not have expression. They're not susceptible to decoration. They are simply what they are, completely honest and without deception. Laying on his chest, the left atop the right, these were Tom's hands. Those long fingers, callused and scarred, were too familiar to be denied away. I couldn't maintain my distance from what was happening. This was my husband, the man that I loved, the father of my child. And he was lying in this box. In five more minutes they were going to close it up and

I was never going to see him again.

A great abyss of loss and longing and regret opened up before me, threatening the very ground I stood on. It would have been so easy, comforting, to simply cast myself in that pit. I knew I could not. Deliberately I stepped away from the casket, determined to keep myself composed and in control.

I was apparently the only person who felt that way.

The Hoffman family, most particularly the women, did not hold back at all. Mama threw herself across her son's body wailing with such plaintive grief, I was forced to look away. I focused my attention on a stained-glass window. It was beautiful, all reds and blues and greens. The Good Shepherd descended a rocky landscape with the lost lamb slung around his shoulders.

Tom's sisters began to cry loudly along with their mother. My eyes narrowed as I carefully memorized every detail of the shepherd in stained-glass. Noting how each tiny leaded piece worked together to create the total picture. I decided that it would be the image to remember. The window would be the memory of that day that I would keep closely. My Tom, not lifeless in a box, but carried away on the shoulders of a great protector.

Whether it was two minutes or twenty minutes that passed, I truly will never know. But eventually the anguish of family mourning began to quiet. I glanced back to see each of the Hoffman women being held and comforted by husbands or brothers or sisters. None of them faced the closing of the box alone.

Only me.

"We're ready," I told the funeral director.

The howling commenced again. Once more I turned my attention to the Good Shepherd window, until it was time to head to the black limousines parked outside.

Tom's brothers and brothers-in-law were all pallbearers. They rode together in a car that followed the hearse. I rode with Tom's parents and his two sisters. They carried on a running conversation all the way to the cemetery.

The new Memorial Gardens had only a few graves near the entrance. The area Tom was taken to was completely empty.

"I went ahead and bought a whole section out here," Papa Hoffman told me as we walked from the car. "Mama and I can be buried near Tom. And there'll be room here beside him for you, too, of course."

"Ah . . . thank you," I answered, a little uncertainly.

"Of course, you might not want to be," he admitted. "As young and pretty as you are, you'll probably marry someone else."

I couldn't think of any kind of response to that, so I simply ignored it.

We gathered under a green awning, the flag-draped casket in front of us. Flowers in every color and description were crowded around. I couldn't look at it. I fixed my gaze beyond the scene to the long row of cars parking along the driveway.

I felt a hand slip into mine. I glanced over. It was Aunt Maxine. I almost shouted with joy as I hugged her. Uncle Warren was beside her. They were strong and solid and dear. I'm not sure I would have made it all the way to the end without them.

When they handed me the folded flag and the minister had spoken the "amen" I feared that they might leave me alone with the Hoffmans again. Uncle Warren did manage to get away, but I grasped Aunt Maxine's arm.

"Can Laney and I stay with you," I said.

"What?"

The question clearly surprised her and

caught her off guard.

"We'll need a place to stay for a few days," I explained. "I was hoping that we could stay with you."

"Well . . . ah . . . I . . ." She fumbled around for a long minute.

"Just for a few days," I pleaded. "Just until I figure out where to go and what to do."

"Well I . . . the Hoffmans have so much more room than we have, Babs," she said. "We've got the boys doubled up in one bedroom and the twins in the other."

"Laney and I can sleep on a pallet in the living room," I assured her.

"I don't know if that would be good," Maxine said.

"It's just for a few days," I assured her again. I leaned closer, whispering so that I wouldn't be overheard. "I can't go back to that house. Please Aunt Maxine. Don't make me go back to that house."

Of course she didn't.

Neither she nor Uncle Warren could understand why I couldn't just stay out at the farm, but they wouldn't force me. I drove from the cemetery with them. We picked up Laney and our suitcases and drove to their house. They put a camping cot in the twins' room for Laney and suggested that I sleep on the living room couch.

"This is just a temporary arrangement," Uncle Warren said sternly.

I nodded.

"I know I need to get out on my own and I will," I promised him.

There is nothing like desperation to push people into unexpected choices.

Laney

Living with Uncle Warren and Aunt Maxine was great. He seemed as constant and dependable as a rock. She was a font of sweetness and simply doted on me. My cousins were great, too. Renny and Pete were in high school. Both were tall and athletic. They didn't pay that much attention to me, but Pete would sometimes give me rides on the handlebars of his bike. And Renny would give me nickels to buy candy. The twins, Joley and Janey, were twelve and they loved the idea of having a younger sister. It seemed like every day we played school and I was the student.

On Sunday afternoons Uncle Warren would drive me out to the Hoffman farm. Most times, I'd get to play with Cheryl and Nicie. Even if neither of them were available, there were always grandkids around. The Hoffmans made a fuss over me, too. I knew I was special. Both because my daddy had died and because everybody was mad at my mother. I didn't know what had happened, but I overheard plenty of snide comments made between my aunts and uncles.

Ned told me directly.

"Your mother is selfish, disrespectful and she never really loved your father."

I didn't really know what the first two things meant, but I knew she did love my dad, so Ned was either lying or the Hoffmans were wrong. I never gave Ned much credit for honesty.

But beyond the few worrisome undertones, my life was great. I had lots of cousins to play with, pretty clothes and plenty of attention.

It didn't make up for the fact that Daddy was gone forever, but it helped.

So, it was unbelievable to me when, just as things were going so well, Babs comes home with the news that we're moving to Dallas. Overnight the homey house filled with comfy furniture and happy people was replaced by a sad little duplex apartment. The entire neighborhood of green grass was exchanged for one small patch between the duplex's two back porches, beyond that it was all concrete driveway.

Everyone was excited and happy. Uncle Warren told Mom how proud he was of her. And Aunt Maxine cheerfully volunteered to help Babs unpack things and line the cabinets with shelf paper. Even my cousins didn't seem sad to see me go.

Babs drove me out to the Hoffmans that Sunday and she stayed and talked with the whole family while the kids all played outside. I didn't hear any screaming or yelling, so I guess it was okay.

She took me aside before she left. "Have a real nice time with your cousins today," she said. "Once we move to Dallas, you won't get to see them so often."

Babs seemed okay with that arrangement. Apparently the Hoffmans were not.

"My parents want to adopt you," Nicie told me.

"Adopt me?" That seemed unreasonable. "Why would anyone need to adopt me?"

"A single woman in the city has no business trying to raise a child," Cheryl told me, undoubtedly parroting adults she'd overheard. "The only way you'll have a chance at any decent upbringing at all is if someone takes you in."

I wasn't sure what a "decent upbringing" was all about, but my cousin did point out some positives.

"You'd have a lot more stuff if you're Nicie's sister," Cheryl told me.

"My mom can't have more children," Nicie explained. "The only way I could have a sister is to make you part of the family."

"I can't be part of somebody else's family," I informed them both. "My mom and I, we're our family."

"Two people is *not* a family," Cheryl said emphatically. "Without your dad, you're an orphan. Your mother will never be able to provide for you."

I hadn't really thought of myself that way, but Cheryl was in first grade. I was pretty sure she couldn't be wrong.

I imagined myself as Nicie's sister. It was a great fantasy. All those clothes, all those toys, they could be mine.

But Nicie and I didn't look much alike. She had big blue eyes and blond curls. Both my eyes and hair were like my mom's, nondescript brown.

"We don't look anything alike," I complained to Cheryl.

She looked at the two of us critically.

"If you had the same haircut, that would help," she said.

Nicie's curls hung down to her waist. My hair was cropped close to my head in what my mother called a pixie.

"You could let your hair grow out," Nicie said.

"That would take forever," Cheryl assured us. "I'd better cut yours to match hers."

Nicie didn't like the idea much, but once Cheryl sneaked the scissors from Grandma Hoffman's sewing basket, there was no going back.

It didn't take Cheryl very long. All of my cousin's beautiful curls were hacked off and thrown in the dirt. And her hairdo didn't look anything like mine.

Nicie cried. Her mother screamed. Cheryl's daddy spanked her. Nicie's daddy spanked me.

Babs was furious. Not at us.

"How dare you strike my child!" she screamed at Uncle Freddie.

"Look at Denise's hair," he growled at her.

Babs only shrugged. "It's hair, it grows back," she said.

Nicie and her mother both began crying again. That just added to the noise of the argument.

Years later I wondered if it just wasn't all too convenient. My mother never came to pick me up at the Hoffmans, Uncle Warren always did. Then, just before we were to move to Dallas she came herself. And the harsh words exchanged gave her an excuse to put aside any plans for future visits.

The ride back to town was quiet.

"Uncle Freddie and Aunt LaVeida wanted to adopt me," I told her.

Babs glanced over at me with a raised eyebrow.

"I guess they won't want me now," I concluded.

"Well, you dodged a bullet on that one," she told me. "I can't imagine that you'd be happy with a family who put so much value on hair. And besides, who would share my cute little Dallas duplex with me?"

We moved in the next week.

Pete and Renny unloaded the heavy boxes. Aunt Maxine helped Babs clean and put things away. The twins played with me. We turned somersaults on the tiny piece of lawn between the pair of tiny concrete back porches and we skipped hopscotch on the wide expanse of driveway in front of the garage.

While everyone was there, the place seemed fun and new. But, at the end of the day they went home and it was just the two of us. I sat, crestfallen at the drop leaf table in the kitchen.

"Well, here we are," Babs said. "Mama and Laney against the world."

I nodded, but I didn't feel much better.

"We have our own room and we can eat whatever we want and get everything as messy as we want and not be bothered by anybody," Babs said.

"But it's so lonely," I told her.

She sat down beside me and rubbed my back.

"It won't be lonely," she assured me. "We'll have friends. We'll have neighbors."

She was right about that. The very next day, the woman in the other side of the duplex, Mary Jane, came over and brought us brownies. She was expecting her first baby just before Thanksgiving. Her stomach already seemed very big to me.

She sat and talked with Babs for hours. I sat in the next room, setting up my own girly gabfest at the coffee table with Tiny Tears and Teddy Bear.

My mom listened to Mary Jane's excitement about the baby's layette. Babs gave advice about bassinets and whitening diapers. When the subject turned to us, she told Mary Jane, very briefly about my father's death, but mostly Babs talked about her hopes for the future.

"I'm going to be working as a dispatcher

for a cement company," Babs explained. "I'll radio the truckers to let them know where they should head next. It's not my dream job, but it's a start."

"Oh, a job like that," Mary Jane said enthusiastically. "Think of all the men you'll meet! I'm sure after . . . well, after a decent interval, you'll be able to find a nice man to marry."

Babs seemed a little surprised by the idea.

"I don't know," she said. "Tom was a very special guy. I loved him so much. I don't think I'd marry for anything less."

"I know what you mean," Mary Jane said. "My husband, Burl, is truly my hero. I can't imagine a world without him. But you have to think of your daughter," she added in a whisper. "All little girls need a daddy."

Babs didn't respond to that, instead she changed the subject.

"What I'd really like is to get on with the telephone company," she confessed to Mary Jane. "That's really my dream job. It's about the most a working woman could want in the world. They pay so well. And there's opportunity there. The supervisors of the women are women themselves. If you're smart and dedicated and work very hard, it's possible to actually move up in the company. Wouldn't that be something?"

"I don't know," Mary Jane said, uncertainly. "But the telephone girls do have lovely clothes. That would be very nice."

A minute later Mary Jane issued a little cry of alarm as a car pulled into the driveway.

"Oh, my goodness, Burl is already home and I haven't even started dinner!"

She rushed out to the man, we could hear her apologizing for her lateness before he even got out of the car. Surprisingly they came to our back door instead of their own.

"I'm bringing my husband to meet our new neighbors," Mary Jane said. Babs eagerly invited them in.

Mary Jane's husband was very tall. He had thick blond hair that he combed back away from his face.

He came through the back door with such a sense of confidence, it was like he felt right at home.

Mary Jane made the introductions. "Honey, this is Babs Hoffman."

"Hi, Babs," he said. "It's great to meet you. Has my Mary Jane been bending your ear?"

My mom laughed. "Some of that and some of me crying on her shoulder."

"Well, you'll have to give that up," he said. "There's nothing but sunshine and happiness in this neighborhood."

"That sounds good to me," Babs said.

"Who's this?" he asked, grinning at me. He had the whitest, most perfect teeth I'd ever seen. "She looks like you. It must be your kid sister."

"I'm her daughter," I told him.

"Daughter!" He pretended shock as he turned back to my mom. "You must have married at the age of twelve."

Babs laughed again.

"Mary Jane," she said. "You'd better get your husband's eyes checked, he's liable to walk straight into a post if he can't see any better than that."

"What's your name, little sister?" the man asked me.

"Laney."

"That's a good name," he said. "I'm Burl."

He offered his hand. I took it just like a grown-up.

"Hi, Burl."

"Laney." My mother shook her head and made the tut-tut sound. "You must call him Mr. Grimes. And Mary Jane is Mrs. Grimes."

He grinned at Babs and then leaned closer to me, like he was telling a secret, but he said it loud enough that anyone could hear.

"She can call me Mr. Grimes if she wants," he said. "But you call me Burl."

He winked at me.

I laughed.

The duplex, I decided right then, was not a bad place after all. And maybe my favorite part of it was Burl. From that day forward he was always around. He was always funny and helpful. Mom and I both liked him a lot. With him around, I didn't miss Uncle Warren, Aunt Maxine, my cousins, the Hoffmans or anyone in McKinney.

Babs

My job at Big D Cement was not easy. It could have been. If I'd only been asked to do what I was hired for, keeping track of the loads. That would have been a full, but do-able eight-hour day. Unfortunately the company didn't mind paying for laborers, but they hated to pay for office work. The owner, Mr. Donohoe, did all the paperwork himself. Except that he didn't.

"Darlin'," he'd say to me. "See if you can make heads or tails out of my chicken scratching."

Then he'd put another pile of work orders, product receipts or time sheets in front of me.

The more I figured out how to do, the more things I would find shifted into my workload. After only a couple of months I began to feel like I started every day running at full speed and didn't catch a breath until closing time. A lot of women might have complained. But truthfully, I was grateful. As the numbness from Tom's death began to wear off, I found myself feeling a desperate sadness and a great sense of being adrift in the world.

I liked Mr. Donohoe. He was an older man with a thick white handlebar mustache. His once muscular frame was now lean and bent, but he still held himself as if he were powerful, protective. Somehow I liked him immediately.

And he seemed to like me, too.

"Six girls," he said. "That's what my wife and I had, six girls. A whole house full. I can't stand working here with these men all day. I need a soft-spoken voice around me. I think yours will suit me just fine."

I liked the job. I liked our little duplex. I liked Laney's little neighborhood school. We were settled in Dallas and we were happy.

We rarely saw Uncle Warren and Aunt Maxine. They had a busy, active life with their own children.

And I'd sworn off the Hoffmans completely.

A couple of weeks after our run-in at the farm, I received a letter from Freddie. I assumed it was going to be an apology, but I was absolutely wrong.

Freddie, Tom's brother just a year older than him, had married LaVeida Raymond, the girl who'd been selected Cotton Queen over me. They'd had Denise a few months before Laney was born. But things had not gone well. After a difficult birth and a life-threatening infection, LaVeida had been given an emergency hysterectomy. That was all sad and I was very sorry. But now she and Freddie had decided that they should adopt Tom's daughter. They simply informed me that they were adopting my Laney.

When Laney had first mentioned this to me, I'd assumed it was some story the kids had made up, but there it was in black and white. They thought that they should take Laney into their family and I should go on with my life as if she'd never been born.

"Of course it's harder to find a husband with a young child already in tow," Freddie wrote. "You can, with a clear conscience, leave Laney with us."

According to Freddie, it is tragic to see a child growing up without a father. Freddie thought he personally could fill the bill. Laney was a Hoffman, he said, and as such she should live with Hoffmans. As if she weren't any part of me and I hadn't given birth to her!

I ignored the letter. That seemed like the best thing to do. Then a second letter arrived, this one on a Dallas lawyer's letterhead. Mr. & Mrs. Frederick Ernst Hoffman were pursuing the adoption of their niece Alana Helen Hoffman.

I was stunned. And I was angry. Laney was my daughter. Mine and Tom's. And she was all of Tom that I had left. I didn't know what to do, who to call, how to protest. I knew Uncle Warren would help me, but they had done enough. I needed to figure out the world on my own. I needed to find a way to manage things myself.

On my lunch break I pored over the attorney listings in the yellow pages. Several times I picked up the phone with the intention to call. But I just couldn't contact a total stranger and spread my whole personal life in front of them. It was just too humiliating.

The solution came, as they often do, unexpectedly. On Sunday afternoon, I was talking long distance to Aunt Maxine. She called once a week to check on us. She also loved to keep me posted on all the happenings in my hometown.

"The Sloan house was finally sold," she told me.

The beautiful two-story Queen Anne with intricate gingerbread moldings and wraparound porches had been sitting and rotting since the death of Old Miss Sloan nearly a decade earlier.

"Oh, I hope they're not going to knock it down," I said. "I've always loved that old house."

"No, it's not being knocked down, it's being renovated and you'll never guess who's doing it."

"Who?"

"Acee Clifton."

"Acee?"

"Yes, he's back from law school and he's set up practice here in McKinney," she said. "He's bought the Sloan house and has an army of carpenters fixing up the place. Though why a single man would want such a huge old house, I don't know."

"Acee Clifton is a lawyer?"

"Yes, honey," Aunt Maxine said. "Hadn't you heard that?"

"I had no idea," I admitted. "I hadn't heard anything about him since high school."

The conversation continued and I made

all the appropriate responses, I suppose, but all I could think of was that Acee Clifton was a lawyer and no stranger.

I called him the next morning at ten o'clock. A woman answered the phone.

"Acee Clifton, Attorney at Law."

"Hi . . . ah . . . hello . . . is . . . ah . . . is Acee in?"

"May I tell him who's calling?"

"This is Barbara Hoffman. He may remember me as Barbara Quarles."

It was less than a minute later when he picked up the phone.

"Babs! What a surprise. It's great to hear from you."

He sounded like himself, but not really. His voice was more confident and upbeat than I remembered. There had always been a bit of an underlying dispiritedness or high school unhappiness that was not now in evidence.

"I . . . I just heard that you are back in town," I said.

"The Sloan house," he replied. "I never imagined that buying that place would make me an instant celebrity in my hometown."

"I didn't know you were a lawyer."

"Yes, I love it. My mother wanted me to study agriculture and take over the family business," he said. "But this is much more to my liking."

"Well, that's good."

Now that I had him on the phone, I was suddenly less eager to share my problems with him.

"So are you and Tom back in McKinney? He's in military service, right?"

I hesitated. The words stuck in my throat.

"Tom was killed last summer," I said, deliberately keeping my voice even.

"Oh, my gosh, Babs! I hadn't heard. I'm so sorry."

I knew how uncomfortable grief was for people, so I quickly moved on.

"Actually that's why I'm contacting you," I said. "I need some legal advice and I wanted to talk to someone that I know I can trust."

"Is there a problem with his estate?"

"His estate?" The word struck me funny. "The only 'estate' Tom left me was a 1959 Ford with a bad water pump," I told him.

There was a polite silence on the other end of the line. I assumed that my financial tightrope was only humorous to me.

"I have a daughter," I went on to explain. "She's in kindergarten. I got a letter from a lawyer here in Dallas telling me that

Tom's brother Freddie is pursuing an adoption of her."

"And you don't want this?"

"I'm not giving up my child," I stated flatly.

"I'm sure a lot of women in your position would consider this a very good solution," he said. "I'm sure that Freddie is more than able to provide for your daughter. And not having a child in tow would certainly make it easier to find another husband."

Both those things were true, of course. No one believed that women needed to be paid real wages. Those who worked earned "pin money." It was assumed that the husbands or fathers would be the ones to provide for them. And men looking for prospective brides tended not to be interested in those who already had children who needed support. It wasn't a fair world, or one that made allowances for catastrophe. But it wasn't as if widows were unheard of.

"I'm not giving up my daughter," I repeated. "She won't be better off with anyone but me. And if her existence runs some man off, well, he'd never be right for me anyway."

There was a low chuckle on the other end of the line.

"Babs, you haven't changed, have you," Acee said. "You're just dad-blamed determined in whatever you do. You never let other people's logic gum up what you're thinking."

The way he said that, it was hard to tell if it was a compliment or a criticism.

"Are you going to help me?" I asked.

"Are you going to need help?"

"Well, they sent me this letter," I said.

"It's a letter," he told me. "It's meant to put some scare into you. To see if you'll just come around to their way of thinking."

"So they can't really take her?"

"Well, they can if . . . if you've been imprudent," he said.

"Imprudent?"

"If you spend your evenings in beer joints or nightclubs," he said. "Or if you've taken up with gentlemen friends who sometimes stay overnight. There'll be a lot of judges that will snatch a child away at the first suggestion of immorality."

"Oh, my goodness! I mean no, no, of course not," I replied, thoroughly shocked. "I've never been inside a beer joint in my life. And men, well I . . . I mean . . . Tom just died. I certainly haven't even thought about . . . about being with another man."

"No, of course not," Acee agreed reassuring me. "Send me the letter from the lawyer and I'll respond. That will be the end of it. As long as you avoid any appearance of impropriety you'll be perfectly safe in keeping your child."

Relief swept over me.

"That's wonderful," I said. "Oh, thank you, thank you. Acee, you don't know how frightened I've been."

"You don't have to be afraid anymore," he said with certainty.

"How much do I owe you?" I asked tentatively. "Or are you going to bill me."

"No charge," he said.

"That doesn't seem right," I told him.

"Can't I do a favor for an old friend?"

We weren't really friends and never had been. But I didn't have a lot of money to spare. Somehow I hated for Acee to know that, to even suspect it. But I thanked him and kept my mouth shut.

As the days passed Laney and I were going along very well.

And a lot of that was due to Mary Jane and Burl. Mary Jane insisted that Laney stay with her after school.

"It's silly for you to pay somebody to keep her, when I would love to have both the help and the company."

I didn't know how much help a five-year-old could be to a pregnant woman, but Mary Jane walked to Bowie Elementary every afternoon at two and kept Laney with her until I arrived home at five. She was wonderful.

And Burl was wonderful, too. When the sink got stopped up or a fuse blew out, he was always there getting things back in working order. He even made a special trip to the salvage yard to swap out the water pump on my Ford. It was great. It all seemed great.

As the birth of Mary Jane's baby grew nearer, I kept close to the phones at work. It was already decided that I would drive her to the hospital and Burl would meet us there. It was a Friday afternoon when the call came.

I gave the news to Mr. Donohoe and he shooed me out the door. It all went perfectly. I got Laney from school. I got Mary Jane to the hospital. Her husband was by her side within minutes of arriving.

Only a few hours later, they were pulling into the driveway of the duplex.

"False labor," Mary Jane told me, disappointed.

"It happens," I told her shrugging.

"I hope it doesn't happen too much,"

Burl said. "I missed a whole afternoon of work for nothing."

"I'm sorry, honey, I'm really sorry," Mary Jane apologized over and over.

I'd cooked a meat loaf for Laney and me. I cut it in half and took it over so she wouldn't have to worry about dinner.

"Thanks so much," she said at the back door. "I'm so very sorry."

"Mary Jane, forget it," I told her. "You can't tell false labor from real labor until it happens. Don't beat yourself up about it."

"I just hate being a bother to you and Burl," she said in a whisper.

"We don't mind," I said. But something in her expression, her demeanor, gave me my first hint that maybe I spoke only for myself.

Over the next few days I was thrown into the company of my neighbors a lot. For the first time, I began to see that everything was not as it had seemed. Burl was not always smiling and helpful. Sometimes Mary Jane appeared almost afraid of him.

It was just anxiety over the coming of the new baby, I assured myself.

The following Tuesday, Laney and I spent a quiet evening together. I read her favorite bedtime story until she fell asleep and then sat up alone to watch *Perry Mason* on the TV. I was just thinking to turn the light off and go to bed when I heard a tap on the back door. It was certainly Burl or Mary Jane and I thought it might be real labor this time. I hurried through the kitchen. I peeked through the curtain and saw Burl. Immediately I tightened the sash on my bathrobe and slid back the bolt.

"Are you going to the hospital again?" I asked.

Before he even answered, he sort of slid past me stepping inside as casually as if he owned the place.

"No," he said. "Mary Jane's resting. I thought I'd come over and see how you're doing."

"Oh." I was caught off guard. What was he doing coming to my place so late?

"I want to thank you for all you've done for Mary Jane lately."

His words were ordinary and he had a big smile on his face, but there was something about them that felt strange.

"Well, you're welcome. Mary Jane has been wonderful to me. She's my closest friend," I managed to mumble.

He shut the door behind him.

"Laney's asleep, I guess." It was more of

a statement than a question.

I nodded.

"Yeah, I was just getting ready to go to bed myself," I admitted.

Burl sort of tilted his head and made a tutting sound. "So sad," he told me. "The beautiful young widow sleeps all alone."

He said it lightly, friendly, jokingly. Still, I was suddenly very conscious of my bare feet and the thin nightgown beneath my chenille robe.

Burl crossed the room and began opening the cabinets. "What have you got to drink in this place?" he asked.

"I . . . uh . . . milk," I answered. "And orange juice, I think."

I moved to the fridge to check.

"I never took you for a teetotaler," he said.

"I'm not. I mean, I don't really drink, but it's just because I was a teenager and now I'm a mother. Tom would sometimes have a beer on a hot summer day. But I don't have anything here, now."

Burl nodded, yet he was clearly annoyed.

"Would you like some orange juice?"

"No."

His reply was sharp.

"Sorry," he said almost immediately. "I just wanted us to have a little drink together, try to get to know each other a little better."

"That would be nice," I said. "Maybe after the baby is born we can have a little welcome home party or something. It would give Mary Jane a nice break and it would be fun for Laney, too."

He chuckled. The sound was somehow unpleasant.

"The party I have in mind wouldn't need my wife or your daughter." He moved to stand right in front of me. "I'm thinking of a little private party for two."

I stepped back.

"Burl, I don't know what you're thinking but . . ."

"I'm thinking about you," he said, his voice velvet soft. "I'm lying in that room over there, and there's just a wall between your bed and mine. It's just a wall and I'm thinking I can almost hear you breathing."

He was so close I could feel his words against my skin. I stepped away again, this time finding my back flat against the refrigerator. I knew what was going on now, I thought. He was making a pass. I could slap his face, but that would ruin any friendship we might have forever. So I pretended not to understand.

"These walls are thin, but I doubt you can hear me breathing."

I tried to edge away from him. He grasped me around the waist.

"I need you, baby," he growled out. "I'm aching, aching for you. And I know you're over here, all empty and needing a man."

"Let me go, Burl."

"You don't want me to," he said. "You've been telling me every way except plain English. Shaking your butt at me night and day. I'm here now, baby, and I'm going to give it to you real good."

"Let me go!" I insisted. "I'm telling you in plain English now, let me go."

"You want to fight a little bit? Okay, that's fun. I like a woman who's a little sassy."

I was annoyed. Burl was disgusting and obtuse. It was clear to me that our friendship was irrevocably spoiled. That disappointed and aggravated me. Unfortunately my sheltered, safe life made me unprepared for anything worse.

"Stop it!"

He grabbed my breast as he pressed me against the refrigerator. I slapped at his hands. He just laughed and ground his pelvis against mine.

"You love it, baby," he said.

He tried to kiss me. I turned my head away.

I was struggling now. I was desperately trying to push him away. He grabbed my hands and held them both in one as he got the other inside my robe, pawing me. I was surprised at how strong he was, how easily he could control me. I began fighting back in earnest. Unable to move my arms, I clawed at him. I aimed a kick at his groin. He brought up his own knee to block my attack. Left with nothing else, his face was close to my own, I sunk my teeth into his cheek.

That made him mad. He cursed vividly and then hauled back and slapped me so hard I saw stars.

"Stupid bitch! This could have been fun for you, but I'm having you either way."

He picked me up as if I were nothing more than a rag doll and slammed me facedown on the kitchen table. I was momentarily stunned as he pushed my nightgown up around my neck. But when he began jerking down my underpants, I grabbed for them. He held my wrists together at the small of my back. I kicked, I struggled, I fought. He parted my legs with his own. He controlled me easily and he laughed at my powerlessness.

"I'll scream," I threatened. "I'll scream, Burl, and it's like you said. These walls are thin. Mary Jane will hear me."

"Yeah, and what's Mary Jane going to do?" he asked me. "I'll tell you what happens if you scream. If you scream your little girl comes running in here to see Mommy getting fucked on the kitchen table. She'll remember it every day of her life. Go ahead, scream your head off, bitch."

I didn't. I thought of Laney. I bit down on my lip. I held my scream. I held my breath. I had only had sex with Tom. It had been sweet and tender, thrilling and satisfying. This was not that. This was mean and ugly and frightening. I laid my cheek against the yellow Formica and I stared across the table. Willing my mind to another place, I focused my attention on the salt and pepper shakers, two little ceramic kids, the smiling icons of a canned soup company. Two happy silent children who watched as he forced himself inside my body again and again and again, greedy, abusive, debasing, until he spilled his seed inside making me filthy for all time.

Laney

I knew the minute that Babs woke me up that something was wrong. Maybe it was the sight of her bruised cheek and swollen lip. Or maybe it was the urgency in her voice.

"Get dressed," she said. "Get dressed as quick as you can."

"Okay."

Normally I got at least a couple of "time to wake up" announcements before I went in and sat at the table, leisurely coming to life over cornflakes and juice. Never was I rousted out of bed to put clothes on immediately. Probably out of sheer novelty I obeyed without question.

"What happened to your face?" I asked.

She reached up and touched it, almost surprised, as if she hadn't noticed.

"I fell," she said and then added slowly, "I was carrying some boxes and I fell." It was weird the way she said it, as if she'd just thought of it. But I didn't comment. She'd walked out of the room and I had more immediate concerns to distract me.

Babs had laid out my clothes at the foot of my bed, a madras plaid button-down shirt and dungarees. Why was I wearing dungarees? I always wore dresses to my kindergarten class. All the girls did. What kind of day was it going to be in dungarees? I went out to ask my mother.

The question disappeared from my lips. The whole house was in chaos. Everything we owned was stacked up, packed up or stashed in brown paper sacks.

"What's going on?"

"We're moving."

"Huh?"

"We're moving out," Babs said. "I don't like this place anymore."

"Are we going back to Uncle Warren and Aunt Maxine's?"

"No."

"Am I going to school today?"

"No."

"What about breakfast?"

"I'll get you something later," she said. "Now you have to help me carry all of this stuff out and get it into the car."

"Why don't we get someone to help us."

"We don't need anyone to help us," her words were stern, almost angry.

"Okay, Mama," I responded meekly.

Her voice softened, too. "Get your shoes and socks on while I pack up the things in your room."

There was no place to sit, every chair was covered with stuff. I sank down to the floor and did as I was told. I could hear her packing in my room. It was not the careful, thoughtful sorting of our things that she'd done at Uncle Warren and Aunt Maxine's. She was just throwing things into grocery sacks as fast as she could. She had my entire room emptied by the time I'd tied my Keds.

"There's not going to be room to take everything," she said to me. "We'll load up as much as we can in the car and the rest we'll just leave."

That didn't concern me very much. I assumed that the stuff we'd be leaving would be her stuff. Towels or dishes or things like that, things that weren't that important. When I saw some of my toys were in the throwaway pile, I didn't go along uncomplaining.

"This is mine, Mom," I pointed out, as I dragged my big plastic shape sorter out of the discards.

"It's a baby toy," Babs told me. "You don't play with baby toys. You're a big girl now."

She was right. Somehow it didn't make any difference.

"I like all my toys," I said. "Why should I leave them here? We brought them from California. We kept them at Aunt Maxine's."

"There's no room for them in the car," she answered.

"We should borrow Uncle Warren's trailer," I told her.

"You don't need them. We're only taking what we need," she said. "We're leaving them here. And that's final."

"But Mama . . ."

"Don't argue."

Her tone was firm, harsher than necessary. So I kept further complaints to myself, but I wasn't happy about it. I continued to sulk even as Babs readied the last of the boxes near the kitchen door.

"Now I want you to be very quiet," she said.

"Quiet? Why?"

"We don't want to wake Mary Jane," she said. "She's probably still asleep and we don't want to wake her."

That seemed a little strange. I thought

87

adults were always up early in the morning. But I figured it had something to do with having a baby and going to the hospital.

Babs opened the door slowly and propped it with the trash can. She glanced at me and put a finger to her lips as a reminder. We began carrying boxes out to the car.

After the novelty of the first load, it wasn't all that much fun. It was hard and boring and my mother insisted that we do it all as if we were walking on tiptoes. I couldn't carry very much. Babs had to do most of the work. It took a half-dozen trips at least. We filled the trunk up first and then the back seat. She crammed the last of it into the floorboard of the front seat passenger side.

"Go shut the door," she told me. "The rest we're going to leave. Hurry! And be quiet!"

Those two commands seemed contradictory to me, but I tried. I made one quiet walk through the home that I was just beginning to feel was my own. I grieved for the things we were leaving behind. The floor lamp that we'd had in the house in California. The rocking horse that had been in my room since babyhood. All my summer clothes, including my swimsuit with the yellow daisies on it. I felt sad and a little lost as I wandered among my now discarded possessions.

Suddenly my mom was there.

"Laney, what are you doing? Come on, get in the car now!" she growled at me through clenched teeth.

I hurried to obey.

I raced through the house and into the kitchen. Babs was right behind me. She moved the trash can to shut the door. I glanced inside it and saw my SoupKids, salt and pepper shakers. Aunt Maxine and I had collected twenty-five can labels to get them. When we mailed them in, I'd licked the envelope. I wasn't leaving them behind.

"Don't touch those!" Babs actually yelled.

I was so startled I dropped the salt one on top of the pepper chipping the little hat.

"Oh, Mama, it broke," I whined.

"Leave it, it's trash," my mom said, her voice adamant.

Just then we heard noise outside. It wasn't a scary noise or an unusual noise, simply the sound of someone moving around outside. Babs paled visibly, her eyes wide in fear.

"Babs? What's going on?" I heard Mary

Jane's voice from the yard.

My mother immediately stepped out onto the back porch.

"I'm sorry, we didn't mean to wake you."

"Wake me? What are you talking about, I've been up for hours."

I was alone for only one short moment in the duplex kitchen. I glanced down into the trash again at my salt and pepper shakers. They were mine. Mine! Babs had no right to throw them away like they were hers. I jerked them out of the trash and stuffed each into a front jeans pocket only an instant before my mother stepped back into the kitchen and grabbed me by the arm.

"We've got to go," she said. The directive seemed as much for her as me.

"I don't understand," Mary Jane said as my mom hurried me across the lawn. "What do you mean you're leaving?"

"Something's come up," Babs told her. "We've got to go."

"Something came up? Between last night and this morning?" Mary Jane didn't seem to believe it. "What about Laney's school? Should I still pick her up this afternoon?"

"She won't be going back to that school."

That statement stopped me in my tracks.

"I'm not going back to my school?"

Babs didn't answer, she hurried me even more forcefully. When she got the car door open, she actually picked me up and sat me inside.

"Where will you be?" Mary Jane continued. "How will I contact you?"

There was an instant of speechless hesitation on my mother's part and then she responded decisively.

"We're going back to California," she said.

"What?" The incredulous response was spoken by Mary Jane and me both.

"Some of Tom's friends have found me a great job," she continued. "But I've got to hurry out there. I'll call you when I get an address."

"It's all so sudden, too sudden," Mary Jane said. "You were going to help me get to the hospital."

The last sounded almost accusing.

"If Burl can't get here to pick you up, maybe you should call a cab," Babs said.

"A cab?"

"Look, I've got to go," my mom told her. "I should have been out on the road at dawn."

"Okay, okay." Mary Jane's voice was

quiet, almost forlorn.

My mom stopped then, next to the car and gave Mary Jane a little hug. "Don't worry," she said. "You'll be fine, everything will be fine. I've got to get on the road immediately. I'll call you, I promise."

A minute later Babs was behind the steering wheel, backing out of the driveway. As soon as we were turned forward in the street, she hit the gas, a little too hard and we squealed away from the duplex and Mary Jane.

"We're going back to California?" I asked.

"No," my mother replied.

I was stunned to think that Babs had lied to Mary Jane. But I didn't question her about that, my curiosity about my future was a much stronger concern.

"Where are we going?"

She glanced over at me, clearly annoyed. "I don't know that yet," she said. "We're just leaving."

I didn't think that could be true. She rushed so forcefully ahead, driving faster than usual and barely pausing at stop signs. We raced through parts of town that were completely unfamiliar. The wind that blew inside my window all new and never seen. The truth of her statement became clear when she pulled into an empty church parking lot. She turned off the ignition and laid her head down on the steering wheel.

"What are we doing?"

"Shhhh!" she answered. "I'm trying to think."

I kept quiet, but her thinking took a very long time. Finally I got my schoolbag out and began to sort through my things. I found some chalk and got out of the car and drew a hopscotch on the concrete. I was really good at hopping. I could even make the circle turnaround on one foot without losing my balance. Nobody at my kindergarten was that good and some of the girls in first grade couldn't do it. I entertained myself with the game. That was okay for a while, but eventually, I got tired of playing all by myself. I wished I was at my school. It was probably recess by now. All the kids would be having fun. I couldn't believe that I would never go back there. That couldn't really happen, I assured myself. Then I remembered our house in California, my sidewalk, my neighbors. One day it was there and the next it was all gone forever. Yesterday I had friends and went to school. And today I was stuck in an empty parking lot. I didn't like being alone, but I didn't get back into the car.

Babs was crying now. It wasn't the little tears of a skinned knee or a broken toy. She was wailing as if my dad had died all over again. I didn't know what to do. So I didn't do anything. I sat down next to the car, leaned my back against the wheel and waited for it to pass. I pulled my salt and pepper shakers out of my pockets. I felt a little bit guilty about having them. I'd never really disobeyed so completely. But still, I was so glad I'd saved them. They were smiling up at me. The one with the broken hat and the one that was fine, they both were smiling, happy to be with me. They were my friends, I decided. My always cheerful, always available friends. From now on, whenever they were with me, I was never alone.

Babs

In the weeks following the move from the duplex, I was acting almost totally on instinct. I tried to stop and reason. I tried to figure out a plan of what to do next. But every time I took the time to think the images and memories of what had happened filled my brain. It made me sick. It made me scared. So I was better just moving forward robotically and keeping my mind in neutral.

I did manage to realize that I couldn't just walk away from my job. I had no money and I knew we wouldn't survive unless I could make some. When I showed up for work three hours late with my daughter in tow, Mr. Donohoe took one look at me and didn't even comment. Maybe he was simply the kind of man who knew when not to ask questions. But what I felt was that what had happened to me must be written across my face.

That was the reason I couldn't just go home. Home to McKinney, to Aunt Maxine and Uncle Warren. That was what Laney wanted. But I was afraid that they would know. They had loved me and cared for me and tried their best and now my life was ruined and there was nothing anyone could do. I began to think about Tom. In the months since his death, I'd been busy, sometimes frantic, and directed toward getting on with my life and supporting my child. That had done much to hold back the grief. Now it washed over me like a deluge and I was drowning in it.

I suppose I let that happen. Even with all the pain involved in thinking about Tom's death, it was better than thinking about what had happened to me in the duplex. And, of course, if Tom hadn't died, nothing would have ever happened.

So, instead of crying about Burl, I cried about Tom. That was more acceptable. The emotions there were strong and could blot out all other feelings. I tried to take comfort in the Good Shepherd of the stained-glass window. But again and again the image of those ceramic salt and pepper shakers on the kitchen table overwhelmed my efforts. The remembrance of evil was just underneath the surface of everything. It showed itself in a new distrust and fear.

Mr. Donohoe was nice to me. I worried about that. The guys in the trucks had always joked around. Now, it seemed as if every glance in my direction was threatening.

I'd moved Laney and myself into a rundown motor court just off Highway 78. It had little cottages with kitchenettes. I made a deal with the old woman who ran the place, Mrs. Petit, to work the after dinner hours and the weekends in lieu of rent. She also kept half an eye on Laney who now came home from her new school on a big yellow bus and was responsible for herself until almost six. Not the finest plan for care of a five-year-old, but it was the best I could manage at the time.

Every evening I sat in the little office of the Shady Bend Motor Lodges sick with fear every time a car pulled up to the entrance. I couldn't trust my judgment anymore. I couldn't count on my instinct to warn me about who might be a threat. So everybody became one.

Or almost everybody.

It was about a month after I moved out of the duplex when Acee Clifton showed up at Big D Cement.

He looked totally different than I remembered, yet I recognized him immediately. He was slimmer, which perhaps made him seem taller than he was. Most of his hair was gone from the front. He was dressed in a very expensive and well-tailored suit. Still, he was obviously Acee. My reaction was unexpected. He should have been virtually a stranger, but he evoked memories in me of a sweeter, safer, less complicated time. The sight of him brought a strange and welcome sense of relief.

"Hi," I said, casually, as if I'd just seen him in the Malt Shop the day before.

He smiled back, apparently just as pleased to see me.

"I'm sorry to bother you at work," he said, giving a slight nod to my boss across the room. "But I needed to talk to you and your phone had been disconnected and the mail came back, Moved: No Forwarding Address," he said. "I went by your house. Your neighbor seemed to think that you'd gone to California."

I didn't respond to that. In truth, it kind of scared me to think of my name even being mentioned back at the duplex.

"I . . . I was running out on the rent," I told him.

I made up the lie on the spot. It wasn't a very good response, but it seemed like a better explanation than the truth.

It shocked Acee. Mr. Donohoe also stopped and looked at me askance, then hurriedly made himself scarce.

"What did you want to talk to me about?"

"I've been in negotiations with Freddie and LaVeida's lawyer," he said. "They haven't dropped the case."

"I thought you said they couldn't win."

"They can't," he assured me. "I mean, they most probably won't unless . . . well, unless they can convince the judge that you're actually doing something terrible. But just continuing with the case gives the Hoffmans some leverage toward involvement in Alana's life. I'm sure they're thinking that perhaps they could get court-ordered visitation or simply get it on record that they are an alternative for her in case you do get into some trouble."

"Okay."

Acee hesitated then lowered his voice in a concerned whisper. "I have to tell you that running out on the rent is not a good way to impress a judge about your fitness to be a mother."

"It won't happen again," I assured him.

"Where are you living now?"

"Out on the highway. Not far from here."

Acee smiled, sort of sarcastically. "That doesn't sound much like a mailing address."

"It's called Shady Bend Motor Lodges," I told him.

His brow furrowed. "You're living in a motel?"

"They're little roadside vacation lodges," I countered, dodging behind semantics.

Acee was nodding, slowly, but he looked worried.

"Babs, that won't sound good to a judge," he said. "Raising a little girl in a motel."

"They're just little cottages," I assured him. "And in the center there's a grassy area with a big tree and a swing set."

"A swing set is not a yard," he said. "And there must be people coming and going all the time. You need to find a better place."

"This is a good place," I assured him. "The old woman who owns it takes care of Laney after school."

I knew I sounded defensive.

"You don't have to convince me," Acee said. "I'm sure that if you like it, then it's fine. But I'm not the judge, I won't be the one holding it up for comparison with that brand-new house of Freddie and LaVeida's, on a nice residential street, with a big backyard."

"I'm Laney's mother," I pointed out, firmly. "That counts for more than all the houses in America."

"That's true," he admitted. "It's absolutely true."

I continued to argue about how good things were. That our little cottage was like living in a dollhouse. Everything was neat and clean and nearly new. I told him about how happy Laney was and how much she liked riding the school bus. It was a huge pack of lies and the more I told it the bigger it got.

Acee listened politely, nodding from time to time.

"Just think about coming up with a more traditional living situation," he suggested finally as he began backing toward the door.

"I'll think about it."

"And call Maxine and Warren," he added. "They were worried about you when I called."

"Of course," I told him. I did feel guilty about hiding out from them.

All in all, I was extremely grateful when he left.

I didn't take up any of his advice. It wasn't that I didn't want to. I thought it was a good idea. I wanted to take up "a more traditional living situation." But other, more immediate and frightening concerns took precedence.

A few days after Acee's visit I was sitting on the dispatcher's stool giving directions to a driver over the radio. I don't know what caught my attention, but I happened to glance out the window. On the street in front of me an automobile, same make, model and color as Burl's, was driving by.

With a sharp intake of breath, my heart was in my throat. My whole body was rigid with fear and nausea churned inside me. I watched the car slowly inch down the street, visibly hesitating at the corner where my Ford was parked.

I convinced myself that it was not him. There were hundreds of cars exactly like his in a big city like Dallas. He wouldn't seek me out. He wouldn't want to see me any more than I wanted to see him. He'd got what he wanted. He'd humiliated me, dominated me, terrorized me. He'd left his filthy stain on my body. He was done. What more could he do?

I comforted myself with that conclusion for several days.

I'd just been to the bank to make the payroll deposit. Mr. Donohoe waved me over to his desk.

"You just missed your boyfriend," he said. "Now, what you do on your own time is your business. But I'd just as soon you didn't run your love life out of Big D Cement."

I was embarrassed and quickly corrected what I thought was his misapprehension.

"I don't have a boyfriend. Mr. Clifton is my lawyer," I explained. "However, I will ask him not to interrupt me during business hours."

"Clifton's the short guy, right?" Mr. Donohoe said. "I didn't mean him. I know he's not your boyfriend. This guy was tall, blond, good-looking. He told me that he was your boyfriend."

My heart caught in my throat. Burl had been there. He had stood in the building where I work and he'd asked about me. The level of my fear went into high gear.

It became harder and harder for me to concentrate on my job. I was making mistakes, a lot of mistakes. At first, I just apologized and Mr. Donohoe was forgiving. But as the days went on and I messed up more and more often, he became less and less patient. So I began to try to hide the worst of my errors. That took up what little was left of my concentration. I fouled up deliveries. I fouled up payroll. Some suppliers were paid twice and some not at all. I couldn't get a handle on what I was doing. I was watching out the window all the time.

I was in the middle of a very serious reprimand when I finally saw Burl pull up and park in front of the building. My emotions were an unblendable mix of panic and relief. No more waiting. Burl was going to do whatever he was going to do to me and then it would be over. But I was terrified at the remembrance of what he could do to me.

"This business competes on its reputation," Mr. Donohoe was saying. "If you hurt that reputation, we lose business."

Burl was stepping out of his car.

"Big D is always on the job when we say we'll be there," Donohoe continued.

Burl was on the sidewalk reaching for the door handle.

"That's our standard, our minimum. I won't . . ."

"Excuse me," I interrupted. "I've got to . . . I've got to go to the bathroom."

I briefly glanced toward my boss. His jaw

had dropped open in shock. I didn't have time to explain.

"Don't you walk away when I'm talking to you," he called out to me angrily.

I wasn't walking. I was running, running toward the back of the building. The restroom was one dark, windowless closet about five feet square. I rushed inside and jerked the bolt across the door. Immediately I looked around for a weapon. There was nothing. The room was empty except for the sink and toilet and a roll of paper hanging from a length of wire attached to a nail. There was nothing with which I could protect myself. I was vulnerable, attackable. I took a defensive position on the far side of the commode. I squeezed myself in between the cold white porcelain and the rough red brick. I tried to make myself small, very small, so small that I would be invisible. I tried to make myself so small that I wouldn't exist anymore.

Bam! Bam! Bam!

The banging of a fist on the door scared me so much I screamed.

"Babs? What the hell is going on?"

The questions came from Mr. Donohoe.

For a couple of seconds I couldn't remember how to speak. Finally I answered, "I'm sick."

There was hesitation from the other side of the door.

"That boyfriend guy is out here wanting to see you," he said.

"Tell him to go away," I answered. "Tell him I'm sick and to go away."

More hesitation, then I heard his footsteps retreat. I didn't move. I didn't get up. I waited. I couldn't be certain that Burl would actually leave. I didn't trust Mr. Donohoe to persuade him. The minutes ticked on. I stayed hidden in my safe spot on the restroom floor.

I don't know how long I was there on the floor. Minutes? Hours? In memory it was a lifetime. Then Mr. Donohoe knocked on the door again.

"He's gone," the man said.

"Okay."

Slowly I got up. I walked to the sink and turned on the water. I washed my face and then stared at myself in the cracked mirror. I was unrecognizable as the happy, carefree young woman who'd come so close to being the Cotton Queen.

I found Mr. Donohoe at the dispatch desk, busy doing my job.

"Sorry," I said. What else was there to say.

He nodded. "You know that you're fired, of course."

The man's brow was furrowed in concern, but his words were unflinching.

"I'm sure you've got a lot of problems," he said. "I'm sorry for that. But I just can't have them here on the job."

I shrugged. "I would have to quit anyway," I admitted, honestly. I was embarrassed about what had happened, but I was more afraid of the future. I could never come back to Big D. If Burl knew where I worked, it was only a matter of time until he showed up again. Even if he never came inside the building, he could follow me to where I lived.

"I'll only beg for one favor from you, Mr. Donohoe," I said. "Please don't tell that man where I live or when I left or where my daughter goes to school."

The man nodded. "I won't say a word," he promised.

Still my evenings at the motel were now all terror-filled expectation. Every car on the road, every person who pulled into the driveway, every door slammed was a threat until proved otherwise.

After the motel had closed for the night and I was not on duty at the registration desk, I was watching from my own little cottage window. Long after the lights were out and Laney was asleep, I sat in silence, cold, scared, watching.

I missed my period. Then I started getting sick. I told myself it was nerves. I had no money. I had to find a job. That was my first priority. I couldn't think about what nausea in the morning could mean. I told myself it was the flu. I hoped that it was a tragic, terminal illness. Finally I had to admit to myself the possibility that Burl had left more in my body than that feeling of uncleanness and violation. I could be carrying his baby.

At first I sat on the toilet, pounding on my stomach to make it go away. I jumped up and down on the bed until I was as high as the ceiling and then went down to land flat on my belly, but nothing happened. I borrowed a huge washtub to set next to the bath. I filled one with ice water and the other near boiling. I sat in one and then the other. I screamed, I went light-headed, but I didn't miscarry.

I knew that there were ways to make it go away. I had heard hushed rumors as a teenager and more as a young wife of people in dark alleys who would do things, for a price. I had no money. But even if I had, how could I find those people. I didn't know who to ask.

My final attempt at ending the pregnancy occurred at an employment agency downtown. The less than helpful owner of the place dismissed me with disdain. Lacking a glowing recommendation from my last job, he was certain that he couldn't help me. I walked down the street to where my car was parked. In the alley beside the building was a rusty metal stairway that provided access to the roof. I stopped in my tracks and stared for long moments. Then taking a deep breath of determination, I climbed those stairs.

They say that just before you die your life flashes before your eyes. I had a similar sensation. With each step upward, I remembered all the things that had brought me to this point. From the most immediate, the child I carried, my mind worked backward. Burl's horrible attack. The death of my sweet Tom. My choice to marry young. My mind wandered back through all that I'd done and those things that were thrust upon me against my will. As I reached the top step and turned to look downward, I knew that my current course of action was very dangerous. I would surely lose the baby. But I could just as easily die myself. And it would probably look like suicide.

Laney would be alone in the world,

just as I had been.

Would Uncle Warren and Aunt Maxine take her in? I was sure they'd be willing to. Or she'd go to live with Freddie and LaVeida after all. That would make the Hoffmans happy.

I thought about all the things I would miss. Watching Laney grow up. Seeing her become a young woman, marry, have children. I didn't want to miss any of that. I didn't want to die. And I didn't want her to be left alone in the world, without parents, the way that I had been.

I sat down on the top step and put my head in my hands. Maybe I was just a coward, but I couldn't do it. I couldn't risk it. There had to be some other way. I tried to think. I tried to pray.

A woman having a baby out of wedlock in 1963 was immoral. Not only would I be a shame and embarrassment to my family, I'd never outlive the scandal. I'd undoubtedly lose custody of Laney. Women who got pregnant went for hurry-up marriages and fudging the date on the birth certificate. But I couldn't marry this baby's father. He was already married. And he was evil.

I knew there were institutions for unwed mothers. Young girls were taken in, fed and housed while their families made up stories about summer camps or visiting relatives in distant states. When the baby was born, it was given up for adoption with none the wiser. But those places were for teenagers, I thought. I had never heard of one that took a grown woman and her kindergarten-age daughter.

What else was there to do? What other options did I have? I didn't know. I didn't even know who to ask.

"What are you doing up there?"

The question came from the bottom of the rusting staircase. It was posed by a stranger, a bum really. A dirty, ragged man looked up at me curiously.

"Nothing," I answered, guiltily.

He started up the stairs. There was something wrong with one of his legs and he held tightly to the handrail and half dragged himself up each step. I hurried down to waylay him, not wanting to put his age and health through the exertion of the climb.

"I was just admiring the view," I assured him as we met at the first landing.

He glanced around and nodded. "It's a beautiful world all right," he said. His hands were grimy, the fingernails black, but his eyes were clear. "Some people like it better from a distance," he said, indicating the top of the stairs from which I'd just come. "But me, I try to admire it close up."

"Yes, I guess so," I agreed. I opened my purse. I only had a dollar and seventy-eight cents. I apologized as I handed him a quarter.

"It's all I can afford," I told him. "I'm out of work and I've got a child to support."

He nodded.

"You should go home, lady," he said.

"What?"

"Go home to your family," he said. "I would if I had some. It's always easier to work things out when you're surrounded by people who love you."

I took his advice. I went back to Shady Bend Motor Lodges, loaded up our belongings and when Laney arrived home on the school bus, I put her in the car and we drove to McKinney.

Uncle Warren and Aunt Maxine were glad to see us. They were so warm, so welcoming, I actually started crying.

"Oh, honey, what is wrong?" Aunt Maxine asked me.

I couldn't tell her.

"Is it Freddie and LaVeida going after custody?"

I shrugged. She took that as a yes.

"You go call Acee Clifton and see if he can see you tomorrow," Aunt Maxine insisted. "You'll feel better."

I did as she told me. It was so late that I was sure he wouldn't be in the office, but he picked up immediately.

"Hi, Acee, it's Barbara Hoffman."

"Babs!" The tone of his voice changed immediately. He was obviously pleased to hear from me.

"I'm in town this weekend visiting Uncle Warren and Aunt Maxine," I told him. "I know how busy your schedule must be, but I was hoping that we could set up a meeting."

"The schedule is the schedule," he said. "It's always crowded and if I try to juggle it, my secretary will throw a hissy fit. How about lunch? A fellow has got to eat lunch and I hate to eat alone. We could talk there."

I agreed to meet him at a downtown café the next day.

It was beautiful and sunny with just the hint of fall in the air. I was wearing a new dress. Aunt Maxine had cut it out and stitched it together that morning. It was just a straight shift in cornflower-blue with three-quarter-length sleeves. I carried a

113

little white cardigan, but the sun was warm enough that it wasn't needed.

I got to the restaurant first. Doris Walker, a tall, big-toothed blonde who'd been in my class at high school was now working there as a waitress.

"Babs Quarles, aren't you a sight for sore eyes!" she announced far too loudly. I felt like every person in the building was looking at me. Perhaps because they were.

"Hi, Doris, it's nice to see you," I responded politely.

"You haven't changed a bit, you know. You look just as pretty as when you were Cotton Queen."

"I was never Cotton Queen," I assured her. "I was first runner-up. LaVeida was the Queen."

"Really?" She seemed genuinely surprised. "I'd have sworn on a stack of Bibles that I remembered you wearing that crown."

"No, but it's sweet of you to think so."

"You all alone today, honey?" she asked.

"I'm meeting somebody."

"Somebody like you want to sit in the back or somebody up here where God and all McKinney can see you?"

She popped her gum and gave a big smile as she asked the question.

"Here in the front window is fine," I assured her.

She showed me to a booth with a perfect view of the courthouse square and handed me a menu. I looked at it eagerly. I felt less queasy today than I had in a week. I didn't know if that was a good sign or a bad one.

"You know, I'm real sorry about Tom," she said, more quietly and with a sympathetic smile. "He was a nice guy. I always liked him."

"Thanks."

Our exchange was barely completed when the front door opened and she turned to greet the newest arrival.

"Acee Clifton. Good Lord, look at you!" she exclaimed. "You're spruced up finer than a prize hog at the county fair."

Her glowing description did not, somehow, sound like a compliment.

Acee actually did look very nice. For Acee, I mean. He was dressed in a very sharp-looking, tailored suit. The double-breasted style and pinstripes made him appear taller and thinner than he was. His crisp white shirt was contrasted by the long narrow line of a navy-blue necktie. Doris's words had brought bright pink embarrassment to his cheeks.

Doris sashayed up to him, and brushed

some nonexistent lint from the shoulder of his jacket. It was as if she was checking out the quality of the material.

"You catching a bite to eat before you go off to wow some jury?" she asked him.

Acee cleared his throat uncomfortably. "Actually I'm meeting Mrs. Hoffman," he said.

Doris shot a quick look back at me.

"Well, well, well," she said loudly.

I felt my own face blushing.

Annoyed, Acee mumbled something about business and took a seat across the table from me.

"Just bring us some iced tea, Doris, and wipe that stupid grin off your face," he told the waitress. "I'm sorry," he added to me.

He certainly had no reason to apologize and I told him so.

We both relaxed a bit.

I expected him to bring me up-to-date concerning Freddie and LaVeida or maybe to lecture me again on how to conduct my private life. He did neither. He was chatty, in a warm, down-home way. He talked about high school. Things he remembered. Specifically things he remembered about me. Things he and I had said and done all those years ago. He recalled the details of a failed experiment in tenth grade chemistry where we'd tried to alter alcohol properties and accidentally made our sample into butyric acid.

"The whole science lab, even the hallways outside smelled like vomit for a week!"

I laughed so hard, I actually snorted.

He was smiling at me across the table. I was more cheered up and lighthearted than I'd felt in weeks. Then suddenly something changed in the air. I don't know if we heard something or felt something. But around us the sound was different and we were both immediately alert.

"What is it?"

"I don't know."

Every person in the place was suddenly looking around, as if they, too, knew something was wrong.

Doris burst out of the kitchen.

"The president has been shot!"

The shock of the words kept everybody paralyzed for an instant, then Acee jumped up.

"Come on," he said.

With only a second to gather up my sweater and my purse, Acee left a ten-dollar bill on the table and rushed out of the café. His hand in mine, he hurried us down the street until we got to Howell's Furniture.

"They will have the televisions on," he told me as we went through the door.

He was right, they did. And we weren't the first people there.

"What are they saying?" Acee asked as we gathered around the big box set with the others. "I know he was supposed to speak today at the Merchandise Mart."

"He never made it," Earl Butzen said. "He was shot driving through Deally Plaza."

"Who did it?"

"It was like an ambush," another man said. "There were shots coming from everywhere."

"How bad is he hurt?"

"We don't know," Earl answered.

"They've taken him to Parkland Hospital," Millie, Ed Finer's wife added.

"President Kennedy is in Dallas?" I asked, surprised.

Acee squeezed my hand. "He'll be fine," he assured me. "He's a strong, healthy man and young, too. He'll be all right."

I nodded, though I felt his words were as much to shore up his own concern as mine. I hadn't voted for Mr. Kennedy. I hadn't actually voted at all. I'd never been that interested in politics and figured that the country, the planet, could pretty much take care of itself without any input from me. All I really knew about the president was that he was fairly young and good-looking. He had a beautiful wife, two cute kids and his newborn son had just died that summer.

Now, as more and more people gathered in front of the TV in the furniture store I waited and worried about his fate.

Then we were seeing Walter Cronkite's ashen face. "From Dallas, Texas," he said. "The flash, apparently official, President Kennedy died at 1:00 p.m. Central Standard Time."

In Howell's Furniture in downtown McKinney several people screamed, a woman fainted. Acee Clifton's arm went around me and pulled me into an embrace. He held me tight against his chest as if he could protect me from all the anger and hurt in the world.

"Damn it, damn it all," he was whispering under his breath.

The next days were jumbled and strange as a new president was sworn in, a funeral prepared, an assassin arrested and then murdered in front of us on live TV. All of Texas was full of rumors. There were Cubans and Communists hiding behind every telephone pole. Gangsters and hit men were supposedly in every car with out-of-state plates. Even the CIA, the FBI and the local police were suspect. The Russians might be preparing to drop a nuclear bomb on us in the confusion.

It was a long weekend of fear and grief and sadness. In small towns in times of trouble, friends and family stick very close together.

Acee was there with us for most all of it. I didn't think much about his presence. I figured that he didn't want to be alone. Nobody did.

When little John John saluted his father's coffin, I cried as hard as anybody. But in all honesty, there was some relief in looking at someone else's problems, in letting my own rest on the shelf while I mourned. Dallas was a very, very dangerous place. But I was forty miles north and completely safe in McKinney.

Monday evening, I sat on the front porch swing with Acee. I was trying not to think about Dallas, trying not to remember all that was evil and terrifying about my life there. I was thinking about Jackie and the children and the loss of a fine man to his country.

I didn't realize that Acee was holding my hand until he brought the knuckles up to his lips and kissed them.

I turned to stare at him. What I saw in his expression caught me completely off guard.

"I don't know where to begin, Babs," he said to me. "I was thinking that we could start seeing each other, get to know each other, find out if maybe someday we could love each other. But now, with all that's happened, it no longer seems prudent to just wait and hope." He hesitated taking a deep breath. "I think I fell for you when I saw you riding in the Cotton Queen Parade. I already knew that you were kind and sweet and pretty. But when I saw you that day, I realized that you were beautiful. I wanted to approach you then, to ask you to be my girl. But I was shy and scared and unsure of myself. Then Tom Hoffman caught your eye. Tom was a great guy. Everybody liked him. But I never quite forgave him for running off with my girl and breaking my heart."

"I . . . I . . ."

"I know it seems sudden," he interrupted. "But it's not sudden to me. And when life is so fragile, so capable of being snuffed out so quickly it just seems foolish to waste time with customary formalities. I love you, Babs. I have for years. Do you think that there's a chance you could ever love me?"

An honest woman would have told him no.

Laney

I often say that what I learned early on about education was to be flexible. I spent my kindergarten in three different schools. The one where we lived in the duplex. The one when we lived at Shady Bend Motor Lodges and then back in McKinney. It was hard meeting new kids all the time, which is why I guess that I spent most of my times with those I already knew, my cousins. Nicie Hoffman was in my class and my very best friend. We never forgot that we might have been sisters. Aunt LaVeida was room mother and brought cookies and planned parties with the teacher. Along with others including Ned and Cheryl who were in classes ahead of me, I was kept conveniently connected to my father's family.

Babs and Acee got married in a small ceremony in the atrium of the courthouse. Uncle Warren, Aunt Maxine and my

Barstow cousins were there. Also the Clifton family, though they were all strangers to me. His mother made the biggest impression. She showed up at the last minute like an arriving queen and seemed to reign over the whole ceremony. None of the Hoffmans were there. I don't know if they weren't invited or didn't show up. Maybe they weren't happy about Babs remarrying eight months after her husband died.

For me it was great. Acee's new house was two blocks from downtown and around the corner from my school. I had my own room, which was bigger than our whole place at Shady Bend! That first Christmas remains one of the most magical in my memory. The huge brightly decorated tree in the front window. The garland winding up the stairway, the stockings hung at the mantel. I suppose my mother decorated the house that way every year thereafter, but it was that first Christmas that was filled with love. Acee laughed all the time. He was obviously so happy being married to my mom. I liked him for that. On the morning of the big day I was showered with new clothes and toys and books. Santa brought me a new pink bicycle with training wheels and silver-and-pink streamers on the handlebars. I rode it up and down the sidewalk in front of our house on that crisp sunny morning.

Dinner was an occasion. Babs set the table with the Clifton family china, a wedding gift from Acee's mother. She was regally installed at her son's right hand. Uncle Warren and Aunt Maxine were also there. I sat next to Renny. He was now Private First Class Renny, dressed in his uniform for the occasion. He'd graduated from high school the previous spring and was home on leave after training with the Army. He was so grown-up and so handsome. I thought him the most spectacular man I'd ever seen, even if he was my cousin. My very first crush, I suppose.

And Renny was wonderful to me. He was always smiling and teasing. He made me feel like I was important and that talking to me was interesting.

The food was great and there was lots of it. Plates were passed round and round the table. I was leaning back in my chair, feeling that stuffed sense of Christmas contentment, when Acee rose to his feet.

"Babs and I are so happy to welcome all of you to our house for this holiday celebration," he said. "I trust that since you've all been good, St. Nicholas has brought all of you exactly what you've wanted."

There was laughter and noises of agreement all around.

I liked Acee at lot. He wasn't anything like my father, I don't suppose. But I did remember how safe I felt with Daddy. I felt safe with Acee, too. And he was funny and always teasing me. He seemed to genuinely like me and I liked him, as well. Not just because he bought me lots of stuff and put up a swing set in the backyard and read aloud to me in the evenings in his deep, strong voice. I liked him for himself. As a stepfather, I didn't think that a little girl could do much better. And it seemed as if most of McKinney agreed. Even the Hoffmans, who I began visiting again on every other Sunday, thought well of Acee. And no one was trying to adopt me anymore.

Our life was like the end of a good story. We were living happily ever after. That joy, hopefulness, good feeling continued for a couple of months. Then our house was suddenly quiet.

Babs and Acee were unhappy. I didn't know why. It wasn't that they were arguing or screaming at each other. In fact, it seemed as if they never shared a word.

They certainly didn't share a bedroom. At first, Babs would come crawl into bed with me in the middle of the night. I liked that. But eventually, she got her own bedroom next to mine. That seemed okay to me. After all, there were a lot of bedrooms in Acee's house.

At the dinner table, I did most of the talking. I'd tell them what was happening at school and what my friends were saying and doing, what I was learning from my teachers. They both listened attentively, even encouraged me to keep up the chatter.

One evening, as I was taking a bite between stories, Acee spoke up.

"Laney," he began. "You should probably hear this from us before you hear it at school."

My mom's head snapped up, her eyes bored into him as if she was giving him a warning. Acee ignored it.

"Your mother is expecting a baby," he said. "You'll have a little brother or sister by the end of the summer."

My jaw must have dropped open in disbelief because Acee, suddenly smiling, reached over and nudged it back into place.

A brother or a sister. It was hard to even

imagine, but it sounded to me like a good idea. We were a family now. And families had more than just one child.

"This is great!" I said.

Acee nodded. "Yes," he said, not quite convincingly. "It is great. Your mother and I couldn't be happier about it."

He looked over at Babs as if he dared her to contradict him.

"Yes," she said, a little hesitantly. "We are happy. But Laney, this is not something that people talk about. If someone mentions it to you, you can tell them that Acee and I are very happy. But you must not mention it yourself."

I nodded, but I wasn't sure I understood.

"I can tell my friends though," I suggested. "And my cousins."

"No," Babs said firmly. "I don't want you saying anything to anyone."

That didn't seem like very much fun.

"Do you understand me, Laney?"

"Yes, ma'am."

That was the end of the discussion. For two people who were very happy, Babs and Acee seemed really sad.

As the weeks passed, I grew accustomed to the idea, even excited about it. Since I couldn't talk about it at school, I talked about it over dinner every night. I told Acee and Babs that I was hoping for a sister.

Acee grinned at me. "If she's as pretty as you, the whole town would envy us," he said. "But the thing about babies is that you have to take what you get."

I nodded. "So it may be a boy."

"And he may be ugly," Acee added, laughing.

We both thought it was a great joke and began calling my mom's tummy, Ugly Boy.

Babs didn't seem to think it was a very funny joke. But she was not in a very good mood most of the time. She yelled at me a lot more than usual. And she was edgy, as if being mad was just under the surface. I felt like I was walking around on eggshells all the time.

"It's just her 'condition,'" Acee assured me one evening as she snapped at me over nothing. "Just try to be as good as you can."

I tried.

Babs got fat. People commented everywhere we went about how much she "was showing." Acee told them that he hoped it might be twins. Babs complained under her breath about busybodies. After a while, she stayed close to the house. She didn't want to see anyone and she didn't want anyone to see her.

I wouldn't have minded that if she'd spent time with me. She didn't. She wandered about the house listlessly all day and sat in front of the TV wearing her bathrobe all evening. Acee stayed in his study. Except for dinnertime, I hardly saw him.

So every day I walked home from school by myself and then played in my backyard or alone in my room. I'd dig up the SoupKids that I'd hidden in the treasure box in the bottom of my closet and played with them as I waited for my kid sister, who would be someone I could really play with.

Marley Barstow Clifton came into the world on July 18, 1964. I'd been dropped off at Aunt Maxine's when Babs went into the hospital. After getting the news, I was eager to see him. I was even hoping to share my backyard swing set with him. But it was not to be.

"Marley is sick," Aunt Maxine told me.

"Like with a cold or something."

"No, he's got a hole in his heart," she said. "I don't think he'll be able to come home from the hospital for a very long time."

My mother didn't come home, either.

When people talked with Aunt Maxine it was always mentioned how Babs never left the baby's bedside. I didn't see much of Acee, either. The rest of the summer I more or less just stayed with Aunt Maxine and Uncle Warren. I didn't really mind it. I mean I loved them and my cousins and all that. But somehow I felt sort of lost, too.

I couldn't go up to the hospital to see the baby. No one under age twelve was admitted. Then they moved him to a bigger hospital in Dallas. No one even mentioned the possibility of getting to see him.

School began. I was off to first grade with Aunt Maxine by my side. Every morning we walked by our big house with my big bedroom, all my wonderful new things inside. It was as if they were lost to me. I shared a room with Janey and Joley. The twins were nice and motherly, but they were freshmen in high school now. It wasn't perfect having me taking up space.

Renny was stationed in North Carolina. He wrote Aunt Maxine a letter nearly every week and Uncle Warren would read it aloud at the supper table. It made the house a little less crowded, but we all missed him.

Pete was now a self-described *Beatle-maniac*. The group's records turned on his record player night and day. And he was combing his hair forward in a Beatlelike manner that exasperated Aunt Maxine and angered Uncle Warren.

Most Sundays, I was sent out to see the Hoffmans. My cousins, Cheryl and Nicie went to my school, so we were best friends throughout the week. Ned was there, too. He called me Little Orphan Laney. I hated that. It wasn't true. I had parents, two parents, just like him. I had Babs and I had Acee. They both loved me and cared about me. They just didn't have time for me.

Marley died the day before Halloween. The twins had already put together my costume. We'd carved a jack-o'-lantern and made plans to get candy all over town.

We didn't go trick-or-treating that year. Everyone went to a funeral instead. Everyone went except me.

I never saw my brother. I never saw him alive or dead. He was like a fantasy. No more real to me than an imaginary playmate.

"Why can't I go to the funeral?" I asked Aunt Maxine before she packed me off to Mrs. Larson, her next-door neighbor and my babysitter for the day.

"Your mother doesn't think that funerals are good for children," she answered.

"All my cousins are going," I pointed out. "Everybody I know is going, except Mrs. Larson."

"Your mother is doing what she thinks best."

"It's not best for me?" I asked. "She's hardly seen me since last summer. I've grown up since then. You should tell her that. I can read now. And I know all my sums. Miss Martin has put me in the Blue Birds Arithmetic Circle. Those are the smartest pupils. It's all boys except me."

"I know," Aunt Maxine said. "You are very smart and we are all very proud. But your mother doesn't want you to go to the funeral. She doesn't want you to remember your brother that way."

"What way am I supposed to remember him?" I asked. "Nobody ever let me see him."

Aunt Maxine didn't have an answer for that. But I didn't go to the funeral. I waited at Mrs. Larson's house until it was all over.

It was late afternoon when everyone returned. I was still feeling a little gloomy, but Uncle Warren perked me up immediately.

"Why don't you get your things together and I'll take you home," he said.

I cheered. Not exactly what was expected of a sister in mourning, I know. But I couldn't help it. I was eager to be in my house again. Eager to see my mother, to laugh with Acee again.

It wasn't at all as I'd imagined it to be. Uncle Warren dropped me off at the curb in front. I carried my dolls, my teddy bear and my suitcase to the porch by myself. I was met at the front door by a stranger.

"You must be the daughter," she said.

I nodded.

She waved to Uncle Warren who was still waiting in the street. He drove away.

"Who are you?" I asked.

"I am the housekeeper," she answered. "But I am not your babysitter and I will not allow you to be noisy and underfoot. Do you understand me?"

"Yeah."

"You will reply 'yes, ma'am' or 'no, ma'am,'" she said. "I do not approve of lax manners."

"Yes, ma'am."

"Do you know where your room is?"

It seemed like a silly question to ask. What kid wouldn't know their own room?

"Yes, ma'am," I answered.

"Then I suggest you remain in there, quietly, until someone requests to see you."

It was a very strange homecoming. Our house, our happy, laughing house, now was big and dark and ominously quiet. I sat in my room and nobody requested to see me. The old house creaked and the furnace made a big whooshing sound when it came on, but mostly it was just silence.

I waited and waited.

I watched out the window at all the people passing by.

I lay on the bed and stared at the ceiling.

I played with my toys — most of which I hadn't seen for months. The dollhouse that Acee's mother had bought for me at Christmas was mostly empty rooms. From deep down in the bottom of my treasure box, I dug out my SoupKids salt and pepper shakers. I decided that they could live in the house. Even in big empty rooms, the two of them together wouldn't be alone or lonely.

I snuck down the hall to go to the bathroom several times. I was genuinely afraid of the housekeeper. I didn't know if I had permission to go to the bathroom. But I wasn't about to find her and ask.

It was after dark when I got hungry and tried to sneak downstairs. I ran into Acee. He seemed surprised to see me.

"How long have you been here?" he asked.

I shrugged. "A while I guess, I came over after the funeral."

"Have you seen your mother?"

I shook my head.

He took my hand and led me to the beautiful nursery at the end of the hallway near my mother's bedroom. Babs had decorated it in bright yellow gingham with Peter Rabbit wallpaper. Sometimes she had let me help. Acee opened the door and I saw her. She sat next to the crib. She looked up with surprise.

"Laney," my mother said. "I forgot you were here."

She forgot that I was there.

"I've been in my room forever," I said. It was a complaint, but nobody seemed to notice.

"Have you had anything to eat?"

"Nope."

"Is Hannah still here?" she glanced up at Acee questioningly. "Maybe she can fix Laney something."

"I'll do it," he answered. "I'm hungry myself. Do you want something?"

Mom shook her head and gazed back into the empty crib.

I was ushered out of his room. Acee took

me to the kitchen and we made ham sandwiches.

"Is that all you can cook, ham sandwiches?"

He nodded. "That's pretty much it for
me," he said, grinning. "Before I married
your mother, I either ate at restaurants or
at my mother's."

He handed me my sandwich and I took a
bite.

"It's pretty good," I told him.

He smiled and nodded. "That goes
along with my philosophy of life," he said.
"If I can only do one thing, I want to do it
better than anybody else."

"I want to do lots of things," I told him.

"Most people feel that way," he said.
"But sometimes it's better to do one thing
really well than to be mediocre at a
number of things."

"What's meaty oaker?" I asked.

"Everything."

"Huh?"

"Never mind," he said. "You'll find out
about the world too soon anyway."

I shrugged and let that go.

"What's wrong with Mama?" I asked
him. "How could she forget I was here?"

Acee reached over and tucked a stray
lock of my hair behind my ear. "She's just
sad, Laney," he said. "Her whole heart is

full of sadness right now. But she'll get better. She'll be fine."

He said it with such certainty, that I had no choice but to believe him.

"For the last few months Marley has been the center of our lives," Acee said. "I hope you don't think that it means that you're no longer important to us."

That thought hadn't occurred to me, but it did then.

"The little fellow was just so sick that we've had to focus all our attention on him."

"I know."

"You are definitely a part of this family and don't think for a moment that you are not."

"Okay."

When we finished our sandwiches, Acee went to his study to catch up on some work. I went back to my room.

I played with my SoupKids inside the dollhouse.

"Are you my brother?" the girl kid asked the boy kid.

"Yes, I'm Marley. I'm your brother Marley."

"How'd you get that broken place on your hat?"

"My mama threw me in the trash," he answered.

Babs

I should have spurned Acee's proposal of marriage. That's what a good, decent woman would have done. That's the course that an heroic, admirable mother would have chosen. I chose the path that made my life easiest. I didn't even hesitate. Acee offered a lifeline and I would have been a fool not to take it.

But I never wanted him to feel like a fool for throwing it to me.

My intention was that he would never know the true origin of our child. A baby is a baby. No one can ever truly know who the child might favor. If it grew up to look like Burl, I would just say he reminded me of my father. No one would argue with me.

I married Acee as quickly as I could. The key to pulling off such a deception would be timing. I'd been unwilling to wait even until after the holidays. If he was surprised, he didn't act like it.

"I don't want a big wedding," I explained. "It just wouldn't be appropriate. It is my second marriage and widows are not blushing brides in yards of white organza."

"We don't want to . . . to insult Tom's family," he said. "There's no need for haste."

I waved off his concern. "I don't want to wait," I told him. "There's no reason for us to delay being happy. Tom would understand."

Acee didn't argue with me. He wanted me to have things exactly how I wanted to have things.

His mother wasn't quite as biddable, but Acee was her only son. She wanted him to be happy and he wanted me to be happy.

It all turned out quite well. The courthouse wedding included all his colleagues and co-workers. It was a very public wedding with both my family and his present and approving. The reception in the Grange Hall was tasteful and refined, rather than lavish and showy. Everyone in McKinney was aware of what was happening. And while not everyone could be invited, no one could truly feel left out.

All in all, I was very pleased with the wedding day.

The wedding night was a disaster.

I suppose I should have anticipated problems, but I didn't. I didn't expect fireworks or the earth to move. I didn't even expect the oneness I'd felt with Tom. But I did expect to be able to tolerate intimacy.

I couldn't.

Acee was very patient, very gentle. I told myself over and over that he was my husband and that he was not attacking me, he had a right to touch me. But my mental arguments made no difference. It felt like I was being violated. And unlike my experience with Burl, I fought back.

Acee was shocked. He stopped immediately.

"What's wrong?"

"Nothing."

"Am I hurting you?"

"No."

"You don't want to do this?"

"Yes, yes, of course I do," I insisted. "I'm just . . . I guess I'm nervous."

"Then we'll take it real slow," he assured me.

That only helped to a point. As long as he was holding me, kissing me, whispering in my ear how much he loved me, then I was fine. As soon as things got more direct, I panicked.

He was gentle. He was considerate. But I just couldn't bear to be touched.

Finally we chalked it up to "nerves" and decided to try again the next night. That didn't work, either, nor the night after that. I began to dread the approach of evening, knowing that we were going to have to try again.

Mostly I held myself in rigid coldness. He attempted to tenderly, patiently arouse me. I didn't want that. Somehow arousal was much worse. When I felt desire, it was a loss of control that was even more upsetting.

"I am so sorry," I told him over and over. "It's not you, it's me."

He kissed my shoulder reassuringly. "I know you loved Tom," he said. "I know the memories of him are strong always, especially at a time like this. But he'd want us to be happy. And I know that we will."

I shouldn't have let him believe it was Tom. I shouldn't have allowed him to think that it was only modesty and reluctance, but once a lie gets rolling, the force of it just bowls over everything that I should have done.

A month later with only two moderately successful encounters, I had no choice but to tell him that I was pregnant.

"That's impossible," he said. "You can't be sure so early."

"I've been through this before," I told him. "I know all the signs."

I tried to be upbeat, happy, cheerful. I thought it would make my deceit less obvious. Acee saw right through my ploy.

He looked down into my smiling face, glancing at my lying lips, and then he stepped backward. He folded his arms across his chest, perhaps angrily or stubbornly, or maybe just to protect his heart from breaking.

"It's not so early, is it," he said.

"I don't know what you mean," I said.

"I mean, that you were pregnant before we married," he said. "You've been pregnant all this time."

"No, no, of course not."

"I wondered why you married me," he said. "I thought, well, it's the money and she has that child to support. 'Fair enough,' I told myself. You want her and she wants security. Lots of good marriages have been based on less. But it was more than that, wasn't it? You were in trouble and any husband was better than none."

"Acee, I . . ."

"Who's the baby's father? Why didn't he marry you?"

"You're the baby's father," I insisted.

"I'm not, I know I'm not," he said. "Surely you know the man. Or were there so many, you couldn't be sure."

I raised my hand to slap him. A man should be slapped for such an insult. But I didn't follow through. The lying was too hard. I was just too tired of it.

"The baby's father was married," I said. "But I wouldn't have him anyway. He forced me. That's the truth. I don't care if you believe me or not."

I did, of course, care if he believed me. If he thought me a slut, he could put me out on the street, drag the truth through a divorce court and everybody in Collin County would know. I'd lose my daughter and everything I'd done would be undone. I'd be ruined. I'd be alone. No decent person would speak to me again. Even members of my own family, Aunt Maxine and Uncle Warren, would have to risk their reputations to stand by me. McKinney was like most small towns, close-knit and caring. But the inhabitants could be brutal to those who strayed from the straight and narrow. Especially so to women, for whom the straight and narrow was very tightly defined.

"I suppose, since you know this man was

144

married that you weren't attacked on the street or assaulted by some masked stranger in an alley?"

I shook my head. "No, he . . . he was a man I knew."

"You led him on?"

"He thought I did," I admitted. "But I didn't, Acee, I swear I didn't. Please believe me. And . . . forgive me."

He didn't answer. He turned and walked away. We didn't speak, except in passing, for two days. Then he called me into his study just after I'd put Laney to bed.

"Is she asleep?"

"Yes."

"No one else is in the house?"

"No."

"Shut the door and come sit down," he said.

I did as he told me, taking a seat on the chair by the window.

I wondered if I should be afraid of him. I learned how violent men could be. And that a cruel man could disguise himself as kind. We were all alone. He could beat me or even kill me and probably get away with it. Worse than beating or killing, he could expose the truth about me, ruin my life and cause my daughter to be taken away.

But it was Acee across the desk from me.

Somewhere deep inside I understood that he would never hurt me. I trusted that the day I'd tricked him into marrying me. And I trusted it now.

"We do need to talk," I admitted.

"*You* have already talked," he said. "Now you're going to listen."

I swallowed nervously.

"I am angry," he said. "I admit to that. And I have a perfect right to be. I was lied to and I was betrayed. There is nothing that can be said or done to undo that."

"I'm sorry."

He didn't acknowledge my words.

"I believe your story about being forced," he said. "I can't, even in the deepest hurt of my heartache, think that you would be untruthful about such a thing."

"Thank you for that," I said.

"Actually it explains a lot about your distaste for sex. I was beginning to worry that you simply found me personally repulsive."

"Oh, no, Acee, no," I assured him.

"I assume you had a more normal intimacy with Tom."

"Yes," I said.

Acee nodded. "Good. Then there is still a chance that we can pick up the pieces of this catastrophe and fashion some sort of marriage out of it."

"That's . . . that is what I want, too, Acee."

"I've decided what we'll do," he said. "I'll go ahead and pretend that this child is mine. I won't have him, or her, inheriting any of the Clifton business interests, but I will feed, clothe, house and educate him. Just as I plan to do for Laney. They are your children, but I have chosen, as their stepfather, to be responsible for them. As far as the ultimate disposition of my property upon my death, we will sort all that out at a later date. You will agree to whatever I decide about that."

His words were very firm, his expression was hard as stone and the formality in his voice distant.

I nodded meekly.

"I can only imagine that your decision to choose me as your husband was based on the mistaken assumption that I would be easily manipulated. That merely by batting your eyes and flashing me that little dimpled smile, I would do your bidding. Let me assure you, Barbara, that I am not that man."

He certainly didn't seem so at that moment.

"Can you ever forgive me, Acee?" I asked.

"I don't know," he admitted. "My first thought was to have the marriage annulled."

The bottom dropped out of my stomach.

"I'd do it, except the truth is I still care for you, I always have. I'm hoping that eventually we can put all this behind us and have the kind of life that I've imagined for us."

"I will try," I assured him. "I will make this up to you. I'll be a very good wife. I can be, you know. I can make your life very comfortable."

Acee nodded.

"After the baby is born and things begin to settle down," he continued. "You will see some sort of doctor. Someone in Dallas. Somewhere unknown to us. You'll take whatever medicine or therapy that's required to make you capable of fulfilling your obligations to me in the bedroom as well as the rest of the house."

I swallowed hard, but nodded agreement.

Acee retrieved some papers from his desk.

"I've put this agreement in writing," he said. "I can't say exactly why. Maybe just because I'm a lawyer. Or maybe it's that your lies have made me distrustful, but I want your signature on this paper. I'll keep it here in the office safe. No one will ever see it but you and me."

I didn't even question that. I took the pen he offered and signed my name.

"We will never speak about this again," he said. "I don't want the slightest chance that we might ever be overheard."

"Yes," I agreed. "We won't talk about it ever."

That sounded wonderful to me. Never to talk about it again, never to think about it again. But, of course, it couldn't be exactly that way. I was still pregnant and Acee and I had to pretend that we were both delighted about it.

"I know it's very early to give this news," he said, making the announcement at a special party with both our families gathered. "But we want you to be as excited and happy as we are."

His mother gasped. I observed his aunts and cousins gossiping together behind their hands. We had been married for only eight weeks. Still everyone was very kind and wished us well.

As the news spread I made a point of saying that the baby was due in September, though I knew I'd be lucky to get past June. I did what I could to undermine McKinney's wagging tongues. I wore a girdle for six months. I followed a strict diet of vitamin pills, hard-boiled eggs and water. It worked pretty well. I gained only twelve pounds for the whole pregnancy. My arms and legs got reed thin. The bones in my face etched my features so sharply, it was as if I'd aged ten years.

Still, nothing could stop the rapid production of life in my womb. I knew that when the baby arrived in midsummer, there would be talk. The world was not a place of tolerance. It's hard to explain what it was like to those who haven't lived it. There were rules that had to be obeyed. And those who broke the rules of society were made to suffer, even those who had been forced. It was how order was maintained. How people were kept in line.

When the baby was born small and sickly, it was like a miracle, an answer to prayers I'd been afraid to ask. Marley was late enough, weak enough, frail enough that no one would dare to question his arrival. I was secretly celebrating my good luck.

Unfortunately that buoyancy did not last past the moment I held him in my arms. It was as if the baby had not been real to me until that moment. He had been only a pregnancy, an unwanted pregnancy, the terrible result of a horrid, sickening experience. If I could have given him away, I would have. But he was here now and he was mine. I had no choice but to take care of him. And he needed a lot of care.

We named him Marley. It was Acee's mother's maiden name. It gave him an instant sense of family and I hoped would get his grandmother permanently on his side.

He needed all the cheerleaders and well-wishers he could get. Marley was tiny, just five pounds, with thick tufts of light-colored hair. He was pale and puny. He hardly cried. It was more a mewing sound, like a frightened kitty.

His weakness, his sickness, could be laid directly at my door. I was the one who failed to take care of myself, I'd not eaten right, I'd worn those girdles. I was the one who had not wanted him.

I tried to want him now. He was so tiny, so precious. His little eyes unable to focus, his tiny fingers and toes, hesitant to grasp. I touched him and kissed him and whispered sweet words of love to him.

I also watched him, scrutinized him,

looked for the mark of evil on him.

Could I hate the man who had given him life and still love the life he'd given?

I didn't know. But I wanted to try. I wanted to be his mother. I wanted to feel for him all those wonderful things I'd felt for Laney. I tried.

For the first few days the doctors were closemouthed and kept Marley away from us most of the time. Finally on the fifth day of his life, as I dressed and readied myself to go home, Dr. Bridges, a longtime and highly respected McKinney physician, came into my hospital room to talk with us.

"You know that we can't let you take him with you," the doctor said.

We both nodded.

"He's getting better, though," Acee insisted.

The doctor was noncommittal.

"We finally have a diagnosis," he said. "I believe little Marley has an anomaly known as Krikor's syndrome."

Acee and I glanced quickly at each other.

"Krikor's syndrome," Acee repeated. "I've never heard of it."

"You wouldn't have," Dr. Bridges said. "It's rare, actually very rare. And it seems to be what's responsible for the hole in your baby's heart."

"I thought you said that the problem wasn't that unusual."

Dr. Bridges nodded. "What I thought at first was that it was atrial septal defect," he said. "It's a relatively common newborn heart problem. It's dangerous, but it frequently corrects itself. Krikor's is a far more serious congenital abnormality of the heart. It's rare enough that we had trouble diagnosing it. I've personally never seen it before. And I've been practicing medicine for twenty-seven years."

He sat down at the foot of the bed and from his pocket he retrieved a plastic model of the heart. He opened the front to reveal the interior.

"There are four separate chambers in the heart," he said. "Each of these has a specific task that it must perform. Sending blood out to the body, receiving the blood back. Sending it to the lungs for oxygen. Pulling the oxygenated blood back into the heart so it can be sent out to the body again."

Acee and I nodded. We'd both been through Mr. Stubben's high school biology class.

"Sometimes," Dr. Bridges continued, "a

child is born with an opening between these valves. The blood seeps across the chambers and cuts down on the efficiency of the pumping. As I said, that usually corrects itself and when it doesn't, we're now trying open heart surgery to correct it."

"So Marley may have to have surgery?" I asked.

Dr. Bridges shook his head. "I don't think so," he answered.

Somehow the words didn't sound as hopeful as they should.

"In Krikor's syndrome, the walls between the valves are very thin and porous. There are numerous holes, some large enough to see, some very small. And the tissue is so thin in places that there is always a danger of new tears. The heart works hard, but it's so inefficient that it just doesn't do the job."

That didn't sound good. It didn't sound good at all.

"Is there some kind of medicine he should take? Some kind of vitamins to make the tissue stronger."

"I . . . I'm not sure," Dr. Bridges said.

"Is he going to be all right?"

"I hope so," he answered. "I truly hope so. I've contacted a specialist at the Southwestern Medical School in Dallas. I'm transferring the baby into his care. He's a specialist in pediatric cardiology. He's up on all the latest therapies and treatments. And he's much more familiar with this syndrome. He tells me he just had another baby born with it last year."

So Marley was moved to Parkland Hospital. I went with him. His tiny little body strapped down to the ambulance gurney. He was hurting and so helpless. He was so dependent on me. Me, his mother, who hadn't wanted him, who'd tried to hide him. It was all my fault. All of it. Somehow I'd lured Burl into forcing himself on me. Then I'd run away from my sins, deceived Acee into marrying me. And now this poor child was sick, probably as much from the way I'd lived during pregnancy as for this terrible disease that he'd inherited.

"I'll make it up to you," I whispered to the tiny open eyes that seemed to see nothing. "I'll make it up to you. And I'll make it up to Acee."

A large brown hand patted my own. I glanced up. Across the width of the ambulance, the paramedic was smiling at me sympathetically.

"A mother's prayers always work wonders," he said.

He'd thought I was appealing to God.

After all I'd done, I felt like I couldn't even show my face to heaven.

The hospital in Dallas was huge. It was all polished tile corridors and closed doors. I always spoke in a whisper there. The slightest noise seemed far too loud.

Dr. Richardson, the pediatric cardiologist seemed young compared to Dr. Bridges and he was brusque and business-like.

"Your son is my concern, not you," he told me. "I'll need to take care of my patient. As long as you don't make a nuisance of yourself or get in my way, you can stay. But I have to tell you, my experience with mothers is that their presence is annoying and they are forever blubbering and whining. If I see any of that, you'll be banned from the bedside. For the child's own good, of course."

With that warning ringing in my ears, I did my best to remain calm.

"I know Dr. Richardson seems harsh," the R.N. told me. "He's blunt and has terrible bedside manners. I guess that's why he takes care of newborns. But he really does know what he's doing. If anyone can save your baby, he can."

I was determined to take comfort in that.

When Dr. Richardson examined the baby, I tried to make myself scarce. Acee decided that he would sit with Marley in the early mornings when Dr. Richardson made his rounds. That worked very well. I would stay late at the hospital, then meet Acee at our little room in the nearby Best Western Motel. He always waited up for me. I would go to sleep with his arms around me. I admit, I didn't love him. But I loved his strength and I needed his stability. I felt so safe in his arms.

Acee was up and in the shower before dawn. He tried to be quiet so I could sleep. I think I slept best when I could hear him getting ready for his day. He'd head for the hospital at first light to see Marley and the doctor before driving into work in McKinney.

It was a strange existence. Each of us just living moment by moment, our moods completely dependent on the current crisis of our very small son.

And he was our son. Acee had not offered more recriminations. From the first moment he'd held that small child in his arms, I knew he had loved him. People from church told us they were praying for a miracle, I knew that Acee's devotion to Marley was nothing less.

To be completely honest, during these weeks I also worried about Laney. I knew she was with Aunt Maxine and Uncle Warren. I knew that she'd be fine. She was just a little girl. She couldn't understand what was happening and I was sure that she would be all wrapped up in playtime and school and other childhood concerns. Still, I needed her. I could look at her and know that I was a worthy person, a good mother, and it gave me strength to face little Marley and all his ills.

Marley suffered what Dr. Richardson described as a mild stroke a few days after we arrived at Parkland. It was the first of many. A few weeks later he had a more serious one. Cerebrovascular accidents they were called. By any name, they were terrifying.

Dr. Richardson shrugged. "Strokes are going to happen," he said. "You'd better just be prepared for that. It's congestive heart failure that will probably be your killer."

His tone was so matter-of-fact it chilled me to the bone.

"Look, I don't believe in giving parents false hope," he said. "This baby is probably not going to make it. And if he does, well, he'll be so damaged, he'll be little more than a vegetable."

That night in the hotel, I could sense Acee's concern and anxiety.

"I just feel so sad about it," he told me. "We've grown so attached to the little guy. I don't know if I can bear to lose him. Why do things like this happen?"

His question was rhetorical. My guilt was abject. I had been more concerned about being found out than about taking care of the child in my womb.

I stood in the little closetlike bathroom and stared at myself in the mirror over the sink. My child was dying and I had only myself to blame. How had I gotten to this terrible place? I thought of Tom and my eyes welled with tears. I had begun to resent him, to be angry with him. If he hadn't died, none of these terrible things would have happened. But he had died and it had all happened. It was still happening.

What Burl had done to me was evil. I'd had no choice but to try to save myself, to save myself and Laney from what would have been an unforgiving and censuring world. I had been victimized. But did that give me the right to spread a blanket of lies over someone else's world? How much deceit could one person cover over? Burl was evil. Acee had been nothing except good to me. He deserved far better than I was giving him. I vowed before God in that bathroom mirror that no matter what happened, I would devote my life to making a good life for my husband.

When I went back into the room, Acee was seated in the desk chair, talking to his mother on the phone. As always, his report was upbeat, hopeful.

"Marley was looking right at me today," he said to her. "And I think he almost smiled."

Acee said nothing of Krikor's Syndrome or the stroke that the baby had suffered. He spoke only reassurance and optimism.

When he hung up the phone I walked up behind him and leaned over to wrap my arms around his neck. He patted me reassuringly.

"Is your mother doing all right?"

"Except for missing us and the baby, she's fine," he answered.

"Acee, you always sound so cheerful when you talk to her," I said. "Don't you worry that she won't be prepared if . . . if something goes wrong."

Acee pulled me around the chair and seated me on his lap. He kissed me sweetly, playfully, like we were just young lovers with no cares in the world beyond each other.

"I'm serious here," I told him. "From talking to you, your mother undoubtedly thinks that everything is going well."

"With a beautiful wife in my arms, how could it be otherwise."

"Acee."

He pulled back a little bit then and looked at me more soberly.

"I don't tell her all the bad news because it's not necessary," he said. "She knows the baby wouldn't still be in the hospital if everything were fine. There is not any way for any of us to 'prepare' for some kind of tragedy. If things go badly with Marley, no amount of worrying beforehand will make it easier."

"You are a smart man, Acee Clifton," I said. "And not just in books, but in feelings, too."

He smiled.

"Smart enough to marry you," he said.

Marley stayed in the hospital for almost four months. One morning, the nurse waylaid us in the hallway and said that Dr. Richardson wanted to meet with us. We went to talk to him, not in the hospital nursery, but in a comfortable book-lined room on the hospital's second floor. His familiar white coat was missing. The gray flannel suit made him seem like a stranger.

"The baby arrested last night," he said without introduction.

Acee and I glanced at each other. I could see the fear in his eyes. I knew it mirrored my own.

"What do you mean he arrested?" I asked.

"Cardiac arrest," Dr. Richardson answered.

When I continued to stare at him questioningly, he gave me the answer more specifically.

"The baby died," he said. "He had a heart attack and he died."

"No," I said, firmly.

"Yes," the doctor insisted.

Immediately Acee rose to his feet. To me it seemed as if there ought to be something more to say, something more to discuss. My husband led me out of the room without a backward glance toward the physician.

Laney

After my brother died, my mother didn't
seem that interested in me. I guess maybe
she'd gotten used to not having me around
or maybe I just started getting ugly. I was
the first kid in second grade to lose a front
tooth. And I was so tall. I was taller than all
the girls in my class, even the boys. I was
taller than Cheryl and Nicie.

Ned Hoffman made a big deal about
that. He started calling me Gargantua Girl.
I didn't know what it meant until I complained to Uncle Skipper. It seems that
Gargantua was a huge monster in a movie.
Cheryl and Nicie thought it was funny. I
didn't.

My mother never commented one way
or another. All she ever said to me was
"Laney do this" and "Laney do that." She
was busy all the time. Actually the word
busy doesn't begin to describe how it was.

My mother was a warrior. Dirt and disorder were the enemy and she was determined not just to get the best of them, but to eradicate both from the face of the earth. I was a foot soldier in this fight, a draftee. Of course, I was not alone. My mother hired maids and housekeepers, constantly. Her perfectionism either drove them away or she was forced to fire them. When our school was integrated in 1966 I was the only white girl who knew a lot of the black kids. I'd met so many of them when the moms worked in our house.

Ultimately, of course, cleaning and decorating were not enough to make a life. Babs turned her attention out to the world at large and began to organize and beautify all of McKinney.

For the most part, I was out of that battle. Or at least I stayed out of it as long as I could. As a little kid, I really couldn't be called upon to fulfill civic responsibilities the way Babs did. But, of course, I was dragged into planting trees at the park for the Garden Club's Arbor Day celebration. And I was her first conquest. But the Owl Club was her goal. The Owls were a bunch of rich old ladies who had meetings in each other's homes and did things around town. I don't mean they actually did things. It seemed like they got other people to do things and they paid for it. They had parties and galas, fashion shows and teas. Babs wanted to be part of that. There was only one sticking point, you had to be invited. That shouldn't have been a problem. Mrs. Clifton, Acee's mother, was a big whoop-de-do in the Owls. But somehow her invitation to her daughter-in-law never materialized. And if her mother-in-law wouldn't invite her, she could hardly ask someone else to do it.

There were few other options for social climbing in McKinney. The Edel Weiss Society was the other ladies' group, almost as prestigious as the Owls. But my aunt LaVeida, Nicie's mom who'd wanted to adopt me, was in that group. So I'm sure Babs wouldn't have been all that welcome.

My mother whined and complained about the injustice of it all. Never to Acee, where it might have done some good. She complained to Aunt Maxine who had no help to offer and failed to see the value in what Babs sought.

"You don't need some club to do good works," Aunt Maxine told her. "Get involved in the church auxiliary or the PTA. They'll take anyone who wants to help."

"It's not *just* about good works," Babs

165

insisted. "It's about Acee taking his proper place in the community. It's a wife's duty to make sure that happens."

Aunt Maxine chuckled and shook her head. "In my day that wasn't what women were talking about when they mentioned 'a wife's duty.' "

My mother gave a startled gasp and glanced pointedly in my direction.

"Laney, why don't you go and play somewhere else," she told me. "It's so warm in here."

She and Aunt Maxine were in her kitchen. The place was steaming hot as they sterilized jars for the apple butter they were cooking.

At her suggestion, I wandered off into cooler areas of the house. I felt perfectly at home in the twins' room. It was smaller than my own and had none of the neat stuff I had in mine. But my room never had the safe, centered feeling that I got in Janey and Joley's nest of yellow gingham and white eyelet.

The boys' room was uninhabited now, but far from empty. Renny was overseas in the Army. Pete was at North Texas State in Denton. The presence of both lingered in the Spartan room with the wagon-wheel bunk beds. Everything was in place except for a box that had been dragged from underneath the bed and left when someone's attention had been distracted. I knelt down to see what was inside. The box was filled with letters, all the same size and blue color. The return address was unfamiliar. But what caught my eye was that they had obviously come through the mail, but they had no stamp in the upper right-hand corner where someone had written in rather sloppy penmanship the word *Free.*

I opened one up to discover they were from Renny. When I'd stayed here with Aunt Maxine and Uncle Warren, they'd gotten many letters from my cousin. But these were different. I opened one and tried to read it. Although it was written in cursive, I could make most of it out. Like letters from him that I'd heard before, this one was filled with funny stories of people. The one I'd picked up was about a farmer and his reluctant water buffalo. But somehow the blue letters seemed different. There was a strange detachment to the incident that felt almost sad.

"You have to give it to these gooks," he wrote. "They work hard and make the most of what little they have. Not so different from folks back in Texas."

That seemed like a strange thing to say.

People in Texas didn't have water buffalos.

"Still, you got to remember that they might be Cong. The women, the kids, any of them, all of them. You got to always be suspicious of everyone."

My brow furrowed thoughtfully. I was pretty sure that being suspicious wasn't in Renny's nature.

That evening at home at the dinner table, my cousin's name came up again.

"How are Warren and Maxine doing?" Acee asked Babs.

I wasn't sure that she could even answer that question. From my observation she'd spent the entire visit talking about herself.

"They're doing all right," Babs told him. "Of course, they are worried about Renny."

Acee shook his head, sorrowful.

"That Vietnam is a bad business," he said.

My mother made a dismissing sound. "The only thing bad about it is those awful protestors," she said. "They ought to not allow that. People ought to be made to keep their mouths shut."

"We've had pacifists in every war we've fought," Acee said. "It's their right to make their views known."

"But this is not a war," Babs insisted.

"This is a police action. And Renny and the other young men are only there as advisors."

Acee raised an eyebrow. "Well, it seems like the kind of advice they're giving can get you killed."

After supper, it was my job to clear the table. Babs washed the dishes the way she did everything these days. With exacting attention to detail. My main concern was that I not be drawn into any big projects. Babs was quite capable of suddenly deciding that all the good silver had to be unearthed from the dining room and polished. Or that the wax buildup on the kitchen floor next to the mopboard was best dislodged with a toothpick.

I hurried up to my room as soon as I could. During the school term I could always claim to have homework. In the summer, I'd say I was tired. Either excuse, I'd stay up late into the night reading or playing with my dollhouse.

Babs would continue working, cleaning, decorating, organizing. I don't remember ever catching her resting or idle. My memory of that time has her constantly busy.

It wasn't such a bad childhood, I suppose. I learned how to do things around

169

the house and I developed a strong work ethic, almost against my will. I guess the bad lesson being taught was the idea that hard work was enough to keep real feelings at arm's length.

Babs

The year after Marley died is mostly a blur for me. I got up every morning. Ate meals. Did chores. Went to bed at night. I existed. Beyond that, I was not living. When they'd closed his little casket, barely bigger than a boot box, I vowed to leave everything I knew about him inside. I promised myself never to think about how he was conceived. Not to remember the day he was born. Not to writhe in agony about the months that he'd suffered. Marley was gone. No guilt, no dreams, no prayers were about to change that. I vowed not to think of him again. I vowed never to say to myself, he'd be three now, he'd be eleven, he'd be twenty-one. He would never be more than four months. He would never be more than a sick infant in a hospital crib.

To keep my vows and my memories at bay, I plunged into near frantic activity. I had a new husband, a new house, a new name and a new position in the community. Added together, they filled my days.

Acee began to pressure me about sex again only a few months after the funeral.

"We could have another baby," he told me. "Dr. Bridges said that's often a very good way to get through the grief."

I wanted to give him another child. I wanted to give him his own child. But my problems in the bedroom had not gone away with time. On the contrary, they seemed to have worsened. Sometimes just a hug or a kiss would cause a small spasm of tightness in my intimate anatomy and with that, a rush of disgust and near panic. I didn't want to be a sexual being. I felt safer just hanging back from personal contact.

Because he had insisted and I had promised, I began looking into what kind of doctor I might see about my problem. From what I could determine, there was no such thing as a sex doctor. The cure suggested in magazines for people with sexual problems was psychoanalysis. Analysis was new, or at least it was new to me. The idea of a "talking cure" made sense on some level. But there was no analyst in McKinney. To take this therapy, I had to make weekly visits to Dallas.

I tried several different therapists. I would spend a couple of months talking to someone and then switch to someone else. I don't think that it was a complete waste of time. I learned a lot about myself. I have abandonment issues. I have low self-esteem. My view of human sexuality had been skewed — puritanical subtexts of a repressed culture. All of those things were good to know. But they didn't really help me.

Of course, that was not the fault of the doctor or the cure. Although I was mostly candid about Laney and Tom, Acee and Marley, my childhood and my problems, I couldn't bring myself to talk about what had happened with Burl. I couldn't forget it. But I could resist bringing it into mind. I had never really talked about what had happened. I had told Acee that I'd been forced. But somehow those words cannot portray what was done to me. Not just physically, more than that. What was done to me darkened my soul. If I couldn't bring myself to discuss it with husband, why would I tell it to some stranger? Some man who seemed nice, but who could easily be different. I would never let my guard down again.

And my problem with going to therapy was much larger than being less than truthful to the expressionless doctor with the clipboard. In the months since moving back to McKinney I had developed a fear of Dallas.

I suppose it had started when Kennedy was shot. I settled upon Dallas as the source of evil in the world. When Marley was in the hospital, familiarity did not make it easier. It actually got worse. I'd see a car or catch sight of someone from the corner of my eye and suddenly my heart would be in my throat, my pulse pounding.

After the baby's death, when I didn't have to go there on a regular basis, I thought it was getting better. But as soon as I knew I was headed in that direction, I became jumpy. I'd be anxious even before I left the house just thinking about the highway. The drive made me so tense, you could have plucked my backbone like a bowstring. The closer I got to the city the more agitated I felt. Once in town, my stomach twisted into a knot of fear at every stoplight. Getting from the protection of the car into the doctor's office was more terrifying to me than a moonless cemetery on Halloween night. Danger lurked in shadows everywhere. Burl could be just around the corner.

In the very reasonable, most rational part of my brain, I could remember when Burl was just a next-door neighbor, an ordinary man, married to a friend. More and more he had taken on superhuman status in subconscious. He was the devil incarnate. He was my night terror, daylight or dark.

As the weeks went on, I just couldn't bear it. I began canceling appointments and I complained about the traffic. I wanted to keep my promise — I was determined to keep my promise. But it was getting harder and harder.

Finally Acee suggested that I talk to our pastor. A weekly visit with a clergyman did not have nearly the negative connotations that were to be expected if I were to be caught going to appointments with a mental health professional.

Reverend Arthur Chester, or as his congregation called him, Brother Chet, was very different from the analysts. The doctors wanted to listen to me talk, they posed questions, they wanted to hear my story. And I had a difficult time keeping it to myself. When I met with Brother Chet, he did all the talking. He didn't pretend to ask questions, he had answers. And if he was interested in why I was the way I was, he never showed any evidence of curiosity.

Brother Chet observed me sternly out of the top lenses of his bifocals.

"Your child did not die because of some sin that you committed," he said. "It's a type of personal vanity to imagine that one's deeds or misdeeds can affect God's universe in such a way."

I nodded, but I was sure that Brother Chet would feel differently if he knew the truth.

"Your little son, Marley, had a life and death that was in every aspect part of God's plan," he said. "You may not like that, but you must surrender yourself to it."

Brother Chet was smiling, feigning understanding and sympathy. But I knew that if he had any real concept of the suffering of the innocent, he could never be so glib.

I changed the subject to Acee and myself, euphemizing our current situation as "bedroom problems."

Brother Chet nodded as if he understood completely.

"I'm sure you're thinking that it's laudable to show respect for your vows to your late husband," he told me.

I tried to keep my jaw from dropping. I'd never mentioned Tom, nor had in any way suggested that he might be the reason that I was having a difficult time making love to Acee. But it seemed as reasonable an excuse as any I could have made up, so I made no attempt to correct him.

"Your late husband's temporal human form is gone to dust," he told me firmly. "He will never seek earthly gratification again. There is no copulation in heaven."

I hadn't really considered that one way or another, but I nodded.

"You have new vows to keep now," he said. "And it's against the law of both God and man for a wife to forsake her husband's bed."

"Well, I haven't really forsaken . . ."

"If you're not allowing conjugal rights in response to his natural desires then you are forsaking him," he stated with certainty. "Such action can lead him into sin and place in peril his immortal soul. Surely you cannot want that? Endangering eternity for the man you've married."

Put that way, my own revulsion seemed like a petty affectation. So that evening, as soon as Laney was tucked in, I went down to Acee's study.

"Brother Chet says that we need to start

sharing a bedroom again," I announced.

He looked up at me, not with anticipation. "Are you sure it's not too soon?"

I didn't answer that. I was afraid that *never* would be too soon.

"It'll be fine," I assured him.

Of course, it wasn't. It was embarrassing, uncomfortable and unsatisfying. But I felt that I had no choice. If I was to be the wife that he deserved to have, then I had to be sexual.

"Close your eyes and pray," Brother Chet suggested.

I found that very disconcerting. Instead I began reading *Cosmopolitan* magazine. I'd heard that the editor had written a book about women having sex and every month there were lots of articles about sexual things. So I bought it at Smith's Drugs, assuring Mrs. Mantee, behind the counter, that I didn't really read it, I just looked at the photographs of beautiful clothes.

I lay beside Acee, spread my legs, tapped down my queasiness and pretended that I was someone else. That I was one of those women in the magazine so concerned with their own pleasure, their own sensuality. With practice, it became tolerable.

Acee never complained. In fact he always thanked me. Proof, I suppose, that he knew I wasn't doing it because I wanted to.

Acee had gotten a bad bargain when he'd gotten me. I knew it and I felt guilty about it. He'd given me a home, a safe haven, security. And the certainty that I would be able to give Laney a good life. For all that, he got a cold, frigid wife, a stepdaughter and a dead son that had been palmed off as his own. Somehow I had to make it up to him.

I chose to do that the way I'd always done it. Uncle Warren and Aunt Maxine had taken in the perfect teenager. Acee would soon discover that he'd married the perfect McKinney wife.

That became my goal. If I could grit my teeth and have sex with him, then I could arrange the rest of his world to near perfection.

His house should be a showplace. His meals should be delicious and nutritious. His standing in the community should be second to none and his wife should be by his side ever lovely, generous and genteel.

Bringing those things into being were easily within my control. All I had to do was pursue, pursue, pursue. My goals were all altruistic and my method was to pursue them.

Of course, I couldn't do it alone. I quickly tried to become the center of female society in McKinney. Not because I wanted that for myself. For myself, I would have been content to live a hermit's life. But the perfect wife for an up-and-coming lawyer required an outgoing nature and an interest in social activities.

I was not a natural for this. For one thing, I hadn't been brought up with an eye toward upward mobility. Uncle Warren and Aunt Maxine were good people, honest and hardworking, but with no pretensions of status. Aunt Maxine still did her own ironing! We'd sewed most of my clothes. And what we'd purchased had been bought at JCPenney. The Hoffmans were no better influence. Tom's expectations for me were to be little different than a typical farm wife. I'd done my own hair and what little makeup I wore came from the drugstore.

I quickly learned that the ladies of the Owl Club bought their fashions at Naomi's Dress Shop. They had their hair done weekly at Miss Lucy's. And the secrets of their facial blemishes were known only to the Cosmetic Consultants at Mary Kay or Merle Norman.

I had a trim figure, nice coloring, good

complexion and regular features. My natural tendency to hang back was probably one of the reasons I'd been runner-up rather than queen. I hadn't known how to make the most of my personal gifts. Now I deliberately pushed myself forward.

I quickly became active in every civic organization that would let me in the door. I was Projects Coordinator to the Garden Club, Bingo Chair of the Methodist Women, a regular at Friends of the Library and, most importantly, I was on the planning committee of the annual Cotton Days Parade.

I didn't have any training or experience for any of these jobs. Except for a short-lived allegiance to *Ye Merrie Stenos*, the business girls organization at McKinney High, I'd never been a joiner. I found it difficult to navigate all the intertwining relationships and rivalries of the other women. But I persevered.

To my thinking, the most prestigious and worthwhile group in McKinney was the Owls. Dating back to the 1890s, this organization of women had done much for the community. But more than that, they were the "old guard," descendants of the original settlers and the elite of ladies' society. Entry into the Owls was by invitation only and I should have been invited. My mother-in-law was a prominent member. For some reason, Mrs. Clifton, who told me to call her Alice, but always seemed surprised when I did, was unwilling to help me.

"It just doesn't seem fair," she explained. "There are so many young women who'd love to be invited but won't be. Bringing you in simply because you're my daughter-in-law seems inequitable."

Equality had never been the byword of the Owls and nepotism ran rampant, but I couldn't budge Alice, so I quit trying.

Like dozens of other worthy young McKinney wives with the Owls out of their reach, I concentrated on the clubs and committees that were within my grasp.

I'm not saying that I was immediately loved and universally accepted. Many in the Delphian Society thought of me as a bit déclassé. Some of the dried-up spinsters at Book Circle considered me a literary lightweight. And the matrons of the Historical Society always remembered that I'd been born elsewhere.

Still, I was Mrs. Acee Clifton. Despite my recent rather hasty pregnancy and my less than impressive choice for first husband, I was an important member of society, an asset to my husband's career, a near perfect wife.

All I needed was to give Acee a son of his own.

Laney

When I think about my years in grade school, I remember my teachers, classroom parties and my friends. In my home life, what I most recall is wallpaper.

Babs could never quite get it right. She would hang a pale floral in the dining room and then see a box print that she liked better. But when the print was up, it clashed with the sitting room, which then had to be changed. The solution to that made the entry hall seem too busy. It went on like that, room after room after room. And it seemed that as soon as it was all finally done right, I'd come home from school to see that she'd ripped the wallpaper down in the kitchen, starting it all over again.

I probably wouldn't have paid much attention if Babs had brought in workers to do the job. Unfortunately she liked doing it herself, but it wasn't a one person operation. When I was still so small I had to stand on a step stool to hand her the scraper, I was her wallpaper assistant.

"Why are we covering up everything all the time? Can't we just strip all this off and paint the walls," I suggested when I was about ten.

She looked at me as if I'd lost my mind.

"Laney, painted walls are for new homes, tract homes." Her tone was dismissive. "We live in a beautifully restored example of turn-of-the-century architecture. We must be true to the era."

That true-to-the era stuff did not extend to kitchens, bathrooms and air-conditioning. It was even flexible for furniture and drapes, but that wallpaper . . . somehow she could never give it up. The smell of paste still reminds me of home.

I was also dragged into many of my mother's do-gooder activities. Monday night bingo in the church basement was as non-negotiable as Sunday morning service. I was going to be there and I was going to help.

The same was true of Christmas festivities and Easter egg hunts and dancing the maypole. My mom was right in the middle of things and I was always there beside her.

That was especially true when it came to the Cotton Days Parade. The annual celebration was a hangover from earlier times when wagons of picked cotton would be lined up along Virginia Street and curve all around the corner waiting to drop their loads at the gin. Apparently it was a very festive time, all the hot, hard work of summer done, the year's wages just ahead of them, adding to the excitement of a day or two waiting in town. The old-timers said that farmers began decorating the cotton carts as sort of an identity and a point of pride. The merchants took the opportunity to serve up roasted corn, berry pies and cold beer. The town was bursting at the seams with crooks, gamblers and confidence men eager to snatch up the money the farmers made.

Over time cotton became less the livelihood of the area, but the celebration lingered. It was transformed into an end of summer festival with a downtown parade, a carnival in Finch Park and a Coronation Party at the Elks Club for the Cotton Queen and her court.

My mother had been in the Cotton Queen's court and she loved all the hoopla and girly giddiness of it all. There were floats to be made from glitter, crepe paper

186

and tissue. Convertibles to be decorated with streamers and bunting. A series of stair-step thrones to be constructed with cut-cardboard backs painted gold. Gigantic white pom-poms hanging from the dance floor ceiling to represent giant cotton balls.

The year my cousin Renny came home, Babs recruited him to help. I was still getting over my childhood crush, I suppose, but I was very excited that he was going to be there. I'd hardly seen him since his return. We'd gone over the night he'd come home. He'd caught a hop into Fort Bliss and Uncle Warren had driven down to pick him up. Aunt Maxine was so excited. She'd baked his favorite, pineapple upside-down cake and put up a Welcome banner that she'd made herself. She'd called Pete at his dorm at college and insisted that he be there. He rarely showed up in McKinney these days. He got lots of ribbing about his long hair and sandals. It didn't seem to bother him.

The house was crowded, noisy, excited as we waited for Renny.

The guest of honor didn't show up until almost midnight. And he didn't seem all that glad to see us. He hardly acknowledged the house full of people. He didn't even recognize his brother, who'd let his hair grow longer than the Beatles ever did. And when his mother offered him cake, he said he wasn't hungry. He went into his room and shut the door shortly afterward.

"He's exhausted," Uncle Warren was left to explain. "And the transition is too fast. He was in Saigon this morning."

We had all left, nodding understanding.

"He's home safe and that's what matters," Acee said.

But that had been weeks earlier. We hadn't seen him. We hadn't talked to him. According to what I overheard from Babs and Aunt Maxine, he never left the house. She would spend all morning trying to coax him out of bed. Then he'd just sit on the front porch swing, reading for the rest of the day.

That didn't seem all that weird to me. If I'd had to be away for a year and only had six weeks of leave, I'd probably sit around myself. But Aunt Maxine was worried, so Babs was, too.

I guess that's why we drove by and picked up Renny on the way to the Nehi Bottling warehouse where the Collin County Bar Association was turning a Chevy pickup truck into a horror movie–size boll weevil, the spurs on its front leg improvised with meat hooks. The parade float required a lot of volunteer effort and Babs was determined that we help.

She dropped us off as she scurried around town to see what was getting done on time and where more help was going to be needed.

I was put on the task of cutting the brown crepe paper into inch wide strips. Renny threaded them through the chicken wire form. Because of his youth and agility, I suppose, Renny was sent up to lie flat on the scaffold so that he could reach down onto the ten foot high back of the big, ugly insect.

We'd worked about an hour when he decided to take a break. I quickly abandoned my job and followed him over to the refreshment table where there was free Nehi, doughnuts and an angel food cake.

Renny's six-foot frame was now more muscular than when he'd played sports in high school. The buzz-cut military-style hair somehow drew more attention to the handsome features of his face. His eyes were the bluest blue, shaded by the thickest blond eyelashes, the kind any girl would have been jealous to possess.

He smiled at me, but didn't look that

keen on having a conversation. That wasn't really a surprise. I doubt that many grown-up military men talked to skinny, gawky ten-year-olds on a regular basis. But I was determined to break the ice.

"I guess all this seems pretty dorky to you after being all over the world," I started out.

His brow sort of furrowed, like he was actually considering my question and then he shrugged.

"I don't know if dorky is the word that I'd use," he said.

"I mean not cool, you know, stupid, stuff like that."

He grinned. "I know what dorky means," he replied. "I just don't know if dorky describes this. It's more like surreal."

"Surreal," I repeated thoughtfully. I'd never heard the word before, but I sure didn't want Renny to know that.

"But these days," Renny continued, "it's like everything is surreal. I just kept thinking that everything would be okay when I got home. But it's still all craziness."

I picked up a doughnut, dripping with chocolate glaze.

"What do you mean?" I asked.

Renny shrugged. "On this same planet,

at this same moment, only a plane ride away people are dying," he said. "They're not just dying. They are dying in gruesome, ugly ways. They're dying from picking up a baby that has a live grenade in his diaper. They're dying from eating some food offered up by a sweet old grandma that happens to have ground glass cooked inside. They're dying because they happen to walk across a piece of the land that the policy map says automatically makes you the enemy. People are dying. And I'm here making a giant crepe-paper bug. What's that about?"

He looked over at me, as if I could answer the question.

I was still trying to take in what he'd just said.

"There's not really any babies with grenades or grandmas with ground glass," I stated firmly. "You're just making that stuff up."

Renny glanced over at me, as if he was seeing me for the first time.

"You're just making it up," I repeated. "Ned does that sometimes. He says things to try to scare me. He's just making it up."

Renny managed a strange little smile. "Yeah, you're right, Laney," he said. "I'm just making it up."

There was something about the way he said it that made me unsure.

Everything he'd said might have gone straight into my *you-can't-fool-me* brain storage area, an area that was already crammed full of crap my cousins had told me. That's probably what would have happened if something more permanently damaging hadn't occurred a few weeks later.

Acee and I were in the family room watching the *Smothers Brothers* on TV. Babs was seated at her secretary writing little handwritten notes on white paper to thank whomever for whatever, whenever.

The telephone rang.

"Hello," my mother said as she picked it up. There was only a short pause before a very frightened and soulful, "Oh, no!"

"What?" Acee stood up and turned to her.

She was still on the phone, nodding, her brow furrowed in worry.

"We'll be right there," she said. "Please don't cry, Aunt Maxine, we'll be right there."

She was already talking to Acee before she'd gotten the phone back into its cradle. "Uncle Warren has had a stroke."

Between Babs and Acee there was no discussion. He got his jacket, she got her purse. I was rushed out to the car with

192

them. They said nothing. I couldn't stop asking questions.

"What happened? What's a stroke? Is he going to be all right?"

I might as well have been talking to myself. No one answered, nothing was said as we made our way through the warm autumn night to the hospital. Downtown there were people on the street headed for the eight-o'clock showing of *Cool Hand Luke* at the Ritz Theater. I watched them silently as we paused at the stop sign. I had an incredible urge to roll down my window and yell, "Stop laughing! Uncle Warren has had a stroke!"

Of course I didn't. I kept my silence as Acee drove on.

We pulled into a parking lot near the emergency entrance.

"You'll probably have to stay in the waiting room," Babs told me. "That's better anyway. I'm sure you don't want to see him until he's feeling better."

As it turned out, we were all in the waiting room. Me, my mom, Acee and the whole Barstow family, Aunt Maxine, the twins, Renny and Pete. Pete's lip was cut and he was holding a wet towel over his right eye.

"What happened?" I asked immediately.

Nobody answered.

Acee immediately took charge of the conversation. "How's Warren? What did the doctor say? Have you seen him?"

It was easy to imagine how Acee might have cross-examined a witness in court. He quickly managed to get the story, in its entirety out of all five available sources. Pete and Renny had gotten into an argument about the war. When angry words had come to blows, Uncle Warren had tried to come between them. His blood pressure, always high, had shot up and blew out a blood vessel in his brain. He'd keeled over and they'd called for an ambulance.

Understanding that people function through a crisis better by having a job to do, Acee sent the twins to get their mother a cup of coffee. He had Babs go with Aunt Maxine to see about the paperwork and billing. He took Pete into the E.R. to get his eye looked at. And he told Renny to stay with me.

I certainly didn't need a babysitter. But I sat down next to my cousin anyway. The knuckles of his right hand were cut and bleeding.

"Are you okay?" I asked him.

"Stupid. Stupid. Stupid," was his response.

I didn't for a moment think that the word was directed at me.

"It was just one of those things that happened," I comforted rather lamely.

"It's been brewing ever since I got home," Renny said. "I just couldn't believe my own brother would turn into one of them."

"One of whom?"

"One of those long-haired, hippie creeps," Renny answered.

I couldn't understand his anger.

"Pete's been wearing his hair long since the Beatles came out," I reminded him.

"This is not about hair!" Renny snapped.

He immediately apologized. I shrugged it off.

"What is it about, Renny?" I asked. "You and Pete always got into fights. It was never a big deal."

"This was a big deal," Renny answered, angrily. "The war is a big deal. I'm fighting for my country and my brother, my own flesh and blood is a traitor."

"Pete's a traitor?" I was shocked.

"Well, as much as one," Renny corrected. "He's one of those filthy peaceniks. He's breaking Mom's and Dad's hearts."

"Really? I thought they were proud of

him. Aunt Maxine is always talking about how he's on the dean's list. How he'll be the first in the family to get a college education."

Renny made an angry dismissing sound. "He takes advantage of the freedoms that me and guys like me are fighting for."

I nodded.

"He says he doesn't believe in the war," Renny said. "Like his opinion should matter. Pete's just a kid. The big decisions of the world shouldn't be up to him."

"No, of course not," I agreed.

"If he's going to live in this country, enjoy our freedoms, then he should do what the government tells him. If he doesn't like it, fine, he's entitled to think what he wants to think, but he ought to keep his mouth shut."

"So this is what you fought about?"

Renny nodded. "I couldn't believe it. He said that he was thinking about burning his draft card."

"Can he do that?"

"If he can, he shouldn't be able to," Renny answered. "But that's not the worst. He said if he was called up, he'd move to Canada."

"Canada?"

"That's when I hit him," Renny said. "I

hit him and I couldn't stop hitting him. All the time I was in Vietnam, when things got bad, I tried to remember that I was there for my family. I was doing all that for you and Mom and the twins and Pete."

He buried his face in his hands for a moment and then looked over at me, his eyes almost as sad as they were angry.

"And I find out that Pete wouldn't do that for me."

"You want him to go to Vietnam, too?"

"No, no, I don't want him to go," Renny said. "It's awful and just . . . just awful. I don't want my brother there. He's my kid brother. I don't want him to go. But I want him to *want* to go. Does that make sense?"

It didn't to me, but fortunately, I didn't have to answer. Janey and Joley returned, each with a cardboard carrier full of coffee and Cokes. They sat down with us, though both seemed wary of the older brother whom they had always loved. Their uncertainty seemed to annoy Renny even further.

"If anything happens to Dad," he told us ominously, "I'll never forgive Pete."

"It wasn't Pete's fault," Joley said. "You're the one that started it."

"It doesn't matter who started it," Renny said. "There's right and there's wrong. I'm right. Pete's wrong."

Babs

Uncle Warren's stroke left him unable to walk and barely able to talk. We were all grateful, but I was very worried. About Uncle Warren, of course, but also about Aunt Maxine. Taking care of him was a full-time job and she had plenty of full-time jobs. Uncle Warren still owned and operated the shoe repair, the dry cleaners, the coin laundry and the Dairy Hut.

From my perspective, the only answer was that one of the boys stay home and take care of the businesses.

"They should probably sell out," I confided to Acee. "But that might make Uncle Warren give up. The only alternative is for Renny or Pete to take over."

Unfortunately I put it to the boys just that way.

Renny was my first choice. He was the oldest, after all. And he'd already done his duty in Vietnam. I was certain that the Army would let him have an early out.

"You weren't really planning to have a career in the military," I pointed out to him as we sat together on the front porch swing outside their house. "And I'd hate to ask Pete to give up college when he's so close to graduating."

I knew immediately that I'd made a mistake. His expression, which had indicated thoughtful consideration, suddenly hardened into stubbornness.

"Oh, yeah," he responded, his tone sarcastic. "Pete's college is so very important and defending the country, that's practically like having no job at all."

"I didn't say that," I corrected him quickly. "And I certainly didn't mean that. You know how proud we all are of you. But you've already done your share for the country. Now you're needed at home."

Renny's refusal was adamant.

"I like the Army. What I do is important. I'm not giving that up to make things more convenient for a shirker like Pete."

Pete was just as difficult when I finally caught up to him with a phone call to his dorm room.

"Babs, I know your heart is in the right

place," he said. "But I think you're over-stepping."

"I'm not," I assured him. "Aunt Maxine has far too much to do caring for Uncle Warren. There is no way that she can care for his businesses, as well."

He nodded. "I agree. But butting in and deciding for them what they should do about it is interference."

"They are too proud to ask for help," I said.

"Maybe," he admitted. "Or maybe they don't really need any. Either way, it's their life. They get to decide all the big things and live it as they see fit. Forcing your view of what they should do is the worst kind of selfishness, Babs."

"Selfishness? Are you nuts, Pete?" I was incensed. "You should want to do the right thing for them."

"I do," he said. "But I'm not convinced that throwing away all I've worked for, all they've worked for, without a specific request from them, is at all what they would want. It may be what you would want. But I'm not sure it's what they would want."

"What they want and what is best may not be the same thing," I said.

"Look," Pete said. "If Mama asks me to give up college and come home, I'll do it.

But I'm not forcing myself into the situation by volunteering."

"Yeah, I know," I told him snidely. "Volunteering is not your big thing, is it."

He didn't appreciate my sarcasm.

"G'night, Babs," he responded, hanging up the phone abruptly.

I was incensed and complained to Acee.

"You know, Pete has a point," my husband told me. "Aunt Maxine hasn't asked you to stick your nose into this."

"Somebody is going to have to do this," I explained. "And if I don't get the boys involved, it will end up being me. And I don't have the time."

Acee looked up from the biography he was reading. That was an unusual occurrence in itself. He prided himself on being able to talk and read at the same time. It was a rare moment in his conversations with me that he lifted his eye from the page.

"Getting out of the house, doing something, that might be good for you," he said.

I stared at him in shocked disbelief.

"Doing something?" I asked, sarcastically. "For heaven's sake, Acee, I am so busy now, I'm near to going out of my mind."

"Yes, of course you're busy," he said.

"But I think it might be nice for you to get involved in some sort of business. You always worked as a teenager. And you seemed to enjoy it a lot."

"I am working at the only career I'm interested in," I told him. "Housewife and mother."

I saw it in his eyes then. An expression that I did not recognize and couldn't interpret. It was almost dismissal. He went back to his paper.

"Whatever you want," he said.

Whatever I wanted? I wanted him to have whatever he wanted. I wanted him to be happy, successful, fulfilled and I was working at it night and day. I was still very involved in serious socializing with the best of the community. And I was making progress. Acee was, of course, already well-known and respected. But I was, slowly but surely, making him the most sought after lawyer in McKinney, at least on the level of entertaining. We were more than simply within the social whirl. We were a prominent cog, fundamental in keeping it turning. We had several parties at the house every month. They were fancy affairs with glamorous dresses and dry martinis. At first I knew that wives dragged their husbands there to see the inside of our house. The beautiful restoration was a natural draw. I made sure that they were never disappointed. I was constantly redecorating, so that there was always something new to see. And I think that it became, for many upwardly mobile McKinney matrons, a point of pride over a lunch at Woolworth to be the one able to describe my new wallpaper.

I was helping my husband. I was creating a happy, healthy homelife, keeping my figure and following fashion. Those things were my job. Of course, I knew that I should be giving him a son. That, it turned out, was not as easy as simply deciding to do so.

I still hated being touched. I hated having sex. Night after night, I would grit my teeth and open my legs, determined to do my duty.

My sessions with Brother Chet became infrequent, as I assured him that everything was now fine. I read my magazines, books, newspaper articles. There was no shortage of information out there. Sex was the topic of the era. Everyone wanted to talk about it. But all that gab was about woman rising up from the ashes of repression and having orgasms.

That didn't interest me. I wasn't seeking

the pleasure of sex, but the product of it. I needed to have a baby. I was letting my husband do that to me several times a week, but nothing was happening.

I didn't know who to talk to or even what questions to ask. Aunt Maxine, the closest person I had to an advisor and confidante, had her hands full, and with four children of her own, I suspected that she hadn't had any problems getting pregnant. Among the ladies in my circle, all the talk was about preventing babies. Discussions of "the pill" took place regularly and all the women claimed it was a miracle drug. I pretended a sophisticated agreement. But I had never tried to prevent anything in my life. Why weren't they developing an antipill? A little tablet you could take in the morning and be with child by afternoon.

After almost two years of trying to get pregnant, I went for a checkup with the doctor. I couldn't face the aging family physician, so I made an appointment with the young upstart in town. I was as nervous as if wading in a creek full of crocodiles. The moment he came into the room I blurted out my concern. Thankfully Dr. Mansfield didn't suddenly turn into Brother Chet and fault me for my lack.

"Let's have a look," he said. "We know that you're capable of conceiving, because you've had two live births to your credit. Let's just make certain that we haven't developed some problem we're not aware of."

I did what I had to do. I put on the ugly cotton gown and climbed up on the table. With my feet in the stirrups, I was completely vulnerable. I hated having to do it. I hated Dr. Mansfield for putting me through it. I closed my eyes and pretended it wasn't happening. But in my mind I saw that set of salt and pepper shakers. It was that table again and it was all I could do not to throw up.

"All right, Mrs. Clifton," he said. "You can sit up now."

I brought myself to an upright position, my legs together tightly. I held back the nausea in my throat. I didn't look at him.

"You can get dressed now and we'll talk in my office."

As I put on my clothes, I pulled my scattered emotions together. It had all been so long ago. I couldn't let it still be there for me. I must just forget it. Too much had happened. It was well past time to put it all behind me.

With my makeup freshened and my lipstick reapplied, I was ready to face the man from across the width of his mahogany desk.

Dr. Mansfield was smiling at me.

"Everything looks normal," he said.

That news both relieved and frustrated me. In my secret heart I think I was hoping that my womb might be full of cancer, a giant abscess or a withering disease that rendered me sterile as only the first step on a ladder to death. I could gracefully exit my world with no one the wiser and everyone believing that I'd done my best.

"You have minimal scarring from childbirth and all the tissues are rosy pink and the picture of health."

"What wonderful news," I lied.

"I see no reason why you shouldn't be able to carry a half-dozen more children if that's your wish."

I nodded.

"Could it be Acee's fault?" I asked him. "I read in *Cosmo* that sometimes men don't have enough of those sperm things."

Dr. Mansfield shrugged off that concern. "Don't believe everything you read in those silly women's magazines," he said with a laugh. "You two didn't have any problem getting in the family way before. I don't see any problem coming up in the future."

I didn't even consider telling him the truth. Doctor–patient confidentiality might seem sacrosanct, but in small towns some truths are *always* too dangerous to reveal.

"I'm sure that it's not physical," he continued. "It's emotional. You need to just stop worrying about it. Relax and let it happen."

That was much easier said than done.

"That's not a bad prescription, now is it," he said. "Build a nice hot fire in the bedroom and don't let the flames go out."

His little suggestive laugh was maddening. I wanted to scream, pull my hair out, rail against God.

Instead I smiled.

"Thank you, Dr. Mansfield," I said sweetly. "You have certainly relieved my mind about that. Oh, and I was wondering, I'm giving a little dinner party a week from Friday. I'd love to have you and your lovely wife join us."

He blushed and his chest puffed out. The Mansfields were new in town, but not so new that they didn't know the social strata.

"We would like that very much," the doctor assured me.

"Fine, I'll give your wife a call and give her the details."

"Thank you," he said. "Thank you very much."

It was better if the Mansfields were in my debt, I decided. It was never good if rumors about me got started. Cultivating his wife as a friend should insure that nothing untoward was ever said.

That's what my life was about. Being beautiful and warding off the prospect of unkind words.

My face to the world was that everything was wonderful and that Acee, Laney and I were the happiest, most perfect little family in Collin County. It was an image I struggled mightily to maintain.

If Acee approved of my efforts, he never said so. The harder I worked to make him a leader in the community, the less he had to say to me personally.

It's not that we were ships that passed in the night. That analogy just wouldn't hold up for us. We saw each other constantly. We ate breakfast together every morning and dinner every evening. We attended all our social functions together. He and Laney had become great friends and were inseparable on weekends. And I was always there. We had multiple conversations on any day of the week. Still, he and I had very little of substance to say to each other.

I believed that to be because I was not his intellectual equal. I was just an ordinary woman with a high school education and limited experience in the world. Perhaps I could have tried harder to think deep thoughts. I could have read more substantive magazines. I could have attended night classes or reached out to embrace culture. But I have to admit that truthfully, I didn't long for more serious discussions. I didn't mind living a life more superficial and less examined. I knew the world could be a darker, deeper place. That little bit of knowledge had been enough to choke out any desire for further examination. I chose to step away from a serious world.

Unfortunately the world has a way of coming crashing into one's door.

Laney

I got my first paying job when I was twelve years old. However, you shouldn't be picturing me in some child-labor sweatshop hunched over a sewing machine. Aunt Maxine hired me to help out Uncle Warren at the shoe shop. Two years after his stroke, he was still not completely recovered. He leaned heavily on a cane and dragged his right foot wherever he went. He didn't go that many places. Aunt Maxine drove him to the shoe shop in the morning and he stayed there all day. In these last years of his life, he lived as he had early on, all by himself, repairing shoes in a tiny shop.

Aunt Maxine had taken on all the other businesses. With the help of the twins and what seemed to be a natural gift for organization, she had taken up the challenge of being the breadwinner and run with it. She hired competent people, paid them a little more than they'd get elsewhere and expected a lot from them. Surprisingly she usually got it.

She never asked her boys to come home and help. Pete graduated from North Texas and got a job at Texas Instruments in Sherman. He was engaged to a very nice girl. She wasn't as pretty as some he'd brought home, but she was out of medical school and working to become a pediatrician.

Renny had become a training instructor in Georgia. He'd also married and had a little baby. We'd only seen them in photographs. He'd never brought his wife back to Texas to meet anybody. They certainly looked happy. And they seemed settled, but inexplicably Renny volunteered for another tour of duty in Vietnam. So Aunt Maxine was back to worrying about him all the time.

The twins were freshmen roommates at Texas Women's University. They had both made enough money from helping run their parents' businesses to afford to send themselves.

I have to admit that I was surprised when Aunt Maxine asked me to work for her. But I was also delighted. I'd started my period. I was wearing a bra. I was becoming a woman. My mother had not noticed. I was so glad that Aunt Maxine had.

The agreement was that I would ride over on my bicycle after school and work until closing adding up the day's receipts and making the charge tickets match what was in the money drawer. It required some math skills, but I was good at that. And it was less than two hours a day.

My mother didn't like it.

"She's a little girl," Babs complained. "She should be doing homework or out playing after school."

Aunt Maxine waved away her concerns. "You weren't much older when we put you to work," she said. "And Laney will have plenty of time to keep Warren's accounts and do homework, as well. And she'll certainly be safer employed on the downtown square than hanging out at the playground with those wild hooligans who spend their time there."

Aunt Maxine was sure right about that. The wild hooligans included my cousin Ned. Now a fourteen-year-old chain-smoker and frequent truant from McKinney High School's freshman class, he'd never liked me and often sought me out for some type of mean trick. I avoided him like the plague. That was easier now that we weren't in the same school.

Babs couldn't really go against Aunt Maxine. And she was so busy with all her clubs and parties, it was probably a relief to have me out of her hair in the afternoons.

I had my own desk that I decorated, as working people do, with memorabilia and personal treasures. There was the five-by-seven framed photo of Acee, Babs and me that had been sent in the family Christmas card. Beside it was a smaller photo of my dog, Bowser, a white Scottie that lived and barked in our backyard. My second place trophy from the Rural Electric Cooperatives public speaking competition was draped with my Fourth Place ribbon for Cornbread Muffins at the County Fair. The only other personal items were my SoupKids salt shakers, Alana and Marley. I felt weird for having kept them hidden in my treasure drawer. My mother, I was certain, would never remember that she'd thrown them away and forbidden me to rescue them from the trash. But I still felt guilty about disobeying her. Here in the shoe shop I could see them every day.

Aunt Maxine noticed.

"You still have those things," she said, surprised. "I remember when we collected the labels from the cans."

"I've always kept them," I told her. "Though the boy got his hat broken."

I didn't say how.

Aunt Maxine and I had become very close. I felt closer to her, in fact, than I did Babs. But that often happens when people share a secret. By necessity, Aunt Maxine had shared hers with me.

It was the first afternoon of my first day on the job. Aunt Maxine took me for a treat at Miss Lettie's Tea Room and gave me a serious talk.

"I'm very glad that you are going to work at the shoe shop. And I know that you'll be perfectly able to take care of things there," she said.

"Thanks, Aunt Maxine," I answered. "I promise to really try my best."

"I'm sure you will," she said. "What I want you to keep in mind is that your job is to help your uncle Warren."

"Oh, sure," I said. "Whatever he asks me to do, I'll do it."

Aunt Maxine nodded. "I know that," she said. "The thing is, he may not remember to ask you."

I frowned, uncertain.

"Uncle Warren is about as recovered from the stroke as he's going to get," she said. "He's come a very long way and we are all so grateful and blessed. But his is not a full recovery. He is not the same man he was before."

I nodded solemnly. "He drags his leg when he walks," I said.

Aunt Maxine smiled sadly.

"That's what everyone notices," she said. "It's obvious and everyone sees it. But what is less obvious is that he's having to drag a part of his brain along, too."

I wasn't sure what she meant by that.

"Your uncle Warren's thinking is not quite up to what it used to be," she said. "He can't count the money accurately or keep sums in his head. He has trouble doing more than one thing at a time."

She smiled at me and patted my hand.

"That's why I want you to help him. I want you to add up the figures that are so hard for him now and keep the books accurate."

"Sure, I think I can do that."

"But there is more to it," Aunt Maxine said. "You must do it without anyone realizing that you're doing it for him."

"Huh?"

"He's a proud man," she told me. "I don't think he's allowed himself to admit his limitations. If people began to treat him

215

differently, and they would, I don't think he could bear it."

I nodded thoughtfully.

"So you must quietly go behind him, fix his errors, cover for his mistakes, remind him of what he's forgotten and never let him know that you're doing it."

"How do I do that?" I asked.

"It's not easy," Aunt Maxine said. "I'd be the first to tell you. It takes patience, it takes practice and it takes humility. But it's a skill that if you learn it and learn it well, it will suit you admirably on life's long road."

So I made a point of figuring out how to help without seeming to and put that knowledge into practice. As it turned out, it wasn't really so difficult. Maybe because I am reticent by nature or because I'd lived my whole life in the shadow of my mother, I found that I could easily correct things and not take credit for it. I took joy in my successes, without needing to take a bow or get a pat on the back. I felt an inordinate amount of pride in how well I could hide my own usefulness. And the only time I was even tempted to tell was at a slumber party.

It was a Saturday night and Nicie's thirteenth birthday. Uncle Freddie and Aunt

LaVeida treated her and seven of her closest friends, which included me, to a slumber party. The evening started out at the new Pizza Inn out at Westgate Shopping Center. We sat together at the big corner booth.

It was lots of fun and I was feeling great. I'd just had my hair done that morning. I'd kept it long, much to my mother's distress because she thought it looked unkempt, but since I paid for it myself, she had no say at all. I'd had the hairdresser frost it a light ash blond. It looked really good. And I felt really attractive and a lot more grown-up as male heads turned my way.

Unfortunately I wasn't the only one to notice.

My cousin Cheryl took offense.

"Twelve is too young to bleach your hair," she stated adamantly.

"I'm almost thirteen and it's not bleach," I told her. "It's just frost."

"There's bleach in the frost," she said. "You can't turn brown hair to blond without bleach."

All the other girls agreed.

"It really looks nice," Nicie told me. "I wish I could do that, but my mom would never let me."

"Your hair looks great just like it is,"

Cheryl assured her. "And your mother is right. We are too young to color our hair and Laney's mother shouldn't have let her do it."

"She didn't have any say in it," I pointed out. "I make my own money, so I do what I want."

That was an exaggeration, but it was meant to shut Cheryl up. It didn't work.

"Oh, yeah, your family gives you a few little chores to do and they pay you for it instead of giving you an allowance," she said.

"No, it's not like that at all."

"Sure it is," Cheryl insisted. "Your mom just wants to keep you busy after school so she won't have to worry about you getting into trouble at the park. Paying you is cheaper than hiring a babysitter."

Her dismissal of my responsibility and the silent agreement around the table tempted me to tell them all. To explain how ill and confused my uncle Warren still was. To point out the level of confidence my aunt Maxine had in me and my abilities. I wanted them to know it all. It was on the tip of my tongue to tell them all.

But part of the trust that had been placed in me was discretion. Revealing the truth might make me look good, but it would make Uncle Warren look bad. For the first time in my life, I suppose, I was forced to truly be a grown-up, to swallow my own pride for the sake of someone else. I managed to do it, but pizza hasn't tasted the same to me since.

After dinner, we all packed into Aunt LaVeida's Oldsmobile station wagon and rode to her house. We were laughing and screaming and hollering at people out the windows. She took the long route through town, which included three complete circles of the downtown square. We were in high spirits by the time we reached the Hoffmans' brick suburban two-story house.

I could never visit Nicie's room without remembering that I could have been her sister. I could have shared the life that was hers. Of course, her room wasn't as nice as the one I had with Babs and Acee. But there was always something about it, something that said she was special, an individual, loved and appreciated for exactly whom she happened to be. My room was a stereotype of what thirteen-year-old girls are supposed to want. It could have been any girl's room. Everything that was out of the ordinary and unique to me I carefully kept packed away in a box in my closet. Once in Nicie's bedroom we changed into our pajamas and began the festivities that passed for entertainment among preteens.

We used Nicie's pink princess phone to call up old people, who were always a little less quick than our parents, and ask them, "Is your refrigerator running?"

If they answered yes, the punch line was, "You'd better go out and catch it!" Followed by a quick hang up and a riot of giggles.

Later we all opened our backpacks, overnight bags and pink duffels to retrieve all our cosmetics and hair paraphernalia. I lay across the bed with my head hanging off the edge, while Trixie Bryan and Cindy Gilbert painted my eyes to look like Cleopatra. Nicie and Charlene Wilkinson were painting each other's toenails. April Harmon and Kathy Cox were giving Cheryl a new hairdo. Even watching upside down, I could see that their outcome was not going to be good.

"I thought ratting was out," I said, hoping to discourage the two from the extensive back-combing that had Cheryl's mousy brown locks standing straight out from her head.

"I don't think it's totally out," April said.

"Yeah," Kathy agreed. "All of the beauty shops still do it."

"They do it for, like, our moms or someone," I said. "I think it's totally out if you want to look cool."

"Oh, it'll never go totally out," April assured me. "I mean if your hair doesn't have shape or body you'll, like, have to give it some."

"No," I disagreed. "All the college girls wear their hair stringy."

"Since when are you the expert on hair fashion!" Cheryl asked, clearly angry. "You have one day when you think your hair looks pretty and suddenly you're telling the rest of us how to live our lives. Well, you're not telling me nothing."

Nicie gave me a wide-eyed caution and I shut up immediately.

As the night wore on, more makeup was applied, more hair was sprayed stiff and more nails were buffed and polished. The more tired we got, the less we did. The less we did, the more serious the gossip became.

We sat, heavy-eyed and painted like harlots among the stuffed teddy bears and ballet slippers.

Cheryl explained the mechanics of sexual intercourse.

"Yuk! That's disgusting," was the universal response.

"That's how it's done," Cheryl said. "It's

totally disgusting, but that's the way it is."

"I can't believe my parents did that," Nicie said with a horrified whisper.

"At least you're an only child," Trixie pointed out. "I've got five brothers and sisters. My parents must have done it six times!"

"Eeeewwww," we all agreed.

"I think if you're married it's different," Cindy said. "I don't know how, but obviously that's the reason that parents are always cautioning teenagers against it."

"I'm sure no one would do it if they didn't have to," April said.

"They say boys always want to do it," Nicie pointed out.

"Why?" Kathy asked.

"Why do some kids eat boogers?" Charlene asked rhetorically.

We all shuddered with disgust.

"It's hard to believe that anyone does that ever," I said.

Cheryl's eyes narrowed. "Are you calling me a liar?"

"No," I assured her. "I'm just . . . just grossed out."

"It's all true," she said. "And people do it before they get married. There are even people that we know who did it before they got married."

There was a startled shock around the room.

"Who?" somebody asked aloud.

Cheryl looked over at me. Her expression was pure venom. "I heard my mother and Aunt LaVeida talking about when your little brother was born. It was only seven months after your mother and Mr. Clifton got married. They both agreed that the only way he would have married her was if he had had to because she was pregnant."

The other girls uttered a gasp.

"So," Cheryl continued nastily, "your mom must have pulled her pants down and let him do that to her just because she liked it."

"My mother never did that!"

"You're supposed to be the math whiz," Cheryl pointed out. "Can't you count nine months."

"My brother was born early," I defended. "You can't say those things about my mother."

"Your mother thinks she's a society hostess," Cheryl said. "But if you ask the Hoffman family they'll tell you that she's a slut. She's selfish and disrespectful to the memory of our uncle. She probably never loved him. He was hardly cold in his grave before she was doing it, probably for

money, with Acee Clifton."
I reached over and slapped her face.
But I never forgot what she said.

Babs

In the summer of 1972 Acee ran for judge. With my duties as chairman of the Cotton Days celebration, the timing wasn't perfect. Of course, he couldn't be blamed for the timing. Old Judge Weatherford, who was at least eighty and had been napping on the bench for years, was, at long last, stepping down. Even when the state legislature had mandated old-age retirement for judges, he'd stayed on the civil court bench and continued to resist. Finally a bout of bad health forced him to call it quits.

In Texas, state and county court judges are elected just like mayors and senators and governors. In theory, they are then answerable to the people and the bad ones can be voted out of office. In practice, once elected, most keep getting reelected. So an opportunity to campaign without going up against an incumbent is not a chance to be passed up.

Early on, Acee seemed like the favorite. I admit to taking a certain amount of personal pride in this. Of course, his reputation was his own. He was smart and honest and well-respected by everybody from the town drunk to city officials. But I had turned those qualities into political capital. I was the person who'd kept his name and his success fresh in the minds of the socially prominent people of the community.

Acee wasn't as interested in political life as he should have been.

"If I'm the right man for the job, the people will vote for me," he said.

"Acee, the people will vote for you because you convince them that you're the right man for the job."

A campaign required little gifts for voters and supporters, something to help them remember your name. Acee came up with the idea of putting his name on fish scales with the imprint: Acee Clifton: Weighing Matters In Collin County. The handy gadgets quickly found their way into the tackle box of every man in town. I wanted him to say Weighing Things Fishy In Collin County, which was funnier and more truthful about what a civil court judge might do. Acee thought that was disrespectful both to the court and the voter.

So I let him do it his way.

"We have to come up with a little something for the ladies, too," I pointed out. "You need their votes as much as their husbands."

He nodded. "I was thinking about a pot holder that says something like Protecting You In Civil Court."

"A pot holder? Oh, Acee please, this is not 1957."

He laughed. "Okay, make a suggestion," he said. "What can I give them that will make me look really cool and hip to the ladies? A subscription to *Playgirl* magazine?"

"Only if you were running in Travis County," I replied.

Finally we settled on tiny flashlights that attached to a key ring. They were so small there wasn't room for any slogan beyond Acee Clifton For Judge.

I enjoyed the campaigning tremendously. We went door to door in neighborhoods I'd never walked in. We attended church picnics and Grange meetings. We stood outside Bird's Supermarket helping shoppers with their bags and asking for their vote.

I loved all of it. I felt as if I'd found my vocation in life. All my training, a decade of social interaction, had been leading up to this point. I could, I was certain, be the perfect political wife.

Our parties had formerly been limited to the higher social strata of the community, those particularly charming couples and a few others that Acee considered his friends. Now I expanded the size and scope of our gatherings to include the less interesting but more powerful businessmen in the county. Many of them were new to the area. They were Dallas men or Houston men. They saw the future of McKinney as the future of America.

"When Central Expressway is completed," one told me, "living in McKinney will be as convenient to downtown Dallas as living in Highland Park."

I smiled, but it honestly didn't please me as much as the man expected. I still avoided trips to the city. I was anxious and jittery every minute I was there. But I smiled politely.

"We're going to develop these old hay meadows and cotton fields into modern, family housing developments," another said. "We'll expand the community to twice the size it is today. Increase the tax base and bring a real boon to local business."

That sounded nice.

One evening as a lawyer representing a big commercial construction company was leaving, he handed me a check.

"This is to help out with the campaign costs," he said. "I know all those flashlights and fish scales don't come free. I want to help."

He gave me a little wink and I thanked him.

Someone else was leaving at the same time and distracted me. The man was long gone before I glanced at the check in my hand. Ten thousand dollars. That was more than our complete budget for the entire campaign. More than the total of all the other money we'd raised.

I was astounded and excited.

When I showed the check to Acee, he was furious.

"Do you know what he wants?" he asked me.

I shook my head.

"He wants to build a big shopping center at the edge of the county," Acee said. "The farmers who own the land don't want to sell. He's taking them to court to have the land reclassified as commercial instead of agricultural so that they can't afford to farm it."

"Oh, well, that's silly," I said. "He can't do that."

"He can if he buys enough legislatures and local officials and . . ." Acee held up the check. "Enough civil court judges.

"I'm going to take this back to him tomorrow and throw it in his face."

"No, Acee," I soothed him. "That's not the way to do it. If you don't want to accept the money, simply don't cash the check. There is no reason to confront him about it."

"Just let him think I'm on his payroll."

I shrugged. "People are free to think whatever they want to think. You're not on his payroll, you have no obligation to do anything for him. But by the time he realizes that, the election will be over. It will be too late to offer support to some other candidate."

"You want me to just let him believe that he's bought me until after I've used him," Acee said. "Babs, where do you get these ethics?"

"This isn't about ethics," I told him. "It's about winning. Once you've won, your ethics will speak for themselves."

He shook his head. "That's not me, Babs," he said. "That's not the way that I deal with other people. It's not the way that I live my life."

"This isn't life, Acee, it's politics."

I couldn't convince him.

The next day he very publicly returned the money given to him by the construction firm. When the farmers in the corner of the county heard about it, they were very pleased and contacted Acee. He wouldn't give them any assurances that he would help them.

"I have to rule based on the cases presented before me," he said. "This issue has yet to be presented, so I cannot possibly say how I might or might not decide it."

To Acee's way of thinking, that was exactly the right and wholly ethical answer, true to both the language and the spirit of the law. But, of course, it was the death blow to his campaign. I'm not saying that the county was overrun with crooks and shady characters. Most of the people were good, honest folks, but they were suddenly suspicious. Before Acee had said anything, it was as if everyone trusted him. But once he attempted to show that he could be trusted, suddenly he was suspect. Virtually all the wealthy businessmen and developers withdrew their support. Even many of the people we'd socialized with for years suddenly made themselves scarce. We knew we'd lost two weeks before the ballots were cast. There seemed to be nothing we could do.

The night of the primary election, we put on our best clothes and our best smiles and went downtown for a party with our supporters and to await the returns.

Acee came in a respectable third. He seemed perfectly okay with that. I was devastated. There was the sense of failure, of course. But somehow it was more. There was also both the sense that your friends had let you down, and the feeling that you'd let them down, as well. I woke up every morning thinking about it. It was the last thing I thought about before I fell asleep at night.

"Let it go, Babs," Acee told me. "It's no tragedy. I've got a great job that I like to do. And the opportunity, by itself, was far more than so many other people get to experience."

Intellectually I knew he was right. But my emotions just couldn't seem to follow my thinking.

"You would have been so much better for this county than either of the men still on the ballot."

He shrugged and shook his head.

"That doesn't matter," Acee said. "Hey,

the first rule of politics is that the best man doesn't always win."

"I know," I admitted with a sigh. "Well, at least we only have to wait a couple of years. And we can use that time to raise money and work out a thorough campaign plan."

Acee turned to me with an aghast expression as if I were out of my mind.

"The new judge's term is six years," he said. "And unless he does something absolutely terrible, it would be fruitless to run against an incumbent."

"Well, of course," I said. "You can't run for judge again anyway. But there are plenty of elective offices out there. We just have to pick one that's vulnerable and go after it."

Just the idea of a new campaign cheered me up.

Acee's reaction was quite different.

"No," he said simply.

"What do you mean?"

"I mean no," he repeated. "I ran for this office because I really wanted to do that job. I'm not interested in politics or public office. I love the law. That's why I went into practice. The lure of the political spotlight doesn't tempt me."

"Oh, you're just thinking that way because we lost this election," I assured him. "You'll feel differently in a few months."

He didn't.

Instead he became interested in something absolutely awful. Sex therapy.

One morning he handed me a piece of the morning paper folded in such a way that it was impossible to miss the article he wanted me to see.

Men And Women Need More, the headline read.

It was paraphrasing, incorrectly, a quote from Dr. William Masters. What he'd really said was, "men and women need each other more than ever before."

The article was about sex clinics and the work they were doing with the intimacy problems of married couples. According to the article, all over the country men and women were rediscovering each others' bodies.

I couldn't quite repress an involuntary shudder.

"I think we need to check this out," Acee said.

"Now dear," I responded very calmly and with a certain haughtiness. "I've told you that I think the talks with Brother Chet help me far more than those highbrow Ph.D.s. I don't want to start going into the city again."

"This isn't for you," Acee answered. "It's for us. We'd both be involved in the therapy. And you can believe me that I'd be a whole lot more comfortable talking about where I want to kiss you with some highbrow Ph.D. than with Brother Chet."

I could hardly argue that.

"This is for younger couples," I assured him with a chuckle. "Newlyweds who are just finding their way. We're old married folks now. Our tenth anniversary is behind us."

He nodded, very gravely.

"That's right," he said. "Ten years and I no longer believe that you're going to get used to my touch. I no longer have hope that one night when I roll off you, you're not going to jump up and race to the shower like the banshees of hell are after you."

I blushed. I was scared. I was humiliated. I didn't know how to defend myself, except with stubborn silence.

"Ladies just like to be clean," I said. "There is nothing strange or abnormal about that. I'm sure that most of the women in this town feel the same way."

"Maybe so," Acee said. "But I'm not married to most of the women in town.

I'm married to you and I would like for us to have a more physically satisfying sex life."

"Eww, Acee please, don't use the phrase sex life, it's just . . . coarse. If you have to mention it at all, say intercourse or better yet, intimacy. Speakers of the English language invented euphemisms for a reason."

"I don't want euphemisms between us," he said. "I don't want anything between us. We're married, we ought to be able to say and do whatever feels good between us."

"Well, I think there may be a discrepancy between what we see as good."

He sighed heavily. "Babs, don't you ever just want me?" he asked. "Don't you ever just feel . . . horny. I mean, right now, this very minute I could lay you across this kitchen table and rip that robe off you and kiss every inch of you. Especially those inches down between your legs that you keep covered up with cotton every minute of every day."

"Acee, for heaven's sake! It is seven o'clock in the morning and Laney is in the house. She could walk in this room any minute. I can't believe that you're discussing such things."

"Honey, darling, sweetie," he entreated. "I love you, but we've got to do better on this than we're doing."

"We're doing fine."

"I want to be a good and faithful husband," he said. "But when I think that this cold, infrequent joining is all that I'll ever have for the rest of my life, it just makes me so sad and disappointed."

"Oh, so now you're threatening me," I said. "Either get better in bed or I'll cheat."

"I never said anything like that and I'd never meant anything like that. I just want it to be better between us."

"The only reason I have relations with you is so that we can have a child," I told him. "If we ever do, I'd be happy to forego that aspect of our marriage permanently."

That statement brought Acee to his feet. He just stood there for a long moment staring at me. I wanted to recall the words. I wanted to begin the entire discussion over again. I should have played along and then let the subject drop. But that's not what I'd done. I'd been honest and I'd crossed the line. I already regretted it.

"Call around today," he said. "Find out who we can talk to and make an appointment."

His words weren't phrased as a request, but as an order.

"No." The word was small, quiet, but I hoped final.

"You won't call?"

I shook my head.

"Then I will," he said.

Laney

Puberty was probably the worst thing that ever happened to my relationship with my mother. One minute she was virtually ignoring me. I was living my life as I thought best. The next she was trying to control every moment of my existence. By the time I turned sixteen, I was near drowning in her words of her wisdom.

"It's better to be out of fashion than caught wearing a fad."

"If you must listen to music, it should be something lovely played on a piano."

"Pierced earrings are only worn by Catholic girls."

"When you're eating in public, no matter what you want, always order salad."

The recitation of these commandments was punctuated by her personal criticisms veiled as questions.

"You're not wearing that?"

"Are you putting on weight?"

"Can you do something with your hair?"

She also maintained complete control of where I went, who I saw and what I did.

"I know you've been close with your cousin Nicie since childhood, but you should really cultivate different friends."

"Other teenagers may congregate in big groups, but you should make a point of being exclusive."

"Traveling to away games isn't necessary. You get plenty of school sports here at home."

Babs wanted me to be popular, to have an active social life. She just wanted it to suit her notion of what teenage life should be like.

"Some people say these are the best years of your life," she told me. "I don't believe that. But these years are the foundation for everything that comes after them."

That statement just sounded like gibberish to me. Of course, all of a person's life is built day by day. But that doesn't mean that if you wear the wrong blouse to class, your reputation will never recover.

"You must think about your future every day," she said. "So many young women just drift through this time with no understanding of their own direction."

I had a complete and total under-standing of where I was headed. I was on my way out of town.

The spring of my sophomore year, Uncle Warren passed away. Aunt Maxine was awakened in the middle of the night and thought she heard something in the house. She got up and checked out every room before deciding that she'd been wrong and then headed back to bed. It was when she returned to the bedroom that she realized that what woke her up was not a sound, but the silence of Uncle Warren beside her.

Everybody came home for the funeral. Renny and Pete and their wives, the twins and their husbands. I think it was the first time everybody was together since Uncle Warren's stroke six years earlier. But it wasn't exactly a peaceful family gathering.

I really liked Sadie, Pete's wife. She was pretty and funny. She worked as a pediatri-cian and their little toddler, Dylan, was a delight. Renny's wife was named Vickie. She was his second wife, but since no one had met the first wife, it was all the same to us. Mostly she just sat out on the porch and smoked.

That was how the first argument got started. Vickie was six months pregnant and Sadie, in her role as physician, suggested that cigarettes might not be the best thing for the baby.

Within minutes everybody was screaming at everybody else.

I didn't know whose side to be on. Renny was still my favorite. I had missed him a lot and I wanted him to be right. But I knew that Sadie was only trying to be helpful to Vickie and that she wasn't the "meddling bitch!" that Renny had called her.

My mother stepped in and stopped the argument.

"I don't care how mad you are at each other," she told the boys. "You both love Aunt Maxine and when you fight like this, you hurt her. Now swallow your pride until we get through this funeral. Then you can go back to hating on a grand scale. But for the next three days, I don't want to hear one angry word."

Maybe it was because Babs was kind of like their older sister, or maybe they just realized that she was right, but they tried to get along. Mostly by keeping a good distance between each other.

I hung out with Renny as much as I could. I'd missed him. The day of the funeral, he had me meet him at four-thirty in the morning. We went out to Lavon Lake where he'd borrowed a boat so we could go fishing.

"It's pretty out here," I told him in a whisper as we sat in the quiet of half-light, the sunrise just blinking on the horizon.

"Pretty?" He chuckled. "Sometimes I wonder at pretty."

"What about it?"

"I'm not sure what it means."

I laughed. "It means something nice to look at," I told him.

He nodded slowly. "Yeah," he said. "A pretty sky, a pretty day, a pretty girl. Do you know what was the prettiest sight I ever saw?"

I shook my head.

"Bombing of the free fire zone from a night flight helicopter."

I was taken aback.

"It was so beautiful," he said. "Like the biggest Fourth of July fireworks you ever saw. We were awed. We were laughing. We were happy. And down below us, people were dying."

He chuckled. "It makes you think about what's really behind all that. Is a pretty sky just light reflected through dangerous clouds? Is a pretty day just the beginning of a deadly drought? Is a pretty girl just a lying, cheating bitch who hasn't gotten caught yet?"

"Renny, why do you say things like that?"

He shrugged. "Sorry."

"Do you think about the war all the time?" I asked.

"No, not anymore," he answered. "It comes to mind sometimes and I still have dreams. But it's more or less behind me."

"You always talk about it."

"Only when I'm here," he said. "When I'm here, it's front and center in my thoughts all the time. The whole time I was in Vietnam, I was thinking about McKinney. Now, when I'm in McKinney, I can't help but think about Vietnam."

"But you're always so angry," I said. "It's like you're angry at us. Tell me why you're like this, you never used to be like this."

"I've grown up, Laney," he said. "You'll get here, too. Grown-up, cynical and angry at the world, eager to shock."

"Is that what you're trying to do?" I asked him. "Make me angry at the world."

His expression changed. He suddenly looked more like the Renny I remembered. "I guess I am," he said.

"Why?" I asked him.

He shook his head. "I'm not sure. I

missed you. I wanted to come out here and be with you. But, when I am with you . . ." Renny hesitated trying to put his thoughts together. "Laney, you're so young and sweet, just like you've always been. In some weird way it sort of pisses me off. I want you to be as angry and cynical as I feel."

"I don't think I understand."

"I don't think I do, either," he said. "I'm just mad at the world and being home, among people who go on living as if there is justice and that things make sense, that just makes me madder."

"Maybe you should move back permanently," I told him. "You could get used to us again."

He shook his head. "Can't," he answered simply. But I knew it wasn't true. He'd mustered out of the Army because of some kind of medical problem and was now working at the shipyard in Norfolk. It was probably a good job. But there were lots of good jobs in Texas, as well.

"You might think about it," I suggested. "I'm sure it would mean a lot to Aunt Maxine to have you close by again."

Renny chuckled. "You're getting more like your mother every day," he told me.

I was incredibly insulted.

"I'm not like my mother," I told him. "How can you even think something like that."

"Oh, Laney," he said. "You're just like her. Talking so sweet like you really care when what you're really doing is trying to bully me around."

"I wasn't bullying," I assured him.

He smiled at me, humoring me. "I can't live around here, Laney," he said. "Because Pete lives around here."

"You're still mad at Pete because he didn't go into the Army?"

"No, I'm mad at Pete because . . . because he's ungrateful. Pete's made a big success of his life and he thinks he did that all on his own. It never occurs to him that he'd never have had a chance at the life he has now if it weren't for me and guys like me."

I nodded slowly, accepting, feeling the rise of that anger myself. I'd always liked Pete. I liked his family. But I was angry at him now, for Renny's sake, I was angry. If I was to be forced to choose between the two, I'd made my choice.

It was only a few days later, after Renny had gone back to Virginia that my conviction faltered.

Aunt Maxine had asked me to meet Pete at the Shoe Shop after school to go over the books. I went in with a chip set firmly on my shoulder. It didn't help that he was already seated at my desk, going through my paperwork without waiting for me to show up.

I sat down and he smiled at me.

"This is really good," he said. "When my mother told me that you'd been keeping the books for Dad since his stroke, I really thought they'd be a mess."

"Oh, did you?"

"Yeah, and I was very wrong," Pete admitted. "You've done a great job with this. We've got accounting clerks on salary at the company who couldn't have done it as well."

I knew I should thank him for the compliment, but I deliberately held it back.

"So what do you think?" he asked me.

"About what?"

"About the shop," he said. "We've got to decide whether to close the shop, try to sell it, or find a shoemaker to employ. Your aunt Maxine said it was up to us."

"Us? You and me?"

He nodded. "She wants me to take a look at her businesses, consult with the managers and come up with plans for the future. She considers you the manager of the Shoe Shop."

"I just helped out around here," I assured him. "Uncle Warren managed the business."

Pete looked at me closely. "You're a very smart girl, Laney," he said. "And a kind and loyal one, too, I think. I know my dad's handwriting. He hasn't done so much as a ledger entry in these books since you started working here."

I refused to comment. He didn't press me.

"Let's not talk about the past, let's talk about the future," he said.

"All right," I agreed.

I found the discussion interesting and Pete's obvious respect for my experience and my opinion was amazingly refreshing. I suppose that, as a teenager, I'd just become accustomed to being dismissed. I was routinely being told what to think, how to behave, what to value. Now, unexpectedly, my cousin Pete was asking me questions, listening to answers and considering my judgments. It was heady stuff.

"There's still quite a bit of business," I told him. "But I don't know if it's enough to pay someone else to do it."

"If we did pay someone?" he asked. "Who could it be?"

I shook my head.

"Well, let's think, if someone got a hole in their shoe this afternoon, where would they have to go to fix it. Lewisville? Allen?"

"Caswell Sargent does shoe repair at his house. Uncle Warren always said he did good work," I told him. "But I don't know how many whites would go to him."

"Do you think white people wouldn't want black people to fix their shoes?"

I considered that. "No, I just think most of them wouldn't make a special trip to that part of town, unless they just had to."

"What if Caswell were here?" Pete asked.

"He'd probably get as much business as Uncle Warren."

In the end, Pete approached Mr. Sargent and he paid cash to buy us out. I remember his nephew, Randall, came that very day to paint the name Sargent's above the Shoe Shop sign.

"What is Pete thinking!" my mother complained over dinner. "This is not Dallas. Black men don't own businesses on the downtown streets."

"They do now," Acee said. He seemed not nearly as bothered.

"Well, it's incredibly foolish," Babs stated. "Sometimes I wonder if all the money Aunt Maxine and Uncle Warren paid for that boy's college was even worth it."

Acee replied without looking up from his book. "Pete's a terrific success, a credit to his family. And a college education is always worth it."

"Well, I suppose so," Babs said. "But selling Uncle Warren's business to a black man. Even you, Acee, have got to admit that's probably not the brightest idea the boy has ever had."

"Actually it was kind of my idea," I said.

"What?" My mother's question was incredulous.

Acee looked up at me. His expression indicated he was both surprised and pleased.

"Nonsense," my mother said, dismissingly. "You didn't have a thing to do with it."

"I did," I insisted. "Pete wanted my opinion and I gave it to him."

Babs gave a little huff of disbelief and reached over and patted me on the hand.

"Honey, that's really sweet, I'm sure," she told me. "But you have to remember that sometimes the gentlemen allow us to believe that they're asking our opinions."

I shook my head, refusing to let it go.

"Pete asked me what I thought, we talked it over and we made the decision together. I was the one who knew about Mr. Sargent. I'm the one who suggested that it would be worth his while to move his business downtown."

"Where would you get an idea like that?"

"I got it out of my head, Mom," I told her. "That's where ideas come from. People just think them up."

"Well, a young girl on the brink of womanhood has a great deal more important things to think about than some old black man running a shoe shop. For heaven's sake, Laney. And what is that you're wearing? Are you putting on weight? If you are, these sloppy clothes aren't going to hide it. And remember, at sixteen we can't excuse extra pounds as baby fat. You've probably had enough dinner already. Maybe you should stop eating."

Deliberately I spooned up a huge bite of scalloped potatoes and looked her right in the eye as I stuffed it in my mouth.

Babs

There is nothing in the world quite as complicated as a mother's relationship with her teenage daughter. I suppose I had never understood that, because my mother never lived to really see me grow through those years. And although Aunt Maxine mothered me as lovingly as any real mother, I suspect that our congeniality together was based, at least in part, on the fact that she was not my mother.

My Laney, whom I'd loved and cherished every moment of her life, whose best interests had always been my first concern, whose future happiness was my highest goal, began treating me as if I was hated. My offers of help and advice were scorned and spurned on every occasion.

She'd get up and dress in the morning, wearing clothes that would embarrass hoboes, her hair stringy and styleless and without so much as a smear of makeup on her face. Blue jeans might be the current fashion, but they were a fad, I was certain. I didn't want Laney to look back at her high school yearbook and cringe at her photographs.

I tried to explain, as kindly as I could, that she looked simply awful and that when it came to choosing brides, young men always appreciated a more traditional kind of girl.

"Babs," she said. She'd begun calling me by my first name. "The last thing I'm interested in is some creep who's choosing a bride."

"Well, of course you don't want to think of it quite that way," I agreed. "But a woman only gets to be choosy when she has a number of fellows who want to choose her."

"There is not one guy in McKinney that I'd waste ten minutes of my time on," Laney said.

"Well, I have to admit, most of them don't seem like much," I told her. "But you have to squint a bit to see their potential. Some don't have much, like your cousin Ned and his friends. But there are some that will do well. Brian Wellman will undoubtedly take over his father's business. And a grocer's wife always knows that she'll eat. Larry Mendal is from a nice family and his mother says he wants to be a doctor. And, of course there's Stanley Kuhl, you can never go wrong with settling upon the top student in the class."

"Babs, you're out of your mind," Laney answered. "Larry Mendal is a jock. We'd have nothing in common. Brian Wellman likes Nicie, I'm not getting in the middle of that. And Stanley? He's the biggest dork in school, dating him would be social suicide."

"Well, all right then, but you have to date somebody."

"Why?"

"What do you mean, why?" I was puzzled at her question. "You have to date so that you'll find someone to marry."

"No, I'm not going to do that," she said.

"You're not going to marry?"

"I might," she conceded. "But not because I have to. I'm going to have my own life and do the things that I want to do. I'll only date to have fun and only marry when I get old."

"That's just silly," I told her. "How will you live? Are you planning to stay in your bedroom until you're forty? By then all the young men in town will be taken. There will be no one in McKinney to make a match with."

"I'm not interested in boys from McKinney," she said. "I'll meet guys in college."

I shrugged. "There might be some you haven't met from Lewisville or Plano, but most of the fellows at the Community College will be boys you know."

"Community College? I'm not going to Community College."

"Of course you are," I told her. "You can live at home and attend classes for a couple of years until you settle on a husband."

"No," she stated so adamantly I was taken aback. "I am going to a real college, a good college, one that's as far away from this town as I can get."

That began an ongoing argument that really highlighted the growing rift between us. I realized that somehow Laney had become selfish and spoiled. She wanted what she wanted and my views on the matter meant nothing to her at all.

That was especially true when, in the summer of her junior year, I managed to get her named Cotton Queen.

It wasn't easy. In any year there are a number of highly eligible and likely young girls . . . 1975 was no different. Candidates were nominated by different social and civic groups in town and then the Parade Committee picked the queen and her court from those applicants. As chairwoman of the Parade Committee, of course, I could not vote. And chose to remain completely silent. Which, of course, always speaks more loudly than a chorus of shouts.

I had Laney nominated by the Owls. I contacted Acee's mother. We both knew that she owed me plenty. She'd deliberately kept me out of the organization for fifteen years, while she lamented to her friends that I wouldn't join.

"Laney must be Cotton Queen," I told her. "It's as important for Laney as for her family."

"The girl's a Hoffman," the woman replied. "I'd be much more interested in putting forward the Clifton name."

The dig was meant to shame me for not giving Acee an heir. I'd long since decided that it must be his own fault. Two men had gotten me pregnant. If my husband couldn't, then there was nothing that I could do about it.

"Because she doesn't carry Acee's name, it's even more vital that we show her off. She deserves it. Our family deserves it and

I just will not see her relegated to runner-up."

"That's what you were, weren't you?"

I was sure the woman knew exactly where I'd come in.

"I was first runner-up," I said, calmly and without regret. "But I was basically an orphan, taken in by hardworking family members. I did well for that social position. But Laney is Acee Clifton's stepdaughter. Anything less than queen would indicate that our social position has declined since Acee lost the election for judgeship."

That was such a direct hit, I could almost see Mrs. Clifton flinch. If there was anything that she and I completely agreed upon, it was that Acee had not gotten what he deserved.

"I can't nominate her myself," Mrs. Clifton said, thoughtfully. "In fact, I can't even show up. I haven't attended a meeting in over a year. If I show up, it would look like I'm there to suggest her. I'll get Florence to do it. She owes me several small favors that no one knows about. But that will only get her name in contention."

"I'll take care of everything else," I assured her. "I've got it all under control."

I wasn't bragging. I'd realized that this

day was coming for ten years. And since the election, I had been able to refocus all my campaigning energies into getting supporters on board. And it all worked well, except for one slight problem, a reluctant candidate.

"I'm not interested in being Cotton Queen," Laney told me. "What I am interested in is a summer job. If I can't have that, I'd rather have nothing."

My daughter was still angry at me for putting my foot down. Without even consulting me first, Pete had offered Laney a summer job working in the company in Dallas.

She was thrilled. I supposed any young girl would be.

"It's a wonderful opportunity," Acee had said.

"It's good experience," Pete insisted.

I shook my head.

"Dallas is a very dangerous place," I told them. "A young girl shouldn't be there on her own."

"She's not on her own," Pete said. "Laney will be living in my house with my family. I'll drive her to work and see that she gets home. She'll be perfectly safe."

I wasn't convinced. I couldn't be convinced. I knew about the world outside

McKinney and I was determined to protect my daughter from it.

"Laney is staying here in town this summer," I insisted. "If she wants a job, Aunt Maxine will find her something to do. If she prefers not to work, there will be plenty of sewing and gardening to keep her busy."

"I don't want to sew or garden," Laney said, angrily. "Pete said I could learn keypunch and work with his company's computer."

"Oh, darling," I told her. "You're much too pretty to need to learn keypunch."

The argument went on for weeks, but I refused to budge.

Laney was furious.

Even Acee was unhappy with me.

"You can't keep her a prisoner in this town forever," he told me. "She has to grow up and leave home sometime."

"She is not a prisoner," I insisted. "But there is no reason that she has to go anywhere."

"Maybe because she wants to is reason enough."

"Acee, she is not your daughter," I stated harshly. "You have no say in what she does or doesn't do. These are my decisions and I'd appreciate it if you'd remember that this doesn't concern you."

His eyes narrowed but he never mentioned it again.

We had plenty of other things to argue about.

Our weekly trip to Dr. Hallenbeck was punctuated by sarcasm and unkind words. Or rather the return was, on the way to the doctor's office in north Dallas, we rarely spoke a word. The drive itself was upsetting enough, but it was followed by those awful sessions. I hated those visits, the probing questions, Dr. Hallenbeck's ludicrous suggestions for "homework." I was, under no circumstances, doing any of it.

I put up with it as long as I could. The subject matter was not all that unfamiliar. I still read the magazines from the drugstore. What was so annoying was how the doctor thought it was all so important.

"I just don't see why we must speak in such descriptive terms," I told him.

"Prudishness hinders," he said.

"I am not prudish," I assured him. "I am merely formal."

The doctor's typically indecipherable expression faltered and he gave a slight laugh. He was laughing at me.

It was at that moment that Acee broke his promise to me.

"Back before we were married," he said, casually. "A man forced himself on Babs."

Dr. Hallenbeck immediately showed interest. I was stunned into silence. Acee had said that we would never discuss what had happened, the circumstances of Marley's conception. Then, right in front of me, he'd told it, all of it, to Dr. Hallenbeck.

I was so sickened and hurt, I could not respond.

The doctor began explaining in his calm, matter-of-fact manner how for some victims the traumatic event can translate its long-term effect into an aversion to sex.

I tried not to hear him. I tried to ignore what was being said. He droned on and on. I remembered the stained-glass window with the Good Shepherd and determinedly focused my attention on those details, not the clinical facts, which the good doctor was trying to acquaint me with.

"Why don't you tell me, in your own words, what happened," he asked finally.

"No," I said firmly.

"I think you need to share it," he said. "You'll feel better if you do."

"I won't feel better remembering," I informed him tartly. "It was a long time ago. I hardly even remember. And I prefer it that way."

"Well, your subconscious hasn't forgotten," he told me. "It's keeping you from experiencing the kind of normal pleasure and satisfaction that you deserve."

"Pleasure? Satisfaction? What is wrong with all of you people?" I asked them both angrily. "Why is the whole world obsessed with sexuality? It permeates the TV and movies, the music. It's all the talk shows chatter about. Have we become animals that this rubbing up against each other is now the meaning of life? It's sick."

"No," he corrected me. "It's not sick. Being able to maintain a loving, physical relationship with your husband is the definition of marital wellness."

I refused to go back after that. Acee pleaded with me. I wouldn't budge.

"You say I betrayed you all those years ago," I told him. "And now you've betrayed me. It seems that we're even."

He tried to get me to talk about it more, but I was finished with talking about sex and I told him so.

"If I never have to do it again as long as I live, that would be fine with me."

That shut him up.

Which freed me up to concentrate on the other giant argument in my home. After no small effort on my part, Laney was chosen for Cotton Queen.

I was thrilled.

Laney was dismayed.

She continued to argue and complain long after it was too late to change anything. I'd assumed that her reluctance to be Cotton Queen was based on some misguided stubbornness.

"You can only be Cotton Queen once in a lifetime, Laney," I told her. "And even then, most girls are never chosen."

"Yes, and they get along just fine," she answered me. "I don't need this or want it. It's a stupid custom, it demeans women."

"Demeans women? It glorifies women. It makes them royalty, to be admired and worshiped."

"I don't want to be worshiped," Laney argued. "Look, this is something that Gussie Goodwife has in her memory book to remind her that she once had a life of her own. I'm going to be an independent woman, a woman with a purpose, a woman of value."

"Of course you are, sweetheart," I assured her. "And Cotton Queen is the perfect place to start. It gets you the attention of the community. When you're in the back of that convertible, you are front and center in the heart of McKinney and every eye is upon you."

"You really don't get it, do you?" she said. "The world has changed. Beauty queens are passé. They're a joke, a stereotype. Wearing that silly rhinestone crown will be an unforgettable embarrassment."

I thought that was probably the most absurd comment that she'd ever made. I repeated it, in jest, at Aunt Maxine's house. We were putting up summer pickles. The twins were there, helping. Or at least Jolie was. Janey had a new baby, fat as a sausage, that clung to her teat constantly.

She was sitting on a kitchen chair next to the yellow table of chrome and Formica. The little fellow she'd named Jeremy was sucking noisily.

"You're going to ruin your figure," I warned her. "Once you've nursed a baby, your bosom is saggy for a lifetime."

Janey chuckled and shook her head. "I'll worry about that later," she said. "Right now I've got all this milk coming in. It seems a shame to let it go to waste."

Aunt Maxine agreed. "If a woman keeps working, she always keeps her figure, more or less. And it's certainly more thrifty to feed with what nature provides than buying that expensive formula."

"The formulas are all scientifically designed to provide the right nutrients," I told her. "You have to keep up with scientific advances, Aunt Maxine."

"Actually, they now say breast milk is best," Joley piped in.

I waved that comment away. "That's just silly," I said.

"It sure is hot in here," Janey chimed in, changing the subject.

She was right about that. The kitchen was hellish. Aunt Maxine had turned off her new central air-conditioning so that she could prop the back door open.

"I've been doing that for twenty years and always prided myself on the quality of my canning," she admitted. "I'm worried that if I start doing the work in comfort, the food just won't taste as well."

It was a foolish superstition and we all laughed, but she still didn't cool the place off.

That's when I told them about Laney's comments about the Cotton Queen. I fully expected all three of them to see the humor in the teenager's warped view of things and agree with me that nothing, not Football Queen, Yearbook Princess or even Senior Sweetheart would do as much to insure her future happiness as being chosen Cotton Queen.

The response I got was an uneasy silence with each of them shooting glances at each other.

"Things are changing," Joley commented eventually.

"Yes, even *Dear Abby* thinks that it's time for women to be more involved in the world," Janey said.

"Laney is a lovely girl," Aunt Maxine said. "But her prettiness is not her best feature. She's the smartest girl in her class and a top-notch worker. She's going to be someone successful in business someday and you should be more eager to help her do that."

"Successful in business?" I was appalled at the suggestion. "I only hope she's clever enough to marry a very successful businessman."

I was genuinely surprised that none of them could understand. But, then I realized the problem. Neither Aunt Maxine nor either of her girls were ever in contention for Cotton Queen. Of course, they had to believe that it wasn't so important.

But I knew the truth. Being in the Queen's Court had been the most important thing that I had ever done. It had more effect on my life than anything else.

Both Tom and Acee had fallen in love with me that day, and I'd only been the runner-up. If I'd been chosen queen . . . I could not even imagine what great things I might have accomplished. I might have married someone else, stayed in McKinney my whole life. Nothing bad would have ever happened to me.

Laney was going to have that crown. I was going to insist upon it, whether she wore it voluntarily or not.

Laney

It was at least a thousand degrees in downtown McKinney and I was swathed in a million yards of scratchy crinoline and sweat-soaked tulle. I looked like an idiot and I felt like a fool. I was sitting on the back of a baby-blue Plymouth convertible. My hair was piled on top of my head into something resembling an ash-blond squirrel's nest, adorned with a sparkling rhinestone tiara. The large silver-and-blue umbrella with the Dallas Cowboys logo that I held over my head was not some kind of weird Texas affectation, but a very real concession to the summer heat. Unfortunately, I would have to give it up once the parade began. That's what I had to look forward to, sunblisters on my bare shoulders.

"Whoa! Shade my eyes, I'm being blinded by the sight of the queen."

I turned to see my cousin, Ned, standing

beside the car. He was looking very Ned-like with his greasy hair hanging loose down his back, a Black Sabbath T-shirt atop ragged blue jeans, and his girlfriend, Judy Bykowski, hanging on him like a body part.

"No disparaging comments today, please," I told him with a fakey smile.

He waved away my concern. "Baby, I wouldn't think about . . . ah . . . raining on your parade, so to speak."

Judy giggled.

"It's not my parade," I assured him. "It's my mother's. Whatever that woman wants, she gets. Even when it's me, dressed up like a cake and driven through town in a half sexist, half surreal motorcade."

Ned grinned. He looked a lot like my daddy. At least Granny Hoffman said he did and she obviously remembered my father better than I did.

He stepped closer to the car and held out an expertly rolled cigarette that he'd been keeping close to the palm of his left hand.

"Take a couple of tokes," he said. "Things will start looking a lot better."

I shook my head. "You'd have to make me comatose to get me through this happily," I told him.

He raised his eyebrows. "That can be arranged," he joked.

"Hey, Ned, what's happening, man?" Brian Wellman called out to him from Nicie's convertible, just in front of mine.

Nicie had actually wanted to be Cotton Queen. It had been one of her goals for high school. Now never to be realized. She was just basically much more traditional than me. And she was genuine beauty-queen material, natural blond, tall, leggy and with the sort of naive sweetness that could declare with complete sincerity that all she wanted was world peace.

Ned and Judy sauntered up that way. He high-fived Nicie's boyfriend and said something to her that caused her to giggle.

Nicie was happy. She always seemed happy. Even now, when my mother had pushed me between her and her goal. She still seemed completely content to play second fiddle or, more accurately, first runner-up.

And, of course, having Brian her steady boyfriend as her driver didn't hurt. He was tall, good-looking, athletic. He was also rich. His father owned a grocery business that seemed to be expanding all the time. Brian drove a brand-new Mustang Cobra, the flashiest car in town. With his neatly trimmed hair and button-down shirts, he appeared to be the ideal Texas teen. Of course, he was a wild hell-raiser. He drank lots of beer and bought drugs from Ned. But his parents didn't know it yet, nor did Uncle Freddie and Aunt LaVeida who were extremely pleased by his romance with their only daughter.

My driver, Stanley Kuhl, came around the corner with a couple of soft drinks in paper cups. He was a strange choice for the parade. Quiet, bookish, the rusty-haired freckled-faced guy had a reputation for sober seriousness that was unmatched at McKinney High.

"Soda pop?" he asked.

I nodded and he handed me one.

"It looks like they're about ready to start," he said. "I sure hope we don't have to wait out in this sun much longer."

I don't know how I got Stanley as my driver. Or actually, I knew exactly how I got Stanley. My mother had decided that I should spend more time with him. Toward the end of junior year, most of the kids in my class had started pairing up. Babs was desperate to see me do the same. Her machinations made me crazy. They were the frequent source of arguments between us.

"She just wants you to be happy," Acee

had explained more than once in an attempt to play peacemaker between us. "Her high school years were very important to her. She met your dad there and he was the love of her life. She wants you to be as happy as she was."

I knew my stepdad meant well. And there was truth in what he said. But it was weirder than weird to have a woman's husband tell you that some other man was the love of her life, even if that man was your real father.

So Babs continued, without my permission, to try to find my Mr. Right among the motley crew of seniors '76. Stanley was her latest choice. And I'm sure she figured that driving my bow-bedecked vehicle would be a great opportunity for him to see me at my best. In truth, it was probably Stanley's only opportunity to see me at all. If my mother hadn't been paying him to ease the blue convertible along the streets he probably wouldn't have bothered to attend the parade.

"Well, if it ain't Mr. Kuhl," Ned called out to him. "Those are pretty impressive wheels you're driving today. Don't let 'em get away from you."

"That's not Mr. Kuhl," Brian piped in. "That's Mr. Uncool. Listen, Dorkface,

272

don't be tailgating my baby and me. You may be driving the queen but, anytime you're following me, you better keep a respectful distance."

From Stanley's behavior, I would have thought that he hadn't heard what had been said to him. He didn't indicate by expression or gesture any response at all. Somehow that made it worse.

"Come off it, guys," I told them.

"Oh, it's a request from the queen," Ned said facetiously.

Stanley glanced back in my direction. "You don't have to defend me," he said. "I've been fending off sticks and stones from Ned Hoffman and his friends since grade school."

"I've been at it longer than you," I told him. "You forget, Ned's my cousin. I was still a chubby-faced preschooler when he started giving me grief."

Stanley smiled. It was a great smile, one that I didn't remember seeing before.

"I thought all you Hoffmans stuck together like glue," he said, still grinning.

I shook my head. "I'm from an offshoot branch of the family," I joked. "If the rest of the family could get away with it, they'd be delighted to either send us off or shoot us."

"We're moving. We're moving," Brian called back to us as he hurried to get behind the wheel of the red Cadillac convertible that was carrying Nicie.

I could already hear the sound of the drums from the McKinney High School band leading the procession.

Ned and Judy wandered up the street to get ahead of the action.

I put down the umbrella and tossed it into the floorboard.

"See that strap," Stanley said, indicating a strip of inch-wide material lying down the length of the upholstered seat back. "I tied it off on the spare tire and ran it up through the back of the trunk lid. It's not exactly seat-belt safety, but if you start to slide off the back of the car, it's at least something to grab on to."

"Oh great, thanks."

"Don't worry, I'll take it slow," he assured me.

"Not on my account," I told him. "I want to get this over with and behind me as quickly as I can."

Stanley's stoic face twisted into what might have been a grin. "All right then," he said. "Why don't I just pass all these slow-poke drivers ahead of us and we'll be through town in a couple of minutes."

"Sounds pretty tempting."

We didn't do it, of course. Two very dutiful teenagers, we headed down the parade route at a snail's pace. Me, smiling and waving, as if I was enjoying myself. He looking straight ahead, pretending he was somewhere else.

It was amazing that people turned out for such an occasion. It either said that small-town folks were very easily entertained or that nobody could resist the sight of people making complete fools of themselves.

I smiled and waved and tried to relax as I put on my best queenlike behavior, but it was a challenge. The crowds along the McKinney sidewalks were no faceless, nameless audience, awed by a fancy dress and a snazzy car. They were all people whom I knew. And people who knew me. They knew me yesterday when I was a gawky teenage girl trying to navigate everyday life during a cultural meltdown, a world oil crisis and a population bomb. And they'd know me tomorrow, when I'd be right back down there on the street, messing up and acting odd, too much of a bookworm for the town of my birth. I didn't want them looking at me, judging me. But there was nothing I could do about it.

As we turned onto Virginia Street nearing the downtown square, I caught sight of my mother and Acee. Acee had his Instamatic covering his eyes as he snapped shot after shot. Babs was holding a huge bouquet of yellow roses. When the car paused at the corner, she stepped into the street, her back straight, her smile bright and she walked up to the convertible as if it were a planned point in the festivities. Stopping to pose for the camera, she handed me the flowers.

"Why don't you just climb in here with me, Babs," I suggested sarcastically.

"Oh, don't be silly, sweetheart," she said. "This is your big day."

It was all I could do not to groan aloud.

As we moved on, I called out to Stanley.

"How am I supposed to wave, hang on to the safety strap and hold these dad-gummed roses at the same time? I've only got two hands."

The question was rhetorical, but he answered anyway.

"You have to make your own choices in life," he told me. "But I'd give preventing a broken neck a high priority."

We managed to make it through the parade without that happening. The end of the route was a chaos of people, floats, bicycles and horses.

"Follow us!" Nicie called as she climbed over the seat to get beside Brian. They turned right and were gone.

"You want to go where they're going?" Stanley asked.

"I don't know, I guess so. Sure."

I slid my butt down onto the upholstery. The entire back seat was swallowed up by my dress.

With a screech of tires and near whiplash, Stanley headed in the direction of the other convertible. We caught up to them just as they turned onto Loop 5. Somehow, I expected Stanley to follow meekly wherever Brian led. I was completely wrong about that. As soon as we got on the highway, Stanley dangerously sped up and pulled directly alongside the car Brian was driving.

"What are you doing?" I cried out.

"This Plymouth has a lot more pickup than that staid, old Caddy," he said. "The idiot is so used to being Mr. Fastguy in his Cobra, he doesn't even know he's in the lesser machine."

Brian was beginning to get it now. His laughing grin had dissolved into fierce determination. Both cars were pedal to the metal. The broken lines on the pavement rushing past like dots. My pulse was pounding. My heart was in my throat. My heavily sprayed hair was blowing all around my head. But there was a strange sort of exhilaration, as well. I loved racing against Brian. I especially loved beating him.

I glanced over at the other car. Nicie was white as a sheet and screaming her head off.

"Let's get out of here," I told Stanley.

"Yes, ma'am," he answered. Immediately the Plymouth began pulling away from the Cadillac, leaving him in the dust. We continued barreling down the road at an astonishing clip until Brian and Nicie were completely out of sight.

I was up on my knees on the back seat, my fists raised high in the air, shouting and celebrating. Stanley pulled off on an unfinished exit ramp. He slowed down significantly when he hit the gravel, but it still stirred a giant cloud of white gyp dust all around us, coating everything, including my fancy dress and the decorated car.

He turned left underneath the overpass and came to such an abrupt stop that I was practically thrown into the front seat. Lying out nearly flat on the seat back, I caught myself with both hands on the glovebox door. I was still laughing when I rolled over and realized that I was in Stanley's arms.

"God, you're beautiful," he said.

And then he kissed me. It wasn't a tentative kiss or a little peck on the lips, it was a real kiss, full of passion and tenderness and raw sensual longing. It lasted only a moment, but it was somehow caught out of time.

When we moved apart, we just stared at each other as we tried to catch our breath.

"Wow," he whispered finally.

"Wow, yourself," I answered.

I smoothed the hair out of my face and felt suddenly too exposed in my low-cut formal.

"I've never felt like that," he said. "I mean, I've felt, you know, the desire part, but that . . . that intensity. I mean, I've never felt anything like that."

"Me, either," I admitted. "I've kissed a lot of guys and I never . . . it was never like that."

"It's kind of scary," he said. "I mean, in a way, it's kind of scary."

"Right," I answered. "It's scary."

"Do you . . . do you think that it's us?" he asked. "Is it us, the two of us together that made it like that? Or was it just the car chase?"

"It had to be the cars," I said. "I mean, us, you and I, there just isn't any you and I. We've known each other since kindergarten and I don't think we've ever been attracted to each other."

He agreed. "Not more than just normal attraction of any guy to a pretty girl," he said.

"There is, I guess, chemistry or something like that."

Stanley nodded. "But even chemistry requires a catalyst. It had to be racing the car. That maybe reacts with our everyday hormones and makes us suddenly crave one another."

"Yeah, that's probably it."

He straightened completely and put his hands on the steering wheel. Slowly he let out a deep breath.

"It was nice, huh?"

"Yeah, it was nice."

He turned and looked at me. "Do you want to try it again?"

To be completely honest, I was tempted. But he was Stanley Kuhl, with all the high school nerdiness that his status represented. He was also my mother's choice as my Cotton Queen companion. It would have been an answer to all her hopes and dreams if I fell in love with a local boy on the day I was crowned queen and lived happily in McKinney ever after.

My hand was still trembling as I held it out to him.

"Stanley, I think that we should stay friends forever and spend our future avoiding fast cars."

He grinned and accepted my handshake.

"It's a deal," he said.

Babs

I was so proud to see Laney take her place on the dais as Cotton Queen. It should have been the perfect start to a perfect senior year. But, of course, Laney never liked things perfect. She wasn't willing to even try out for cheerleader. She wouldn't use her musical talent for marching band. She wasn't interested in elevating her social position at school or even being named Most Likely to Succeed. Laney was completely focused on her life after graduation. And all the arguing in the world wasn't changing her opinion one bit.

"This is the best year of your life and you're intent on wasting it," I told her.

"If this is the best, I might as well put my head in the oven right now," she answered.

She was not overly dramatic. I didn't worry that she was unhappy. Laney just had no sense of what things could make her life easier. And she was stubbornly unwilling to take advantage of her advantages.

I had to work all through high school. There was no wiggle room in that. Uncle Warren and Aunt Maxine needed me and I owed it to them to help out.

Laney, on the other hand, made a choice to work. I could understand helping Uncle Warren after school. But he'd died and the Shoe Shop was sold, so there was no reason why she couldn't quietly step back from Aunt Maxine's businesses. But she didn't. She continued to run errands, keep books, help with taxes and inventories and fill in wherever and whenever she was needed.

I complained to Aunt Maxine about it.

"Laney wants to work for me," she said. "I appreciate the help and I'll miss her when she goes away to school."

"She's not going away to school," I told her. "She'll go to community college here in town."

Aunt Maxine laughed and shook her head.

"You don't talk to that girl much, do you?"

"I talk to her every day."

"Well, you must not be listening," Aunt Maxine said. "She's applied to colleges all over the country. She's even talked about Harvard and Yale. I didn't even know that girls went to those schools."

"Laney is not going to Harvard or Yale," I stated with complete conviction. "She's not leaving home. She'll get all the education she needs by being a wife and mother right here in town."

"I haven't heard her say anything about wanting to be a wife and mother," Aunt Maxine said.

"Young girls will have their silly fantasies," I explained. "They'll talk about wanting to be ballerinas or fashion models. But when it comes right down to it, women are still women. And the measure of their success is still the man that they marry."

Aunt Maxine shrugged, unconvinced. "That was sure true in my day. And in yours, too. But the world has changed. These gals today, they look at things differently."

I shook my head. "All that 'I Am Woman' nonsense is just that, nonsense."

I'm not sure I convinced my aunt, but at least she didn't argue with me. My husband maintained no such restraint. He'd sided with Laney numerous times, but our disagreement became serious one week-night in late January.

It began, ordinarily enough, at dinner. Laney had, once again, brought up her plans for going off to college. She and Acee discussed the different colleges from across the table as if it were all settled. I tried to just ignore it. They both knew my thoughts on the matter. The last thing I wanted to do was ruin a lovely meal with another huffy tantrum from my daughter. But after listening to her buoyant enthusiasm for nearly twenty minutes, I was strangely reminded of her father. For a moment I felt a warmth in my heart, a remembrance of the foolish, hopeful young love that we'd shared. I had gone out into the world because I had to. Tom had been excited about leaving home. He wanted the adventure of discovering life beyond McKinney. And he'd come home to his parents in a box.

"Just stop this daydreaming," I blurted into their conversation abruptly. "Laney, you are not going anywhere. You're going to attend community college and stay in your very nice room upstairs."

"I'm going away to college, Babs," Laney said. "I've already decided that."

"You aren't going anywhere," I replied.

"You can't make me stay here," she said.

"I most certainly can," I answered. "I'm your mother."

"I'll be eighteen this summer. After that, I do what I want, whether you like it or not."

"You would go against my wishes?"

"I *am* going," Laney said. "And I'd hope you'd wish me well."

She stomped off and I began clearing the table. I hoped that would be the end of it, but Acee followed me into the kitchen.

"It's normal for a child, any child, to want to get out from underneath parental wings."

"She can be on her own once she marries," I explained.

"If she's married, she won't be on her own," Acee replied. "Laney is a smart, responsible, well-adjusted kid. She's earned the chance to pursue her own goals."

"She can pursue whatever she wants," I assured him. "She'll just pursue them here, in McKinney."

"No, she can't pursue them here," he said.

"Why not?"

"Because one of the things she wants most to pursue is putting some distance between herself and this town."

"What a terrible thing to say!"

"It's not terrible. It's truthful and it's natural," Acee said. "You've made McKinney a prison for her."

"Oh, don't be so overly dramatic. I have not."

"You know you have," he answered. "She's been trapped inside these city limits since you moved back here."

"That's silly."

"It may be silly," he said. "But it's true. You brought her home from Girl Scout camp on the third night away. She's had to beg for every beach weekend or shopping trip. Even football games are off-limits if the other high school doesn't come here to play. You never let her go anyplace."

"She went to Austin just last week," I said in my defense.

"It was a school field trip to see the state capitol and she got to go because she brought the permission slip to me for signature. She was afraid you would come up with some excuse for her not to go."

"Well, she *was* sniffling. She said it was just allergies, but she might have been coming down with a cold."

Acee took a deep breath and shook his head, sadly.

"Babs, some time, sooner or later, we're going to have to deal with the elephant in the living room."

"The what?"

"The elephant in the living room," he repeated. "The thing that's so big, but that we never talk about."

"Oh, for heaven's sake," I said, running the hot water in the kitchen sink. "You're not going to bring up sex again, are you? Do I need to remind you, I'm almost forty years old? I'm approaching the menopause. At this stage of life most couples have stopped anyway."

"I'm not talking about sex," Acee said. "I gave up on that, on us, a long time ago. What I'm talking about is your inexplicable fear of the outside world."

"I don't know what you mean."

"Oh, yes, you do."

I tried to walk away, but he followed me back into the dining room.

"First it was just Dallas," he said. "You didn't like the traffic, you didn't like the lonely stretch of highway. Okay, I thought, she doesn't like going to Dallas alone, that's fine. But then, you didn't like going with me, either. And it wasn't just Dallas. It was Dallas, Fort Worth, Austin, Houston, New Orleans. We haven't been on a vacation in ten years, because you're afraid to leave town."

"You never said anything about wanting to go on vacation," I pointed out.

"This is not about vacation." Acee raised his voice. "It's about some craziness within you that's getting worse and worse."

"I am not going back to counseling," I stated flatly.

"I'm not asking you to," he said. "But I am insisting that you do not limit your daughter's life based on your own irrational fear."

"Irrational?" I was suddenly angry. Acee thought he had something to be mad about. Well, I was mad, too. "You think my fear is irrational. Do you have any idea what's going on out there?"

"Out where?"

"Out there. In the places outside of McKinney, do you have any idea what that's like," I said.

"I think I know more about it than you do," he said.

I shook my head. "Out there people are getting kidnapped and killed every day, Acee. There's guns and drugs and young people who are totally insane. Charlie Manson is out there."

"Charlie Manson is in jail," Acee said.

"Well, there are plenty more just like him, I'm sure," I said. "You just don't know, Acee. There are men, terrible men, that would take advantage of a sweet, young girl like Laney."

"There are men that would take advantage of her right here in McKinney," he answered. "She's just smart enough not to let that happen."

"So you think that sort of thing only happens to stupid women?" I screamed at him.

"I didn't say that," he yelled back. "I said that it could happen anywhere and you can't keep someone, anyone, but certainly not someone you love, locked up for their protection."

"Well, you can try. Laney is my daughter. You don't understand that. She's not yours. You don't love her the way I love her."

Acee flinched as if I'd struck him. "She's not my flesh and blood," he admitted. "But how dare you suggest that I don't love her. Laney is my daughter, the only child I ever expect to have."

"I know you care about her. You're a good provider. But you're still just a stepfather."

"No, I'm more. I've given my heart, my

life, to raising that little girl. I didn't just buy the food she eats and the clothes on her back. I've listened to her stories, sympathized with her little childhood heartbreaks. I've been the one who she's been able to talk to. The one she's felt safe enough to share her dreams with. Don't you dare suggest that my commitment to her is casual or superficial. The only reason I'm still here, living this dead, miserable marriage with you is because of her. She's lost one daddy already. I just couldn't have her feel abandoned a second time."

"What on earth are you talking about?"

"I'm talking about leaving you," he said. "I wasn't going to bring it up until after Laney left home. But now that I've started you might as well know my plan."

I just stared at him. My brain was incapable of connecting the dots.

"I've been making arrangements to divide our assets," he said with a calmness that could only be described as matter-of-fact. "I have no illusions about your ability to support yourself financially. I realize that I'll have to continue that and I fully intend to. But I'm convinced that the only chance of happiness that either of us has will come with permanent separation."

"What do you mean by permanent separation?"

"Divorce."

That word certainly cleared up the fog in my head.

"I'm not giving you a divorce," I stated adamantly.

He just stood there looking at me for a moment and then he chuckled. "Do you think that surprises me? You've always been about as selfish and self-centered as a wife could be. You wouldn't *give* me a drop of water if I was burning in hellfire. But I'm getting a divorce."

"Selfish? Self-centered?" I was astounded at the suggestion. "I've done everything for you. I've cooked a million meals, washed tons of dirty clothes, I've made your home a showcase and your name respected all over the community."

"You're right," he said. "You're absolutely right. You've done all that and I'm sure there are plenty of people in this town who think that I'm a lucky man. But I never asked for those things, Babs. I never asked for them, I never wanted them. All I ever wanted was for you to love me. Can you say you gave me that, Babs? Can you say that you ever loved me?"

"I married you, didn't I."

"Oh, yes, oh, yes, you married me," he said. "Have you forgotten why? I haven't forgotten. I haven't forgotten that tiny helpless little baby."

"Stop it."

"I haven't forgotten that precious little child," Acee said. "He wasn't my seed, he wasn't my blood. But I couldn't help but love him. My name is on his gravestone. Have you ever even been out to the cemetery to see it? It reads Marley Barstow Clifton."

"Don't talk about that!"

"Don't talk about what? I thought you'd forgotten he even existed."

"It was a long time ago," I said.

"Yes, it was. And you've put it behind you, haven't you, Babs," he said. "You put it behind you and you never think about him. You do that because if you thought about him, it might hurt and you're not willing to be hurt. You're not willing to be hurt by anyone."

"You don't know that!" I screeched at him. "You don't know anything about me."

"That's right, I don't," Acee said. "I only know about myself. I know about the kind of man that I am. I am the kind of man who likes small animals and remembers to feed the birds in the winter. I'm the kind of man who loves children, even little children who are not my own. I'm the kind of man who would stay married to a cold, heartless bitch for twelve long years because at one time, oh so very long ago, she needed me for one small moment of her life."

"It was not exactly like that," I said in my own defense.

"Then tell me what it was like, Babs," he said. "Tell me about when you gave your heart to me. Tell me about when you shared your tender feelings. Oh, that was not on your to-do list, was it? You never bothered. Not even one casual, insincere word of love has ever passed your lips. I've lived with that, Babs. I've waited and wanted and hoped. But I'm done with that now. Now, I'm just hanging on until Laney gets free of you. Then I'm off on my own."

"I'm not giving you a divorce," I stated flatly.

"I guess you've forgotten that piece of paper in my office safe," he said. "It's never too late to have your reputation ruined, is it, Babs?"

Laney

Rice University is located just south of downtown Houston amid a parklike atmosphere of trees and secluded walkways. It was the quiet center of my new, very noisy life.

I loved Houston.

Yes, I noticed that it's so hot and humid in summer that it's hard to breathe. I am aware that people in Houston spend more time sitting in their cars trapped in freeway traffic than they do at all of the arts, music and cultural events of the city combined. I still liked it.

Everything about the place seemed new. Even the old staid halls of the university were all twentieth century. There was a building boom in every sector of the city. It was as if Houston, and everyone in it, were under construction.

I fit right in.

I arrived in September of 1976, alone and on my own. I drove down in my new red Chevy Chevette, a graduation gift from Aunt Maxine. My mother was furious about Aunt Maxine providing my getaway car, but there was nothing that she could do about it. Everyone had sided with me and Babs just had to lump it.

She and Acee were getting a divorce. That had come as a surprise to me, but I guess it shouldn't have. Acee was a great guy. He was thoughtful and caring. He was always willing to listen. And he actually respected me. My opinion had value with him. My mother was cold and controlling. I could talk to her until I was blue in the face and she heard nothing. She was always in charge and things always went her way.

That is, until I left home.

My freedom was so new, so hard won, that I reveled in it. I dressed however I wanted. I stayed up late. I ate junk food. I drank beer.

I don't suppose I was a wild child by any stretch of the imagination.

I never missed class. I turned in assignments. I wrote papers. I studied for tests. I was definitely not going to shortchange myself on my own investment.

Acee had offered to pay for college. I'd been banking most of my paycheck for years, so I had more money than anyone expected. I'd been offered scholarships at several small colleges, but I wanted a more prestigious school in a big town. So, I managed most of my own expenses. But my stepfather wrote my tuition checks.

Dorm life was great. I expected to experience a certain amount of claustrophobia among the crowd, having been an only child. But I took to large communal bathrooms, cafeteria lunching and the complete absence of privacy or quiet pretty well, I think.

I had an interesting roommate. Interesting in the sense of observing animals in the zoo. She was nothing like me, but I found her truly fascinating as an anthropological study. Her name was Carl Anne Coyle and she was from a tiny ranching community in west Texas. As a roommate she was perfect, neat, tidy and quiet. As a person, she was kind of a mess. She vacillated from being a serious Christian immersed in Bible reading and prayer and an in-your-face lesbian, out of the closet for the first time.

"I'm a homo, lesbo, in the know and on the go," she'd announce in the singsong rhyme that made her a legend on campus. "I'm a gay gal. I'm butch, I'm dyke. If you're not cool with that, then take a hike."

The homo-lingo would accelerate through the week until Saturday night when she became completely absorbed in it and headed out for a long, wild night of partying.

Sunday morning, she'd be up early, her short brown hair twisted into hot rollered curls to go with her modest skirt and a smudge of pink lipstick. She'd take a bus across town to a distant church where nobody knew her to confess her sins and pray for forgiveness. All her friends from 4-H and rodeo had gone to A&M. They'd been surprised when she'd chosen Rice. She wasn't ready for anyone back home to know.

Because we were good roommates, there was gossip that I was a homosexual, as well. Surprisingly I was not bothered by what other people thought — one of the advantages of growing up in a small town. When you've become accustomed to having your every move critiqued, you stop paying attention to it.

Carl Anne and I were great roommates because we both wanted the same thing, to stay in Houston and never see our families.

I was, more or less, able to do that. I never considered driving home for a long weekend. I took summer semester. I went to South Padre for spring breaks. I made excuses for Thanksgiving. And even for Christmases, drove home on the twenty-fourth and back to Houston the next day.

Of course, it wasn't possible to completely shut McKinney out of my life. I had to come home for a long weekend in the autumn of 1978 for Acee's mother's funeral. I'd never felt very close to the woman. The answer why could probably be found in the fact that the highlights of her eulogy included her membership in the Daughters of the Republic of Texas and her forty years of service to the McKinney Owl Club.

But except for those kinds of special circumstances, I stayed in Houston.

Aunt Maxine, who still thought long distance was only for emergencies, wrote me long newsy letters about all the goings-on in town. The place was booming. There were new housing developments and shopping centers going up everywhere. The courthouse, downtown's center hub, was shut down and all of its offices and hearing rooms moved to new facilities on Mc-

Donald Street. The farmland all around the city was being snapped up and subdivided. And an industrial corridor had sprung up along the expressway between McKinney and Dallas, bringing in new jobs, new people and a lot of new money. One of those new companies was my cousin Pete's new start-up. He'd gone out on his own to make advanced software for personal computers. The new little machines were mostly for playing games, but Pete was convinced that the future was more than Pac-Man.

What I didn't hear from Aunt Maxine, I heard from my mother. Babs called often, too often, to cry and worry and complain. She'd gotten a great deal in the divorce. Acee had let her have the house, the car, a bank full of assets and a monthly income. Babs could only whine about the loss of her status in the community and her loneliness. In my sophomore year Acee remarried. Babs screamed over the phone like a crazy woman. Doris Walker, Acee's new wife, was a two-time divorcée and former waitress with two teenage boys. I remembered her as a friendly, loud-talking, big-toothed, big-boobed, big-haired gal. My mother called her "common," a serious insult from Babs. And somehow Acee's ability to find happiness with such a person, when he didn't find it with Babs, was the ultimate betrayal.

Acee called me, too, with the news.

"This doesn't mean that you're not still my favorite daughter," he teased.

"I'm still your only daughter," I pointed out.

"But a clear favorite," he insisted. Then added more seriously, "I don't want to lose you. I don't want you to feel like there's no place for you in my life."

"I don't," I assured him. "If you're happy, then I'm happy. You are happy, aren't you?"

He chuckled lightly. "Amazingly so," he told me. "Dorrie makes me laugh every day. We just have fun together. Who knew marriage could be fun? She says she's been in love with me all her life. I never guessed."

"Yeah, the guys are always the last to know," I told him.

"What about you?" he asked. "Have you met anyone?"

That was one of the things I loved about Acee. No matter what was going on in his life, he was always interested in me. He always asked about me. What my life might be like, never crossed my mother's mind.

"I have met a guy," I told him.

"Oh, yeah?" No pressure to spill the beans, just a willingness to listen.

"His name is Robert Jerrod, not Bob, Robert."

"Okay, where'd you meet this Robert."

"He's my teacher."

"What?"

I laughed. "Not really," I answered. "He's a grad student that proctors in my Intro to Economic Theory class."

"Ah, so he's a little older than you."

"Yeah, a few years," I admitted. "But the guys my own age are such immature jerks."

"Oh, I'm sure that's always true," he agreed, teasing.

"No, seriously," I said. "I like it that he's a little further along than me. I feel so far ahead of most of the other students. I've had a lot of work experience, kept accounts and done actual management. Most of these other kids have never held a job. Some of their preconceptions make me half-woozy."

"Well, we can't have that," Acee said. "So how serious is it with this fellow?"

"Oh, moderately serious, I guess."

"Serious enough to bring him to McKinney?" Acee asked

I couldn't imagine that I could ever get

that serious with anyone.

Robert had been a complete surprise to me. I'd seen him in class. He was Dr. Vonderhaar's assistant. I should have known I'd get noticed. I was a standout in discussions, I was very confident about my lessons.

I was less of a social success.

I dated. Guys were always asking me out. I went to movies and discos and parties of every type and description. The relationships always came up short. I either broke things off abruptly or we just naturally drifted apart.

I was sitting on the green, soaking up the sunshine of a sunny winter day when he plopped down beside me, leaning back on his book bag. He was very good-looking with green eyes and dark brown hair that was long enough to be fashionable without being unkempt.

"Ms. Hoffman, right?" he asked.

I nodded. "Mr. Jerrod," I replied.

He offered a smile and a handshake. "Robert."

"Laney."

Once we began talking, we couldn't stop.

He was a Houstonian, or as much of one as anyone I'd met. His parents had moved to the city in the early 1960s when his dad

303

went to work for NASA. Robert had grown up in town and around in the suburbs. He was a city boy. I really liked that.

I told him about my life, growing up in McKinney and my desperation to get away from the place. He seemed fascinated by everything I said and interested in everything I'd done.

On our first real date, he met Carl Anne. She looked him over on my behalf. He was charming, but not patronizing. After we left he turned to me.

"She's a lesbian?" he said.

"Is that a statement or a question?" I asked back. "Because if it's a question, it's none of your business."

"It's a statement," he said. "You don't mind having her as your roommate?"

"We get along great," I told him, truthfully. "The only time it ever comes up is when people ask me about it."

"You're pretty sophisticated for growing up in McKinney," he said.

I laughed. "I don't think McKinney had anything to do with it," I told him. "There aren't any homosexuals in McKinney. Or if there are, I never knew about them."

"I suspect the latter," he said.

"Yeah, I guess I do, too," I admitted.

Our first dates were ordinary, traditional.

We went out dancing and to movies. Slowly we began to graduate to less typical dating spots. He took me to art exhibits, smoky blues clubs and to the opera.

One Saturday night, between the end of the semester and summer session, we went to a party. It was at the home of friends. Everyone was older, closer to Robert's age than my own. They were graduate students or newly working. They all seemed nice, welcoming. They also all seemed very smashed. There was drinking, plenty of drinking. There were also joints of marijuana and little pipes of hashish being passed around. There was even a mirror on the living room coffee table with little lines of cocaine snorted up through a straw.

None of this slowed the conversation, which was all about money. Buys and deals, speculations and margins, were on everyone's lips. With the price of gasoline having gone straight through the roof, there was money, a tremendous amount of money in Houston. And everyone at the party had a personal plan for getting a little more than their fair share. Somehow I'd imagined the world of business to be staid and serious, gray flanneled and buttoned down. These people were wild. A

new generation, more groupie than hip-
pies. They were not flower children putting
daisies in rifle barrels, but entrepreneurial
nonconformists into free markets as much
as free love, eager to take their chance at
putting dollar bills in Wall Street's G-string.

Greg, a guy who was introduced to me
as Robert's best friend, grabbed my hand.

"Come with me, we've got to talk," he
said.

We wandered through the house for a
few minutes. All the rooms were noisy and
were occupied. Finally he pulled me into
the tiny front bathroom. It was hardly
larger than a good-size coat closet and decorated with black and pink wallpaper, like
some Victorian bordello.

"You look good, Linda," he said, his
voice somewhat slurred. "You look real
good."

"Laney," I corrected. "My name is
Laney."

"Yeah, whatever," he answered. "Robert
is my best buddy. We've been together
since high school and we're headed to the
top."

"That's great. That's really great."

"You see, Linda, there are two kinds of
people in the world, there are winners and
there are losers. Robert and I, we're going

to be winners. If you hang with us, then you can be, too."

I didn't like the narrow confines or the stench of expensive bourbon on his breath. I made as hasty a retreat as I could manage. And later, back at Robert's apartment, repeated the conversation to him word for word.

He laughed.

"Greg was way too drunk to talk to," he said. "I'm sorry that was your first exposure to him. He's really an okay guy. I think you'll learn to like him later."

"I hope so," I told him.

Robert's apartment was pretty nice for a grad student, most of whom lived in a near slum environment. His little efficiency was modestly decorated by bookshelves and interesting pieces of household staples, arranged like art. He had a television and a nice stereo. There was a rug on the floor and a wine rack atop the refrigerator. It was not anything like a dorm — it felt like a real home. And it made me feel, somehow, that Robert was all grown-up, an adult. While I was still a kid.

He put in a Barry White cassette and a low, sexy love song began to play. He snuggled down beside me on the Hide-A-Bed couch and we shared a few sweet kisses.

"Did you have fun tonight?" he asked after a few minutes.

"Sure," I answered.

He chuckled. "That's not very convincing," he said. "The drugs and booze, that freaked you out, didn't it?"

I shrugged and then nodded.

"They didn't have drugs and booze in McKinney, I suppose."

"Well, yeah, I guess they did," I told him, thinking of my cousin Ned. "I just never got involved in that."

"And that's a good thing," he said. "It's easy to get all caught up in that and end up frying your brain and ruining your life."

He ran one long finger along the line of buttons between my breasts.

"What about sex?" he asked. "Did they have that in McKinney? Did you get involved in that?"

Sex, not necessarily as a subject for discussion, had been coming up in our relationship more and more. I had always managed to scurry around it and go home safely. But I was becoming less and less interested in doing so.

"I'm sure that they must have sex in McKinney," I told him. "Considering the number of children born there year after year. But I never got involved in it."

308

"And since you've been here in Houston?" he asked as he ran his hands along my neck and down to my collarbone.

"No, I haven't really gotten into it with anyone here, either," I admitted.

He was stroking me underneath my blouse. My nipples were as hard and stiff as little buttons.

"And why was that?" His words were a hot whisper against my throat.

I didn't really have a good answer and it was getting more and more difficult for me to think clearly.

"I don't know," I said. "I didn't have a steady boyfriend or anything like that."

His hand stopped abruptly and he pulled back to glare at me.

"Steady boyfriend," he repeated with a generous amount of sarcastic disdain. "Is that what you've been waiting for? You want me to give you my class ring?"

"No, I . . . I didn't mean that."

"Babe, if that's all it takes for you, I think it's up in the top drawer of the chest. You can have it."

"I wasn't . . . I didn't think that . . ."

"It just seems to me that if a woman's going to put a price on it, that's a pretty economical one."

"I'm not putting a price."

"Then what is it about?" he asked. "It's not that you don't want it." He shoved his hand up my skirt and clasped me intimately. "I knew you'd be wet. I could smell it. So if you want it and I want it, what are you holding out for."

"I'm not holding out," I insisted.

"Well, you're not putting out."

"I just . . . I just haven't ever done it," I tried to explain. "I want it to be special."

His face softened. His annoyance disappeared as quickly as it had come.

"I haven't done a virgin since high school," he told me. "But I promise you, babe, I can make it special."

And he did.

Babs

The city limits of McKinney, Texas, had been my world for most of my life. After everyone left me; Laney, off to college, Acee, tying himself to that low-class waitress, I found my area of comfort growing smaller and smaller. By 1979 I was no longer leaving my house. But then, I didn't need to. I had no job, no activities, no friends, no one I wanted to see. Since I didn't go anywhere, I didn't need clothes. I spent most days in my bathrobe. Bird's Supermarket delivered groceries to my door. Aunt Maxine or one of the twins occasionally dropped by to make sure that I was still alive.

It was a nice life, actually. I didn't mind it at all. I had the new cable TV installed and thirty channels were suddenly available in my living room. I spent my day watching old reruns of *Donna Reed* and

Perry Mason, Make Room for Daddy and *Father Knows Best.* It was so pleasant to just step back into those times. If I closed my eyes and just listened to the dialogue, I could almost put myself back there. Back when I was runner-up for Cotton Queen, Tom Hoffman's steady girl, a happy, hopeful young woman, ready, eager for whatever the future might bring.

At night, however, with all the house lights off, I sat in the shadows beyond the dining room window and stared out into the darkness. It was the same darkness that I'd hidden in at the Shady Bend Motor Lodges. What I was watching for, what I was fearful of, was no longer as clear cut and definable as it had been. But it was still there. It was very much still there.

I might have lived out the rest of my life just like that, fantasy all day and fear all night. That was working perfectly until Laney called me in early June. After a few requisite inquiries about my health, she got right to her point.

"Robert, the guy I've been dating for a while, he got his M.B.A. a few weeks ago," she told me.

"Oh, well, isn't that nice," I said. "When are you going to bring that young man home so I can meet him?"

"I don't know. One of these days," she answered. "Anyway, with Houston's economy booming, he got offered some really great jobs. And he's accepted one with an energy finance company."

"Uh-huh," I responded, already more or less bored with the personal details of some young man I didn't even know.

"It's a great job," Laney told me. "And they paid him a big hiring bonus. So he's made a down payment on a house in West University."

"Really?" I said. "I suppose a home is a very good investment for a single man."

"Well, Robert's not exactly a *single* man, Babs," Laney said. "He and I have been together for over a year now."

There was something about the way she used the phrase "been together" that was disconcerting, but I ignored it.

"It's certainly nice then that he'll be staying in town and living so near the campus," I said.

"I've moved in with him," Laney stated.

"What?"

"I've moved in with him," she repeated. "We're living together. There's no reason for me to pay expensive room and board at the dorm when I can live with him and still ride my bike to classes."

313

"Honey, you can't do that," I told her.

"Of course I can."

"What must people think?"

"They think whatever they think," Laney answered. "I don't really care."

We continued to argue for several minutes. I got angry and slammed down the phone. Then I called her back and we wrangled even more. I couldn't budge her. I couldn't make her listen to reason. I was furious. I was frustrated. And I was frightened. I was frightened for my daughter. I had never wanted her out there where men could hurt her, misuse her, take advantage of her. I had tried to keep her safe, but she seemed determined to run headlong into danger.

After walking the floor with worry all night, I called Aunt Maxine for help. I decided that the only way to handle the situation was to have Aunt Maxine go down to Houston and shame Laney out of such a terrible decision. I thought that if they laid it on thick enough, they might even be able to get her to give up her last year at college and move home immediately. In my own mind I was convinced that the only thing that would be required was the sight of some member of her family. That would bring Laney to her senses and cause her to realize that she was being duped by this Robert person.

Aunt Maxine hurried over as soon as I called her. She came in, rather out of breath and looking pale and tired.

"Are you ill?" I asked her.

"Not any more than usual," she answered.

"Well, you look terrible," I told her.

A ghost of a smile flittered across her face. "Trust me, Babs, I'm perfectly capable of returning the compliment."

I glanced down to see that I was still wearing my bathrobe. That it was frayed and worn and had a dribble of unidentified food stain down the front.

"I'm sorry," I apologized hurriedly. "I was just worried."

"I'm worried myself," she said. "Renny's wife is divorcing him."

"The new wife?"

"She's not all that new anymore," Aunt Maxine said. "She's keeping the house and the kids and virtually throwing my son out on the street."

"That's terrible."

"Apparently that's how it's done," she said. "I don't know what to do. I called Pete to see if he could help. He said that Renny would never take anything from him. And he's probably right about that. It just breaks my heart that those two boys can't get along."

Aunt Maxine was so upset, so distracted that I just couldn't tell her what Laney had done.

After she left, I decided that if she couldn't help me, maybe I could help her. I picked up the phone and called Renny's home. His wife answered. I was extremely gracious and friendly, using all those social skills honed in community service. She gave me a number where I could reach Renny. I tried it on and off all day. Finally late that evening, I lit a lamp in the darkness and called again. He picked up on the second ring.

"Renny, it's Babs," I said.

"You heard, I guess."

"Yes, Aunt Maxine was here this morning."

"So now you know it all," he said. "You know I'm a lousy husband, a bad father, I can't hold a job, I can't keep a wife."

"Your mother needs you, Renny, come home."

"I've heard all this before," he said.

"Yes, you have. And it's more true now than ever."

"She has Pete."

"Yes, and she loves Pete," I said. "But she loves you, too. And she wants you back."

"I can't come back there," he said.

"Why not?"

He hesitated.

"I'm scared," he said, finally. "I'm just flat-footed scared of the place. It holds a lot of bad memories for me."

"Sometimes we have to do the thing that scares us," I told him. "Sometimes that's the only way. Come back. It doesn't have to be permanent. Stay in McKinney until you get on your feet, until you figure out which way to go from here."

"Is that what you're doing?" he said. "I heard you don't step a foot out your front door anymore. Are you trying to figure out which way to go from there?"

The conversation continued on for some time, but we never got much beyond that.

After I hung up, my own words kept replaying in my head. I knew that I was right about Renny. He needed to come home and face what frightened him here. He was never going to be a whole person again until he did.

I flipped on the light as I went in to use the toilet. I caught sight of myself in the mirror and was startled. I stopped to stare in near disbelief. Looking back at me was a wild, haggard old woman. Her lifeless hair was graying at the temples and hung like a mop down past her shoulders. Her face was pudgy, lined and splotched, her teeth were yellow. Her clothes were ragged, worn and dirty. She looked like one of those homeless women they showed on the TV news. Except she had my eyes.

"My God!" the startled whisper escaped my lips.

No wonder my daughter was throwing away her life. She had a mother who was throwing away hers.

I stood there for a moment, thinking about the enormity of the hilltop I needed to scale. Trying not to be daunted by the task ahead of me. I remembered the words I'd told Renny. He needed to face the thing that frightened him. I apparently needed to do the same. With a trembling hand, I rifled through the top drawer of the vanity until I found a pair of scissors. I took a deep breath and started cutting my hair.

The first steps were only tiny. I went into the hairdresser's to get some style for my sheared locks. I bought a new outfit, casual but clearly fashionable in vivid red to give me courage and picked up some fresh makeup. I called Ritters Garage and they sent a couple of men to try to get the car started, tuned up and in shape for a drive. I packed my overnight bag and set it by the back door. Long days and house darkened nights followed while I succumbed to fear once more.

Then one morning dawned with a brilliantly lit blue-and-pink sky on the eastern horizon. I knew I should go. I walked past the suitcase a half-dozen times before I finally picked it up and carried it outside to the car. I was trembling as I started the engine. I kept telling myself how foolish and silly I was behaving. But no rational arguments could override the genuine terror that gripped me as I set out that Saturday morning on an all-day drive.

I'd planned my route carefully. It was very circuitous. I would head north to catch Highway 69 to Greenville. From there I'd go south through Tyler and Lufkin. For any other person, the trip would have been straightforward. Due south through Dallas and Huntsville, arriving in Houston in about five hours. My way meant an additional two hours, minimum, but I didn't mind. I was determined to see my daughter, but I was willing to do a great deal to avoid driving through Dallas again.

Even bypassing it, I was still afraid. But as always, I couldn't say of what. I tried to rationalize it, intellectualize it. What's the worst that could happen? I'd ask myself. I could be involved in a deadly accident. I could get a flat and be stuck by the side of the road until a stranger/serial killer stopped to abduct me. Either of those outcomes would involve pain, suffering, terror. But they'd be over soon enough. My heart would surely give out early if I were injured. And a killer would dispatch me within days when he realized how useless I'd be at fighting him.

If that was what I was afraid of, why was I so afraid?

As I drove I recognized my own answer. That wasn't what scared me. At every small-town stop sign, every station selling gasoline, every car that passed me, I glanced at the faces. I was looking for Burl. After all these years, I knew he was still out here and I feared that he still stalked me.

I arrived in Houston in late afternoon. I found my exit easily enough and drove into the part of town near Rice known as West University. It had a sweet, small-town feel with cute little cottages and bungalows, many under renovation. I had expected Houston to be big, urban, frightening, like the *Streets of San Francisco*. But the residential area seemed not so different from McKinney after all.

I got lost a couple of times before finding the address. Even then I might have missed it if I hadn't seen Laney's little red car. I pulled my aging Buick to the curb and turned off the ignition. I hadn't realized how tightly I'd been holding my body until I relaxed it. I was exhausted already and my mission was just beginning.

I mentally toyed with the idea of driving away, finding a nice hotel and getting a good night's sleep before facing my daughter. But the thought of getting out on the road again was almost as daunting as carrying forward. With a determination born of maternal love and absolute necessity, I got out of my car and headed to the front door of the slightly shabby 1920s home that had a childlike quality about it. Perfect, I thought, for a couple who weren't really a couple, only playing house.

There was a piece of tape over the doorbell with a note in Laney's handwriting that read Broken, Please Knock, so I did. I waited for what seemed like a long time and then knocked again.

"Coming!" I heard an annoyed voice call from inside.

An instant later I was standing face-to-face with a young man. He was sweaty and his clothes paint splattered. He was handsome, I suppose. His dark brown hair was a little long for my taste and although his features were regular enough, I didn't find them particularly pleasing. Perhaps I was predisposed to dislike him. Whatever the reason, I detested him on sight.

"Yeah?" he said, by way of greeting. And then added, "If you're collecting for some charity, we're not interested."

"I'd like to speak to Alana Hoffman," I said, as haughtily as I could manage.

For a moment I thought he might refuse and try to chase me from the porch. Of course, he did no such thing. Instead he turned back into the room and yelled out her name.

"There's some woman at the door," he explained when she'd hollered back.

"Just a sec," I heard Laney say.

I waited.

Robert walked away from the door, but left it ajar. Inside I could see a bland, boring living room with lots of drab walls, books and black plastic. It was completely a man's room. I was pleased and relieved to see nothing of Laney in it. I wouldn't be asking her to give up so much.

The door opened wider and there she was, my Laney. She hadn't come home at Christmas. It had been over a year since I'd seen her pretty face. It was smeared with yellow paint. Her hair, that she'd allowed to grow back in its natural brown color, was now twisted into an untidy ponytail at the crown of her head.

"Yes, ma'am?" she said, before recognition dawned on her. When it did, an instant later, her jaw dropped open in complete shock. "Mama?"

Her use of that word was almost equally as startling to me.

"Babs," she corrected herself. "What are you doing here?"

"I came to see you," I said. "I came to meet your young man."

She glanced out at the car at the curb. "You drove yourself here?"

"Yes."

"I . . . I don't know what to say," she sputtered. "You should have called us, let us know you were coming."

"Mothers don't have to call first," I told her. "Mothers have full immunity just to pop in. So I am."

Laney just stood there, staring at me, apparently dumbfounded.

"Invite me inside, darling," I said. "You

don't leave your mother standing on the porch."

"Yes, of course," she said, opening the door more widely. "We're painting the kitchen this weekend. Everything is a mess."

"Um, I see."

"Come on in, I'll introduce you to Robert."

Something in her tone suggested that she'd prefer being devoured by wolves.

Laney

It wasn't as bad as I would have imagined. But I'm not sure I would have imagined it at all. In the almost four years that I'd lived in Houston, my mother had not stepped a foot out of McKinney. Now suddenly, without warning, she'd come to stay the weekend.

Robert was not amused.

"What's she doing here?" he asked me in a whispered question behind her back.

I shrugged like I didn't know. But I knew.

There was nothing in life that could have stirred my mother to leave her beloved McKinney. Nothing except life and death. And it was my independence that she was determined to try to kill. She'd finally realized that I was having a life of my own, pursuing my own goals and just being happy with neither her input nor her consent.

I brought her into our kitchen.

After three years of dorm living, I'd thought it the ultimate of luxury. Now, seeing through my mother's eyes, it was a tiny postage-stamp kind of a room with ancient appliances and cracked Formica countertops.

"We're going with yellow," I said, stating the obvious. "It seems very sunny."

"It's very fumy," she said, wrinkling her nose in distaste.

I nodded. "Yes, but I much prefer paint. There is something slightly unhealthy about just wallpapering over dirty walls."

It was a deliberate dig considering the literal forest of colorful print that she and I had glued up over the years. Unfortunately Babs appeared oblivious to it.

"Is there somewhere we can talk?" she asked me.

"Not right now," I told her. "We've got to get this done. It takes forever for anything to dry in this humidity."

It was probably one of the ten least hospitable comments I'd ever made in my life. Amazingly my mother failed to take offense.

I tempered my nastiness with a more warmhearted suggestion. "Why don't you have a seat in the living room. I'm sure you need a rest after such a long drive. I'll bring you a nice glass of ice water."

"No, thank you," she said. Instead she picked up the roller that Robert laid down and began to paint the kitchen.

Robert was taken aback. His own mother was such a princess, she never put her hand to any type of manual labor. He was just becoming accustomed to my handiness. Clearly he found it disconcerting to have a woman of an older generation being equally comfortable at doing a "man's job."

"You don't have to do that," he told her, almost taking offense at her willingness to help.

"I don't mind," Babs said. "I'm here to talk to my daughter and my daughter is in here. Why don't you take a little break? Go out for a smoke or something."

"I don't smoke," he said.

"Well, why don't you pretend that you do," she suggested with a very bright smile.

Robert shot me a helpless glance. I could almost have laughed. He always seemed so in control. He was the center of attention in every room he ever entered. But with Babs, he was out of his depth. With her, I knew he could never protect me.

"I'll . . . I'll be out in the backyard," he said.

Babs dipped the roller and continued her job.

I did mine as well, picking up the narrow brush, I carefully edged a thin border around the baseboards, the tile, the ceiling, allowing my mother the freedom of broad strokes that covered a lot of space in a short time.

We were silent. The longer that it lasted the worse it became. Finally when I could no longer stand it, I started up a neutral conversation.

"How long have you been driving?" I asked her.

"Since I was a teenager."

"No, I meant how long today."

"Oh, well, all day, I suppose," she answered. "I left a few minutes before eight."

That was a lot longer than it should have taken. "You must be exhausted," I said.

She nodded. "I am rather tired," she said, dipping her roller in the paint tray once more.

I reached over and stopped her movement.

"Then stop doing this," I said.

"No, no, I mustn't," she said. "Painting this kitchen is apparently very important to you and you're my daughter. What's important to you is important to me."

"Really?" I said. "I always thought it was the other way around. What was important to you was supposed to be important to me."

"That, too," she said.

We lapsed back into a working silence. When I couldn't bear it anymore, I tried to take the initiative again.

"If you're going to do this, maybe you should change into something you don't mind getting paint on."

She glanced down at her clothes. "Do you like it?" she asked. "It's new."

"It's pretty loud," I told her. "I know you haven't been keeping up with fashion much, but people are wearing more muted colors these days, browns and grays and navy."

"Bright colors give you confidence," she said. "You should really try it, darling."

I gave her a hard look and then commented nastily. "My confidence comes from inside me, Babs. I don't need to try to find it hanging in my closet."

"Right," she said after a moment.

I realized that I was trying to start an argument and my mother was not cooperating. She was here to intrude on my life,

.dicule my choices and discount my decisions. I knew that. And I was ready for her
to just get on with it.

"Look," I blurted out. "I know what
you've come here to say, and you might as
well just say it and get it over with, because
it's going to be nothing but a waste of your
time."

Babs glanced over at me. She was calm,
thoughtful.

"If you know what I've come here to
say," she said. "You might as well say it
yourself."

"You've come here to express some kind
of moral outrage about my living with
Robert."

"Moral outrage," she repeated. "Is that
what you think? I'm very upset about this
living arrangement, but moral outrage
isn't enough to get me to drive to Houston."

"Then what is?"

"Love for my daughter, wanting what's
best for her," she said.

"Since when do you have any idea about
what's best for me," I said.

"Since the day you were born," Babs answered. "You are young and very smart.
You think you understand the world, but
you don't."

"I don't understand the world?" I shook my head, incredulous. "Babs, you're the one who has been holed up in McKinney for two decades. News flash, the world has changed while you weren't paying attention."

"Things haven't changed that much," she said.

I rolled my eyes. "It's all changed completely," I told her. "Completely. All those narrow gender roles that women of your age were forced into, they don't exist anymore. Maybe people have not started living together in McKinney, but in the rest of this country, Babs, there has been a revolution. Women have been empowered. We've got the pill. We've got equal rights. We've got opportunities. When you were my age your only choices were being a nurse, a teacher or a housewife. My choices are unlimited. I can be and do anything that I'm capable of."

Babs shook her head. "You are naive," she said. "Men still own everything and run everything. They only let you think you have power. When it gets down to the gritty details of life, they still have the upper hand. And it's the whip hand, Laney. Never forget that it's the whip hand. Getting along with them or staying

331

clear of them are the only choices a woman ever has."

"That's crazy."

"It's not crazy, it's how life is."

"Who has hurt you so much to make you think this?" I asked her. "Was it my father? 'Cause I know it wasn't Acee."

"You always defend him, don't you," she said, chuckling humorlessly. "He takes your side against me and you'd take his side against me. But that's okay. I don't mind. And I don't want to talk about Acee. I want to talk about Robert."

"What about Robert?"

"You talk about making choices, being empowered. But isn't he still in charge here? Isn't this his house? Doesn't he set the rules? Doesn't he make the decisions? Has he ever mentioned marrying you? No, of course not, it doesn't suit him."

"It doesn't suit me, either," I insisted. "It's his house because he's already working. I'm still in school. Once I have my degree and start making my share of the house payment, it will be my house, too. As for the decisions, we make them together. He's older and more experienced, so I listen to what he has to say. As time goes on, I'm sure that will evolve."

"Will it? Won't he always be older than

you? Won't he always believe that he knows more?"

"No, he won't."

"Do you know that?"

"I do, because I love him and trust him, Babs," I said. "I realize that it's hard for you to understand that, having never loved or trusted anyone in your life."

"What a terrible thing to say!"

"It's true," I pointed out. "You rely completely on yourself. You never let anyone in. Acee is such a great guy, crazy in love with you and would do anything for you."

"Oh, yes," she said. "That's why he left me."

"Yes, he divorced you. Yes, he married Dorrie. But it wasn't like you really cared. I watched for twelve years as you dismissed him, discounted him. In all those years, I never saw you initiate one encounter with him. He started the conversations, he took your hand. He asked about your day. If you two kissed, it was him kissing you. You never gave him so much as a scrap of your time or your affection. You treated him like a prison cell mate. Trapped in a narrow space, you didn't want to share anything going on inside you. You don't know anything about love and trust, so don't even try to lecture me on it."

"I've always loved you," she said. "You've never doubted that."

"Frankly, Babs, from time to time, I have. You've been as secretive with me as with everyone else in your life. Now here I am, finally happy and getting what I want from life. Are you here to celebrate that with me? No, you've come to try to make me feel bad about the good things I've found."

"No, Laney, no, that's not why I'm here," she insisted. "I'm here because I love you. I can't bear to see you hurt or unhappy and this road that you're on, that's the only place that it can lead."

I shook my head. "Babs, I'm sure you think you know what you're talking about, but you don't," I told her. "It's not like it was when you were my age. America has changed. We don't have that 1950s mindset anymore. Women like me, who are bright, intelligent, motivated, we're allowed now to go out and seek our own goals. We don't have to marry someone to make a life."

"So you don't believe in marriage? It's because of my divorce, isn't it?"

"No, don't be silly," I told her. "I'm not angry at you or at Acee. You both love me and gave me a good home. I'm grateful for that."

"But you don't want it for yourself."

"I do want it. I think. Eventually."

Babs nodded as if she understood, but her words were sarcastic. "So you don't want to tie yourself down to the vows and commitments of marriage. You want to be free to just have sex with people."

"I am not 'having sex with people.' I am having sex with Robert. I love him and I'm committed to him. I'm just not *legally* committed to him."

"And he's not *legally* committed to you," Babs pointed out. "I don't suppose you've found this out yet, but men have a difficult enough time staying faithful and true when they're legally bound to. Without any sense of obligation to you, the *best* that we can expect of this man is to merely break your heart."

"Maybe I will end up hurt and miserable," I admitted. "Then you can pat yourself on the back and say you were right all along."

"I don't want to be right," she said. "I want you to be happy."

"That's what I want, too. I'm not like you, Babs. I have hopes and dreams and ambitions. There's a big, wide universe out here and I want to see it, experience it, understand it. Do you think that I can come back to McKinney, marry some throwback to another era and put up wallpaper for the rest of my life?"

I hadn't meant my words to be such a stinging indictment of her own life, but the high color in her cheeks and the hurt expression on her face indicated that it had come out that way.

Bravely she held up the roller and eyed me sternly.

"I don't mind if you paint," she said.

We continued through the rest of the day. Robert ordered a pizza for supper. Babs had never had food delivered. And seemed to relish the novelty. With Robert she was social matron in full battle gear, alternately charming him and putting him down. She manipulated him so easily, I was thoroughly annoyed.

As the evening wore on interminably, she finally rose to go.

"I'd better go find a hotel," she said.

"You're very welcome to stay here," Robert told her.

I could have kicked him.

"No," she told him, smiling so brightly that he apparently couldn't hear her words. "I couldn't stay here. That would be like condoning, wouldn't it?"

Robert laughed as if they were having a little joke. He got in his car and had her follow him to the Shamrock Hilton Hotel at Main and Holcombe. By the time he returned, I was already in bed.

"I had my doubts about your mom at first," he told me. "But she's delightful. You two are a lot alike."

"What? That's nuts," I told him. "Robert, she's here to break us up. She doesn't like you and she's playing you."

"Don't be silly, Laney," he said. "I'm far too shrewd a businessman to be 'played' by some small-town housewife."

"Babs may never have ventured into corporate America," I explained. "But she's had lots of experience running civic groups and organizing fund-raisers, doing big social events. She even ran my stepfather's campaign for judge."

Robert chuckled. "I'm sure she can give a lovely dinner party," he said. "That's what those women do, isn't it? Wow each other over bouillabaisse. I'm not likely to be outmaneuvered by your middle-aged mother."

I was a bit surprised at Robert's dismissal of Babs's competence. I never doubted her abilities.

My point was proven the next morning when she showed up before eight. I hadn't even had my coffee.

"I thought we might all go to church to-gether," she said.

"We don't go to church," I told her.

"Of course you don't," she said. "But I'm your guest and I want to go. You have to humor me."

"No," I stated firmly. "You're not my guest, you're my mother. You showed up uninvited and you're not making me go to church with you, just so that you can try to make me feel bad for 'living in sin' with the man I love."

" 'Living in sin,' " she repeated. "Remember that I did not say that, dear, that is your description. And you may love this man, but it seems to me that if he loved you, he'd want to declare it publicly and put a ring on your finger to prove it."

"Robert doesn't need to prove anything to me," I told her. "And he doesn't have to prove anything to you."

"Oh, Robert dear, good morning," she said a moment later as he came out of the bedroom. His hair was standing straight up and he was still unshaven. "I was hoping that you and Laney could take me to church this morning. I hate to go alone, but of course, I will, if you could give me directions or let me follow you in your car again."

"No, no, you don't have to go alone," he told her. "Laney and I will be happy to go with you."

I wanted to kick him. I wanted to insist that I wouldn't go. But I knew that Robert wouldn't, couldn't, back down after he said he would take her. And the last thing I wanted was for my mother to be able to talk with him about me behind my back. We showered, dressed and went to church. Afterward, Robert bought us both brunch at the Warwick.

"By the next time you come to visit," he told Babs, "we'll be able to cook for you at home."

I had high hopes that she would never come again.

After lunch, we went back to the house. I thought it was time for Babs to head out. I didn't want any excuse for her to linger.

"It's a long drive to McKinney," I mentioned several times.

She didn't take the hint. Instead she made herself busy in my kitchen, where the paint was dry and the cabinets and shelves were ready to be reloaded. She laid down shelf paper and unpacked boxes. I didn't like having her take the lead.

"You don't know where I want things," I told her.

She nodded. "So, I'll unpack and hand them to you and you can decide where they should go."

That seemed reasonable, though I still thought the most reasonable thing was for her to get in her car and drive away.

Neither Robert nor I had a great deal of dishes or utensils. Which was actually a big plus when it came to the two small cabinets in my freshly painted yellow kitchen. The work went quickly and within a half hour we had all of Robert's meager possessions shelved and most of mine. I was straining to put a nest of mixing bowls on the top shelf when I heard a startled intake of breath behind me.

I turned to see Babs, standing wide-eyed, pale and still as she stared at my SoupKids salt and pepper shakers. She looked as if she might dash them to the floor at any second. I couldn't believe she would still be angry at me for rescuing them from the trash. I reached over and took them from her hands.

"I see you found Alana and Marley," I said. "You remember, Aunt Maxine and I saved soup-can labels and sent off for these. That's what I named them." I placed them on the windowsill and smiled at the sight of them there. "All the SoupKids are collectors items now," I told her. "The ones in good condition go for fifty bucks, minimum. Of course, Marley's hat is broken so that really cuts down on the re-sale value."

Babs made a strange, almost inhuman noise that seemed to come from deep within her chest. Then, inexplicably, and to my horror, she rushed to the sink and vomited.

Babs

When I returned to McKinney, I was determined not to allow myself to retreat again
into the isolation that I'd been living. My
visit to Houston had not been a success.
There were so many things that I wanted to
say to Laney, so many arguments I wanted
to make against wasting her life on a man
who had no commitment to her.

Unfortunately my own demons had followed me to their place. After the incident
with the salt and pepper shakers, I couldn't
get to my car and get out of there fast
enough. Home was where I wanted to go.
Home was where I was headed. In fact, I
was in such a hurry that I went directly up
the interstate driving right through the
middle of Dallas, as if that city was no
longer any more dangerous than the rest of
the world.

Amazingly, in terms of the conversations

that I'd had with my daughter, Laney's words had more effect on me than mine seemed to have on her. My daughter couldn't see herself marrying someone from McKinney and putting up wallpaper for the rest of her life. Well, for myself, I couldn't really view that as my future, either.

I was forty years old. My daughter was grown. I had no prospect of grandchildren on the horizon. I had no real friends or social position. I was uninterested in remarriage. But, unless some tragedy occurred, I was likely to live for thirty years. I realized that I had to do something.

I went to see Aunt Maxine. The day hadn't yet heated up as we sat on her front porch sharing coffee. She was happier and more optimistic than I'd seen her in months.

"Renny is moving home," she told me.

"Really?"

"Yes," she said. "He called me last weekend. He asked about you and I told him that you'd gone to Houston. He said he'd been thinking about starting over and that the best place might be home."

"That's wonderful."

She agreed. "I'm thinking about giving him the house."

"What?" I'm sure my jaw dropped open.

"It's not easy for a man to live with his mother," she said. "That treads on a man's self-respect, somehow. I've been thinking for some time that this place is too big for me. I'm going to sign over the deed to Renny and move into an old-folks place."

"A nursing home?" I was shocked. "Aunt Maxine, you're much too healthy and vital to move into someplace like that."

"Not a nursing home," she answered. "There's a new kind of place they've come up with for old people, Senior Living they call it. They call us seniors instead of old coots. They have these places in Dallas. Every resident has her own apartment and some privacy, but there are group activities and help as well if you need it."

"You're moving to Dallas?"

"Oh, no, I could never leave this town," she said. "I want to live in a place like that here in McKinney."

"There's no place like that here."

"Not yet," she said. "But you know what your uncle Warren and I always did. If we decided McKinney needed a drive-in or a Laundromat or a dry cleaners, we just built one."

"You don't know anything about run-

344

ning a Senior Living Center."

"Warren didn't know anything about shoemaking until he got his leg blown apart in the war," she said. "He needed a more supportive shoe to allow him to stand, so he learned how to make one. Everything we've ever done, we've started from knowing nothing. I'm not too old to begin with that again."

I nodded. "That's what I wanted to talk to you about," I told her. "I've decided that I need to go to work."

"Praise the Almighty!" she exclaimed. "Babs, I was beginning to worry that you were going to sit in the house until you became a piece of furniture."

"Why didn't you say something to me?"

"It wasn't my place to say," she answered.

"I'm hoping that you'll give me a job," I told her.

She shook her head. "Not a chance," she said. "You don't need to be working for me. People who work for me do it because they need money. Seems to me you're set up well enough that money's not your chief concern. You need to be out there doing something that brings you satisfaction."

"If only I knew what that was," I said.

"Surely you've done something that you

really liked," she said. "I know you've done something that really captured all your thoughts and made you feel helpful, useful. Maybe decorating or some such."

I shook my head.

"Maybe you could open a little dress shop, you've always loved clothes."

"No, I don't think I'd want to do that," I said.

"Well, there's always running the Cotton Days celebration," Aunt Maxine said. "You can volunteer to do that again."

"You know what I really liked," I said. "I really liked Acee's political campaign."

Aunt Maxine rocked thoughtfully in the swing as she nodded. "They're always needing people for that kind of thing," she said. "Warm bodies, they call them. With a big election coming up, they'll be needing plenty."

Aunt Maxine was exactly right. On the way home, I detoured over to McDonald Street to the former gas station on the corner that now bore a huge sign that read Collin County Republican Headquarters. I parked the Buick and walked inside.

There was only one guy in the building, a stranger. There were so many strangers in McKinney these days. The growth of the subdivisions on the edge of town meant lots of new faces. I figured that not knowing the man was both good and bad. Good, because he'd not think of me as Acee Clifton's ex-wife. Bad, because he'd have no idea of the level of my competency at community organization.

"Good morning," he said. "Can I help you?"

"Actually I've come in to see if I can help you," I said. "I have some interest and experience in political campaigns and I thought that perhaps you were looking for volunteers."

He smiled broadly, revealing the perfect, gleaming white teeth that are only available with caps.

"So you're a supporter of Ronald Reagan."

"Ronald Reagan?"

"That's who we're supporting for president," he said.

"Ronald Reagan, the actor?" I asked.

The man's smile disappeared. "Ronald Reagan, the governor of California," he replied rather sharply.

"Oh sorry, I guess I'm confused," I apologized profusely. "I haven't really been keeping up with the newspapers. And I'm a Texan, so I'm not familiar with who's governor in other states. The only Ronald

Reagan I ever heard of was that actor on *Death Valley Days.* Remember him? The guy who sold the Twenty Mule Team Borax, he had that same name."

The man's face was beet-red, obviously furious. "Governor Reagan used to be an actor, but now he's a governor."

"Oh, it is the same man, oh I'm. . . . I didn't know, I . . ."

The interview, such as it was, went downhill from there. I knew so little about the election, who was running, what the issues might be. My ignorance appalled even me. The last straw was when he asked if I was a registered Republican. I had no idea and had to check my voter registration card.

I left the place feeling stupid, embarrassed and humiliated. I peeled out of the parking lot, directly in front of an oncoming car. I screamed, as I realized he was going to hit me. The sound of screeching brakes was near deafening and he swerved off the road, managing only to give my car one startling jolt.

I sat there behind the wheel, trying to catch my breath.

The door jerked open.

"Babs, good God, are you all right?" a familiar voice said beside me.

"Acee?"

I looked over to see my ex-husband squatting down beside my car. Without any thought, agenda or motive I wrapped my arms around him, grateful for the warmth I knew was there. He hugged me back. It felt wonderful for one long, pleasurable moment and then he pulled away.

"Are you all right?" he repeated.

I nodded, remembering that he was not my husband anymore. "I guess, you just scared the bejeezus out of me," I said.

"Here, let's get your car off the road," he said, helping me to my feet. It was only then that I realized how traffic had begun to back up around our near accident. "Stand on the sidewalk," he said.

He moved my car off the street. His own was parked far out of the way on the middle of somebody's lawn. A young motorcycle cop showed up. Acee knew him. I didn't. We both told our stories. He appeared pretty bored with them until he realized that we were former spouses. Then he was determined to make sure that neither of us had targeted the other.

Ultimately, I was given a ticket. There was some damage to both vehicles, but when Acee told the policeman that he was the one who paid insurance on both cars, the man went on his way. Acee and I lingered.

"You're looking good," he told me.

"Thanks. I got a new do," I admitted. "I went down to see Laney and her boyfriend last weekend and I wanted to look my best."

He nodded. "Yeah, she called me after you left," he said. "She told me that you'd gotten sick and she was worried about you. I said I'd check on you this week. But I hadn't intend to *bump into you* quite this way."

We both laughed.

"Why aren't you at the office?" I asked him.

He looked at me strangely for a moment before he replied. "It's Marley's birthday," he said. "I was going out to the cemetery to put flowers on his grave."

"Oh! Really?"

"I do it every year," he said. "You knew that."

"No," I told him. "I had no idea."

"I used to ask you to go with me," he said. "You never wanted to, so I quit asking."

I thought about that for a long moment, nodding.

"You know, I haven't been out there

since the day we buried him," I admitted. "I doubt if I could even find his grave if I wanted to."

His brow furrowed and his expression was incredulous. "He's buried next to Tom," he said. "Don't you remember, you insisted that he be buried next to Tom."

"No, I didn't remember that."

"You haven't been out to visit Tom's grave, either," he said.

"No, no I guess I haven't," I said.

He reached down and clasped my hand. "Come with me," he said.

"What?"

"Come with me to the cemetery. Please," he added.

I really had no interest in going, but I couldn't think of a good reason to refuse. I got into Acee's car. A fragrant bouquet of lilacs and baby's breath lay on the back seat. The meaning of it disturbed me so much that I found myself talking nonstop.

I told him about my encounter in the Republican headquarters. He hooted with laughter.

"Most people who want to help with elections know who's running," he pointed out.

"I just enjoyed your campaign so much," I said. "So much of it is organizing events and getting people and places set up. I really thought I could do that. You're not thinking of running for office again, are you?"

"No," he assured me. "Dorrie's great, but she wouldn't make a good politician's wife, she's way too honest. Maybe you should find a cause to support. They have campaigns that are just as intense and political as any election."

"I'll think about it," I told him.

The conversation drifted to Laney and Robert.

"She's got to find her own way," Acee said. "I don't know if this guy is right for her or wrong for her. But until they both know, maybe it is best if they don't get married."

"Acee, think what people must be thinking, what they must be saying," I said.

He glanced over at me and chuckled. "You and I, probably one of the most well-known divorced couples in McKinney, just drove through downtown together in the same car. Can you even imagine what people are thinking or saying about that?"

He had a point. If anyone had seen us, the gossips' tongues would be wagging nonstop.

"But we know we're just driving together

352

to the cemetery," I pointed out. "It's all innocent. With Laney, well, I didn't ask for specifics, but I'm fairly certain that she and Robert are not sharing a bed because of a shortage of sheets."

Acee shrugged. "I slept with Dorrie before I married her," he said.

"I don't want to know that."

"I didn't sleep with her while I was still married to you," he said. "You probably do want to know that. But is it so terrible to have sex before you're married?"

"Yes, the whole thing about marriage is that married people have sex," I told him.

"I don't think it's the whole thing about marriage," he said. "I mean if sex was everything, I'd never have stayed with you twelve years. Our sex life was simply terrible."

I was so shocked at his statement, I gasped.

"I hope you're not going to pretend that's not true," he said. "You hated my touch. I've heard lots of jokes about women who fake orgasm, but you're the only woman I've ever known or heard of that had to fake affection."

It was on the tip of my tongue to deny it. But I didn't bother.

"Sorry," I said, simply.

"Me, too," he said.

The cemetery was huge, much larger than I'd remembered with webs of new roads and whole new sections of graves. Acee drove to a part more familiar. The giant trees hung over the lawns with stark shadows in the heat of midday. Acee pulled up to the curb.

"Come on, let's say happy birthday to the little guy," he said, grabbing the flowers from the back.

It felt strange, otherworldly, as I followed Acee. The little grave was exactly where I had left it. The tiny lamb carved into the stone was just as I had remembered. *Marley Barstow Clifton* it read, *July 18– October 30, 1964.*

"Babs, are you okay," Acee said beside me.

The sight of the stone blurred as tears filled my eyes.

"My baby!" I choked out and dropped to my knees at his tiny grave.

I remembered everything about him, his little hands and his little toes, the tiny mewling cries and the dark eyes that never once focused on my face. He had been so small, so helpless, so dependent upon me. I'd failed him.

For the second time that day, Acee

wrapped his arms around me. He knelt at my side, holding me, lovingly, tenderly.

"It's okay," he whispered. "Let it out, it's okay."

"It's not okay," I told him. "I killed him. I killed this precious child."

"You did not kill him, Babs," Acee said.

"I did," I insisted. "From the moment I knew he was inside me, I wanted him dead. I was so afraid that someone would find out where he came from. Someone would suspect that he was conceived out of wedlock. Someone would think that I'd had sex without marriage. What a stupid crazy deceit. Here we are twenty years later and people brag about doing it. I was so ashamed. I was so dirty. I didn't want him to live. I didn't eat, I bound myself up. I pretended that I wasn't pregnant with him. Because I hated him. I hated him until the day he was born."

"Babs, oh Babs," Acee said. "He had a heart defect. That didn't happen because of anything that you did. It was hereditary. It was there already and nothing you did or did not do would have made any difference."

"But I could have loved him," I said. "If I'd been a decent person, if I hadn't been so frightened I could have loved him. He was not someone else, not anyone's son. He was just himself, our little Marley and all those months he was in my body I didn't know that. I thought . . . I thought he was . . . I thought he was someone else."

Acee held me in my sorrow. After a few minutes, I got ahold of myself. He gave me his handkerchief and I blew my nose.

"Sorry," I said.

"You did love him," he said. "You think you held back, but I was there, Babs. I saw you hold him, feed him, caress him. I knew that you loved him. And he did, too."

"He was too little to know anything."

"Even a newborn feels a mother's love," he said.

I didn't answer. There was nothing to say.

He shook his head. "You never cried for him, you know," he said. "I always wondered why you never cried for him."

"Guilt," I answered. "I felt such guilt about him that I just couldn't cry."

"I guess you've finally punished yourself enough," he said.

We sat there together on the grass for a few more minutes. He nodded toward the nearby gravestone. "That's Tom," he said. "Would you like me to leave you alone for a few moments to be with him?"

I glanced over and then shook my head. "No, that's okay," I told him. "I have no guilt about Tom. I loved Tom."

"I was always jealous of him," Acee said. "He got the girl that I wanted."

I nodded. "The runner-up for Cotton Queen," I said.

He shook his head. "That lively, laughing, daring, optimistic young woman whose effervescence could hardly be contained in the staid traditions of the Cotton Queen coronation. That's who I fell in love with."

I shook my head. "I hardly even remember that young girl," I told him. "I'm not sure that was me."

"It was, Babs," he said. "I know it was." He sighed, heavily. "I guess some people are just meant for one person. Tom was your soul mate. He brought out all the luster in you. And when he died, you just could never give your heart to anyone again."

His words caught me off guard somehow. I lost the drift of the conversation for a moment, unsure who he was talking about. I sat in silence, soaking it in.

"Is that what you think?" I asked finally, incredulously.

"What?"

"Is that what you think was changed in me," I said. "That Tom died and I was nothing without him."

"I didn't mean it quite that way," Acee said.

"I loved Tom," I said. "He was a good husband. But his existence didn't make me more than I was. Losing him was a tragedy, but I was still capable of loving, caring, living. I know that I'm just an empty shell now. That for all I did to make your home happy and your career successful, I was never really much of a wife, but I can't have you blame Tom for that."

"I wasn't blaming Tom," Acee said, hurriedly. "I know there was that incident, when . . . when you were forced."

"I was raped, Acee," I told him. "I told you that I was forced. But the word 'force' doesn't describe it. It was rape. One night in my own house on my own kitchen table with my baby girl asleep in the other room. A man who I thought was a friend forced his body into mine against my will. That's it. That's my story. That's why I could never love you. That awful sex therapist was right about that. I can't bear to be touched."

"I'm so sorry, Babs," he responded.

"I can't believe that I just told you that,"

I said. "All these years, I have never said it aloud."

"You never talked to anyone about it?"

I shook my head. "Not anyone," I repeated. "Not Aunt Maxine. Not the doctor. Not even the psychologists or Brother Chet. No one."

"And not me," Acee said.

"No, not you, either," I agreed. "I couldn't say it aloud. I tried never to think about it. But I couldn't stop thinking about it. I can't imagine how I ever voiced it. Now that it's out, I don't know how I ever kept my silence."

"I wish you would have trusted me with it, Babs," he said, quietly. "Maybe if I'd known we might have had a chance."

"I think he ruined any chance I might have ever had," I told him.

"Would you still have married me if that had never happened?" he asked.

It was a strange question to ponder.

"Yes, I think so," I answered.

"The truth is, we'll never know," he said.

"No, I guess we won't."

"I'm sorry about what happened to you, Babs," Acee said. "I hate that such violence and cruelty ever touched your life. But I'll never regret the time we had together."

Laney

My graduation was strangely anticlimactic. With all our friends out working in the world, I felt slightly out of step and left behind. I would have been fine just to ignore the day completely. It wasn't mandatory that I attend commencement and my degree would come in the mail. Robert and I could privately open a bottle of champagne to toast my success.

That was, of course, not at all how it was going to be. My mother drove down to Houston, this time bringing along party plans. The entire family would be coming to share the event. Aunt Maxine, Renny, Pete and the twins, along with their spouses and children, even Acee and Dorrie and their boys. Babs spoke with Robert about our friends and before I realized what was happening virtually everyone that we knew was on the guest list.

And almost all of them planned to attend. The big holdouts, and this was, of course, significant, were Robert's parents. Mr. and Mrs. Jerrod had yet to acknowledge me in any way as Robert's partner. I was simply his girlfriend. No, it was worse than that, I was his live-in girlfriend who they were hoping he would dump for some nice, old-fashioned virgin.

I was hurt at their refusal to come, but I put on a big smile and pretended it was fine. Of course, this was exactly what Babs had warned me about. That even if I thought living together was perfectly okay, there would be plenty of people who wouldn't be so laissez-faire, who would judge me harshly and I would have no recourse but to put up with it.

Fortunately my mother didn't say, "I told you so." Quite to the contrary she rallied to my defense.

"Let me give his mother a call," she said. "A personal invitation might sit better."

I had my doubts. And as Babs schmoozed and cajoled Mrs. Jerrod, I could tell that it wasn't all going as well as she'd hoped.

"Oh, I do understand, I do," my mother said to his mother on the other end of the line. Babs's huge smile of false geniality

361

was projected through her voice. "Yes, schedules do get crowded this time of year. And it will all be fine. In fact, it might even work out better. There are so many people coming from Robert's company and even some of his clients. They are certainly not the kind of people you're accustomed to in Pearland. And I know you'd never want to put your brilliant, successful son at any social disadvantage."

My jaw dropped open. But I was more quick-witted than Mrs. Jerrod who apparently didn't realize that she'd been dealt a very choice and elegant insult until after my charming mother had said goodbye and hung up the phone.

Babs turned to me, her expression transformed to extreme annoyance.

"Your future mother-in-law is a self-righteous, ignorant twit," she told me. "Keep that in mind if you have children. You'll want to overcome any inherited traits as quickly as you can."

I laughed. But the term future mother-in-law was beginning to sound really good to my ears. I had not minded living with Robert. I felt like our commitment was as strong as any marriage. But, as I finished school, ready to set out in the world, my feelings changed. We'd made our point about not being restricted by the repressed mores of our parents' generation. And we proved that we were together for better reasons than just a piece of paper. But I was beginning to question why it couldn't just be a marriage.

I wasn't angling for six bridesmaids and a white dress, and I wasn't interested in changing my name, but didn't see any reason why it shouldn't happen. At the very least, it would give me legal standing in Robert's life. And hopefully it would be more. It would be a public declaration of our love and commitment to each other.

I had not said anything to Robert to clue him in on my thoughts, but I was optimistic that he was thinking along the same lines. And I was hoping, wishing, that as a graduation gift, he'd bought me an engagement ring.

The day was typical for Houston in May, stifling hot and unbearably humid. We all took the six-block walk to the stadium to avoid the nuisance of having to park. It was a curious feeling having all these relatives suddenly thrust into the mini-universe that I'd created with Robert. They seemed accepting of him, friendly with him. He appeared somewhat stilted and cold. I was unaccustomed to being around people who were close to me. Perhaps for the first time, it occurred to me that all our friends were actually Robert's friends. I rarely saw any of my personal girlfriends, outside of class. The only acquaintance of mine who'd ever even been to the house was Carl Anne. Even she made a point of visiting when Robert wasn't there and left quickly as soon as he showed up.

I shrugged off the unwelcome realization with a reasonable rationalization. In any relationship there will be a more dominant person. Just because Robert was that dominant person, didn't mean that his friends weren't my friends, as well.

"So, have you lined up a job yet?" Pete asked me. "We could really use somebody like you."

"Did Babs tell you to suggest that?"

"Babs? No."

"That's exactly what she'd want," I told him. "There is nothing she'd like more than for me to get a job that would move me back to McKinney."

Pete shrugged. "Well, it's a growing place, lots of good stuff happening out on the expressway, a Texas version of Silicon Valley. It's not like you'd have to live downtown. We have hundreds of employees who don't set foot on the square twice a year."

"It's a great place," I agreed. "But Houston is really bursting at the seams, too. It's all so dynamic now and Robert is here."

"Ah . . . Robert," Pete said, glancing back to see him in conversation with Acee. "When is he going to make an honest woman of you?" he teased.

"I am a very honest woman," I assured him.

He chuckled. "That's why I'd like to have you in my company," he said. "Whether Babs would like it or not."

My family took their seats in the bleachers, while I found my chair on the field. From that distance, I'm sure I was unrecognizable from the other hundreds of robed and mortar-boarded graduates. Standing out among the sea of unrelieved black were yellow ribbons blowing in the breeze from every conceivable location. With the Americans held captive in our embassy in Tehran, their fate and the fate of our nation, was not far from anyone's mind. But all of the commencement speakers were upbeat, eager and optimistic.

I lined up to hear my name read and walked across the stage. I shook hands with the deans and the speakers and accepted an empty leather folder, the actual certificates would be mailed to us.

After we'd thrown our hats in the air and hugged each other goodbye, I met up with my family at a prearranged location across the street. To my delight, I'd acquired two more guests. Nicie and Cheryl were among the group. I hugged them both eagerly.

"Brian and I had planned to come," Nicie told me. "Then at the last minute he canceled. I got Cheryl to drive down with me."

"That's great," I said. "It's so good to see you."

It *was* good to see her. And it was interesting, as well. Nicie had the life my mother had wanted for me. She'd gone to community college in McKinney and was now engaged. She seemed very happy with that.

"Let's see this diamond," I said, picking up her hand.

Her ring was big and shiny and bright, everything that it should be. I made a fuss over it and encouraged everyone else to do the same. That actually worked out well. I felt more confident when all the attention wasn't focused on me.

As we headed back to the house, Cheryl fell in beside me. We chatted amiably for a few minutes. I asked her about her life. Cheryl was living in her own apartment in Dallas, working for a utility company. She seemed pretty happy.

"Your guy is really a hunk," she told me.

"Thanks. I think so, too."

"Is it serious between you two?"

I gave her a look of disbelief. "Cheryl, we're living together. You'd have to call that rather serious."

She shrugged. "A shack-up is just a shack-up," she said. "It's a perfect setup for guys. If I were you, I wouldn't get my heart set on anything permanent."

"Well, thank you, Cheryl," I said sarcastically. "If you ever get to be me, then you can take your own advice."

I excused myself and hurried up ahead. I snagged Renny's arm. He smiled at me.

"Congratulations, kid," he said.

"Thanks. And congrats to you, too."

"To me?"

"For moving back to McKinney," I said. "How's it going?"

"Pretty good," he said. "Too good, really. I like the work I'm doing. I'd gotten so used to being a nobody from nowhere. It's really kind of uplifting to walk downtown and have people know my name, ask about business. I feel like somebody again. It's great having the house. My ex is going to let the kids come out to spend some time with me this summer."

"That's great!"

"Yeah, it's all great," he said. "Even being in the same town as Pete is not so bad. We won't ever be friends. We don't have anything in common except family, but I don't mind him so much anymore."

We arrived at the house and I was barely able to change my clothes before being absorbed into the giant party. The worst thing about having a gathering of a hundred people you'd really like to talk to, is that there is very little chances of getting to talk to anyone more than a couple of seconds.

There were our friends, clustered together at a table in the backyard. They were all heavily invested in wine drinking, the guys smoking expensive cigars. The women were equally as game and talking just as tough. There was lots of joking and laughing going on, but I was too distracted to keep up with the direction of the conversation.

I talked to Doris for a few minutes. Acee's new wife was not her typical loud, boisterous self. She seemed a bit intimidated by the company. I'd always liked her around town, but could never honestly see her and Acee as a couple. But they do say opposites attract and if she suited Acee, then she suited me. Apparently a little uncertain about her place in the celebration, she fell back on her former vocation and began passing plates of hors d'oeuvres and getting drinks for everyone.

"You don't have to do that," I assured her. "You're a guest."

She patted me on the hand and flashed me that big toothy smile. "It gives me something to do, honey. I've been slinging hash so long, it's second nature to me."

"Well, you needn't sling hash for me," I said.

"It's an honor," she said. "Acee is so proud of you. He thinks of you just like a daughter."

I nodded. "He's really the only father I've ever known," I told her.

"Your real daddy, Tom, he was a nice genuine guy," Doris said. "I know everybody says you're just like your mama, but I see plenty of Tom Hoffman in you."

The last part of that statement sort of muddled in my mind as I took offense at the beginning. "I'm not anything like my mother," I assured her. "I'm not anything like her at all."

As the party progressed I chatted with

Acee, the twins and their husbands, Pete's wife, all of the kids from little Janey's youngest, a toddler to Doris's teenagers. Nicie regaled me with all the latest plans for her June wedding. Aunt Maxine gave me the current contracting woes of the new Senior Retirement Village she was having built out on the Loop. I was interested in all of it and wanted to talk to everyone, but not all on the same day.

I was making a retreat to the bathroom when my former roommate, Carl Anne, caught up with me.

"Listen, I just wanted to check," she said, glancing around to make sure that we were alone. "Your friendship is like really important to me."

"Yeah? For me, too," I assured her.

"You know I wouldn't want to risk it for anything, so I thought I'd run it by you first, to see what you think."

"Run what by me?"

"I'm . . . well, I'm thinking about making a play for your cousin," she said. "Are you cool with that? I mean, I won't so much as wink if it bothers you. But if it's no big deal for you, I'd like to make a move."

"My cousin? Renny?"

"No."

"I hope it's not Pete, Pete's married."

"What are you talking about? Renny? Pete? This is me, Carl Anne," she said. "I'm thinking about making a play for your cousin, Cheryl."

"Cheryl?" I was stunned. "Carl Anne, I don't believe Cheryl is gay."

She chuckled. "Lots of folks don't believe the earth is round, but it keeps spinning on its axis all the same."

At that point I began to suspect that my own world must be hurtling out through space. I gave Carl Anne my blessing and went on to the bathroom. What I found there was not pleasant.

Hilary, one of Robert's friends and the housemate of Robert's best buddy, Greg, was splashing her face with cold water. The room reeked of vomit.

"Sorry," she said, before I even made a comment.

"There's a little candle here," I told her. "I'll light it and the place will be back to vanilla bean before you notice." I hated the sound of my own voice. It sounded like my mother on a hostess high. "Too much wine?"

She shook her head. "None at all."

My brow furrowed.

"I'm pregnant," she said.

I was so surprised I'm sure my jaw dropped open like some cartoon character. It was very hard to imagine this edgy, hard-nosed businesswoman as somebody's mommy.

"Oh, Hilary, that's wonderful!" I managed after a moment.

She waved away my congratulations. I realized that she was crying.

"Don't say anything to anybody," she said. "Not even to me."

"No, no, of course not, if you don't want me to."

"I haven't decided if I'm going to keep it," she said. "It's just the worst possible time. I have this absolutely incredible deal with Stinson Intercont and the next twelve months will make it or break it. I don't have the kind of career where I can take maternity leave."

I nodded sympathetically.

"What does Greg say?" I asked.

Hilary gave a derisive snort and laughed as she shook her head. "Oh, he's a lot of help. He said, 'I thought you were on the goddamned pill.'"

Greg's attitude should have surprised me, but it didn't.

"I don't know what to do," she said. "I just don't know. How can I do this? How can I throw away everything I've worked so hard for? How can I just give up the biggest deal I've ever seen to become Mommy and bake cookies for the PTA?"

"Lots of women have careers and kids, too," I pointed out.

She nodded. "They either make so much money they have full-time nannies or so little money, they can lay the kid on the cotton sack as they drag it through the fields."

"Oh, Hilary, I'm really sorry," I told her.

"Yeah, me, too." She stood up straight and plastered a bright smile across her face. "Hey, this is your big party. Let's go see if we can have a few laughs."

"Okay."

"And . . . and don't tell anyone," she reminded me. "I should never have fallen apart like this."

"I'm glad I was here. And don't worry, I'll never say anything," I promised.

And I didn't.

Though, I do admit it was on my mind later that night. The guests began clearing out about nine o'clock. The cousins from McKinney left first with their long drive up the interstate. The friends and colleagues left next. Acee hung around as Doris insisted on helping with the cleanup.

Once they'd gone, Babs finished up and left for her hotel. It was just me and Robert alone in our house.

"Doesn't that sound wonderful," I said.

"What?" he asked.

"The silence, it's practically music."

"You're nuts," he told me.

"That's Bachelor of Nuts to you, sir."

He laughed. "Okay, Bachelor of Nuts, go get your panties off and I'll meet you in bed."

I ran a quick bath and scrubbed off the day's grime. Found a very frilly, feminine nightgown in pale blue satin, the front pleats were sheer enough that my nipples showed through. I brushed my hair. I looked good. I smelled good. And I felt good.

The vanilla bean candle was still burning. I blew it out and thought once more of Hilary. Or rather, I thought of myself and what I might do in her place. I certainly was not interested in having a baby. But if I did get pregnant, Robert would stand by me, he'd do the right thing. Greg was just not as committed to Hilary as Robert was to me. I was sure of that. She and Greg were just a live-in. What Robert and I had was more like a trial marriage. Still, I was ready to make it official. It would simply be easier to have that part of our lives settled. That way we could concentrate more fully on our careers without having to concern ourselves about the relationship at all.

Just before I reached for the doorknob, I deliberately stopped to get a handle on the direction of my thoughts. *Things don't always happen the way that you think they will,* I reminded myself. I took a deep breath. *Don't be disappointed if he doesn't have a ring.*

I stepped into the bedroom. Robert was sitting on the edge of the bed in gray boxer shorts. He had a gift-wrapped package in his hand. The box was too large. I knew that right away. Still he could be deliberately deceptive.

"What is it?" I asked, being a little coy.

"You'll have to open it up to find out," Robert said.

"It doesn't look big enough for a blouse or pajamas," I told him. "It's probably like underwear or socks."

"Nope."

"If I guess it will you tell me?"

"Mmm . . . yeah, I guess so, if you guess it."

"Do I get a hint or something?"

"You want a hint? Okay —" he held out

the package to me "— Laney, my sweet Laney, what's inside this box is . . . is your future."

The words went through me like a bolt of electricity.

There was no guessing then. I grabbed it out of his hands and ripped it open.

Inside there was no tiny velvet box hiding among tissue. I stared, uncomprehending at a leather-bound book.

"What is it?" I asked.

"It's a Day-Timer, sweetheart," he said. His voice brimmed with excitement as he eagerly showed it to me. "It's a whole system of daily organization and time management planning," he said. "It allows you to maintain control of your appointments, schedule, client lists. If you're going to make it in corporate America, you've got to have a Day-Timer."

Babs

After Laney's graduation, I was officially a woman without purpose. My daughter was making her own way in the world, without my help and resisting my interference. I had no career, no volunteer work, no hobby. I had nothing. I spent almost a year redoing my house, making its huge elegance seem cozy and clean. I moved my bedroom down into Acee's office and closed off the second floor completely. I redid the landscaping, every trowelful of dirt I turned myself. I put in a flower garden, like nothing I'd imagined in my girlhood gardening dreams. It included a granite serenity bench and a koi pond. In the far north corner of the yard, I had homegrown vegetables, tomatoes, pole beans and lettuce, onions, radishes and carrots.

I was healing, finally, at long last I believed that I was healing. Admitting the truth to Acee, speaking those bitter words aloud at last, had lanced the wound that had festered in my soul for so very long.

I wondered at times, as I sat in my quiet retreat and watched the fish gracefully moving through their lives, if I had spoken up earlier might my life have been different?

I tried to imagine it. Mentally I put myself back on Aunt Maxine's front porch explaining to Acee why I needed his help. He probably wouldn't have married me. My pregnancy would have been a local scandal and Freddie and LaVeida would have taken Laney away.

No, I couldn't have done that.

Perhaps later, when Marley was born. Acee and I had been so close then. Maybe I could have unburdened myself and he would have understood. Maybe I could have told him then, but our focus was so much on the baby.

There had been happy times in our marriage. No couple could stay together as long as we had without some good laughs and some shared fun. But was I supposed to interject into one of those rare islands of good feeling the sordid humiliation and evil of being raped?

Merry Christmas, darling husband. For your special gift this year I want to share with you the single most horrible and degrading experience of my life.

Surely during twelve years of marriage there should have been one moment when it would have been exactly right to tell him.

Or I could have told someone else. The relationship between a husband and wife is already so complicated. If I'd spoken of it with another person, it might have given me the courage to share it with him.

Who could I have told? Aunt Maxine. Yes, I was absolutely sure that my aunt would have stood by me, loved me, helped me all she could. But it would have hurt her so much. It would have been like selfishly giving her my pain so that I could find relief.

What I should have done, all those long years ago, was confess the truth to one of those therapists. Not Brother Chet, of course. I couldn't tell him anything. It would get all over town. But one of those strangers I saw in Dallas.

Of course that was the reason that I hadn't. They were strangers and I couldn't trust them. They might have been familiar with every mental illness on earth. But that didn't mean that they would understand. Among all of those framed diplomas on their walls, there was no guarantee of compassion or even benignity.

Dr. Hallenbeck had known, he'd wanted me to get it out, to say it aloud. He said it was the only way to start healing. But I hadn't been ready. That was the point, wasn't it?

Maybe I should have told somebody. Or maybe there had been no one to tell. Either way, it was done. That part of my life was behind me. I needed to find a way to make what was ahead work better.

It was probably sheer boredom that had me taking an early-morning stroll downtown in the middle of the week. I'd put on a cheery outfit in honor of the day. Pink slacks with a beautiful pink-and-turquoise top that had a fancy beadwork design. The collar extended into a draping scarflike attachment that was tied in a bow at the neckline. I felt good and looked good. It was the only way to face the world these days.

I turned the corner onto Pennsylvania Street when I spotted some activity in front of the Coin-Op Laundromat. A big truck was blocking most of the street as they unloaded brand-new machines. As I got closer I could see Renny, observing.

I called out a greeting. He turned and smiled, pleased to see me.

"What are you doing out this early?" he asked me.

"Oh, you know us old ladies," I said. "We don't sleep much."

He bent his head down and eyed me critically over the top of his glasses. "You're only nine years older than me," he said. "And I'm just now hitting the prime of life."

"Well, don't hit it too hard," I teased him. "It's been known to fight back."

He chuckled.

We looked at the new washers as they were being installed.

"In the fall, I'm replacing the dryers," he told me. "It's too much capital outlay at one time, but if I spread it out over six months, it's less of a crunch on my finances."

"You know, Renny, if you need money, you can always come to me."

He laughed and shook his head. "One thing about my family, you can't accuse them of being stingy. My mom, Pete, the twins and now you. Dad is probably rolling in his grave over all the money that's been offered up to me."

"We all know you're good for it," I said.

"I am good for it, that's why I'll just take it slow, pay for things as they make money," he said. "Besides, how could I borrow from a woman with no visible means of support."

I shrugged and laughed. "I'm still living off my ex," I said. "I haven't brought home a paycheck in twenty years."

"How long can that go on?" he asked.

I was surprised at the question.

"Acee's agreed to support me," I said. "It was in the divorce decree."

Renny nodded. "Yeah, and I'm sure he'll do it, though I'd imagine it's already pretty tight supporting two households. What will it be like when he starts paying to send Doris's boys to college."

His words made me feel bad, ashamed, like somehow I was underhandedly getting something I didn't deserve. I never handle criticism well and I didn't appreciate his.

"I don't believe that my financial affairs or those of my ex-husband are any of your concern," I told him flatly.

He nodded. "You are absolutely right," he said.

"You are obviously thinking of your own challenges in scraping together enough cash to meet your child-support obligations." My tone was as sharp and dangerous as broken glass.

"Actually I wasn't," he said, still not reacting to my obvious anger. "I was only thinking about you. You did me a good deed once, you know. You told me I had to come back here. You said that sometimes we have to do the thing that scares us. You're scared to be responsible for yourself, but it's time that you do that. Acee's support was offered in the spirit of fairness. You've managed to turn it into a crutch."

"You don't know what you're talking about," I said.

"Probably not," he answered. "But I do know that my widowed mother, will be sixty-five next week. And how is she celebrating? By opening a brand-new business. All of the money that went into that, she made on her own, after my dad died. She didn't have to do that. She could have just hunkered down at home and piddled in her garden the way you do."

"Gardening is hard work," I insisted.

Renny nodded. "It is. And it's important. But it's not enough to make up a life. Both my parents believed in the healing power of work. It helped my mother. It's helping me. You're going to be around here for a very long time, Babs. Figure out something to do from here on out."

I was still mad when I stormed out of the place. How dare that little weasel, who'd been handed the family business on a silver plate, criticize me. This women's lib thing was going to everybody's head. What was I supposed to do to make a living?

I maintained my anger for the better part of the day. But eventually I had to look at what Renny had said.

Acee made a good living. He always had. The house had been signed over into my name, but he still paid the mortgage on it. He paid the electric bill and the heating, my beloved cable TV, he made sure I had gas and groceries. I got a generous allowance of spending money.

Acee and Dorrie lived in a nice house, but it was significantly smaller than mine. Acee's car was the one he had when we divorced. The one Doris drove was even older than that. They lived nicely and dressed well, but she was no longer working. It couldn't be easy for Acee to support all these people. I began to feel guilty about what everything cost.

Still, it was no easy task coming up with some scheme where I might make some money. There wasn't exactly an abundance of job opportunities in McKinney. Every divorcée in town was running a little dress shop on the square. Virtually all the other businesses had moved out to shopping centers near the highway. If I was going to drive as far as the highway, well I was practically in the next town anyway.

Ultimately my guilt drove me to an employment service. Dressed in a lemon-colored silk suit with a long mandarin jacket and shoulder pads that might have appealed to Bette Davis, I drove out to an office in Plano. I didn't want to see anyone I might know. I couldn't bear for people in McKinney to know that I was looking for work, at least until I could actually find some.

I'm sure it was the vivid yellow suit, set among the boring black and gray of the younger women around me, that captured the eye of the older, more experienced manager of the place.

I was invited into her semiprivate cubicle, framed by two bright corner windows at the far end of the building.

"Please have a seat, Mrs. Clifton," she said, not looking up from my paperwork in her hands. "I'm Katherine Garnett and I'll be happy to help you find work."

She was dressed, very chicly I thought,

in a sweater dress. The vivid teal color was charming and the huge cowl neck drew attention to a very lovely face, a few years older than my own.

"What job skills do you have?" she asked me as she seated herself on the other side of the desk.

"Well, I can type, I suppose, though I haven't done it since high school. I knew shorthand back then, too, though that's been twenty-five years, as well."

The woman smiled at me, a little too patiently, I thought.

"We don't say 'typing' anymore, we say 'keyboarding skills,' " she told me. "And shorthand, well there's not much call for that since they invented the dictaphone."

"Oh."

"Don't worry about it," she said. "With all the new personal computers around, companies are closing down the typing pools and foregoing secretaries for executive assistants. There's not a lot of opportunity there right now anyway."

"Okay," I said.

She was reading the papers I'd filled out. She turned over one sheet and then glanced up at me.

"Is this your complete work record?"

"Yes," I admitted, embarrassed.

The only job I'd ever had that wasn't part of Uncle Warren's family business was working for Big D Cement. I was pretty sure that even if Mr. Donohoe wasn't dead, he probably still wouldn't rehire me.

She took a deep breath and sat back in her chair. I expected her to say something like, "thanks for coming in, we'll keep your name on file." Instead she said, "Tell me about yourself."

I was startled.

"Ah . . . well there's not much to tell," I said. "I've just been a housewife and mother."

"I'm sure that there is something exceptional about you, something you've done that's, in its way, extraordinary."

I smiled. "I was runner-up for McKinney Cotton Queen in 1956," I blurted out.

We both laughed.

"It's pretty embarrassing to have that as the only bright spot on my résumé," I admitted.

"At least you were runner-up," she said. "I came in third place for Miss Luling Watermelon Thump."

She and I both nearly howled. People from other desks were glancing, our way.

"So sorry," I said. "Mrs. . . . ." I glanced

down at her desk looking for her nameplate.

"Call me Kathy," she said. "I think we former gems of Texas had better stick together."

We talked for several minutes about my life. She was interested in my volunteer work and encouraged me to put that on my résumé. But when I began to talk about how much I enjoyed Acee's campaign, she perked up. She asked a number of questions about what kind of things we did and how they were run.

"The bottom line, of course," I told her, "is that we didn't win."

"I wouldn't call it the bottom line," she said. "It's more like a starting point." She was flipping through her card file. "I want to send you on an interview. There's no posted opening right now," she said. "But I just want these people to meet you and talk to you. Do you want me to set it up?"

Within twenty minutes I was out in my car with a scheduled appointment, map and directions to a place called Ardith Eden Events. It was located in HiLo Park Shopping Center in Dallas.

My palms were sweating. I was nauseous. I'd driven through Dallas several times since coming out of my self-imposed exile. But I'd never driven *to* Dallas. Never walked around in a shopping center where people of Dallas might see me.

I managed the impetus to pull out of the parking lot. But every foot of the rest of the drive was a battle.

They didn't even have a job posted.

I could never take a job in Dallas, the commute is too far.

I don't want to do this.

Kathy's directions were impeccable. Although I had driven as slowly as I possibly could, I arrived in front of the building exactly on time. I scurried inside.

I met Ardith herself and her assistant, Geoffrey. They were surprisingly down-to-earth considering the pricey chic events that they put together.

I didn't make any attempt to impress them. I knew I was a small-town girl in a very trendy, expensive part of the city. I already knew they didn't have a job. And if they did, I didn't want it.

I talked about the campaign. Things that I liked. Things that went wrong, problems that I had.

"Most of the women we talk to," she told me, "only have experience with weddings. We don't do a lot of weddings and we feel that they are a much more proscribed event than what we do. Anyone working with us would have to be flexible, creative and capable, as comfortable dealing with the waitstaff as with Ladybird Johnson."

"And hopefully when they're not being forced to share the same fish fork."

Everyone laughed. Ardith gave a meaningful look to Geoffrey who nodded.

"We are planning, perhaps early next year, to open a second store site in Plano. The north area is just booming and we think we could get in there early and establish a good base."

I nodded. "I would certainly like to be considered for your staff if you make that move," I said. "Although I'm not sure that I can wait until next year to go to work."

"Of course not," Ardith said. "Besides, you need to learn the business from Geoffrey and myself. We'll put you on staff here. I know it's a long way from McKinney and with the Expressway eternally under construction the commute is horrid. So you'll come in two or three days a week, learn a few things, make a tad of money. If nothing else, it will perk up your résumé."

As I walked back out to my car, I felt a strange disconnect from reality. I'd found a job, doing something I might actually like and be good at. And I'd just agreed to come into Dallas two or three days a week indefinitely.

That couldn't be good.

Laney

Getting my first job was so exciting, it was like anticipating a great romance. I had all the thrill, butterflies, angst and enthusiasm of any love at first sight. And I felt just as certain about the prospect of a happy ending. You would have thought by my eager jitters that I'd never put in a workday in my life, when I'd actually had a longer and more varied work experience than most of my bosses. And you would have thought that all those years would have taught me to be wary of guys who seemed too good to be true.

That was my boss. Mr. Thrushing, or Larry, as he preferred me to call him, was looking for a smart, ambitious young woman to put on the fast track to executive status. He thought I was just what he was looking for. And my lack of a corporate résumé just meant, he told me, that I hadn't learned any bad habits in what he termed "Willie Loman's world." Of course he was mistaking the character from *Death of a Salesman* for one in *The Man in the Gray Flannel Suit*, but I knew what he meant. I also knew that his actual reading was limited to *Baron's* and the *Wall Street Journal.*

It was all so great. I dressed in my basic black suit, carrying my Day-Timer in my briefcase as I went to my own tiny postage stamp of an office with a little window that looked out into the branches of a big tree. My name was on the door with my fabulous title, Assistant Director For Special Projects.

Larry was the director for Special Projects. I figured out pretty quickly that was a euphemism for stuff-nobody-else-in-the-organization-wants-to-do. My boss was the cleanup man. Every situation that was prickly, icky or sticky got dumped on his desk.

I found him generally unsuited for the job. Larry was a glad-hander. He could remember people's names and their wives' names and whether they played golf or racquetball. He spent a great deal of company time both on the course and on the court. You could mention the latest news on some obscure business or market phenomena and he always had the low-down scoop, the most up-to-date gossip and the grimy details. I'm certain he was a true asset to the company team.

But he didn't like his job very much, nor did he seem to appreciate its value. Almost from my first day at my desk, he delegated most of it to me.

In the beginning I felt swamped, nearly overwhelmed as dozens and dozens of tedious, thankless tasks were piled in my In-box. But I worked through that. I took each wrinkle that came my way and, one by one, I carefully ironed its problems and set them aside. I discovered that I was getting a fast and thorough education on how the actual operations of the corporation worked and where they didn't work.

Larry was very pleased with my efforts. He heaped tons of praise on me and even got me a very quick raise in salary. I felt very safe in confiding my thoughts on how the guys in the computer center, ever bogged down and understaffed, might be able to hand off much of their in-house application education through a tandem training system.

He listened intently and encouraged me.

"Write it up," he told me. "Write it up as

a proposal and get it to me on a floppy and I'll see what I can do."

I spent almost two weeks putting together my research and my speculations. I was worried about my numbers, simply because they were so good. But after reworking them a dozen times in every possible mode, I felt that I'd pinned them down.

"What's this?" Larry asked as I handed it to him one morning.

"The tandem training."

He took the disk from my hand.

"I'll look at it," he said. "Polish it up a bit, if I think it needs it, and pass it on to the next level. It's hard to be patient, but things take time."

I nodded and I waited.

It was almost six months and several excellently written proposals later, that I finally heard. Or rather I read, in the company newsletter, that T-Training was the newest innovation in network-wide I.T. compatibility. And heading up this project was the new vice president for Information Technology, Larry Thrushing.

I confronted him only after I'd seen with my own eyes the proposal he'd submitted. It was exactly what I'd handed him on that floppy. The only polishing I detected was the change in authorship. And he didn't even have the generosity to list me as a contributor. I was stunned. I felt that for all my hard work I'd been stabbed in the back.

Larry didn't even blush when he gave me his explanation. "It was a good idea," he said. "I knew it wouldn't go anywhere if they thought some low-level nobody had come up with it. Without my name on it, it was dead in the water. Now, don't worry, Laney. I'm going to continue to take care of you. I'll still be your boss, just on a higher level."

So Larry was promoted and Mr. Carmington was given his position. He was older, slower and less knowledgeable about virtually everything.

"You and I are going to get along fine, Lucy," he told me.

"Laney," I said. "My name is Laney."

"All right, Laney," he replied, as if he were almost annoyed at having to use my actual name instead of what he thought I was called. "That will be fine. Please remember this, maybe you should write it down . . ."

I grabbed a pencil and a yellow pad.

"I take my coffee with one teaspoon of sugar and a single dollop of half-and-half.

Do not, under any circumstances, bring me coffee that's been whitened up with powdered creamer. It sours on my stomach. Half-and-half is what I want. Make sure that you always have that in the break room refrigerator and that it's fresh."

That night when I complained to Robert, he howled with laughter.

"At least you don't have to speculate on where his priorities lie," he said.

"I don't think this is funny," I told him. "The guy doesn't seem to know anything about anything."

"That's probably why Larry put him in there," Robert said. "The old guy would just get in the way and Larry's confident that you can handle the department on your own."

"Then why wasn't I even considered for the director's job?"

Robert shook his head. "Baby, don't get mad at me," he said. "You've got to be realistic. You're barely twenty-four years old. And you're gorgeous. Nobody on senior staff is going to look at you and think to themselves, 'that's director material.' It's just not going to happen. You just keep working at it. You just keep exceeding the mark day after day, covering for Carmington and keeping things smooth.

Eventually somebody is going to notice."

"I don't get a lot of satisfaction in making my boss look good," I told him. "It's what I've been doing since Aunt Maxine first put me to work. And I was a lot more willing to help Uncle Warren shine than any of the Bozos I'm currently spinning plates in the air for."

Robert laughed again. These days he laughed about almost everything.

Unlike myself, Robert was not having to work hard and wait patiently in someone's shadow. He was making money hand over fist. We both worked sixty to seventy hour weeks, but while mine netted me a comfortable salary, Robert got huge bonuses and stock options.

The price of oil had gone through the roof. The boom was big and with the Reagan administration cutting back on federal regulation, there were big profits to be made in the industry.

Robert worked on the finance side. Small independent oil companies who had leased prospects contracted with him to come up with investors to pay for the expense of drilling. Since nearly everybody wanted a piece of the action, working guys with their life savings and ancient old widows with their husbands' annuities were lined up to buy in. If the well came in, everybody made money. If it didn't, the investors lost everything, but the companies, who had so little of their own capital invested, were in a good position to lease more land elsewhere that new investors would pay to develop.

Robert was good at finding the people and selling the shares. Greg was, too. They were close colleagues and friendly competitors. Both making more money, more quickly than they'd ever imagined.

Hilary, Greg's girlfriend, was out of the picture now. I never knew what happened to her. After my graduation party, I never saw her again. Several weeks afterward we went to a weekend gathering and he was with someone new.

"What happened to Hilary?" I'd asked Robert.

He shrugged. "They broke up," he told me. "Greg didn't give me any details. But he doesn't seem to be suffering from a broken heart."

No, he didn't.

He was showing up with a new girl on a bimonthly basis, each one blonder and bigger breasted than the last. Greg was drinking deep and laughing long. And my Robert was, too.

One afternoon the two of them had taken off early, gone by the car dealership and both showed up at our front door in brand-new BMWs. Robert's was fire-engine red, Greg's was powder-blue.

"I can't believe you bought that car," I told him later that evening. "You just went out and bought it, without even discussing it with me."

That irked him. "Why would I discuss it with you?" he asked. "It's *my* car. Are you going to try to tell me what I'm going to buy for myself with my own money?"

"I wouldn't tell you what to do about anything," I said. "But with the renovations that the architect has come up with for the house and that big vacation you've been talking about to the South Pacific, I thought that at least you'd want to talk about it. We're supposed to be sharing each other's lives."

"We are. We are, babe," he insisted. "Don't be mad about the car. I know you're worried that I bought it to pick up chicks. Well, that may be why Greg bought his, but I bought mine because I really like it. I like having a snazzy, good-looking vehicle to drive. Damn, don't you think I've earned it?"

"Of course you have," I said.

We made up. We made love. And I forgot all about it. I had just been jealous. The man I loved was more successful than me and I should be proud instead of resentful.

A couple of months later, on a gray and boring Thursday, I'd forgotten some papers that I'd been working on at home. It had been a horrendously busy week and I'd hardly seen the inside of my home, but I needed those papers. I just couldn't do without them. So in lieu of a lunch break, I went home to get them. I was annoyed to find a Datsun 280Z taking up the space directly in front of the house, its vanity plate read Perfect 10. I rolled my eyes and found another parking spot down the street. When I walked back to the house, I was surprised to see the BMW in the driveway.

Once upstairs, I was more surprised to see one of Greg's cast-off buxom blondes bouncing her silicone titties over my new king-size bed while she rode my Robert screaming, "Go, stud! Go! Go! Harder! Harder!"

If before that moment someone had asked me what my reaction might be to finding Robert with another woman, I'd have honestly answered that such a sight would have me bursting into tears. That's not at all what happened.

I was calm. I was dry eyed. And I was out for revenge.

Robert's overpriced graphite tennis racquet was leaning up against the wall next to the door. He was always just leaving it there and I'd hang it back in the closet for him. I picked it up and without bothering to remove the protective cover, I delivered a forceful forehand return directly on the sex cheerleader's big gaping mouth.

She jumped and screamed. Her nose was bleeding. I began pounding the racquet into Robert who was scrambling to escape. I managed one direct blow to his private parts that had behaved so offensively to me. Then he was screaming, too.

I was screaming. They were screaming. I was still lobbing and backhanding. The girl had blood dripping all over her and the next blow I landed had her scurrying out of the room, down the stairs and out the front door, stark naked. Robert was half bent over, holding his jewels, trying to fend me off with one hand. He managed to wrench the racquet away from me before I did much more damage.

"Stop it! Stop it!" were the words I finally deciphered coming from his mouth.

When I finally stopped, he threw the expensive racquet across the room.

He remained bent over, cursing and complaining about his injury.

I was ready to complain about my own.

"How could you?" I asked him. "How could you, *stud?*"

That word, at least, captured Robert's attention. He wasn't going to be able to lie about it or weasel out of it. I'd believed my eyes and my ears.

He shook his head. "I don't know. Laney, I'm sorry. I don't know why I did it. It was just so easy. It seemed so basic and simple. I never thought you'd find out. I never wanted to hurt you."

None of his answers made me feel any better.

For two long days we wrangled over it, two long days of pleadings and recriminations. I wasn't interested in his excuses. I was unmoved by his tearful regret. In the end, there was only one apology that seemed sincere enough for me to accept.

"Laney, let's get married," Robert said to me finally.

"What?" I was incredulous.

"I think all this freedom, all this not having things tied up and settled down, I think it's not good for me," he said. "If I'd actually vowed to be faithful, I'm sure I would have been."

I didn't know what to say. I didn't know if I even believed him. I wanted to throw his too-little-too-late offer back into his face. But I didn't want to lose my little house that I'd come to love. I didn't want to admit to my mother that she was right and that I did get hurt. I didn't want Robert to become Greg, moving happily on with his life, forgetting all about me. I think it was those reasons more than his insistent declarations of love that led me to my answer.

"All right," I told him. "I'll marry you. And we'll forget that this ever happened."

Babs

Like firefighters running into a burning
building or soldiers patrolling the war-
zone perimeter, I grew accustomed to
driving into Dallas for my new job, always
aware of the danger there. I liked what I
was doing. My job was not the most creative, I suppose. All the exciting planning
and design details were done by Ardith or
Geoffrey. I was involved with the grunt
work. Making sure the table setup was exactly as planned, the caterers were fulfilling their commitments and that the site
crews followed through with cleanup. The
locations I worked were mostly downtown
or at one of the country clubs. Our clients
were wealthy, corporate or both and they
were willing to pay a great deal not to have
to think about whether the napkins would
clash with the posters from the new ad
campaign.

And I have to admit that it was a very good feeling when I was able to call Acee and tell him that I was no longer going to need my stipend.

"I'm not making enough to take on the mortgage yet," I admitted. "But I'm working toward that goal."

He didn't make light of my efforts or tell me that it was unnecessary. Acee, being Acee, expressed thanks and applauded my efforts.

So despite still having that queasy stomach on the morning drive every day, I was feeling pretty good about myself and my life.

That was until Laney called me.

"Guess where I'm calling from?" she asked me.

"Where?"

"Fiji."

"Oh, my heavens! That's fabulous."

"It is, Babs," she said. "It's totally fabulous. You just can't believe how beautiful it is here. And guess what else?"

"What else?"

"Robert and I got married three days ago."

I was so stunned I just gasped, for a moment I couldn't speak.

"Babs? Are you there?"

"You got married?" I finally managed. "In Fiji?"

"No, we actually got married in Houston before we left," she said.

Somehow that was even worse. My only daughter, the most important person in my life, had made the most important change in her life and she hadn't even invited me to share it. As a mother, somewhere I'd gone really, really wrong.

"Oh, don't worry about it," Ardith told me when I confessed the news to her. "It happens all the time. These kids don't do anything like we'd hope they would. When they get back, we'll throw a lovely party for them, as fabulous as any wedding reception and we'll be saved all the white dress and thirteen bridesmaids nonsense."

But upon Laney's return, she made it quite clear that she was not having any big fancy party.

"You can have a small celebration at your house," she told me. "No catering. No cake. Family only."

It wasn't enough, but I accepted what I was offered, a small, intimate family gathering. Fortunately the family was growing larger all the time. And I defined it on a grander scale, inviting the entire Hoffman clan, as well. With all the cousins now married, the inclusion of the spouses and their families, they pretty much made up half the town's population.

Robert and Laney drove up that morning. He had never visited McKinney and spent some time wandering around the downtown neighborhood. He liked it very much, but not in a way I particularly appreciated.

"The place is like a time capsule," he said. "It's a throwback to another era. It's completely frozen in the fifties."

"Most of those buildings are turn-of-the-century," I pointed out.

"Yeah, but the fact that nobody's figured out a better use for downtown space since then, it's just wild," he said. "You could just put a fence around it and sell tickets. Welcome to Retro World! Maybe you could make a two for one deal with Six Flags Over Texas."

I just tried to ignore it and think the best of him. He was Laney's husband and therefore I was obligated to get along. But the man just wouldn't let the subject drop.

"We like it the way it is," I heard Pete telling him that afternoon at the party. "The good news is we can still walk around and window-shop and have everything close at hand. The bad news is, these old buildings can't be refitted for a business like mine where lots of high-tech equipment is used."

"So, you just leave the downtown alone and build out on the perimeter?"

"Yeah," he said. "That's what we've done so far."

"Well you'd never see that in Houston."

"I'm sure you're right," Pete agreed. "The land values downtown are through the roof. They're knocking down everything to put up all those new skyscrapers. I guess you could say that we're lucky here. We're booming, but not so fast or so successfully that we're going to choke on it."

"Canapés?" I said, offering a plate between the two.

The party was going very well. The children were running wild in the backyard, giving their parents an opportunity to converse at normal volume in the living room and the den. The entry hall was a virtual mountain of packages for the newlyweds. And on the formal dining table I'd laid out my pièce de résistance. Laney had refused to have a cake. So, in substitution, I had five dozen tiny marzipan swans swimming among edible flowers on sterling silver trays.

She'd groaned aloud at the sight, but I

was certain that in the long run it would make for lovely memories. With that in mind, I shot an entire roll of film just of the table.

I expected Aunt Maxine to help me serve. But she seated herself in the den recliner and allowed the festivities to come to her. Doris filled in and, as always, she was amiable and competent. Her older boy was now a freshman at U.T. and she was very proud of him. She chattered on about his classes and his activities to anyone who would stand still long enough to listen. But when the two of us were alone in the kitchen, her topic of discussion changed abruptly.

"I wanted you to know that Acee is really pleased about how you're getting on with your life again," she said.

"Thanks," I said. "I'm glad about it, too. And I'm sure that with two boys to educate, the last thing you and Acee need to worry about is supporting his ex-wife."

Doris shook her head. "Oh, it's nothing to me," she said. "It's Acee's money and even when things get tight, I just laugh, 'cause I've seen a lot worse times in my life."

"Yes, I guess you have."

"I think it's funny when people whine

about having to pay bills," she said. "I love to pay my bills, 'cause it's such a thrill to have the money to do it."

"I think you may be right, Dorrie," I said. "I get a bit of a thrill out of paying mine, too."

I was chuckling and glanced over at her. She was looking at me intently, thoughtfully, seriously.

"What?"

"You do know, Babs, Acee is still in love with you."

I didn't know what to say. My first thought was to deny it, but how could I presume to know Acee? Doris did know him and she was not the kind of woman who needed to fabricate drama in her life.

"Oh, don't worry," she assured me quickly. "I know that he'd never do anything about it. He'd never leave me or hurt me. He loves me, too, I'm sure of that. I just wanted you to know that. In case, well, in case you ever needed to know that."

I tried to be honest with her. As a woman who is basically unsure of her own mind in terms of relationships, I tried to be as open as I could on how little I understood of my feelings.

"I love him, too, in my own way," I said. "I guess I always will. But I was never able

411

to love him the way that you love him, Doris. And I was never able to make him happy. These days, he seems very happy."

"Thank you for that," she said.

Laney burst into the room with two arms full of dirty dishes.

"Here you two are," she said. "I was wondering if the serving staff had deserted in the line of duty."

"Of course we haven't deserted," I said. "And you shouldn't be picking up, you're the bride."

"You say that, Babs, as if I'm likely to forget."

"Did you see who Renny brought?" she asked us both in a whisper. "Judy Bykowski. What's that about?"

"Probably just what you think," I said. "At least she didn't bring the baby. She must have left it with her mother."

"Baby?"

Doris gave her the news. "Judy had Ned Hoffman's baby, but he wouldn't claim it. So the Hoffmans act like the child is nothing to them. But there's not a soul in town who can't recognize that kid as a Hoffman from five hundred yards."

"Oh, how horrible."

"So now she and Renny are dating," I said.

"Oh, it's more than dating," Doris corrected me. "She and that baby are living down there with him in Maxine's house."

"People are *living together* in McKinney," Laney said. "It must be the scandal of the decade."

"Oh, it's more than a scandal, darling," I told her. "It's an epidemic. There are these unmarried couples all over town now."

"What's the world coming to," Doris said, feigning shock and dismay. "In my day, if you weren't married to a fellow, well you did him in the back seat of the car while you were parked behind the Jiffy Dog, not in the privacy of your own bedroom where the whole town could speculate about it."

Laney responded to that very inappropriate comment with the most delighted giggle I'd heard from her all day. It sounded so good to me that I couldn't scold her. It was then I realized what had been missing in this wonderful celebration. It wasn't the solemnity of the ceremony or the gaiety of a grand reception, it was that neither the bride nor groom displayed any of the giddy optimism that typically accompanied a wedding.

When Doris headed back out to the punch bowl with a pitcher of Agua Fresca,

413

I pulled my daughter aside.

"Are you happy?" I asked her.

"Of course I am, Babs," she answered. "What a silly question."

I nodded. "It's just that both you and Robert seem, I don't know, a little subdued."

"It's the price of oil," she told me. "The glut on the market has driven everything down. It's a problem for Robert. It means trouble on his job, that's all."

"I thought cheap gas was supposed to be good."

Laney shrugged. "I guess it is for anyone who doesn't work in the energy industry. Don't worry, Babs, it will rebound. And it shouldn't affect you much anyway."

She was wrong about that, of course.

In the next year, lavish entertainment, and therefore the events business, took a tremendous hit. Ardith and Geoffrey had less and less need for me. And the plan to open the store in Plano went completely by the wayside.

"Things will pick up," Ardith assured me. "But until they do . . . well, if you get offered some other kind of work, I think you should take it."

That seemed rather unlikely as unemployment was way up all over town. But it was worse in Houston where the oil industry was the base of the entire economy. Robert lost his job. Laney was hanging on by her fingernails.

I knew that I was lucky to get as much work as I did. But I was no longer willing to spend huge blocks of time sitting at home. I began to comb through the classifieds, going out for interviews, even pestering Kathy at the employment agency to find me something. Jobs were, in the Texas vernacular, slim pickings. I was willing to talk to most anyone about anything. That was probably why Kathy contacted me about a position that had just been posted.

"It's part-time work at a nonprofit agency," she told me. "They get funding from United Way, philanthropical foundations and community and business sources, but what they need is somebody to manage a year-round campaign that's both fund-raising and public awareness. They want to get their name and their number out there."

"That sounds interesting," I told her over the phone. "And I wouldn't mind part-time. That way I would still be able to do things with Ardith and Geoffrey."

"That's what I thought," Kathy said.

"And a lot of this work you could do from home. I know you're not crazy about the McKinney/Dallas commute."

"So great, when can I talk to them?"

"How about tomorrow," she said. "It's always good to jump on these things as quickly as you can."

"Sure," I agreed. "Go ahead and set it up. What's the agency called?"

"It's the North Texas Rape Crisis Services."

My heart momentarily caught in my throat. "Rape Crisis?" I finally managed to blurt out. "What do they do?"

"Oh, I don't know, really," Kathy said. "Let me look at this flyer they sent me. They do victim advocacy. They monitor legislation. Here's the mission statement, 'To provide comprehensive services to victims of sexual assault and their families.' I know they have a hotline. Women who've been raped can call in anonymously and talk to counselors."

There was a strange sort of buzzing in my ears. And my hands were shaking so badly, I could hardly hold the phone.

"What . . . what a wonderful idea," I managed to get out.

"What?" Kathy said. "I didn't get that. Are you interested in this?"

No! was the first thought that screamed through my brain. A job was supposed to take my mind off things I didn't want to remember. I couldn't take a job that would remind me every moment of every day of the most traumatic event in my life. It was long past time since I should forget that it had happened. It was ridiculous how that one awful night continued to color my decisions. This was a job, a job I would certainly be able to do and to do well. It was for a good cause. It shouldn't matter that it touched me in a personal way. I should do this. I couldn't let the past imprison me forever.

"Yes," I said, and then more forcefully. "Yes, I'm very interested. I think this might suit me perfectly."

Laney

Robert and I had been living large in the early eighties. Our clothes were from the best designers. Our gadgets the coolest and most up-to-date technology. We'd turned our modest cottage into a three-thousand-five-hundred-square-foot showplace. He had his BMW and I had my BMW. We had a boat that we moored at Galveston. We worked like Energizer bunnies all week and we partied hearty every weekend.

When the North Sea oil came into production at the same time Mexico started exporting, the OPEC monopoly couldn't maintain its market share. The price of crude, that had been flying so high and us with it, dropped like January temperatures and those who were hoping for an early spring thaw seemed doomed to disappointment.

The company Robert worked for was

one of the first casualties. Without profits to be made, investors couldn't be cajoled to put money down. And without that capital, independents went under.

My husband was shocked, but ultimately philosophical.

"This is not the only game in town," he said, and then chuckled. "Well, maybe it's the only game in *this* town. But Wall Street is buzzing big-time. I can make money in the stock market just sitting here in the house in my pajamas."

So we pared down our lifestyle, retrenched our finances and tried to ride things out.

Robert started his day at 4:30 a.m. at the close of the Nikkei in Japan. By the time he got their business day analyzed, Wall Street would open. He would buy early in the day those things that he thought would go up and sell them for a profit at the close of trading. It was intense and exciting. Not that different from high stakes gambling, and just as addictive.

Robert was good at it. And he was having a great time. Several of his buddies, including Greg, were also in the game. And after the bell in the afternoon, they met at Kazoo's, a local bar, to rehash their successes and one-up each other.

I continued to go to work every day. My former dreams of climbing the corporate ladder and becoming a female CEO were being replaced by more temporary goals of staying employed. In a way, I was lucky. All the men who'd supervised me, Carmington, Thrushing and the rest, were the first ones to get their heads on the chopping block. What had once been accomplished by entire department staffs was now being handled by myself and a few other low-level managers, desperate to scrape by.

The end came for me in the spring of 1986. I went in one morning to find that employment for everybody but the lawyers and some of the accounting staff was severed immediately. I had been expecting it, but I was still crushed.

"Hey, don't worry," Robert told me. He was so happy and jazzed up that evening that he couldn't manage to conjure up even a smidgeon of sympathy for me. "Let's see it as an opportunity."

"An opportunity? An opportunity for what?" I asked. "I can't be a day trader, too."

"Well, you can be something else," he said. "Haven't you said to yourself a million times, 'if I didn't have to go to work every day I could . . .' Haven't you said that?"

"Sure."

"So think about it," he said. "Take this time off as an opportunity to do something you've always wanted to do."

I resisted the idea that was in my mind. For some reason it took me months to speak it aloud. Finally near the end of summer, I let Robert in on my thinking.

"If I'm just going to be stuck here at home," I said. "It seems like a perfect time to start a family."

His jaw dropped open and he just stared at me for a long moment. I wished the words back in my mouth, but they wouldn't go.

"Gosh," he said, finally. "Is that what you want? You've been so into your career. I wasn't even sure that you were even interested in motherhood."

I shrugged. "I'm already not working," I pointed out. "I could have a child now. And by the time the economy picks up, he'd be ready for day care or something."

"Fine," Robert said. "It's not like we don't like kids."

"Right."

"I guess we both always thought we'd do that someday."

"Exactly."

With that seemingly brilliant plan and less than optimum commitment, I quit taking the pill and began preparing my life for this mommy temp job. I read some books, looked at some furniture. And waited for my periods to stop.

Getting pregnant took longer than I expected. It wasn't completely for lack of trying. Robert had always been interested in sex and continued to come home from Kazoo's ready to jump my bones. But I began to notice that with the amount of alcohol he was consuming, he was less and less able to complete the process he started.

So I began to nag.

"Don't drink," I'd tell him as he headed out the door one afternoon.

"Two beers only," I'd remind him the next day.

"This is becoming a habit," I warned him the evening after that.

Finally I confronted him. "You are drinking too much," I told him.

"Don't be silly," he said. "I have a couple of brews to take the edge off and that's it."

"No, that's not it," I insisted. "You're getting drunk every day. There is something wrong with that."

"I'm celebrating," he said. "When you day-trade, there's something to celebrate every day."

Since Robert wouldn't see what was happening, I decided I would talk to Greg about it. The two were still best friends, still doing the same jobs, still friendly competitors. If I couldn't get my husband to listen, then maybe his best buddy could.

"I want you to start hanging around the house here," I said to him. "When you guys go off to Kazoo's Robert's drinking too much."

Greg chuckled and shook his head. "He's not drinking that much," Greg insisted. "He's just downing a few beers to chill, level out a bit, you know. You can't blow and not drink, it makes you too speedy."

"What?"

"The coke has more than just the high," he said. "It has this jittery thing going, you've got to get some booze with it to even that out."

"Coke? Robert is doing cocaine?" I was staggered.

Greg looked at me as if I was crazy. "Where have you been?" he asked as a facetious joke.

I confronted my husband that very day.

"I didn't tell you because I knew you'd react just this way," he said. "It doesn't seem to matter that you've lived here in

Houston almost ten years. You're still not much more sophisticated than the day you left McKinney."

"Sophisticated has nothing to do with it," I told him. "There is nothing sophisticated about addiction."

"See, that just shows how little you know about it," he said. "Cocaine is not addictive. It's a recreational drug. It's not like heroin or speed. It's just a nice, fun high. It feels great and then it's over."

"If it's so over, then why are you doing it every day."

"I do it because I enjoy it," he said. "When I quit enjoying it, I'll quit doing it."

He continued to discount my arguments, to ignore my complaints. I was so worried, so upset, so angry, so consumed by this unexpected serpent in my Garden of Eden that at first I didn't notice my own symptoms. I'd been waiting for months to feel queasy. Now I was throwing up in the toilet every day and thinking it was only nerves. As soon as it dawned on me that it might be something more, I hurried to the doctor and had my condition confirmed.

"You can't continue to do this with the baby coming," I told Robert. "This is an ultimatum. If you want to be a father, then you have to cut out the drugs and the drinking and all of it."

"Laney, be reasonable," he said.

"I am being reasonable," I insisted. "I don't want our child to grow up around this. If you really can give up the drugs, then you have to do it. If not . . . if not, then we're out of here."

Those were tough words, it was a tough stance, but I was completely serious. There are times and situations that simply brook no argument. Fortunately Robert didn't try.

"Okay, babe," he said. "I can see that this is really important to you. Stay calm. If you don't want me to do coke, I won't. It's as simple as that. You and the baby, you'll need me around the house more anyway. I'll quit going to Kazoo's. I'll start doing more stuff around here. In fact, I was thinking about starting my own business. Things are still bad in energy, but there is so much money to be made in the stock market, I'm thinking that I might get into it on a bigger scale. Start managing other people's money as well as my own."

He reached over and pulled me into his arms. He patted my still very flat tummy. "It's amazing what a guy can accomplish if he's got the right kind of incentive at home," Robert said. "You and this little guy in here, they are just what I need."

I believed him. Probably because he wasn't lying. He believed it himself.

But as I prepared my nest and readied myself for the upcoming blessed event, I lost sight of what was happening around me. In my self-involvement with maternity clothes, prenatal classes and discussions of Lamaze vs. epidural anesthesia, I failed to notice that Robert was disappearing. Not just from the house and from my life, but his entire person was slowly being obliterated from the face of the earth.

One afternoon in mid-October I was in the doctor's office. I'd just had an ultrasound and she said that the baby looked great.

"Is it a boy or a girl?" I asked.

She scooted the wand across my stomach a few times more. "I don't see a penis," she told me. "That's not definitive, of course, but I'd say there's a good chance that this is a girl."

I hurried home to give the news to Robert. I was full of excitement and enthusiasm.

It died as soon as I got into the house.

My husband was high, obviously, seriously, high, but there was nothing upbeat about his mood.

"It's all over," he told me.

"What's all over?"

"Everything," he said. "It's all gone, every bit of it, gone. It's all nothing. Nada. None."

I tried to make sense of him for several minutes, then gave up in frustration.

"I'm not talking to you when you're like this," I said. "When you come down from wherever you are, we'll discuss why you've been into the drugs again."

"I'm never coming down," he said. "There's nothing to come down to. There's nothing left."

I waved away his words as nonsense and went upstairs.

The truth of what he was trying to tell me came in jolting pieces of information over the next few days. Robert had lost a fortune in the Black Friday crash. Not just our fortune, which would have been bad enough. He lost the fortunes of the investors of his new fledgling business. He lost a fortune in money borrowed against our house, our cars, our household goods, our credit cards. Robert was right. There was nothing. Overnight we'd gone from being trendy, upwardly mobile yuppies, to homeless, jobless debtors. The only thing that stuck solidly with us was Robert's drug addiction.

I tried to help him. He didn't want help. He and Greg sat in the living room day after day, doing drugs, drinking beer and watching TV.

I was eight months pregnant, not exactly a great job candidate. I had thirty days or less to get my life in order before my child was born. I begged Robert. I pleaded with him. Finally I threatened.

"If you don't do something, make some effort to get ahold of yourself and start working through some of this disaster, then I'm leaving you."

"Don't let the screen door hit you on your way out," he said.

Greg laughed raucously, as if that were really funny.

"If I leave, I won't be coming back."

"Promise?"

More laughter. I went upstairs and started packing. As each suitcase was filled, I kept expecting Robert to show up at the door. I kept assuming that when it came right down to it, he'd never let me go. Once I had all my things, all the baby's things in suitcases or boxes, there was no choice but to face him again. I went back downstairs to give him another chance.

Greg was sleeping on the dining room floor. Robert was sitting in front of the TV with a beer in his hand.

"I'm going to call my mother to come and get me," I said.

"The phone's dead," he answered. "You'll have to walk down to the Mini Mart."

The store was four blocks away. We had no cars, Greg's BMW was in the driveway, but I didn't even ask to borrow it. I walked.

At the pay phone, I made a collect call.

"Babs, it's me."

"Hi, honey, I'm so glad you called," she said. "How are you feeling? How's my little grandbaby."

Her warmth and welcome, the tenderness and care in her voice, broke through the iciness surrounding my heart. I began to cry.

"Come get me, Mama," I managed to mutter.

When I got back to the house, it was locked. I had no key. Robert, Greg and the BMW were gone. My suitcases were piled up by the front step. I sat down on the front porch and waited almost five hours on that cold winter night before Babs arrived to rescue me.

I never saw Robert again.

Babs

The Rape Crisis Center was, in almost every way, a surprise to me. I had not imagined that there were so many people; thoughtful, knowledgeable people, eagerly waiting to help women, children and men who'd been abused. And the gamut of things that they were willing to do to help was impressive. They would stay with victims in the emergency room, stand beside them while they talked to police. They would help them get back to living at home, or if they were at risk in that place from their spouse, family members or neighbors, they would assist them in finding a new, safe place to live. They made sure the victim, and sometimes her whole family, had access to appropriate counseling, both immediately after the attack and later, if the aftermath overwhelmed her.

They gave public education programs on

sexual assault to schools and civic groups, giving real life information about prevalence, prevention and protection. The organization made it a goal that every person in the community had the most up-to-date information, free of recriminations, myths and prejudice.

What drew me most strongly was the hotline. Twenty-four hours a day, trained volunteers manned the phones. A person who'd been attacked could call anonymously and talk to someone. They could verbalize their horror, their terror to another human being, without any fear of the long-term ramifications of doing so. How wonderful that must be, I thought to myself, to be able to just talk to someone. I'd carried the burden of silence for almost fifteen years before I was able to speak about it. Keeping those words inside me had been, in some sense, as soul killing as the rape itself.

"All our volunteers go through a very rigorous training," Analisse, the director told me. "And it's not the kind of job that anybody can do. So when we're trying to raise money and awareness, we're also trying to attract those people who can be just right on the phones."

I nodded and wrote that down. I was

taking extensive notes on the requirements of their promotional campaign.

"Many of our volunteers have been through this themselves and know very well what the clients are going through," she said.

I blanched and gave a hasty glance through the office glass at the main work area.

"Some of these people were victims themselves?"

Analisse smiled. "I don't think you can tell who they are by looking," she told me.

She'd misread my sudden panic. I was suddenly nervous that someone might suspect me.

"I suppose I thought that most of these volunteers were . . . social service workers or counselors or . . . or . . . professionals of some kind."

"Some are," she assured me. "Anyone with the desire to help will find some much needed job to do."

"But many of these people are victims themselves."

"We prefer to be called *survivors* of sexual assault," she said.

I wrote that down.

"It's just . . . everyone seems so upbeat,"

I said. "You'd never know."

Analisse took a deep breath. "That's what we're working toward, I suppose," she said. "If we could prevent every sexual assault, we would. Failing that, we want the people who've been through it to know that they're not alone. That what happened was not their fault, they don't need to feel guilt. And that they have control of their lives. Their attacker had that control for a few moments or a few hours, but doesn't control them now. That, on its own, is a lot to be upbeat about."

I nodded thoughtfully.

"Will I need to go through this training that you offer?" I asked her.

She hesitated a long moment. So long I began to get nervous. I began tapping my pencil against my collarbone. When I realized what I was doing, I stopped.

"Yes, I think you should," she said, finally. "It will give you more insight into what we do and what we need. You'll get familiar with supportive, nonjudgmental language and the basic first aid for those who've been attacked. Yes, I think you'll have to take the course."

"Certainly," I said, nodding.

My fear of it warred with anticipation of it. Perhaps I could learn something while revealing nothing. That's not what happened.

I did fine in the classroom. I took copious notes all during the four-day information sessions. Little information lightbulbs were turning on so quickly in my head, I was probably in danger of some inner power shortage. Virtually all of the terrible, life-altering, happiness-crushing effects I'd suffered through had been typical, normal, even predictable. And they would have been so much easier for me to understand had I known that.

Even when other members of the class shared personal experiences, I managed to keep my thoughts and my memories hidden inside. But on the final day, we participated in some mock phone interviews. Some of us pretended to be callers, while others answered the phone and practiced hotline listening response.

Since I was not going to be working the phones, I was picked to be a caller and given an identity and an incident on a five-by-eight card. I was to be Sally, a twenty-two-year-old single mother who'd been raped by an acquaintance at a community gathering. The perpetrator was known and well liked by family and friends. He was an upstanding family man with a lovely wife and two children, his youngest a playmate of Sally's own child.

I began my bit of playacting without much trepidation. I said the things that we'd learned to expect victims to say. The person training for the hotline did her part to be an encouraging, supporting listener. As I went on, I got more into the character. I began to feel what she must be feeling. I got to saying what she might actually be saying.

"He's a horrible man," I said into the phone. "But nobody knows that. Nobody will believe it. If I tell, everyone will think that it was me. That I led him on. That I was trying to ruin things for his wife, for his family. That I let him think that it was all right. That I wanted it. At best they'll think that I was too stupid not to recognize what he was, too stupid not to protect myself."

"It's not your fault," she responded correctly. "I'm just so glad that you're safe. I'm so sorry that this happened. You did the best that you could do at the time."

"I should have done something else," I insisted. "I should have never opened that door. I should have never got friendly with those people. I should have stayed in McKinney where I belonged instead of trying to venture out into the world. Instead of trying to stand on my own."

I looked across the table at the other trainee on the mock telephone and I realized that I had somehow shifted unexpectedly from Sally's pretend rape to my own very real experience.

"I . . . I'm sorry," I blurted out, realizing that I'd inadvertently revealed feelings that I'd so carefully kept hidden all those years. "I didn't mean . . ."

"It's okay," she said to me, more forcefully. "I'm so sorry that this happened to you, but you are very, very brave to come forward to say so. You are going to be better from saying this. And we are all going to be better for having heard it."

I knew she was right.

After I put the phone down, Analisse came up to me and hugged me.

She wasn't the only one to openly show support and affection. Every man and woman in that room was there for me. And didn't hesitate to say so.

"I kind of thought you were one of us," she admitted. "And no, I don't think it's because you have some kind of mark on your forehead. It's just that I've dealt with plenty of business people on campaigns in the past. And I just knew from the concern and intensity of your interest that this was more than just business to you."

"Yes," I admitted finally. "It is more than just business."

All of this was on my mind the evening Laney called me from Houston and asked me to come get her. I hardly hesitated long enough to go to the bathroom. I grabbed my purse and was out the door.

I'd known that things were not right with Laney and Robert. That unsettling feeling I'd had about them almost from the day they'd married, had only intensified with time. Even when she'd called me with the exciting news that she was carrying my first grandchild, I got the sense that things were not as they should be.

Not that I could discuss this with Laney. Our relationship, as it had panned out, was not one with a great deal of sharing or trust. I blame myself for this. Or at least, I lay the blame, in part on my own secrets so closely kept so long. I knew that Laney loved me, but I was fairly certain that she didn't understand me. And that was exactly how I had always wanted it. Protecting her from the ugliness that I'd experienced was what a mother should do, I was certain.

But I couldn't protect her from the ugliness that she found on her own.

When I got to her house in Houston she was sitting on the porch with everything she owned packed into three suitcases. Heavily pregnant and shivering from cold, I wanted to take her to a doctor to have her checked out.

"Just take me home, Babs," she said. "I just want to go home."

Laney strapped herself into the passenger seat and I tucked a blanket around her. She was sound asleep before I got six blocks away from her house. She slept much of the way home. I forced her to go into a restaurant for dinner in Huntsville. But she had very little to say to me. I didn't press her for details. She'd talk when she was ready.

We arrived in McKinney in the middle of the night.

"We'll bring this luggage inside in the morning," I told her. "Let's just go in and go to bed."

Laney slept all night and most of the next day.

I brought the suitcases in myself and dragged them upstairs into the hall in front of her room. I brought her dinner, but she wouldn't get out of bed to eat it.

When the next morning arrived and she

still hadn't stirred, I went into her room and opened the curtains.

"Leave me alone," she moaned from the bed.

I felt sorry for her, but I was still her mother.

"Laney," I said. "If this was just you, I'd let you lie in bed for as long as it takes. But it's not just you. So, you are going to get up, wash up, come down to breakfast and take a walk around the block."

She gave me the evil eye.

"Get out," she said. "I'm tired. I need to rest."

"That baby inside you needs food and fresh air."

Her answer was to roll over and pull the covers up over her head. I stood looking at her for a long moment and then walked over and jerked them off.

"Get up, Laney!" I insisted.

"Go away!"

"I'm not going anywhere."

"You always think you know what's best for me," she snarled. "But you don't, Babs. You don't know anything about me."

"Maybe not," I agreed. "But I know a few things about your baby. If you don't take care of yourself, it's your baby who's going to suffer."

"My baby is fine," she insisted.

"But he won't be if you don't start thinking about him first," Babs said. "Believe me, this is one of the things I learned the hard way."

"What are you talking about?"

"Marley."

Laney eased up on one elbow, hair wildly tousled, but eyes clear.

"Marley? My brother, Marley?"

"Marley died because I didn't take care of myself," I told her.

Laney grabbed for the covers once more. "Don't be so dramatic," she said. "Marley died of a heart defect."

"Yes, he did," I told her. "But he might have been stronger, he might have had more strength to fight for his life if I'd taken better care."

"Yeah, right."

"It's true," I said. "I didn't want Marley. He was unplanned and a shame and embarrassment to me. I hid my pregnancy. I didn't eat right, I wore girdles. I tried every way I could think of just to miscarry. When he was born weak and sickly, I thought it was a miracle. But it wasn't. It's what happens when a baby is deprived in the womb."

She sat up then, staring at me.

440

"I heard from the Hoffmans that you were pregnant when you got married," she said.

I nodded. "I guess my secret wasn't as safe as I thought."

"But even if you were embarrassed," she said. "I can't believe that you didn't want Acee's baby."

I stood there for a moment that seemed like a lifetime. There are things in every mother's life that she hopes never to share with her daughter. This was one of them. I didn't want her ever to know, but somehow it now seemed important, for her own sake and the sake of my grandchild, that she did.

"Marley wasn't Acee's baby," I said.

"What!"

Laney's mouth dropped open, her expression incredulous.

"Who? How? What?"

"I was raped," I answered to all three questions. "When we lived in Dallas, I was raped."

My daughter just continued to stare at me, completely dumbfounded.

"I can't believe that it came out that way," I said. "I never meant for you to know. I've kept the whole sordid story inside me for twenty-five years."

She nodded. "And you never told anyone?"

"I told Acee," I said. "He knew rather generally, but not with any detail until just a few years ago. When he was already my ex-husband."

"Was he supportive?"

I nodded. "Yes, he was. He . . . he saved my life back then. In those days, single women weren't allowed to be pregnant. I was going to have a child by my rapist. And I was probably going to lose you because of it."

"Oh gosh." Laney's expression was stricken. I wasn't sure if it was sympathy or disgust.

"When Marley didn't live . . ." I began in explanation. "I have so much guilt about that. Maybe if I'd wanted him more he might have survived. Maybe if I thought more about the child and less about what had happened to me. I was just so scared."

I sat down on the side of her bed. I stared down at my hands, afraid to see what might be in her eyes.

"Acee knew that it wasn't his baby?" she asked.

I nodded. "I was already pregnant when I married him. I told him that the baby's father had forced me. But I never revealed . . . the reality of what that meant."

"That you'd been raped," she said.

"Yes. Raped." I let out a deep breath and shook my head. "I've been working for the Rape Crisis Center in Dallas. It's really helped. I have been a lot better since I found out that I'm not alone and what I feel is not . . . weakness or craziness or . . . or my own fault."

"Oh, Mama."

Laney reached over and wrapped her arms around me holding me so tight. I felt the tears welling up in my eyes. Once I started crying, she did, too. The two of us sat there, hugging and bawling. It was a great feeling, letting go and expressing my emotions with my daughter. I wanted to really get into it, but I knew that probably wasn't good for the baby, either.

Deliberately I fished the tissue box out of the bedside table. We wiped our eyes and blew our noses and tried to straighten up.

"I was always sorry about Marley," she said. "I'm really sorry about all that happened."

"Thank you."

"I've heard that something like this affects women like posttraumatic stress disorder. Have you had problems like that? Long-term effects?"

"Oh, none really," I answered quickly. And then as she continued to look at me, her expression completely devoid of condemnation, I felt compelled to add. "Except for my sex life. Or my lack of it. I haven't been able to . . . to have pleasurable sex since it happened."

Laney's eyes widened.

"So, no matter what you think the reasons were for my break-up with Acee, you can add close to complete disaster on that score."

"I'm so sorry."

"And there was the travel thing," I continued.

Laney looked at me questioningly. "You mean, how you would never go anywhere?"

I nodded. "I started becoming afraid of any place unfamiliar. It got worse and worse, until I was practically a prisoner here in the house," I admitted. "I still get jittery every time I drive into Dallas."

"It happened there?"

"Yes, when we were living in the duplex near Cummings Park."

Laney drew a startled indrawn breath. "I remember when we left there," she said. "I remember you had bruises on your face."

"Yes," I said simply.

"So, what happened? Did someone break in the house?"

"I let him in," I told her. "It was the man who lived next door."

"Mr. Grimes?"

"Oh God, Laney," I said. "I hoped you wouldn't remember him."

"I don't much," she said. "But I remember his wife. I stayed with her after school."

"Yes."

That afternoon we went for a stroll. Just getting outside made us both feel better. I helped her unpack. She'd brought all of the baby's stuff and most of her own clothes, but she'd left the rest of her things in the house.

"I don't know what I was thinking of," she said. "I should have at least brought some of the china and crystal. Robert will get nothing for it at the pawn broker's. And there were pictures and books, so much I should have gathered up."

"Well, you did the best you could and at least you are safe."

I was struck by how much my words sounded like something I would have expressed at the Center.

"I even left my SoupKids salt and

pepper," Laney said. "And I've had them since we first moved in with Aunt Maxine. They are the only thing that's been with me all this time. Well, except for you."

Except for me.

"Maybe it was time to let them go," I told her.

"Yeah," she said. "Maybe so. Have you ever been back by there?"

"Where?"

"The duplex."

"No, never."

And at the time I told her that, I never would have imagined doing so. But as the weeks passed I began to be intrigued with the idea of revisiting the scene of the crime. I imagined myself stealing back the power that the place had robbed from me.

Laney

Laney Rachel Maxine Jerrod was born on January 8, 1988, in McKinney Medical Center. I made some comment about having three eights in her birthday so Doris brought me a paperback from the drugstore on numerology.

"Eight means new life, new beginnings," she said.

I smiled at her, pretending to be pleased, but it was hard to feel that way. I'd failed at marriage, failed at a career, failed at my life outside McKinney. And now I was back here, living off my mother and bringing a child into the world to live with me in my girlhood bedroom.

My relationship with Babs was better than it had been in years and I was grateful for that. I needed her and she stepped up to help without a word of complaint. But that wasn't enough to make me content.

I wanted my old life back. I wanted my stressful, thankless job, my distracted addicted husband. I wanted my foreclosed house in West University. But that was all gone.

Acee handled the divorce for me. He handled it way too efficiently from my perspective. Somehow I'd imagined that there would be lots of face-to-face confrontations and disputes, that opportunities for long discussions and an airing of my grievances would occur. And then finally, at long last, we would face each other across a courtroom.

None of that happened.

I asked Acee to file my petition. The next time we discussed it, the divorce was final.

I remember the moment with almost inhuman clarity. It was midmorning in Babs's living room. Acee was spreading the papers out on the coffee table. Rachel was contentedly rocking back and forth in her little swing. The tinny strains of "The Farmer in the Dell" were playing as a background score. *Hi-ho, the derry-o, you are now divorced.*

"How can it happen so fast?" I asked him.

"Both of you were agreeable to it," he

said. "And there was nothing to contend. No remaining assets and Robert's biggest concern was that he was not going to owe you big child-support payments. I told him basically what you told me. That you weren't as interested in his money as much as his relationship with his child. And that he needs to be free of drugs for any visitation."

I nodded. "What did Robert say about that?"

Acee hesitated a moment and my heart sank.

"He says he'll pay the minimum," Acee answered. "He's not interested in having contact with the baby at this time."

Acee spoke the words in a brusque, businesslike manner as if getting through them quickly would hurt a lot less.

So that was it. My marriage was over. My dream was gone. But there was Rachel and she needed me, so I had no option for quitting or hiding. I had a child to raise. I may not have felt like getting up in the morning, but breast-feeding every four hours certainly limits one's ability to wallow in a grand funk.

"Thanks, Acee," I said to him. "It's a good thing that you still think you're my stepfather, 'cause I sure can't afford to pay you for your services."

"You just gave me my first grand-daughter," he said. "That's more riches than any bank could ever hold."

I knew he meant it. He was a real schmaltz, baby-talking, goo-goo, ga-ga kind of guy. He was Rachel's number one fan.

"There is one thing that you could do for me," he said.

"Anything," I responded.

"Dorrie's not been well," he said. "She's so tired, she doesn't really have the energy to get about town or come visit you. If you'd visit her occasionally, it would mean a lot to me."

"Sure," I told him.

I was surprised. I hadn't realized that Doris was sick. But it became clear to me over the next few months that she was more than just tired. Her lethargy was vir-tually debilitating and she ran mysterious low-grade fevers two, sometimes three times a week. This went on for months and months. The doctors were stumped. They ran tests for everything from meningitis to dengue fever. Finally they settled on her liver.

"It's some new kind of hepatitis," she ex-plained to me as I drove her home from the doctor. Rachel was hungry and shrieking in her car seat. "It's not Hepatitis A or Hepatitis B. So they're calling it Hepatitis, non-A, non-B. Isn't that funny?"

I didn't know if it was funny, but Doris was so upbeat I was encouraged.

"So they can treat this non-A, non-B stuff," I said.

She shrugged. "They don't know much about it, truly," she said. "But it's definitely not cancer, so that's a big relief. I was really afraid that it was cancer."

The fevers were from peritonitis, a result of decreased liver function. Once that was treated, Doris began to feel significantly better. But she continued to have lots of weird, unanticipated symptoms and Rachel and I spent more and more time over at her house.

That was just as well. Because Babs was never home.

I understood that my mother worked for a living. I'd had a career myself, I knew that it took a lot of hours. The events firm that she worked for had decided at long last to open its second store. The original idea was to locate it in Plano. But as suburban growth crept ever northward, Babs convinced them that McKinney was the best place.

This should have meant she was home

more. Certainly she was putting in a lot of time getting the business off the ground, but at least she shouldn't be commuting back and forth to Dallas.

Unfortunately she still was.

Babs refused to give up her part-time job with the Rape Crisis Center. She was putting in long hours in McKinney and then commuting downtown to put in more time at the Center. It was crazy and I told her so.

"I know the Center is important to you, Babs. But you have a granddaughter," I said, stating the obvious. "Any other woman your age would *want* to spend some time with her."

"I do want to spend time with her," Babs said. "And I hate missing anything she does. But I have other priorities, as well. Rachel has her mommy with her. And I'm pretty certain that this is one of those circumstances when I'm not going to come out well either way."

"What do you mean?"

"If I saw her more you'd accuse me of hovering," she said. "So I see her less and you accuse me of being neglectful. This is just one of these times when I'm not going to be able to do the right thing, no matter what."

"You always manage to make it about you, don't you, Babs," I said.

She chuckled derisively and shook her head. "I'm paying the bills around here, Ms. Mom-Of-The-Year," she said. "I'm making it possible for you to be a full-time mother and I'm not interfering in your life. You should thank your lucky stars and not try to change a thing."

She did have a point. I was feeling annoyed at our role reversal. I loved motherhood. I loved Rachel. I wanted to be with my baby. But I was also feeling a little cheated. Babs was supposed to be the Betty Crocker housewife, the 1950s mom who stayed home and baked. I was the hard-bitten career woman. I was supposed to be a mover and shaker. I was going to make CEO before I was forty. Now she was off to work in her power suits and I was stuck at home scraping oatmeal off the ceiling.

I talked to Aunt Maxine about it.

"You can't have everything," she told me. "Lots of young women these days think they can. But I always worked. I had to. You don't have to work all the time to keep your hand in."

In the spring after Rachel turned two, I approached Pete about a job.

"I could use you," he admitted. "We're under phenomenal growth pressure. And a person with your qualifications as a part-time employee would be a great asset to the company."

I'd get no benefits, no insurance, no stock options, no bonuses. But I could limit my work schedule to two mornings a week while Rachel attended the Mother's Day Out at the Presbyterian church.

It was sort of like leaving her with family. Nicie was the childcare supervisor. Brian had walked out on her and she had three kids to support. Still optimistic and up-beat, she doted on Rachel as much as her own little ones. And Rachel was one of the few toddlers who waved goodbye to her mom without any fuss at all.

I loved being back at work, even if it was only ten hours a week. It forced me to slim down enough to fit into my business ward-robe and encouraged me to be consistent with Rachel on potty training. Both of us profited from the effort.

Pete's company had grown into a huge campus of modern glassy buildings that abutted the expressway. Their innovative software had made commercial applica-tions on the Internet quick and easy. They were now into dot-com merchandising programs in a big way. I was not all that familiar with the Internet or computers generally. But I was able and willing to learn. And, as always, I found my forte in the company's crumby cleanup. I was always able to find work that was unglamorous enough not to tempt anyone else.

Pete seemed pleased with my efforts.

I'd only been working there a few months when I was in the main building one morning, waiting for the elevator to come down from the executive level. When the doors opened, I stepped inside and did a double take at the occupant already there. The face was familiar, but the expensive suit and good haircut were not.

"Laney," he said, his voice deeper than I remembered.

"Stanley? Is that you?"

He chuckled. "Only you and my mother would still call me Stanley," he said. "You look good."

"Thanks, so do you," I said. "What are you doing here?"

"I was upstairs talking to your cousin Pete," he said. "Trying to sell him some computers."

"Oh, you're a computer salesman," I said. "I guess that explains the great suit."

There was a flash of something in his expression and then it disappeared. And he gifted me with that wonderful grin that I remembered from the day of the Cotton Days Parade.

"You like the suit," he said. "I guess it is a great improvement over the blue jeans and plaid shirts of high school."

I nodded, but the smile had caught me up short. A flood of memories had assailed me, centering around that kiss, that one fabulous kiss that the two of us had shared that day. The thought of it had sent a jolt of sexual energy through my body and had me staring at the man's lips and feeling like my panty hose were way too tight.

Jeez, Laney, get a grip! I admonished myself. It had obviously been way too long since I'd had sex, if the confines of an elevator could suddenly give me the hots for some guy I hadn't seen for well over a decade.

"So, are you married, Stanley?"

I wished I could have cut my tongue out for asking the question.

"Divorced," he answered.

"Me, too."

"I know," he said.

There was an uncomfortable moment of silence between us.

"Maybe we could grab a cup of coffee sometime," I said.

"Or dinner," he suggested. "Would you like that? I could take you to dinner."

"Yeah, yeah, that would be great," I said. The elevator stopped and the door opened. "Let me give you my number." I began scrambling through the folders in my arms, trying to come up with a scrap to write a note. I managed to drop a whole sheaf of papers. When I bent down to grab them, I lost my Day-Timer and my pager. Stanley squatted down to pick up everything. I hurried to help and managed to hit him in the head with my purse.

I felt like an idiot and I was acting like one. We were in the middle of a very busy office building. The building where I worked. Our heads just inches apart I realized I was easily just one brain cell away from jumping his bones right there in the elevator.

"You're living with your mother, right?" he said.

"Right."

He handed me the last of my fallen valuables.

"I'm sure her number is in the phone book," he said. "I'll give you a call."

I replayed the entire encounter a dozen

times in my brain as I drove over to pick up Rachel. I was a complete moron, plus being a sex crazed maniac. What kind of desperate divorcée had I become that I had the hots for the biggest nerd in McKinney High School?

I related the encounter to Nicie with most of the relevant detail.

"I'm so sex starved," I admitted with self-deprecation, "that I practically attack the first single man I see, even if he is the local dweeb."

"Stan Kuhl is not a dweeb," she said. "He's the most eligible guy in town."

"Stanley?" I was incredulous.

"My God! Don't tell me you don't know," Nicie said, clearly astounded.

"I don't know what?"

"Come here," she said and had me follow her into the church office. "Look." She pointed to the desk. There was nothing there but a mess of papers and a computer.

"What?" I asked her.

She tapped on the metallic logo pressed onto the front of the monitor. My attention focused on it for the first time. It read: *Kuhl Computers.*

Babs

The year after Laney moved home and Rachel was born I took off with a wish of good luck and a shoestring budget to open the McKinney branch of Ardith Eden Events. Expecting nothing less than hard work and long hours, I started scrounging up local business. Amazingly I was good at it. All those friends and acquaintances I'd made during my years as a local social climber and celebrated hostess had evolved into an impressive contact list. I knew everyone and everything, including who needed parties and programs and a planner to put them together.

Mostly it was small gatherings with few expectations and not much budget. But from time to time, a really good job would come my way.

It wasn't she-crab soup at the country club, but I did manage to put together a corporate retreat for the city, where they had managers from big companies in town for a weekend to be wined and dined and shown the advantages of locating or relocating part of their business on the McKinney corridor. It was a lot of hard work and the city's outlay for it barely covered my expenses, but it was my own operation and, at the worst, I got to show off for the people I might work for if they did choose McKinney.

Over the years I expended much of my energy building a business and a reputation. And I was enjoying it. I tried not to neglect my home life. It felt good to have Laney home. We were closer than we'd been for decades, even if our mother/daughter relationship continued to have its challenges.

And my Rachel, she was a delight. It's amazing how, when you have your own baby, you think that it is impossible to love any other child in the world that much. But when you become a grandparent, you find out differently. There is all that tremendous wash of love and devotion you felt for your own baby. But with none of the worry, anxiety and responsibility that weighs so heavily upon parents.

I loved little Rachel as I had Laney. But

when I got up and got ready to leave in the morning, I could kiss her goodbye without so much as a thought as to what her day would be like. Her mother would keep her safe and warm and fed. She'd see that she learned her colors and her numbers and how to navigate across the back lawn without falling in the fishpond.

Laney consistently said that she wanted me to spend more time at home, that she wanted me to do more babysitting, that she wanted me to stop working so much.

She may have actually believed that was what she wanted. But I thought differently. From my perspective, the only way that the two of us could ever manage to share that house without killing each other, was for one of us to have someplace else to go.

At first, it was just me running off and leaving the house and all its operations in her care. Once she started part-timing for Pete, we shared more responsibility. But I wouldn't cut back on my schedule. The McKinney branch of Events was just beginning to really pay off. And I was certainly not willing to give up my work at Rape Crisis. I continued to spend countless hours coordinating promotions and doing events planning for them. Most of these efforts were off the clock. I spent far more time and effort than anything they actually had budgeted. I saw this organization as my mission. It was a way that I could turn all the negative energy that surrounded my rape into a positive force to help someone else. I was completely unwilling to give that up.

I was there at the Crisis Center office one cold, drizzly winter day working out the details on a huge golf event for which we were one of the recipient charities. Analisse was helping me.

"We're going to need to switch caterers," I told her. "These guys are not going to be able to bring this in on bid. I think we should go with Grimaldi."

"You're the one who knows about this stuff," she said.

I nodded. "I need him to commit now," I said. "And, naturally, his shop doesn't answer. It sure would be nice if everybody had cellular phones and not just me."

"It'll never happen," she said. "People like their privacy too much. Why don't you see if you can find his home number. At worst you can leave a message on his answering machine."

Agreeing, I jerked open the white pages of the telephone directory and began leafing through the pages, searching for the number. Unexpectedly my glance was captured by a name at the top of the page: *Grimes, Mary Jane.*

And just that quickly, my demons that I'd chased so far from my everyday life returned.

"What's wrong?" There was genuine concern in Analisse's voice.

"Huh?"

"You just turned as pale as a sheet," she said. "What happened?"

I hesitated only an instant. I'd grown accustomed to being straightforward with people from the Center. I'd learned that in this very safe place keeping secrets was not necessary.

"This is the wife of the man who raped me," I said.

Analisse glanced at her name.

"Okay," she said, thoughtful, nodding. "She's listed by her own name. Must mean she's divorced. Maybe she figured out what an evil bastard he was. See if he's listed separately."

Slowly, with my heart in my throat, I turned the page back and followed the name Grimes up to the top of the alphabet. Edward. David. Charles. Buddy. Albert.

I stopped. Stared at the names a moment. Then I looked through the entire Grimes listing. There was no one named Burl. There was no one with initials that included B. There were probably seventy-five listings, but none were him.

"Maybe he's moved," Analisse said.

"You mean he could live somewhere else." My heart was suddenly pumping.

"Don't panic," she said. "You're safe. Just because you don't know where he is, doesn't mean that you're in danger."

"You're right," I said. "Of course you're right. I'm acting stupid."

"It's a natural reaction," she said. "You've gotten used to thinking he was in one place. Now you're dealing with the idea that he might be somewhere else. But it might be somewhere else good. Maybe he's in jail where he belongs."

I managed to choke out a small bit of humor on that.

"That would be all right with me," I said.

"Hand me the phone book."

I did and she immediately picked up the phone.

I gasped.

"It's okay," she assured me.

"Hello, Mary Jane." She waited, listening to the person on the other end.

"Oh, hello, Cassie," she said. "This is Analisse Grey, I'm an old friend of the family. Is your mother home?"

Another pause.

"What about your dad? Is he at work?"

This time the silence from Analisse seemed to go on forever. My heart was in my throat. In my mind's eye I could see Burl, as he had been that day walking into my kitchen. Now in my imagined fears he was walking toward the phone to talk to Analisse. I couldn't let even his voice touch her. I reached out to grab the phone. She pulled away and began speaking.

"Oh, I am so sorry to hear that, Cassie," she said. "I didn't know. Listen I won't take up any more of your time. I'll call your mother back another day."

There were a few more polite words exchanged between the two before Analisse settled the phone into its cradle.

"He's dead," she told me.

"What?"

"That was his daughter. She says that he's dead," Analisse repeated. "He was killed in a car accident in 1964. He's been rotting in hell for a quarter of a century."

Intellectually I understood what she was saying. But emotionally, I couldn't quite accept it.

"He can't be dead," I insisted.

"Babs, this is good news," she told me.

I knew that it was. But I couldn't shake my very unsettled reaction to it. All these years when I'd been afraid, all those miles I'd driven quaking with the idea of happening upon him unexpectedly, all that time he'd been dead. My fear of him had nearly destroyed my life. But he hadn't been there to fear. He had died the same year that Marley had died. A few months before or a few months after, they'd both been gone for most of my life. It was disturbing that I hadn't known that. It was frustrating. But it was more. By the end of the day, I'd finally figured out what I was feeling. Anger.

I'd been cheated. In some deep-seated place in my soul, I'd imagined, against all reasonable possibility, that somehow, someday, someway, I would make Burl Grimes pay for what he did to me. That in the end, I would have justice. I would have vengeance. And the hope of that had somehow kept the hate alive in me.

But now, that hope was gone. Burl had escaped my wrath, my revenge. He had done what he had done. And now there never was nor would there ever be any opportunity for me to make it right.

I chuckled to myself as that thought went through my head. Did I actually think that anything could have made it right? If I had tied him down and done exactly to him as he had done to me, would I have felt better about it? Impossible.

Nothing could unring the bell. Nothing could return the woman that I'd become to that trusting place I'd been before he walked into my kitchen. But the woman that he'd broken all those years ago, could that woman be mended?

Without even the slightest consideration or weighing of risks, I drove over to the duplex as soon as I got off work. I had not been in that neighborhood since the day I'd scrambled out of there with my daughter and my secondhand dishes. But I found the place without so much as one wrong turn. If it hadn't set on the corner, I'm not sure I would have recognized it. The house was so much smaller, drabber, than I remembered. The yard was unkempt, as was much of the neighborhood. The screen door sagged miserably. Next to the street was a homemade sign that read: Duplex For Rent with a phone number below it. I parked at the curb and walked up to the back porch. There was no curtain in the door. I put my face up to the window and peered inside. The empty kitchen looked much the same. I reached down to turn the knob. It was locked, just as it should have been.

I just stood there. Remembering the first day I'd seen the place. Recalling when we'd moved in and how thrilled, anxious, excited, I'd been to have my own place. This place had been the first spark of life in me after Tom died. It had been like the Good Shepherd window. A way to get on in the world without thinking about what I'd lost. It had been me and Laney against the world. That was how hopeful it had begun. All of that had been overshadowed by how it had ended.

The back door on the adjacent porch, Mary Jane's porch, opened. An aging black man stepped out.

"Can I help you with something?" he asked me.

I didn't know quite what to say.

"You looking for a place to rent?" he tried again.

I manage to shake my head. "I used to live here," I explained.

A smile brightened his expression. "Is that right?" he said, assuming incorrectly that good memories had brought me back. "I've got the key, you want to look inside."

"Oh, no . . ."

"It's no trouble," he said, turning back in the house he called out to someone. "Shandra, bring that key by the front door, the one with the tassel on it." He turned back to me. "My granddaughter will show you inside."

The girl, about fourteen, opened the door for me and we walked around for a few minutes. The rooms were empty now. The furniture that had been part of the place had gone to some landfill years ago. The rooms were open, the walls were scarred, the floors were dirty. I kept waiting for some feeling to envelop me. Waiting for fear or flashback or relief or something. There was nothing. This was just an old house in an old neighborhood. It had nothing to do with what existed inside of me. Just as Burl had nothing to do with the fear that had held me prisoner in McKinney for so many years. He was already dead. He had been beyond the ability to hurt me. All that fear, I'd managed on my own.

"Thank you," I told the young girl and handed her a five-dollar bill. "Buy yourself a popcorn and soda next time you're at the movies."

"Thanks," she answered.

I walked out to my car, unlocked it and

got inside. I tried to take stock of what I was feeling. After a few moments I realized that I didn't feel anything at all.

That was good.

Laney

I had sex with Stan Kuhl on our first date. I don't say that with any pride of accomplishment. I had every intention of behaving like a proper and somewhat priggish McKinney matron. Especially after I found out that according to Nicie, every single woman in town was after him and half the married ones would dump their current husbands in a heartbeat if he looked in their direction. It's amazing how attractive money can make a man. With that in mind, my plan, if I had any kind of plan at all, was to simply be interested, but not that interested.

Unfortunately things got a bit out of hand.

My mother was home for once and eagerly agreed to babysit. It was a freebie, but I would have paid a lot not to hear her talk.

"Stan Kuhl," she said. Then a few moments later. "Stan Kuhl." Again. She kept repeating his name. What she didn't say, of course, was, *wasn't Stan Kuhl the guy I wanted you to hook up with, but he was way too far beneath you to even be considered.*

It just made me crazy the way Babs could imply an "I told you so" without even bothering with the words.

She also didn't say anything about my dress. It was several years old, from my prebaby days. It was red, short and clung to me like skin. I expected her to either comment on the age of the garment, the changes in my body since last I'd worn it, or to tell me, truthfully, that I looked like a slut.

When she didn't say anything, I was forced to goad her.

"Do I look like a slut in this dress?"

"You're not a slut, sweetie," she said. "You're a lovely young woman in the prime of her life."

"I didn't say I was a slut, I asked if I looked like one."

No comment.

"You think I look like a slut?"

"Laney, if you feel like you look like a slut," she said. "Then go change."

"I like this dress," I insisted.

"Then wear it," she said. "If you're comfortable with how you look, that's all that's important."

The woman was positively maddening.

Stan arrived exactly on time. He looked good. Not *GQ* good, more like *Parents* magazine good, but good nonetheless. I wanted to just run out the door with him. That would probably have been the smartest thing to do. But it's not what I did.

"Would you like to meet my daughter?" I asked.

"Sure," he said.

Rachel was already a little beauty. Her dark blond hair was thick and long, hanging down past her waist. She had a bright smile and chubby cheeks, very squeezable. She and Babs, along with Rachel's favorite stuffed animal Boogie Bear were having a lovely little tea. Stan and Babs exchanged polite greetings.

"This is Rachel," I told him. "Sweetheart, come and meet this nice gentleman."

My daughter didn't seem in any way eager to do so. Instead she clung to my leg and peered out at him from the safety of my skirt.

He squatted down to her level and offered his hand. "Hi, I'm Stan," he said.

Rachel didn't make any move toward him. But she did blush and giggle.

Stan looked up at me. "She's a flirt, just like her mother," he said.

"I'm not a flirt."

He looked back at Rachel. "Your mother claims to be a changed woman," he said.

She didn't understand him, but she was obviously pleased with the attention.

"I'm going to take your mom out," he said. "Feed her some dinner and talk to her a while. And I'll have her back here before you even miss her."

Rachel obviously believed him, because she didn't cry, scream, or throw a tantrum, all of which she was perfectly capable of doing. I got my jacket and we headed out into the night.

"Have a good time," Babs told us.

I was surprised at his car. It was nice, clean and new, but it was an ordinary sedan. A man with his money and position should have been cruising about town in a Mercedes or a Porsche. Even Robert's old BMW was flashier.

"I thought we'd drive into the city," he said.

"Not any restaurants good enough in McKinney?" I asked.

He hesitated before he answered. "Everybody in McKinney knows us," he said. "If we're seen together at any restaurant downtown the gossips will have us hooked up in twenty minutes. Poor Cindy Gilbert, I ran into her on Virginia Street one noon and bought her lunch. It was just a half hour of do-you-remember-old-what's-his-name and they're still talking about how I never called her back, dumped her after one date."

"So you're a heartbreaker these days."

"No," he said, firmly. "I'm not a heartbreaker. I'm not a player looking to score. I'm not a rich jerk out to buy some pretty arm candy. I'm not 'local nerd makes good' looking for revenge on the girls who scorned him in high school. I am ordinary Stanley Kuhl who'd like to take an attractive woman to dinner without becoming breaking news for bored McKinneyites."

"Okay," I agreed.

"I suspect you discovered that I'm not a computer salesman."

"Yes," I admitted. "I got the whole scoop, I guess. You married a college professor and it lasted about a semester. No kids, no ties, certifiably the most eligible guy in town."

He snorted skeptically at that. "I got the

lowdown on you, too," he said. "Eight years with the same guy. Two of them married. The oil bust busted you up."

I chuckled. "Who'd you hear that from?"

"Pete," he answered.

"I thought guys didn't gossip."

"We only share the facts, ma'am," he said. "Where'd you get your information?"

"My cousin, Nicie, filled me in."

"Ah, Nicie, how's she doing?"

"She's hanging in there," I said. "It's not easy, three kids and Brian acting like a jerk."

"Brian's not acting," he said. "He's always been a jerk."

"I heard he's running his father's business into the ground."

"He's just got it set on automatic pilot," Stan said. "Unfortunately that doesn't work well for long periods of time."

Our conversation continued like that. People we knew. Old times. We discussed the changes in McKinney, the efforts to make downtown flourish again and the pros and cons of its current fashion mall concept. We had already exhausted most of the inconsequential conversation topics by the time we parked in Dallas's Deep Ellum district. The formerly industrial area on the east side of downtown was the latest new hot spot in the city. Rapidly filling up with art galleries and nightclubs. It was not the kind of neighborhood I would have expected a prosperous yuppie to take a first date to impress her. We went down an alley and he directed me up a narrow flight of stairs.

"I've heard the ribs in this place are fabulous."

I nearly stopped dead in my tracks. Apparently Mr. Eligible Bachelor of McKinney had never heard that you don't feed a woman barbecue on the first date.

The place was dark and noisy and crowded. Stan got us a table in a corner next to a window that overlooked the brightly lit and busy pedestrian-only street below.

I have to admit it was fabulous. The food was, I believe, the best I'd ever consumed in my life. The taste was smoky and spicy, tender and juicy. And extremely messy. The few pitiful paper napkins they gave us couldn't begin to do justice to the amount of sauce I managed to get on my hands, my face.

As soon as I'd finished my dinner, I hurried to the bathroom to try to clean up. I felt sticky all over. I washed away virtually all my carefully applied makeup and had to scrub my arms practically all the way to my armpits.

Feeling at least clean and with nothing in my teeth, I returned to the table. The restaurant was now filled to the brim and I could hardly weave my way through to Stan in the corner. I arrived to find my chair had disappeared.

"I've moved you over here for safe-keeping," he said, indicating the chair that now sat right next to his.

I scooted in, finding myself all too close to him. I felt jittery, nervous, somehow exposed.

"Do you have any idea how attractive you are?" he whispered close to my neck.

I suddenly had this strange vision of myself. I imagined myself sitting in this crowded place, right beside him, but my little red dress had magically disappeared. I was casual, legs crossed sitting unnoticed in this noisy room wearing only my bra and panties, my thigh-highs and four-inch heels. Only Stan was looking at me. Only Stan could see me.

I tried to shake off the suggestive fantasy. My mouth was as dry as cotton. I was wet everywhere else.

"I think we'd better get this over with,"

he said. "I know you're as anxious about it as I am."

"What?" I managed to get out in one soft breath before his mouth came down on mine. The touch jolted me like a high-voltage wire. His mouth was on mine and I was on fire. We were kissing and kissing. I felt him trying to draw back, and dug my fingers into his lapels and pulled him tighter against me. In my mind's eye, I was down to just the stockings and heels and I couldn't get him close enough. I squeezed my thighs together tightly against the ache there that was getting out of control.

He wrenched himself away.

"Let's get out of here."

He threw some bills on the table and grabbed my arm. I was barely able to retrieve my purse before he dragged me out of the building. Out on the staircase, he pulled me into his arms and kissed me again. This time I could press my whole body against his. And I did.

"Oh, my God!" he kept saying. "Oh, my God! I can't believe this. I told myself it wouldn't be so good. Not like I remembered. I was just a kid. I imagined your kiss better than it could be. But I didn't and it isn't."

His words meant nothing to me. I

wanted his lips. I wanted his hands. I was on fire. I was in heaven.

"For Christsake, get a room!" somebody complained as they squeezed by us trying to enter the restaurant.

"Come on," Stan said. We hurried down the stairs. "We'll go to my place. No, that's an hour away. We'll find a motel."

We didn't make it that far. Maybe it was because it had been so long. Or maybe I really am a slut, but when we got to his car in the shadowed lot we started again. I was so ready, I so wanted him. I couldn't remember ever wanting a man more. He lifted me up until I sat on the car. I wrapped my legs around his waist. He was caressing my breasts. I jerked down the top of my dress, trying to make it easier for him. I let my hands explore the front of his trousers. What I found there was impressive and eager.

The moments were too frantic and our appetites too ravenous. He bent me forward over the passenger side of the car hood and we had desperate, aching, incredible sex that had me screaming my head off with appreciation.

After it was over, he managed to get the car door unlocked and we got inside, still breathing heavy, still half numb with pleasure and incredulity.

"I can't believe I had sex out in the open in a parking lot," I said.

"I'm never selling this car," he responded. "I want to be buried in this car."

We sat there together for long moments, catching our breath, talking, kissing. The kisses were more play now than passion, but just as pleasurable. He pulled my dress down to my waist and put little love bites on my nipples.

"I love how this dress just goes up or down so easily," he said. "It's quicker and more efficient than the drapes in my house."

"What happened to my bra?" I asked him.

"I think I threw it down," he said. "It's probably out on the pavement, I'll look for it before we go."

He feathered a long string of little nips and pecks from my breast up to my throat. And then he put his mouth on mine again, this time seriously. It was wonderful. I moaned aloud.

"You are so good at this," he said, as our lips parted.

"No, it's you," I said. "You're the one who's doing it."

"Me? I'd hardly even kissed a girl before

that day I kissed the Cotton Queen in that convertible," he said. "All these years, no woman I've ever kissed measured up."

"It was a very good kiss," I admitted. "It ranks pretty high."

"It does," he agreed. "But that sex, wow, Laney, you are way off the map."

I smiled with some pride, but some embarrassment, too.

"I'm not usually like that," I assured him. "It's just . . . it's just that it's been so long."

"I think we're going to have to test that statement," he said.

"Test it?"

"I don't suppose you're on the pill, or anything responsible and reasonable like that."

"I will be tomorrow," I assured him.

He nodded. "There's a box of condoms in the glove compartment," he said. "Why don't you get one out. I'll wear it and you can prove to me how boring you are having sex when it's only been a half hour since you had it last."

"You keep condoms in the car?" I asked.

"It's a brand-new package," he assured me. "I just bought them, with you in mind, I swear it."

"Pretty sure of yourself then?"

"Let's just say, I'm an optimist."

I got the prophylactic.

"We're doing it here in the car?" I asked.

"It's been lucky for us so far," he said.

He unzipped his pants and sheathed himself in the thin latex. "Come on, Laney," he said. "Climb on and show me how boring and ordinary sex with you can be."

I failed dismally at any attempt at that.

We didn't get home until the predawn hours. There was nobody on the streets of McKinney but the garbage trucks and the paperboy, but I knew that didn't mean that my arriving home at such a disgraceful hour would go unnoticed.

"Are you okay?" he asked me as he walked me to the porch.

"I'm a bit sore," I admitted. "But it kind of feels sort of good."

He chuckled. "Does this mean I can call you again?"

"You'd better, or I will be just like poor Cindy Gilbert."

"No," he said, feigning thoughtfulness. "Sex with Cindy was never this good."

My mouth dropped open in shock.

"Kidding," he assured me quickly. "I was just kidding."

I decided that he was.

At the front door, he gave me a sweet little smooch on the tip of my nose.

"I'd better go," he said. "Your mother may start flipping the lights off and on at any second."

I nodded. "She's probably sitting up for me in the living room at this very moment."

He laughed like it was a good joke.

She was waiting for me. But at least she was in the kitchen. And there was coffee.

Babs

I knew that Laney was having an affair with Stan. I didn't condemn her for it. In the years since she'd moved in with Robert, most of the world had changed on that issue. All over McKinney, and probably the rest of the country, couples were casually cohabiting with no consequences from the community. So, I didn't condemn her. I did worry about her. Feminism and equal rights may have changed the way women looked at the world. But I was afraid that how the world looked at women was not all that different.

I worried that making herself so available to him, no strings attached, made it easier and easier for him to avoid strings at all. If I'd been less interested in her happiness, I might have been able to keep my mouth shut. But I just kept talking and she didn't appreciate it at all.

"If you make that cow and milk state-ment again," she said. "I will have to kill you."

She'd just gotten home from another all-night date. I'd had to take Rachel to pre-school so she could get a shower and dress for her day on the job. She was working for Pete full-time now. And spending two to three nights a week keeping company with Stan Kuhl.

I poured the dregs of the coffee into my cup. "You can't go on like this," I said.

"If you don't like babysitting, just say so," she said, primly. "I can afford to have someone else do it."

"This is not about babysitting and you know it," I said. "You and Stan can't keep doing this."

"Doing what?" She feigned ignorance and then added crudely. "Oh, you mean screwing. Oh, yes, we can, Babs. We can do it a lot."

"You are not going to dissuade me from talking to you by being smutty," I told her. "It's time to either marry Stan or move along."

"My personal life does not concern you," she said, very focused and business-like.

"You're living in my house. I'm helping

raise your child," I pointed out. "And you'll always be my daughter. That gives me the right to speak my mind."

Laney rolled her eyes. "You never fail to take that opportunity, do you?"

"It's time for Stan to make things right," I said. "If he has any consideration for your reputation, he needs to show it now."

"Babs, women these days don't have reputations," she said with heaps of pithy condescension.

"You think they don't? You're on your way to being the next Judy Bykowski," I told her. "Is that what you want? Ned Hoffman would rather father a bastard than give her his name. Now she's living with Renny, cleaning his house and working in his businesses and Renny won't marry her, either."

"Maybe Judy wants to be single," she said.

I shrugged. "Who cares what Judy wants," I said. "I know you, Laney. I know what you're made of. I know what you went through with Robert. You want love, commitment, stability. Don't even try to pretend that you don't."

"I'd like to be married to Stan someday," she admitted.

"Someday is never going to happen unless you get firm with Stan, insist on making it official."

Laney's eyes narrowed. I knew I was really annoying her.

"What do you want me to do? Ask him to marry me? I thought you were opposed to women's lib. Isn't the man supposed to make the first move?"

"Yes," I told her. "And he will. But sometimes a fellow needs a little push."

"I have no intention of pushing anyone," Laney said. "I don't have to have a husband. I don't need a man to define my life. I'm not going to twist Stan's arm to make him conform to some expectation of yours. You don't know me, you don't know Stan, you don't know what you're talking about."

"I know that making yourself sexually available to a man who has no long-term commitment is the worst kind of low self-esteem behavior."

"Low self-esteem? Good grief, Babs, you're talking to me. I'm the woman in this room who actually *was* the Cotton Queen, not just runner-up pretending she was the real deal for all these years. When it comes to low-esteem issues, you're the clear winner there."

"I certainly have my problems," I admitted. "But I'm not some man's hussy on call, ready to drop my panties whenever it happens to be convenient for him."

"You look at everything through your own weird, warped view of the universe. You, drop your panties? Not a chance. Tell me, did you ever in your life have sex just because you wanted to?"

I felt myself blushing. "If I did I was very young," I told her truthfully. "And I'm certain that I never allowed my own carnality to trump my responsibility as the mother of a young child."

"Give me a break," Laney said. "My relationship with Stan doesn't hurt Rachel. She loves Stan. And he loves her."

I nodded. "I believe he does love her. But that's not enough to make him marry you. For that he has to love you."

"What a crappy thing to say!"

"What a crappy reality that it's time you faced," I shot back. "Has the man ever once told you that he loved you? Has he even mentioned marriage in casual conversation?"

Laney blanched and I knew I was exactly right. It was killing me to wound her. I felt I had no choice.

"Sweetie, I don't want to hurt you," I said. "I love you. But I worry that while you're wasting time making inroads on this highway to nowhere, you're not meeting any men who might actually want to marry you, to make a life with you. You're missing a man who might be interested in being more than Rachel's buddy, someone who'd be willing to be her daddy."

She shook her head, refusing to see it. "Stan and I are very happy with our relationship," she insisted. "We like where we are and how it's going. When the time is right to move things up another notch, we will. Until that time, you should just butt out. You're wrong about me and Stan. You've got it completely wrong."

But the weeks turned into months, turned into years and Stan made no move to elevate their now rather well-known affair to anything legitimate. I took no pride in having been right.

In the summer of 1991, the doctors came up with a new name for what ailed Doris. She'd been living with non-A, non-B hepatitis for almost five years when the specialist, Dr. Berlin informed Acee, with a bit too much self-congratulation I thought, that his wife was McKinney's first case of Hepatitis C, a heretofore unidentified strain of liver inflammation.

"How did she get it?" I asked Acee.

He shook his head.

We were sitting together in the hospital waiting room. He'd brought her into emergency. For several days her belly had been swelling and she looked six months pregnant, but she hadn't wanted to see the doctor. This morning when her brain was so foggy she couldn't figure out how to make the toaster work, Acee had finally convinced her that they had to have help.

"She doesn't have any of the risk factors for this," he told me. "She's never had a blood transfusion or used drugs. She's never had a sexually transmitted disease and she tests negative for all other types of hepatitis. The doctors are stumped. Doris simply shouldn't have this disease. But she does."

Acee looked tired. He looked old. He looked scared.

"The doctor assured me that this problem she has with thinking and remembering is temporary," he said. "The inability of her liver to function properly is causing toxins to build up. One of them is ammonia and it rises and accumulates in the brain, making her muddled."

I nodded, sympathetically.

"She isn't able to really eat anything," Acee continued. "She was down to ninety-three pounds before she started retaining all this fluid. Dorrie weighed one thirty-five when I married her."

"Oh, I'm sure she was lying to you about that," I told him, feigning snideness. "Doris weighed one hundred forty pounds if she weighed an ounce. Her hair alone probably accounted for half of that."

Acee chuckled. I was glad to give him even the briefest of respites from the worries that drained him.

"Thanks for coming here," he said to me. "I called the boys, they're both on the road. When I couldn't get Laney on the phone . . . well, I know it's probably not good manners to call my ex-wife to hold my hand. But you're the closest friend I could think of."

"I'm glad you called me," I assured him. "And you're right, we've always been close friends."

The disease, or what they knew about it, seemed very confusing and complicated. It progressed very slowly, they assured us, but Doris was very far along. They'd only just discovered its existence, but she may have been walking around with it for twenty years. They could treat it with interferons, but the prognosis for someone Doris's age with her level of infection was very bad.

"The way I like to explain the liver," Dr. Berlin said, "is that it's like a window screen. It has lots of little bitty holes. Fluids pass through the liver the way air passes through the window screen. Now, if a fly hits that window screen and dies there, well that plugs up a few holes, but doesn't really affect the airflow enough to notice. This hepatitis C is like a huge swarm of flies hitting the screen and dying there. There's so many tiny fly corpses, that everything just backs up on either side, practically nothing gets through."

Dr. Berlin's folksy explanation may have worked wonderfully on ignorant, uneducated country people, unfamiliar with modern medicine. I found it condescending at best. And the image of poor Doris filled up with dead flies was extremely disturbing to me and not a bit comforting to Acee.

It was midafternoon when her sons arrived. I waited in the hallway so they could have time with their mother alone. Laney showed up, anxious and frazzled.

"I was in and out of meetings all day," she told me. "I saw Acee's number on my phone, but I figured he was just calling me to set up a lunch."

"It's okay, Laney," I told her. "You're

here for him now and I know he appreciates it."

That was true. When he came back to the waiting room, she ran into his arms. He held her tightly and cried against her hair.

I know that some would say I treated Acee unfairly when I married him. I had even felt that way myself many times, stung by my own guilt. But at that moment, seeing the relationship between father and daughter, I knew that I'd given Acee a gift, a very valuable gift. For that alone, our marriage had been worth it.

Later that evening they did a needle aspiration of Doris's distended belly. They drew off a liter of fluid making her much more comfortable and able to sleep.

I held her hand and sat with her while the three men and Laney were huddled in the corner, in consultation with the doctor.

"At this point, the only thing I can suggest is a liver transplant," he told them.

"They transplant livers?" Laney asked. "I've only heard about hearts and kidneys."

"It's new," the doctor admitted. "There are only a few hospitals in the country that perform the operation. I'd recommend Johns Hopkins in Baltimore."

"All right," Acee said. "So we take her to Baltimore? In an ambulance or what?"

"No, we'll put Mrs. Clifton on the transplant waiting list," he said. "I can get her listed there tonight. We keep her here a few days to get her stabilized then we'll send her home."

I could hear Acee's sigh of relief from across the room.

"She gets to come home," he said.

"Yes," Dr. Berlin told him. "If . . . when she gets close to the top of the list, you two can fly up there and wait nearby."

"Mom's never been that far from home before," her eldest son pointed out.

In fact, she never did go that far.

Doris got better and went home. She followed the doctor's instructions to the letter, trying to get ready for the surgery. It was as if she were in training for the Olympics, and Acee with her. Doris took medication. Watched her diet. She walked every day. She had a couple of bouts of peritonitis and returned to the hospital several times to have fluid buildup drawn off. But she seemed to be getting better.

Then it was all over. She awakened Acee in the middle of the night and told him that something was very wrong, her back felt hot along the line of her kidneys and her lungs were congested like a really bad cold.

He raced her to the hospital. Within an hour she'd slipped into a coma. She died the next day.

Laney

Sometimes you lose people before you ever fully realize how much they mean to you. That's how it was with Doris. She was more than just the woman my stepfather had married. In my life she'd been the unmother, the grown-up, worldly-wise female who, unlike my real mother, always knew the right things to say and when to say them.

"Don't you worry," she told me once. "Stan really loves you. How can he help it, you're so good for him. Just give the boy time. I was in love with Acee almost twenty years before he ever thought of marrying me. And most of that time he was married to somebody else."

I knew she was right. I knew she was. But in the deepest, darkest part of my heart, I feared Babs might be right, too. Stan had gotten comfortable in our relationship. He liked having me as his . . . ah . . . girlfriend? too old . . . companion? too young . . . date? too insignificant . . . lover? too much information. I feared that I was, as Babs had so unkindly phrased it, his hussy on call.

That wasn't really true, either. Our relationship was a good deal more involved than just sex. And Stan never said anything to indicate that that was the major role I played in his life. I was beside him on civic occasions as well as family ones. We took vacations together at Port Aransas. And shared chaperone duties on a Sunday School trip to Six Flags. He showed up at Rachel's soccer games and patiently sat through her piano recital. And at Doris's funeral, he was at my arm, quietly, considerately making himself available for whatever I needed. It was more than a lot of women expected from their husbands.

You should be happy with what you have! I admonished myself. *He's a great guy and he genuinely likes and cares for you. That should be enough.*

It wasn't.

I was tired of living with my mother, but I'd put off getting my own place. Every time I thought of moving, I thought of moving into Stan's house. I'd never bothered to change my name, I was still going by Laney Jerrod. I hated that, but I didn't want to be Laney Hoffman, I wanted to be Laney Kuhl. I was only thirty-three, I was still young enough to have children. I wanted a brother or a sister for Rachel. Stan was the kind of guy who ought to be married. Why didn't he ask me? It was a mystery. Could I just wait around indefinitely until he decided to tie the knot? Could I risk having him decide to tie it with some woman other than myself?

How do you get a man to marry you?

I thought about the way I got Robert to propose. Just the idea of Stan with another woman made me physically sick to my stomach. I don't know how I'd forgiven Robert. I don't know how we lived over that betrayal. But I knew I'd rather stay single than see Stan with someone else.

After the prayers at the cemetery, Doris's flower draped casket was lowered into the ground. Her sons and their wives joined Acee in the black limo, I hung back. Not wanting to leave Stan behind.

"Let's walk," I said to him.

As nearly a hundred McKinney citizens made their way to cars, Stan and I strolled among the gravestones in silence.

I didn't really know my way around the

cemetery. I'd never spent much time there. I'd certainly never wandered aimlessly reading headstones as I did now. So I certainly surprised myself at having walked directly to my father's grave. *Thomas Henry Hoffman, 1939–1962*

"This is my dad," I said to Stan.

He wrapped an arm around my waist. "You were very young when he died. Do you even remember him?"

"Yes, a little," I admitted. "Most of what I remember is when he died."

"I guess that makes sense," Stan said. "Really strong emotional moments would make more vivid memories than day to day ones."

"I guess that's why my mother didn't want Rachel at the service. We had a big fight about it last night."

"I'm so sorry," Stan said.

I shrugged. "I'd wanted her to come with us, because she and Doris had been close," I explained. "I thought Rachel deserved some closure. I just hated the idea that Doris would just disappear without a trace and she'd not understand why."

"Yeah, that does seem very sad," he said.

"Babs went ballistic when I mentioned it. She has very strong feelings about kids and funerals. I remembered how she'd fought to keep me away from my father's. She lost her own parents when she was young, I guess she knew that the image of Doris in that open casket would be the one that stayed with Rachel all her life."

"Your mom is a very wise woman," he said.

I nodded, accepting that, in some ways, that was very true.

"You'd better not sing her praises too highly," I said, turning the conversation. "She doesn't have your best interests at heart."

"What do you mean?" he asked, smiling, recognizing the teasing note in my voice.

"She keeps nagging me to get you to the altar," I said, smiling a little too broadly and feeling as if I was perched on a high wire without a net.

His expression changed abruptly to something indecipherable.

A silence lingered between us.

"Are these your grandparents?" he asked, indicating the newer Hoffman graves next to my father's.

"Yes," I said. "Grandma died the year Rachel was born and Grandpa only lived a few months after."

"And this little grave with the lamb?"

"That's my brother," I said. "He died as a baby."

Stan nodded.

"So, do you need to go back to Acee's house?" he asked me. "I really need to get back to the office."

"Sure, drop me off at my place and I'll get my own car," I told him.

We walked back across the cemetery to where we were parked. I kept smiling, talking, pretending everything was fine. My heart was breaking. He really wasn't going to marry me. I was just his . . . whatever I was. And I was never going to be anything more.

I truly didn't understand it. Every moment we spent together was a testament to his love for me. But he never spoke the words and he never asked for anything permanent.

Over the next few days and weeks, I tried not to care.

I was determined to focus my life on my daughter and my job. Each was, in its own way, perfectly capable of absorbing every moment of my attention. Rachel was the star of her preschool. She had a better vocabulary than most kindergartners. And she'd taught herself to read because Babs kept falling asleep during her bedtime stories.

At work, things were buzzing. The company was in the forefront of creating software programs to capture and clean code with Y2K errors. Back when computers had been new, the internal operating codes were designed with six-figure date bars. March 12, 1965, was stored as 031265. Storage space for detail was at a premium and this seemed perfectly all right. That is until someone began to ask what would happen when January 2000 rolled around. Would the computer think it was January 1900? And if so, what kind of errors might that generate? Everything was hypothesized from bank systems failing to planes falling out of the sky, even to computers inadvertently launching nuclear missiles.

A change was easily rectified in the new systems, but there were so many old systems still in use. Pete had us pouring more and more of our time, our energies and our staff into the project.

It was at this point that he took me aside.

"Laney, I just need a clear signal from you," my cousin told me. "You have the talent and the ability to be a major player in this company. But executive levels are never part-time or even full-time. They require a complete life commitment."

"Pete, you know I have a daughter," I pointed out.

He nodded. "That's why I'm telling you this," he said. "I want you to achieve your ambitions. I know you would be good for my company. But you're important to me as a friend and relative as well as an employee. I don't want you to make a choice here that you can't live with."

"You're only saying this because I'm a woman," I told him. "Men have families and they don't drag them down."

"Don't they?" he said. "Name me one chief exec in this country who is raising a child on his own. I'm not aware of any, even among the group that could afford an entire platoon of nannies. The ones that are married don't even spend time raising their children. They have clear division of labor with their wives. Believe me, I know what I'm talking about."

I'm sure he thought that he did. He and Sadie had been having a rocky time of it the last few years. She was as successful at her practice as he was with his business. Their children were all teenagers now, a difficult time for parents everywhere, but especially so when both are consumed by jobs they love.

"Think about it, Laney," he said. "It's

not about the status of women in America, leading the feminist march through the glass ceiling or even having it all. It's about you and Rachel, your little family. Forget about what you've always wanted and try to figure out what it is you want right now. I'll back you either way."

I appreciated his support, though I had little time for life introspection. I was back to working very long hours. I'd put in a full day at the office, come home for family time with Rachel and then after she'd gone to bed, I'd pull out my laptop and work until the wee hours of the morning.

Maybe all that was on purpose. I had very little time left for a man in my life.

And the man in my life seemed to have very little time left for me. Stan seemed to be even busier than I was. I did wonder if perhaps he was just seeing someone else, but whenever I'd call him, he was at work. Something was going on with his company, but he never talked about it. At first, I just thought it must be a stressful business cycle. But when it didn't seem to let up and Stan continued to be silent, stoic and wound very tightly, I finally mentioned it to Pete.

"I think the only person in the country working longer hours than you and me has got to be Stan," I told him one evening as we were leaving work after 8:00 p.m.

"Yeah, he's in a pickle, all right," Pete said. "I hope he didn't give you a piece of the business for Christmas last year."

He chuckled and I smiled, but I had no clue what he was talking about.

I couldn't help thinking about it, though.

By the time I got home, Rachel was already in bed, but she'd waited up to kiss me good-night.

Babs, who'd had a long day herself, headed for the TV in the den.

"I'm going to watch Sipowicz and go to bed," she told me, referring to the lead character in *NYPD Blue*, her favorite nighttime drama.

"Okay, I'm going to work on a few things," I said.

But ultimately, I couldn't. My mind kept going over and over what Pete had said.

I got on the Internet and pulled up the Web page for Kuhl Computers. No help there. It was all fancy flash sequences, the only information was about the capabilities of the machines. No financials were listed at all. Since it was a privately held company, there were no stock prices to graph. And even a search of news stories about the company revealed nothing. But something was happening.

Pete knew about it and assumed that I knew, too.

He assumed that I knew, because I should know. I was Stan's *whatever* and he should share important stuff with me. But he hadn't. In fact, as I thought about it, he hadn't said much to me about anything lately. What did that mean?

I grabbed up my keys and a minute later I was walking to the car. As I drove down the street toward his house, it occurred to me that, like Robert, I might find him with some silicone sister. That thought was terrifying enough to get my foot off the gas pedal. But then I remembered Pete's words. If big things were happening and I wasn't in on it, then Stan had already left me. And I might as well find out about it.

There was no car with a "Perfect 10" license plate in front of his house. The lights were all on, although it was now after eleven o'clock. Not a typical time to drop in for a visit. I rang the doorbell.

He answered dressed in a T-shirt and pajama bottoms. His hair was mussed and he looked tired, but I was sure that he hadn't been asleep.

"Laney? What are you doing here?"

"I'm beginning to wonder about that

myself," I told him. "May I come in, or do you just want to have this conversation on the porch."

He stepped away from the door and motioned me inside. Once he'd closed it behind me, he sighed heavily.

"Who told you?" he asked.

Not your best icebreaker.

"Nobody has told me, that's the problem," I said.

"I always knew it could happen," he said. "This didn't catch me unawares. The potential was always out there and I thought that if it ever did turn out badly, well, I'd just start all over. It wouldn't matter that much, I'd be none the worse for wear. But then we came together and the stakes got higher. Damn, Laney, I'm sorry. I'm really sorry."

I could hardly breathe.

"So there is someone else?" I managed to get out.

His brow furrowed.

"Someone else?" He looked at me quizzically for a moment and then shook his head. "No, no," he said. "I resisted all offers. Maybe I shouldn't have. I might have got out clean with plenty of start-up in my pocket. I knew if they couldn't buy it they'd kill it."

Buy it? Kill it? They who? I was confused.

"Wait a minute," I said. "Just wait a minute. Are you breaking up with me or what?"

He stood suddenly perfectly still. I watched him swallow. Then he raked a hand through his hair and heaved a sigh. "If that's what you want, Laney," he said. "I don't have the energy for a big, scary blowup. If that's what you want, then suit yourself."

He stalked off into the house. I stood there alone in the foyer for a moment before I followed him. I found him in the dining room. The area had been turned into a giant office. Files and paperwork completely hid the six-foot-long table. On the sideboard, he'd set up a whole line of computers hooked together paralleling.

"What are you working on?" I asked. "A moon shot?"

"It's not a joke," he said. "I may be going down, but I'm going to make this the foulest, most bitter poison pill those bastards have ever tried to swallow."

"Stan, stop, look at me."

He did.

"I still don't know what is going on? What's happening here?"

For an instant I thought that he wasn't going to tell me. He moved away from me again. But then he returned to face me. "As you've undoubtedly suspected I'm losing my company," he said.

"What?"

"The *bigs* have quietly, unofficially gotten together and conspired to run the little guys out of the industry. You may have been too busy to notice, but the price of new computers has been falling dramatically for months. Businesses are out there spending lavishly, getting new equipment ahead of Y2K. But instead of profits, instead of supply and demand, the big computer makers have slashed prices and are taking losses. They have deep pockets and can afford to do that. It's a strategy to increase market share. My pockets are not so deep. I never planned for my company to sell computers to every mom or high school kid. These machines weren't designed to sit on the secretaries' desks for checking e-mail. These are high-quality, high-function tools, primarily for engineers and scientists. What Vincent was to motorcycles, I wanted to be for computers. But apparently even geeks are not immune to pricing strategies."

There was a sigh in his voice and a

slump in his shoulders.

"If I'd gone public, they might have taken me over. The name might have survived, but I'm pretty sure the quality wouldn't have. So I'm gone. And all this . . ." He spread his arms indicating all the controlled chaos around him. "Well, I'm making sure that every jiggle I've ever done to make my machine better, has my patent on it. It won't stop them from pilfering what they want, but at least it will make it more complicated."

"Why are you doing it here? Why aren't you at your office and why don't you have some help?"

"I'm not the only one who knows we're going down," he said. "I have seventy employees that realize they're going to be looking for work very soon. They are good people, loyal and hardworking. But their families come first. I can't put them completely in the know and then expect that they wouldn't use their information to gain favor and employment with another firm."

"So you're doing it all yourself."

He nodded. "Pretty much."

"I'll help," I told him.

"I can't ask you to do that," he said.

"Why not? I hope you don't think that I would steal your secrets."

Stan shook his head. "I just know you've already got your hands full at your own job."

I shrugged. "Pete will give me the time if I ask for it. The advantage of working for a family business. In the morning, I'll ask for it."

"Are you sure?" he asked.

"Never more sure of anything in my life."

We worked the rest of that night and most of the morning. We collapsed into bed together just before noon. I got up to pick Rachel up from school. I took her with me back to Stan's house. And she splashed around in his pool and built a fort of towels and lawn chairs in the backyard until Babs came to get her.

It took two more days like that before Stan felt comfortable about the patents and was ready to start deconstruction of the company.

"Instead of flooding the market with the last of my inventory," he said, "I'm going to hold it back. I think there may be collectors, ultimately, that may be interested in it. And if I'm not relying on last-minute sales to pay off debt, then I can be up-front with the staff."

I nodded, sad for him.

"You'd better go back to your own office,"

he said. "Before one of my good employees convinces Pete to let them do your job."

I laughed, threw my arms around his neck and stood on my tiptoes to give him a kiss.

His reaction was a bit less than enthusiastic, but I convinced myself that his mind was still completely engaged with business matters. We'd get our relationship back on track as soon as things began to calm down a little.

I went back to my own work as he made his official announcement, made financial arrangements to sever his employees, got his equipment and real estate on the market. Another company, down in Round Rock, was positioning itself to take on the *bigs*. They absorbed much of the Kuhl workforce. So although those people had to leave McKinney, they did, for the most part, find good jobs doing the work they'd been trained for.

The whole dismantle took less than six months. Kuhl Computers went the way of the Studebaker and the Moped.

Stan did a lot of traveling. I assumed on business. He didn't talk much about the future or what his plans were. And he still seemed distant.

On a Saturday in early October, he returned from a trip. I knew he was home and I just kept pacing the floor.

Babs couldn't ignore it. "What are you doing?" she asked me. "Trying to drive me crazy?"

"I'm . . . waiting on a phone call," I said.

"Who from?"

"From Stan, if it's any of your business," I said.

"It's not any of my business," she agreed. "Of course, it's hard not to notice that the man is never around much anymore."

"If you're going to make some snide comment about how badly I've handled our relationship and how stupid I've been to get involved so deeply without any commitment on his part, well . . . well just don't. I know what a mess I've made of my life, I don't need you to tell me."

Babs was silent for a long moment.

"At the risk of being argumentative," she said finally, "I don't think you've made a mess of your life. You're raising a wonderful daughter, you have an impressive career and you've found a lot of personal happiness. Most women never manage so much. But I think you're being silly to sit around here waiting for him to make a move. Who taught you that you can't just call him?"

"You did," I pointed out.

"And what did I ever know about men?" she asked me.

I walked over, picked up the phone and dialed his number. He answered on the third ring.

"Hi," I said. "Did you just get home?"

He made a few comments about the trip. Inquired politely about Rachel and things at my office.

I suggested that we have dinner.

"I'm really tired," he said.

"Let me come over to cook something for you," I suggested.

"No, no, that's not necessary. I'll just fix a bowl of soup and go to bed."

I hesitated a second and then glancing over at Babs, seated at the kitchen table, I screwed up my courage.

"That sounds good to me, I'll be right over." I hung up before he had a chance to comment.

I ran upstairs, repaired my makeup and brushed my hair, assuring myself that I was as attractive as a thirty-four-year-old single mother and former McKinney Cotton Queen could be.

"Wish me luck," I said to Babs on my way out.

"Laney, you don't need luck," she assured me. "You're a bright, hardworking and determined individual. You're also a caring, giving and empathetic woman. If a man can't fall in love with that, then he's simply unworthy of you. And if you'll remember, I thought Stan was the right one, long before you ever got the idea."

By the time I got to Stan's house, I was determined. No more tiptoeing around things. This was going to be the showdown. He was swimming laps in the pool. I didn't wait for him to get out and dry off. As soon as he pulled up to the side, I went directly to it.

"What is wrong with this relationship?" I asked him.

"Huh?"

"You've been pushing me aside for months now," I said. "I thought it was someone else. Then I thought it was just the problems with the business. Now I don't know what to think."

At first it seemed as if he wasn't even going to answer. He turned his back on me and went to the ladder. He climbed out and got a towel.

"Think what you want," he said.

"What do you mean by that? What's going on?"

"I guess I'm waiting for the other shoe to

drop," he said. "I lost the business, so I'm waiting for what comes next."

I just stared at him, wondering what he was talking about.

"What comes next?" I asked him.

"Look, Laney," he said. "I know that I'm a nice guy, but I'm not exactly hunk of the planet. When I was trotting around town with lots of cash in my pockets, women were interested in me. Not geeky women, like my ex-wife. Gorgeous women, like yourself. Those women who never gave me a second look when I was selling ice-cream cones at the drugstore. Now my fifteen minutes is over. I'm not in bad shape. I've still got this house, I'm not in debt and I think I've still got a few good ideas that I might be able to make a living on. But I'm not Daddy Warbucks anymore. I'm more like M. C. Hammer."

"So? Do you think that makes a difference to me?" I asked him.

He shrugged. "Well, it sounds like you dumped your husband when he went bankrupt."

"What?"

"That's what Pete said," he told me. "I didn't want to believe that about you, but I kidded you about it once and you didn't deny it. I'm . . ." He hesitated for a mo-

ment, then his chin came up, almost de-
fiant. "I'm just as down now as he was
then."

I was hearing him, taking it in, finally
getting it.

"You're right," I said. "This situation is
much the same situation as what happened
with Robert. You'll be starting over with
little or nothing. I've been used to nice
gifts, fancy evenings and expensive
weekend getaways. I have a child to support, a life to live, dreams I want to fulfill.
All of that was true with Robert and with
you. But you know, there is a big difference
between the two relationships."

He looked at me, a question in his eyes.

"I'm in love with you, Stan," I told him.
"And I don't believe that I was ever in love
with him. I know he wasn't in love with
me. But I'd kind of thought that you were."

"I am," he said. "I am in love with you."

"Then prove it," I said.

"Prove it? How?"

"Marry me. Live with me. Be a father to
my daughter, give me more children to be
her brothers and sisters. Make a life with
me, Stan. A life for better or worse, richer
or poorer, until death do us part."

Cotton Days
McKinney, Texas
2004

Laney watched as her beautiful daughter, Rachel, now seventeen, stared at the tea leaves in the bottom of her cup. She was so young and so sweet. She was smart as the dickens, but Laney worried that she was naive. It was so easy for any girl her age to be deluded by popularity and image. Laney felt compelled to impress upon her the importance of having her dreams rooted in reality.

"It's tempting," she said. "Very tempting, to get carried away with all the attention. As a young woman you want to believe that because you're a nice person, a good person and attractive as well, that you're special and that the world just falls at your feet," Laney said. "You get chosen as Cotton Queen, you wear a crown on your head, people applaud and you live happily ever after. That's not how it is. Life is not a fairy tale or a romance novel. If you start out believing that it is, you're doomed to disappointment."

Rachel rolled her eyes.

"Mom, I'm not an idiot," she said. "I know it's not that simple. Adversity, injustice, tragedy, I see those things — even in high school. I know they're there. But I can't see how walking around, anticipating them, is going to make living with them any easier."

"No," her mother agreed. "I suppose it's not. I just worry about you buying into this outmoded queen image."

Rachel chuckled and shook her head. "Believe me, Mom, I don't feel much like a queen," she admitted. "I feel like a gawky, awkward kid, pretending to be a queen."

Her mother laughed. "Now that's the most honest thing I've heard anybody say about this in weeks," she said.

"Is this the way you felt?"

"Yes, I think it was," Laney said.

"Mom, I've noticed that it's a new millennium," Rachel told her. "I'm not into some weird retro subset. I just think it's kind of cool to get all dressed up and wear a crown and pretend to be royalty for a day. It's fun. It's like a part in a play. It doesn't mean that I'm not going to college and become a scientist or a journalist or a photographer. I know I'm going to spend most of my life working on particle physics or accounting or practicing law. Someday I want to get married and have a family. I know that's my real life, Mom. But this, this is just a day out of ordinary time. It's just for giggles and a great page in my scrapbook. And I'd really like you to be there with me."

Laney sat across the table from her daughter, wavering. This sweet, little child, her baby, that she'd brought into the world when she'd felt so very much alone had managed, almost in a whisper of time, to grow into a beautiful and wise young woman.

"We won!" The screech came from the doorway as two rambunctious screaming boys tumbled out onto the deck. They both held up small trophies of faux-gilded plastic. The younger of the two, stuck his right in front of Laney's face.

"Look, Mom, look," he said. "Read it."

Laney complied. "Cotton Days Soccer Tournament 2004, Eight to Ten Year Olds Division, First Place."

"First Place!" he repeated.

"Very good, Connor," she said.

"He sat on the bench most of the game,"

his older brother related, unkindly. "He's the worst player on the team. I scored two goals, Mom. Two."

"That's very good, Thomas," she said. "I'm always proud when you do your best. And I'm sure Connor did his best, as well."

The older brother snorted. "Too bad for him that a guy can't *read* his way to a championship."

"Stupid jock," Connor shot back.

"Connor," Laney said, firmly. "We do not use that word to each other in this house."

"We can't say jock?" Thomas asked, deliberately misunderstanding. "Don't worry, Mom. I'd never say that about my kid brother."

The two boys were very alike physically, Thomas just a taller version of Connor, but their personalities and interests were as different as night and day. Connor had all his father's geeky brilliance. Thomas was, Laney suspected, a throwback to the Hoffmans. Athletic and good with his hands, he would protect his brother and sister against anything in the world. But he would also spend most of his time with them being a major annoyance.

Across the table Rachel sighed with impatience.

Thomas heard the sound and turned his attention to her.

"Hey, if it isn't the Rotten Queen, all done up for the big day," he said. "What's with the hair? Are you trying to trap small animals in there?"

"Eat dirt," she responded.

Thomas reached out and grabbed a curl of her carefully perfected updo and jerked it down from the elegant coiffure.

Rachel screamed. Thomas laughed and tried to run away. Stan arrived just in time to catch everybody in midargument and sorted out crime and punishment. Thomas was sent to his room. Connor grabbed a book and made himself scarce. Rachel and Laney went upstairs to repair the damage.

When Laney returned to the deck to collect the dishes, Stan was seated where Laney had been. She sat down across from him with a heavy sigh.

"Her royal highness is not completely damaged," she reported. "Though her supply of brotherly love may have been bruised."

"They say eleven is the hardest year," he said to her.

"Yeah, if we can just hold on until he's sixteen then we can stop worrying," she teased.

Stan chuckled.

"Rachel looks wonderful," he said. "She's going to be the prettiest queen since . . . well since I was driving in the parade."

"Flatterer."

"Just being honest," Stan said. "About both my wife and my daughter. Rachel has turned out to be a very pretty girl. And she's got a good head on her shoulders, with or without the fancy hairdo."

"Yes, I think she does," Laney admitted.

"And she has excellent taste," he added. "Wait until you see the dress she and I picked out. It's going to look fabulous."

"Dress? What dress?"

"Your dress."

"Stanley?"

"Truth is, I just couldn't see you turning her down," he said. "You're going to love the dress. It's your color, a kind of deep scarlet, the exact shade of red roses."

"Stan, I have made it absolutely clear from the beginning that I was not going to be in this parade."

"They need you for the float."

"Why do they have to have a float?" she asked. "In my day riding in a convertible was elegant enough."

"Well, time marches on," he said. "Now

there's a big float and if you're not on it, there'll be a big empty spot."

"I don't want to," Laney said stubbornly.

Stan shook his head. "Just because it was your mother's idea doesn't mean you're allowed to disappoint your daughter."

"You know how I feel about this entire queen extravaganza," she said.

"I do," he said. "And I know how much you want to protect Rachel from it. Just like Babs tried to protect you from things that she didn't care for. You are so much like your mother."

Laney's eyes narrowed dangerously.

Stan laughed.

And so it was that two hours later, Laney stood on a sidewalk near downtown dressed in a vivid red dress that was a bit too loose in the top and a bit too tight in the hips.

"You'll be sitting down," Rachel said. "Nobody will notice."

The float, made of white pom-pom bows on the top of sticks was meant to represent a cotton field ready for harvest. It had waves of hills, each higher than the other and three chairs. Around the lowest one the sign read, *Barbara Quarles, 1956.* The one in the middle, *Alana Hoffman, 1975.* And at the top a huge, glorious looking throne that read, *Rachel Jerrod, McKinney Cotton Queen, 2004.* Rising up from the back of the throne was a huge banner that ran the width of the float. *Three Generations of Cotton Days Royalty.*

"I feel like an idiot," Laney said under her breath.

"Well, you look fabulous," Babs said beside her.

She looked over at her mother. "Thanks," she said. "You look very nice yourself."

Babs was gowned in royal purple, a small tiara on her head. "I brought one of these for you," she said.

Laney shook her head. "I don't want to wear a crown," she said.

"Please?" Babs asked. "It will look silly if I wear one and you don't. And I need the accoutrement. There are bound to be some people in this crowd old enough to remember that I wasn't actually the Cotton Queen in 1956."

"Aunt LaVeida passed away three years ago," Rachel said. "I think that clause about when the queen can't fulfil her duties definitely comes into effect."

"Wear it," Babs pleaded.

Laney hesitated.

"Come on, Mom," Rachel said, overruling whatever deliberations her mother was still making. "Scrunch down."

Laney allowed her daughter to secure the rhinestone decorated circle upon her head.

"There," Rachel said. "You really look like a queen."

"She always did," Babs piped in behind her.

"Okay beautiful ladies," Acee said as he came up beside them carrying a step-ladder. "Time to load up. The queen goes first."

Rachel scampered up the steps and then held up her acres of pale pink organza as she carefully climbed the hills to her seat at the top. Under the voluminous feminine skirt she had on well-worn sneakers.

Laney, in heels, stepped more carefully and settled into her place.

Acee offered his hand to Babs.

"You are more beautiful today than you were all those years ago," he told her.

To the surprise of everyone, including Acee, she wrapped her arms around her ex-husband's neck and kissed him.

Laney's jaw dropped open at the unprec-edented display of affection. When her mother shot a glance toward Rachel, Laney turned as well, just in time to see her daughter give Babs an enthusiastic thumbs-up.

In the distance they could hear the high school band begin to play.

"We're starting," someone called out.

But it was still several, nervous minutes before the huge float began to inch its way down the street.

It had been so many years and so much had happened, so many things had changed. The population was twice the size of what it had been the last time Laney paraded through the streets. Downtown McKinney once abuzz with hardware stores, shoe shops, banks and butchers was now an antiques Mecca, the preferred shopping day-trip for affluent Dallasites. The quaint old buildings and cute lunch counters were now more familiar to tourists than the locals. But amongst the applauding throngs of strangers in the square were faces well-known to the women riding the float.

Renny had cordoned a full section in front of one of his buildings for the seniors from Aunt Maxine's center. Maxine sat in the middle of them. She was still in her wheelchair since her fall last spring, but she was excited and waving eagerly as they passed. Renny and Judy had been happily married for ten years. They were now pillars of the local business community. If anyone remembered their rocky start, it was never mentioned. Home from college for the summer was their son, "Big" Bykowski, a former McKinney High School basketball star, now on athletic scholarship at St. John's. Laney always had a soft spot for the cheerful, well-adjusted kid who was a taller, more muscular version of the faded photo of Laney's dad.

Halfway up the block, she spotted Pete. He was all alone and looking gray and older than his years, but he was smiling. That was good to see. When the dot-com bubble burst, his business had been forced to restructure and downsize. He managed to hang on to a small niche market that he'd kept in operation, but he lost a lot, more than just money and power. He and Sadie had finally called it quits. They were both still in town, neither dating, but everyone expected imminent divorce.

In front of the old Ritz theater Laney saw Nicie and Cheryl. She'd expected to see Nicie today, who was now remarried and helping her husband run a restaurant out on the lake. She was still Laney's best friend and the two tried to have lunch together every week. But Cheryl was someone who folks in McKinney rarely saw. In fact, Laney suspected that those who were seeing her now probably didn't recognize her. Pumped up, with a mannish haircut and an armful of hunky tattoos, she looked more like her brother, Ned, than the young woman they'd gone to school with. Ned had drowned a decade earlier. Out fishing on the lake and stoned on methamphetamine, he'd apparently become disoriented and jumped out of the boat to swim to shore.

As they rounded the corner near the old bank building, Laney spied her husband, Stan, and their two young sons. The boys were hooting and hollering, as was their nature. Stan was busy snapping photos with the digital camera. She waved and she smiled. He lowered the shiny metal box from his view and just gazed at her for a long moment. Laney felt the love and tenderness in that look spread over her like warm molasses.

He turned then, prompting the boys. The two grabbed up something behind them and came running into the street. As if on cue, the driver stopped the procession and waited as the two young Kuhl brothers delivered a long-stemmed yellow rose to each of the three women on the float.

Thomas sort of tossed his up to Rachel whose clean catch was probably due to summer softball. Connor was so short that Babs got up from her seat and went over to retrieve the flowers he carried. She kissed her grandson on the top of his head, embarrassing him completely. Then as she returned to her throne, she handed the second rose to Laney.

"Thank you for doing this," Babs said to her.

"Thank you for making me," Laney replied.

Babs took her seat and the giant crepe paper barge began sailing down the street once more.

In the distance the band played, the twirlers tossed batons, the soldiers marched with flags, the clowns rode on go-carts, the cowboys on horseback, onlookers ate sno-cones and the queens waved and smiled. Laney had never felt like a queen. That's what she'd told her daughter. And she didn't feel like one now. Maybe that's what this was all about. Coming to the realization and appreciation that, after all the rush of celebration, the excitement of being the center of attention, the glamour of an elegant gown, the fantasy of reigning over friends and neighbors, after all that, you're able to recognize yourself as just an ordinary woman with a crown on your head.

The employees of Thorndike Press hope you have enjoyed this Large Print book. All our Thorndike and Wheeler Large Print titles are designed for easy reading, and all our books are made to last. Other Thorndike Press Large Print books are available at your library, through selected bookstores, or directly from us.

For information about titles, please call:

(800) 223-1244

or visit our Web site at:

www.gale.com/thorndike
www.gale.com/wheeler

To share your comments, please write:

Publisher
Thorndike Press
295 Kennedy Memorial Drive
Waterville, ME   04901